Eighteen Days Till Home

by Shirley Latessa

*To Doug,
With much affection
and thanks*

WAVERLY PRESS
NEW YORK

Published by Waverly Press
P.O.B. 20624
Columbus Circle
New York, New York 10023

Book design by Jennie Reins
Cover design by Barbara Richey

ISBN: 0-9657922-0-X (U.S. Edition)

Acknowledgments

I'd like to thank the many people who gave me encouragement while I was writing and rewriting this book, and to mention by name those who took time out of their busy lives to read it and to offer me their comments.

My heartfelt thanks to: Douglas Sloan, Fern Sloan, Jane Gelfman, Marsha Post, Rochelle Fang, Annette Lancy, Jim Hindes, and Chris Bamford.

But especially to Faye Moskowitz, Rebeccah Schacht, and Yael Gani who read and reread this book and then offered me such valuable advice.

My thanks also to Jennie Reins for her helpful suggestions about type and layout, and to Barbara Richey for the myriad beautiful covers she designed, and for the one that now envelops this book.

And much gratitude to Jonathan Hilton and Yael Gani for shepherding this book through all the stages of publication with confidence and quiet encouragement.

Dedication

To my children, Rachel, Gabrielle, Gina, and Dave, with much love.

The entire novel takes place in the months of April and May in the year of 1990.

The day after seeing her daughter, Rebecca Layton Warren and Becky's new husband, Edward Warren, off at Kennedy Airport for an extended honeymoon, fifty-three year old Elizabeth Layton, known to her family and friends as Beth, took to her bed.

It was time to mourn her losses. One husband, dead of a heart attack. One daughter, dead of leukemia. Her surviving daughter, married and gone.

Before getting into bed, Elizabeth did the following. She wheeled her shopping cart to the Gristede's near her Greenwich Village apartment, filled it up with food, drink, and other sundry supplies, then pulled it home and stuffed the contents into her cupboards and refrigerator. She asked her doorman to hold all her mail because she would be gone for an indefinite period of time. She canceled her *New York Times* delivery "until further notice," then she put a terse, "I can't come to the phone right now," message on the answering machine in the living room, unplugged the phone in her bedroom, pulled down all the window shades, undressed and went to bed.

Sleep came quickly. When she woke up some hours later, she began finally, mercifully, to cry. She cried until she could sleep again and slept until she needed to cry again. That was the first day of her two weeks of mourning.

Once each day of those two weeks, she plugged the phone back into her bedroom outlet, and dialed her sister, Merle Brody, in Scarsdale.

"You sound like shit," her sister invariably told her.

"I'm fine, just tired after the wedding."

"Are you working on your book?"

"I started a new poem yesterday. The book's almost complete," Elizabeth said.

"Why don't you come up here for a few days. You can write up here."

"No, not now, really, I'm fine. I've been looking forward to this, to the empty nest, to my own space," Elizabeth carefully built the lie brick by brick. "Tonight I'm having dinner with a friend," she added for good measure and tried to keep the misery out of her voice.

"Well, you sound terrible," her sister said. "Call me tomorrow."

This was the conversation, or some variation of it, every day for two weeks. After each conversation with her sister, Elizabeth unplugged the bedroom phone, climbed back into bed and slept or wept. After four days and nights of alternating periods of napping and crying, she experienced bouts of insomnia.

On the fifth day of her *rest*, Elizabeth panicked. She knew that something dreadful had happened to Becky and Ed on their honeymoon. She couldn't drive away the anxiety until, after a day of near hysteria and frenzy, she finally reached them by phone in their hotel room in Hawaii. The honeymooners assured her they were having a fantastic trip.

Rebecca told Elizabeth that she had never been happier. And Elizabeth assured her daughter that she too was fine. Asked by Rebecca if she was writing, Elizabeth answered that she was. On the sixth night disturbing and vivid dreams interrupted the little sleep she was getting, so Elizabeth tried to stay awake by watching late night TV. But the old scary movies made her more agitated, and the romantic movies depressed her. When she found herself sobbing over "The Road to Morocco" with Bob Hope, Bing Crosby and Dorothy Lamour, she turned off the set and crawled back into her bed.

She slept, and for three nights running she dreamt of her dead daughter. Not since the first few days after Alicia's death had she dreamt of her, not that whole terrible year while robot-like she had planned Rebecca's wedding. Cruelly, in these current dreams Alicia was alive and healthy, even laughing. Each time Elizabeth woke up, the irrevocable fact of her daughter's death hit her again with such brutal force, with such a harsh sense of loss that the precious dream-conversation she had been having with Alicia was immediately driven out of her memory. It was inevitably superseded by a picture of Alicia's pale, fearful face as it had been just before she had died, lying in that hospital bed, a little cap knit for her by her younger sister covering the nearly bald head that had once been luxuriant with dark curls. Clutching her mother's hands Alicia had died, a cry of "Oh, it's dark," on her lips, a gasp, and then nothing, only a forlorn, empty, used up body, twenty-seven years young, and gone. And Elizabeth had not been able to keep her from disappearing irretrievably into that final darkness. No love, no powerful mother-instinct, no furious mother-will nor prayerful promises to a nonexistent God had been enough to keep her daughter alive.

But Elizabeth had not fallen apart. She had stayed strong for Becky because there was no one else to hold her up. She had stayed strong for Alicia's lover, strong for her own useless mother, who had given up one of her piano engagements in Florida to come to the funeral and had carried on in her usual dramatic and damaging way. Elizabeth had stayed strong for James, her brother, and for Merle, her sister, and for their spouses and their numerous inconsolable children, strong for all of Alicia's friends, her old college and high school classmates. Mostly Elizabeth had stayed strong because it was expected of her. She had stayed strong when her husband, Matthew, had died four years earlier. And she had pulled herself together one more time for Becky's marriage to her college sweetheart, only a year after Alicia's death.

But enough was enough. So all the while Elizabeth had been planning a small but elegant wedding at the Waldorf Astoria, she was also planning this *rest*. For months she had planned it, to close her door and let go. To finally, finally let go.

On the seventh day of her mourning Elizabeth stopped crying. She got angry. She stormed about the apartment, knocked over chairs, kicked the silk orientals that had been her father's joy, and raged, raged at her husband, Matthew. She had needed Matthew so desperately. He should have been with her when the doctors told her that Alicia had leukemia, and not dead a whole horrible year. He should have been with her through the three years of hopefulness and hopelessness, of hospital stays, and difficult treatments. He should have been with her at the end, holding her, Elizabeth, even as she had held Alicia. And when Becky married, Matthew should have been there to walk down the aisle with her to give Becky away instead of Elizabeth's brother, James.

But mostly she was furious because of Raven who, in the last year of Matthew's life, had almost succeeded in taking Matthew from her.

That afternoon, she threw their wedding picture across the living room, leaving glass shattered on the floor and a black streak on her white walls like a disintegrating comet. Her own capacity for rage made Elizabeth sicker.

That first week of her mourning she showered every night as had been her habit. The second week she didn't bother, couldn't bother. After the dreams came, she almost stopped eating. She did drink an occasional cup of tea. Occasionally she ate an apple. Occasionally a piece of dried Jarlsburg and a cracker. The one thing Elizabeth remembered to do was to call Merle daily. But she remembered less and less of what she said to her or what her sister said back. Then two weeks after Elizabeth had gone into mourning, Merle showed up at her door.

"Beth, if you don't open this damned door, I'm getting the police, do you hear?" Merle shouted.

Elizabeth hated scenes so she opened the door.

Her sister took one look at her and said, "Jesus Christ!" First she held her in her arms while Elizabeth sobbed and sobbed, then she scrambled some two-week-old eggs and made a pot of strong coffee which she herself drank. While Elizabeth was soaking in a hot tub with the bathroom door propped open, Merle straightened up the apartment, changed the sheets on Elizabeth's bed and made a phone call.

By evening their brother, James Norton, was up from Princeton and they were eating fresh salads, cheese, fruit and sourdough bread from Balducci's.

"That's my proposal," her sister was saying. "You either opt for that or we put you in a hospital. You can't keep on like this."

"I hate cruises," Elizabeth said.

"This is not a cruise, this is an art tour."

"Like the one Merle and Phil took two years ago," James said.

"It's on a boat," Elizabeth eyed him belligerently.

"A ship," her brother said, "really a yacht." James was a sailing enthusiast.

"Think of it as a floating hotel," her sister said.

"I'm not up to it."

"Then which hospital will it be, Paine Whitney or Beth Israel?" Merle said, and Elizabeth knew she meant it.

After a moment Elizabeth asked, "Where does it go?"

"Greece, Turkey, Crete, Italy. You'll love it. Plenty of sea air, glorious art, ancient artifacts, interesting people who don't know anything about your problems," her sister enumerated the trip's virtues. "Eighteen days of rest and recuperation, with company that's stimulating and art that will be a feast for your mind." Art was one of Merle's passions and she was a member of all the New York museums.

"It's sponsored by four museums," her sister poked the brochure that now sat in front of Elizabeth with one long red-nailed finger, "The Barry Collection here in New York, the Tremont Archaeological Museum...where is that?" She looked up at her brother.

"Minneapolis," he said.

"Right, and the Starling Museum of Art in San Francisco. There's one other..."

James picked up the brochure sitting untouched in front of Elizabeth. "The Brilling Institute of Greek and Roman Art..."

"...up in Boston," Merle said. "Therefore it's going to be wonderful. There'll be an art historian from the Brilling to give lectures aboard the boat." She retrieved the brochure from her brother and opened it to the appropriate page.

"Ship," her brother said.

"I don't want to go on a trip," Elizabeth told them.

"What do you want to do?" her brother asked.

"Brood and make herself sick," Merle said. "She can't stay home so it's the trip or the hospital. I'm not standing by while she mourns herself into a nervous breakdown or starves herself to death. She's so thin now, you could write with her." Merle glared at her brother. "And don't you dare offer to take her back to Princeton with you. Nina has her hands full, and there are four teenage boys in your house." It sounded like an accusation.

"They love Beth."

"James," Merle's voice moved up several decibels. "Your house is chaos. Total, unbelievable chaos. No one would recommend a mouse take up residence with you, much less someone as stressed and as vulnerable as Elizabeth is right now. Look at her!"

So James looked at her and said, "You're right."

Next Merle turned a fierce eye on Elizabeth. "If you give me a hard time about this, Beth, I'm phoning Becky and telling her to come home immediately."

"No!" Elizabeth stood up quickly, rattling the cups on the table. "Don't you dare. Don't you dare interrupt Becky's honeymoon. It's only been two weeks. They haven't even gotten to Australia yet," and she sank back into her chair and began to sob.

"I have no choice, honey. Becky would never forgive me if she thought I let you starve yourself to death while she was gone."

Elizabeth had no answer for that.

"Where's your passport?" Merle asked.

"In my safe deposit box at the bank."

"We'll pick it up on the way to Scarsdale tomorrow morning."

And so the next morning James returned to teaching at Princeton while Elizabeth and Merle, Elizabeth's passport and suitcase in hand, boarded a train to Scarsdale.

The next two weeks passed in a haze of activity. Merle, who loved a project, devoted herself entirely to Elizabeth. She registered her for the trip, helped her select a cabin, and sent the check Federal Express to the Smith and Smith Travel Agency in New York City. Smith and Smith, in turn, fed-exed them all the pertinent information including a book list and clothing suggestions. Merle took Elizabeth shopping for clothes. She took her to bookstores for books.

Every afternoon, while she prepared the dinner, Merle propped Elizabeth up on the living room couch, turned on the radio to the classical music station, and surrounded her with history and travel books. Elizabeth dutifully leafed through them, staring at the pictures, reading bits and pieces of the text trying to absorb some information. When her brother-in-law, Phil Brody, came home from his dental office, he always gave Elizabeth a warm hug. When he said good night to her, his eyes filled with tears. Once she overheard the two of them talking in the kitchen.

"Do you think this trip is such a good idea?" Phil asked.

"Do you have a better one?"

In her niece's old bedroom where she slept, Elizabeth wept quietly each night, careful that her weeping not disturb anyone. She didn't dream about Alicia while she was in Scarsdale. She dreamt but the dreams were chaotic and painful and the images disappeared quickly, sliding behind the hill of recollection as soon as she woke up.

Once she and Merle took the train to New York where they arranged for Elizabeth's mail to be held and for a neighbor to come in and water the plants while Elizabeth was away. They carted back clothes and the few books Elizabeth thought she might want on the trip. Elizabeth had stopped protesting. She would dutifully navigate her way through this trip, then the family would leave her alone. She would be careful, very, very careful, in the future. It was only eighteen days, the whole of the trip, and then she could go home again.

The night before her departure, Elizabeth phoned Rebecca, who was now in Australia, to tell her she was going on a vacation and would return a week or so after Becky and Ed came back from New Zealand. "I'll visit you in Philadelphia as soon as I return," Elizabeth told her. Becky was thrilled her mother was finally going on a trip. "Mom, you've always been tough. You're the strong one in the family. Thank God for that, but now it's time for you to have a little fun."

"That's just what I'm going to do," Elizabeth said.

Only Hank, after Matthew's death, had not thought of her as tough or strong.

Beth, don't think about Hank now.

The next day Merle drove Elizabeth to the airport talking all the way about how marvelous a ship the New Odyssey was and how well Smith and Smith ran a tour. Elizabeth said "uh-huh" several times and tuned her out.

It was a late afternoon in May. The day had been unseasonably hot. The sun was shining. And, somehow, Elizabeth Layton was on her way to Athens.

At the security check-in Merle made a scene, but they wouldn't let her go through to the gate without a ticket. She finally gave up, embraced Elizabeth, said, "You'll be fine," then turned and quickly walked away.

Paul Burrows was watching a woman.

His plane to Athens was late. It had not yet arrived at the gate. And the plastic seats in the TWA terminal were not very comfortable for someone as tall as he. His back felt stiff and the leg he had injured in World War II began to throb, so he decided to walk around, to see if he could figure out who in this steamy, unair-conditioned and overcrowded terminal might be with his tour. It was an idle game, he knew, but it would help to pass the time until the plane took off.

For a moment he had thought it was Annie. He had stopped, startled. And then wondered what it was about her that made him think she looked like Annie? His Annie had been tall and ample. This woman was of average height and rather thin. The thinness of grief, he decided, noticing the hollow of her cheeks, the black circles under her eyes. Annie's hair had been long and she had worn it twisted and piled high on her head. This woman's hair was cropped very short. It was gray. That was like Annie's. However, none of her features looked like Annie's. Really she didn't resemble his dead wife at all.

So what was it? What was it about her that had stopped him? Something about her face, yes, about the expression on her face. This woman had a wide mouth and large expressive eyes. He couldn't tell from this distance what color they were. Her nose was small and her chin jutted out giving her a look of strength. It was the play of emotions that crossed her face again and again, he finally realized, that reminded him of Annie. As if the woman were having an inner debate. No, more like a heated argument.

Paul stood behind a row of plastic seats and watched her. Where could this sad woman be going? To a funeral? To visit someone who was ill? She did not seem like a candidate for his tour though she was sitting at Gate 31, his gate. But that didn't mean anything. The terminal was crowded and people were sitting wherever they could find seats, even on the floor.

Paul's left leg was beginning to ache from standing still, so he was glad when the woman stood up, picked up her carry-on and her raincoat and moved away. He followed her to the women's bathroom and then waited until she came out. She circled the terminal obviously looking for a seat but there was none to be had. Finally she entered the long cafeteria line. Paul got into line right behind her. When at last she arrived at the drinks, she opened the case and took out a bottle of mineral water. Paul, too, took a bottle of water. There were no more trays, no napkins. The cashier was a heavy, gum-chewing girl with bovine eyes whose fingers moved as slowly over the computerized cash register as if they were performing their task under water. A small fan was blowing on her, rippling her long scraggly mouse-brown hair.

"You'd better remove the bottle top," Paul said to the woman as she started to walk away. "The cashier has the opener."

"Oh, thank you," the woman said, barely glancing at him. She turned back and found the bottle opener on a chain next to the cashier.

At that moment he heard the announcement squawked over the PA system. His plane had finally arrived at the gate. It was being cleaned and serviced and they would announce the boarding directions soon. The woman moved back to Gate 31 and stood near the boarding gate, her carry-on on the floor between her feet, clutching her bottle of water.

She must be on my plane, Paul thought with pleasure.

An hour later they boarded the jumbo jet. The woman whom Paul had been watching was seated across the aisle from him. Now that was interesting, fortuitous even. Paul surreptitiously watched her as the plane loaded up. She looked unhappy, rather anxious. Perhaps she didn't like flying. She sat there clutching a book while feelings flitted across her face as if it were a movie screen. How vulnerable she looked.

When the doors were finally closed and the plane began lumbering toward the takeoff runway, he heard her gasp.

"My dear, just try to breathe normally, in-out, in-out," he said to her.

The woman, startled, turned her head to look at him. Her eyes were green and huge.

"Don't be embarrassed. Many people fear flying."

"Oh, I'm sorry," she said. "I mean, I'm not afraid of flying. At least I never have been before. It's just that…" She didn't continue.

"Lean back. Close your eyes and try to breathe rhythmically," Paul told her.

The woman did as he suggested.

"Now try to picture the sun sitting in your heart and radiating light, pouring light throughout your limbs."

The woman opened her eyes and looked over at him.

"Just an exercise that some actors I know do to help them get centered and calm before a performance. Can't hurt," he said.

"No, probably not," she made an attempt at a polite smile, then closed her eyes and opened them again. "Do you mean *the* sun or some other sun?"

A meticulous mind, he thought. "Think of your heart as your own personal sun and it's sending light to all your limbs, to all your nerves. Feel yourself bathed in a warm, peaceful light."

"My heart is not a sun. There's no light there." She shook her head. "Sorry." Her laugh was apologetic.

"Then imagine one," he said. "Place one there."

"I can't. I'm fine now. Thank you," and she picked up her book.

Leave her alone, Paul, he told himself.

The announcement came to prepare for takeoff and in a few roaring moments they were airborne.

Paul smiled at the woman when she returned from the bathroom later but he didn't attempt to speak to her again. He dozed, drank club soda, ate his dinner and snack, each in their turn. During the movie he closed his eyes and slept fitfully. While he slept he dreamt of Annie. "Some meetings are important, Paul," she said. "I know that," he answered, "but she doesn't want to talk to me and once the plane lands that will be the end of it." "Is that what you think?" Annie said, and kissed him on the forehead and he woke up. It was morning. Breakfast was about to be served.

Unlike the marble and dark wood lobby of the Hotel Helene, the furniture in Beth's hotel room was modern, blond and new. She and her fellow travelers had been met at the airport baggage area by two American escorts from Smith and Smith holding yellow 4-M signs ("4-M" for the four museums sponsoring this trip). Their baggage was collected on great carts from off the baggage carousel. They boarded two large buses and were driven through Athens to the hotel. In a haze of fatigue Beth had watched the approaching modern Mediterranean city. She had been too tired to do more than glance around at her fellow passengers. She would meet them all at a cocktail party that evening at the hotel. All she wanted now was a bath and a nap.

Beth unlocked the small refrigerator next to her bed, took out a club soda and drank it gratefully. Her luggage appeared miraculously ten minutes later. She unpacked, showered, set her alarm for 5 P.M. and immediately fell asleep.

Paul slowly unpacked his suitcase and hanging bag. His tour group would be in the Hotel Helene for three nights.

No point in leaving everything to wrinkle in his suitcases. He was tempted, of course. But he must stay attentive, awake and alert, must remain firmly in the present. That's why he was here. Better to do things the right way, not the easy way. He must not dream through this trip. That would render it useless. This trip was perhaps a last chance, and he had to take hold of it. Annie knew.

Pay attention to details, he instructed himself. So he spent a groggy hour making the elegant room livable. The Hotel Helene was located near Constitution Square. It was a grand hotel, far costlier than any he and Annie had ever stayed in on their several trips. There had been fruit and flowers waiting for him. He felt a twinge of regret that Annie had not lived to enjoy this luxury, then quickly pushed away the sentiment. Annie's illness had been terribly debilitating. She was in a better place now, free of the body with its pains, its restrictions. No, he missed Annie, but he certainly knew better than to feel sorry for her.

After he unpacked, Paul stood for a moment uncertain what to do next. He looked longingly at the bed, but knew that if he crawled into it now for a nap he would be up and wide awake in the middle of the night. Old bodies didn't take kindly to rapid changes. A walk might help. Yes, definitely a walk was in order. Paul put on his jacket and left his room, carefully locking the door. He rode the elevators down to the spacious lobby and walked past the Smith and Smith table where several people had gathered, no doubt, to get information about the city. In a few hours there was to be a reception. He had decided not to go. If he could stay awake until, say, five or six, he could order up his dinner, take a shower, and go to sleep at 8 P.M. That would pull him toward a normal schedule.

Outside the hotel, he turned to his right. Modern Athens was pleasantly familiar—he had been here with Annie. It was filled with hurrying people and traffic and noise. Not unlike Boston, he thought. Sleepy as he was, Paul walked briskly around the block, detouring to look at Constitution Square. He was too tired to sort out what he was seeing, too tired to feel, to think. But that was all right. He was about to pass his hotel for a third go-around when he decided he had walked enough. He had made it to Athens, after all, and that was good in itself.

And something deep in his soul answered, yes, yes, and he knew it was Annie.

Paul entered the hotel and approached the girl sitting at the Smith and Smith table. He stooped toward her, extended his hand, and said, "I'm Paul Burrows. Can you tell me what time we are to meet tomorrow morning?"

The young woman, who was still in her twenties, smiled brightly at him. "So nice to meet you, Mr. Burrows. I'm Colleen MacMurray. We're meeting in the lobby at 9 A.M.

"9 A.M." Paul repeated. "Thank you."

"Mr. Burrows, several of our guests are going to skip tonight's reception and are going to turn in early. It won't be a problem if that's what you want to do." Again she smiled. "You missed a night's sleep, after all."

"Though I'm looking forward to the trip," he said, "these old bones are protesting mightily right now. I'll see you in the morning, 9 A.M."

"See you then."

Paul returned to his room, took a long leisurely shower. At 5 P.M. he ordered up a light dinner, watched the English news channel on the TV, and at seven set his alarm for six-thirty in the morning, and quickly fell into a deep sleep.

Beth woke at 5 P.M. and put on a lavender paisley dress that she had purchased for the trip. At five minutes to six she went down to the small reception room for the welcome cocktail party. She was tired. She didn't want to be there. And when she stepped into the long, rather plain rectangular room, with dozens of people she didn't know, panic hit her. She was about to turn around and go back to her room when a waiter came by with a tray of wine. She took a glass and gulped down a few swallows.

Look at the people, Beth, she told herself. Keep your mind busy. Do what you've always done in new situations. So she began to observe the individuals who would be her companions for the next two weeks.

Her fellow travelers were mostly over forty, as she had expected. However, here and there she noticed a younger face. A daughter was traveling with her mother. How alike they looked. The daughter in her twenties, the mother somewhere in her forties, maybe fifty, and very attractive. A woman with white hair piled high on her head was there with a young man. A lover, Beth speculated, then dismissed the thought. Probably a son or maybe a grandson. She continued her perusal. There were less than forty people in the room even though she knew there would be about sixty or sixty-five passengers aboard ship. Perhaps some had been too tired and had simply gone to bed. Fatigued as she was, Beth admired the ones who had ignored this event. She admired their casualness in following the schedule. But she needed the schedule, the structure of the trip, what followed what. The planned events were like stepping stones in a river she must cross to get to the other side. One at a time, a little leap to the next stone, step by step, one foot after the other. And then she would be safe on the other side. And home. Seventeen days.

Beth put some pieces of bland-looking cheese on a plate with a few crackers, took another glass of wine, and found an empty table. She intended to stay to hear the announcements about their two days in Athens and then leave. The 4-M travelers were on their own for dinner that night. She wasn't hungry, the cheese would be enough. She wanted only to sleep and so end another day.

"May we join you?" an elderly female voice broke into her musings.

"Oh, yes, please," Beth answered, mechanically putting on a smile.

A woman in her seventies, with thin sharp features, wispy dyed auburn hair and black agate eyes, introduced herself, "I'm Lucy and this is my sister, Doris."

Doris was rotund with a wide, open face and dyed light brown hair that frizzled about her face.

"Nice to meet you. I'm Beth."

The two women put their drinks down and settled themselves into the small chairs.

"We're sisters," Doris said with a grin, "but don't ask how we came from the same parents." Her laugh was like an approaching train. The sound filled the small reception room.

"Oh, Doris," Lucy scolded but her tone was mild.

"Of course, I wasn't always fat, and Lucy had a little more meat on her when we were growing up. I'm from Kansas City," Doris went on with the introductions, "and Lucy's from Rockport, Mass, that's near Boston."

"I'm from New York."

Doris said, "We do this every year and, oh, it's such fun."

"You come every year to Athens?" Beth asked.

"Oh, no, I mean we travel together," Doris's laughter bubbled up again. "I just leave Frank home with the house and the garden and the dogs, and Lucy and I go somewhere exotic."

"Doris is the married one," Lucy said.

"Oh," Beth nodded and covered her own ringless finger with her right hand. It had taken her eight months after Matthew's death to remove the ring. That had been at Hank's insistence.

"Come with me to Greece..."

Good God, don't think about Hank now.

"Not much of a reception," Doris looked down at the innocuous cheese on her plate and the few crackers. "If you want something else besides wine, they make you pay for it. I love my gin and tonic before dinner and the price I just paid is outrageous."

"I've switched to vodka," Lucy said. "Vodka and tonic. Gin is bad for you." She looked disapprovingly at her sister.

"Lucy is a health nut," Doris said, and put a whole cracker in her mouth.

"The wine is free," Beth said.

"It's Athens. It's the Greeks," Lucy nodded. "They absolutely don't know how to make a cocktail party."

"Now don't you go blaming the tour company," Doris patted Beth's hand, "Smith and Smith do the best they can. Wait until you get on the New Odyssey. There everything is first rate."

"Top of the line," her sister agreed.

"You've traveled with Smith and Smith before?" Beth asked.

"Our sixth trip," Doris said.

Beth looked up and noticed an attractive man on the other side of the room standing with a group of people who were engaged in an animated conversation. The man, however, was staring at her. When he caught Beth's eye, he smiled broadly at her, and gave her a little nod.

"If you're not a raving beauty, you can't afford to be too fussy..."

Beth looked away, pretending not to see him and felt a flush of anger. When you're not pretty, she had long ago decided, and men whom you do not know and have not spoken to, stare at you, you can be sure they're after one thing. And she had heard about men aboard cruise ships who look for women to sleep with for the duration. Women who would not expect much. Plain women.

My God, Beth, you're beginning to sound like an old maid school marm.

"You know you're chicken shit," Hank scowled across the table at her.

Beth pushed the unbidden memory away and focused, with some force of will on Lucy, who was speaking.

"Oh yes, this is the sixth time we've taken one of the Smith and Smith tours, and it's our third time on the New Odyssey. You'll love it, my dear. There'll be lectures—that's her over there, the lecturer," and Lucy gestured with her head at a woman talking to the man who had been staring at Beth.

"She's very bright, very important. We've traveled with her before," Doris nodded her approval.

"She's from the Museum that Doris and I belong to in Boston, the one that has all that Greek and Roman art."

"I don't get to the Brilling very often," Doris said, "but they do sponsor good trips so it's worth joining. That's her husband next to her."

Oh, Beth thought, and looked again at the handsome man the lecturer was talking to. You misread his smile, he's married.

And then she was shocked that she felt disappointment.

"That balding man who stands like a pretzel," Lucy said. "He paints, we've been told, but he's not anyone important." Her mouth became a thin line.

Beth looked again. The balding pretzel was, of course, a different man, not the one who had smiled at her. She was relieved. And irritated with her own ridiculous feelings. Jet lag, she told herself severely.

"Smith and Smith organize such wonderful trips," Doris said. "We took one with the Geographic Society last year. Remember the cocktail reception party we were given in London?"

"The food was extraordinary. Fresh, exotic fruit, all kinds of fish and cold salads, bread..."

"Free drinks..."

"And service. Only the British know how to give good service, wouldn't you say so, Doris?"

"Well," Doris looked thoughtful for a moment, "there's the French."

The two sisters continued to talk. Beth asked a question now and then and listened with half an ear and was grateful that good travel manners didn't allow one to pry into strangers' lives. Through a cloud of exhaustion, she watched the others in the room, routinely noting faces, hairstyles, and clothes (a mix of spring and summer, dressy and casual, skirts and slacks, city chic and country casual).

"*...is this need to categorize, to find large boxes to put things in, to carve up the world into digestible chunks.*"

The laughter in the room reverberated loudly as drinks loosened tongues. Sounds in particular slipped past the barrier of Beth's skin. Something wanted to scream inside her. She could barely contain the shout that was growing like a vine from her chest down through her legs, and up through her arms. Her fingers felt brittle. She grabbed the nearly full glass of wine clumsily in her wooden hands and swallowed and swallowed. She began to breathe too rapidly. And stood up. "I'm sorry," she said, "I'm sorry but I have to leave."

"They're just about to make the announcements," Lucy said looking toward the platform as the man from Smith and Smith, microphone in hand, stepped up to it.

The room became silent. Beth breathed in deeply. She could wait for that. Yes, she could do that. That's why she had come. For the agenda. That's what she needed. What followed what. Step by step through the next two days. The Screamer became silent. Her fingers felt like her own again and she began to breathe normally. She could feel the wine spreading like warm butter just below her skin. She was all right. Of course, she was all right. Nothing threatening here. Nothing at all. Beth sat down again and willed herself to listen.

The young man introduced himself and then his colleague from Smith and Smith. "Hi, my name is Bill Orbach. This is Colleen MacMurray. We'll be making this trip with you right through till we finish in Rome. Our job is to see that everything goes smoothly and that you don't have to worry about anything except being on time for the next event."

A small ripple of laughter.

"We're always available to talk to you. We'll be at the desk in the lobby whenever you're in the hotel. We can give you information about where to shop and where to eat in Athens, if you can find the time and the energy after we're through with you."

Again knowing laughter.

"Of course on board ship we'll be available whenever you need us. We'll accompany you on all the excursions. So relax and enjoy yourselves. You're in good hands."

A round of applause.

"Before I tell you about the plans for our two days in Athens, let me introduce you to Marion Levitt. Some of you who have been on other trips with us probably know her. She's our accompanying lecturer from the Brilling Institute of Greek and Roman Art in Boston and she'll be giving you some background to the exhibits we'll be seeing and to some of the archaeological sights we'll be visiting."

Marion Levitt, a tall woman in her early forties with a nice face and dark brown hair which she wore in a bun, smiled and nodded from where she was standing and got a polite round of applause. She looked efficient and academic. Bill then introduced Marion's husband, Gary Levitt.

"And finally let me introduce Eric Halsey from the Barry Collection in New York City. Eric is responsible for all the marvelous new art that the Barry has been purchasing. Some art connoisseurs say that the Barry, small as it is, has the best collection of post-modern art in the world, largely because of Eric Halsey. He'll be traveling with us as a kind of representative of all four museums."

There was a buzz of interest around the room.

The man who had stared and smiled at Beth now grinned and waved at the crowd. Beth blushed and didn't know why. It's the wine, she told herself. It's the wine. As Bill did not introduce any wife or traveling companion, Beth assumed Eric Halsey was traveling alone. Which doesn't mean anything, she told herself severely.

"You pull away from life and all its marvelous experiences."

"Oh, my goodness," Lucy said, "that man's famous, really very famous. I saw him in People or one of those magazines not so long ago. And once on one of those interview shows on public television. He knows everybody who's important in New York City."

"Really?" Doris asked.

"Yes," her sister nodded, "he's part of the New York scenario."

"You mean the scene, Lucy, the New York scene."

"Whatever," Lucy waved a hand at Doris.

So you see, Beth, he couldn't be interested in you. Probably thought he knew you. It happens all the time.

Colleen, a bright, cheerful woman in her late twenties, outlined the next two days. Beth listened carefully to the instructions, then the moment the announcements were over, politely bid the two sisters goodnight, and left. All she could think of was that she wanted to sleep. How stupidly she had behaved. How ridiculous to have a panic attack for no reason. Jet lag and wine don't mix, she decided. And that man Eric What's-His-Name was merely being polite. Had she made a fool of herself? Had she looked too disapproving? It didn't matter. She didn't have the energy to worry about it.

She returned to her room, undressed, washed, cleaned her face, set her alarm and went to bed. It was eight-thirty P.M. Athens time. She was exhausted but after turning and tossing for over an hour, she got up and opened the little refrigerator and took out a lemon drink. She poured it into a tumbler and sat down in the arm chair a few feet from her bed. She wanted to be angry at Merle, but she was just too tired. She started to cry. Then scolded herself. She had seventeen days to get through, she could do that. She had gotten through Matthew's death and Alicia's death and Becky's wedding. She could do this. Just follow the schedule and be polite. Beth turned on the TV and watched a drama in Greek and finally fell asleep.

Paul Burrows, seated in one of the two buses that was to take the 4-M tour group to the Benaki Museum, wasn't sure he was rested. Some part of him was still over the Atlantic, winging its way east, and he felt unusually buoyant. His left leg, with its injury from the war, didn't bother him, nor did any of the minor arthritis pains that he usually felt, particularly in the morning. Of course this body lightness wouldn't last, but for the time being it was rather pleasant. On the other hand the wooliness in his head he could do without.

Paul's alarm clock had awoken him at the appropriate time. He had breakfast in his room and was down early for the tour. He was pleased when he saw the woman from the plane board his bus. She came in head down and took a seat a few rows ahead of him. She hadn't noticed him. Perhaps she wouldn't remember him. Yesterday he had been surprised when he saw her board the other 4-M bus at the Athens airport. The sad lady with the face of glass was on his tour. Before falling asleep last night he had thought about it. First, he had been drawn to her at the airport. Then she was seated near him on the airplane. And now she was on his tour. I shall get to know her, he decided, as he drifted off to sleep. Good, his wife Annie said.

Beth was looking at crocheted lace in the lower level of the Benaki Museum. She had come out of sleep that morning anxious, miserable and filled with fear, but that was, she told herself firmly, to be expected. After arguing herself into a tenuous equanimity, she had showered and dressed, then had descended to the dining room where she had eaten a small breakfast. She was aboard the bus at the appropriate time. Just follow the schedule, she told herself.

The Benaki had the most extensive display of crocheted items Beth had ever seen. She herself owned several crocheted pieces with some of the same patterns, an inheritance from her Italian great-grandmother. She began to feel better. It did help to look at things that individuals had made with their hands. History was after all about people.

"I'm giving Great-Grandmother Antoinette's crocheted doilies to Elizabeth," her mother told the two sisters two weeks after she had sold the house in the wake of their father's death, *"because Beth truly likes old things. Merle, you and Phil can have Grandmother Norton's Royal Albert. You entertain the most. I'm giving the Persian rug that was in my mother's dining room to James and Nina. The boys won't be able to destroy that old warhorse, I hope. I won't need any of these things in Florida."*

When Beth moved in front of a display case to look at the wedding costumes their guide was talking about, her eyes caught sight of a middle-aged couple. They were holding hands and whispering to each other.

"I never meant it to go so far, Beth, really I didn't. I saw it first as a little attraction that would pass..."

"The wedding costume on the left was worn by a lady of the upper class, the one on the right by a lady of the lower class," their Greek guide, Irene, told them.

Suddenly, Beth felt wretched watching the handsome couple. This was all a mistake. One shouldn't be all alone, shaky, on the other side of the world. Pull yourself together, she told herself sternly. Just follow the guide. Get through the day. It's only sixteen days till home. One step, then another. That's all.

"The skirt for the lady of the upper class is embroidered with imported Venetian gold thread, whereas the other one is embroidered with simple silk thread."

"You can at least try to look pretty at Merle's wedding."

Beth stared hard at the costumes trying to recover their appeal.

"The father as well as the bridegroom were obliged to give specific gifts to the bride. The father gave her a necklace of coins that was worn around her neck. The more coins the better."

Hank had given her a bracelet made of pennies and copper wire that he had purchased from a street vendor.

"You know you're chicken shit..."

Please don't let's think about Hank.

"After all," Irene said, "it was also a display of personal wealth. Of course, the stones are just glass. The bridegroom gave the bride the belt. Homer tells us that Aphrodite kept her philters of love in her belt. In the Minoan Civilization, the belt kept away the evil eye. In the Byzantine culture the belt was a means of class distinction."

"Mother, is it awful? Is it too soon? I really would like a wedding with a white dress and bridesmaids and flowers, all that corny stuff," Becky looked apologetic. They were sitting in their

favorite Indian food restaurant, only a few blocks from their apartment. "If it's too soon or if you can't manage it, I'll understand, and so will Ed. We could elope or have a small wedding for just the immediate family. Isn't he terrific, mom?"

"The best," Beth managed a grin. *"And you're going to have a perfect wedding, Becky, with cousins and friends and white gown and all. I wouldn't want it any other way."* Poor Becky, she thought, how hard it's been for you. *"How would you like my wedding gift to you to be Great-Grandmother Brewster's set of Wedgwood? And how would you like to have your Grandmother Layton's silver cutlery set?"*

Who else was there to give it to now?

And Becky leapt up and leaned over the table dragging her scarf in the yogurt sauce and gave Beth a big hug. "Yes, to everything, yes, yes, yes!"

Beth drifted away from the wedding gowns to look at the jewelry. Beautiful, she thought. She peered into case after case. She loved handcrafted jewelry. It was one of her passions. She was casual about clothes, not indifferent, but casual. Earrings, however, were her love. And if she was rather plain, if she didn't have her mother's beauty, at least she had nice ears. And with short hair, her earrings dangled for all to admire. She was particularly taken with the long earrings which were not worn in the ears but had been hooked to one's hair or one's headdress.

From there Beth moved on to look at the bedspreads and embroidered tablecloths.

"And, of course, this collection is not all from Mr. Benaki. It was added to by other people who donated to the museum as well…"

"Lovely, aren't they?" a vaguely familiar voice said behind her. "My grandmother had a bedspread like that one. It weighed a ton."

Beth turned around and to her astonishment there was the old man from the plane, the one who had tried to help her through her panic attack. "Hello!" She smiled with genuine pleasure, and felt a sense of relief as if she had suddenly found an old friend. "I didn't know you were on this tour."

"And I didn't know you were on it," he said. His blue eyes were unusually clear and his six foot lean frame stooped slightly to look at her. "But now we know."

Beth laughed. "I mean, I didn't see you at the cocktail party yesterday."

"I had an early supper in my room, took a leisurely shower, and then went to sleep. I may look like a forty-year-old," he said, and winked at her, "but these old bones let me know I'm seventy-six when I've missed my sleep."

"You probably made the right choice."

"Paul Burrows, from Gloucester, Massachusetts," the white-haired man introduced himself with a little courteous bow. "I have to confess I did see you get on the bus this morning."

"Did you? I'm still in a bit of a jet lag fog, I guess. But we're practically neighbors, I grew up in Beverly. Well, not quite neighbors, I've been in New York since after college." She extended her hand and introduced herself.

"It's nice to meet you, Elizabeth."

"Call me Beth."

"Thank you. I will."

And they shook hands.

"Was your grandmother Greek?" Beth asked him as they moved slowly past the crocheted items.

"Great-grandma on my mother's side was Greek," he said. "The others were French, Scotch-Irish, English, some German. In other words, I'm a typical American mongrel. Oh, yes, did I say Scandinavian?"

"Sounds like my background. Only *my* great-grandmother was Italian."

"This is a lovely museum," he said.

"You've been here before?"

"Yes. Well, to Athens and to parts of Greece, but not to Macedonia or Istanbul, or Turkey or Crete."

"For me it's all new."

"Exciting, isn't it? I'm terribly happy to be on this tour," Paul told her.

They moved around the displays, pointing out items to each other, moving in now and then to listen to their Greek guide. Finally their group followed Irene up the stairs and into a room with icons.

"An interesting part of Byzantine history is the War of the Icons. Have you heard about it?" Irene gathered her group around her.

A few people mumbled, yes. Some said, no. Most just shrugged.

"Well, it was a bloody war, a religious war, about whether icons were being worshipped as if they were magically the incarnation of God, of Christ, of Mary or the Saints. This was very sacrilegious to many people. And very pagan."

Beth watched Paul as he listened to their guide. A new friend, she thought. When she thought the word *friend,* she suddenly became anxious. She didn't need any friends, didn't need anyone prying into her life.

Beth, stop it, she chided herself. He's just a fellow traveler, like Lucy and Doris. It is not good travel etiquette to ask personal questions. And Paul certainly had good manners, a kind of old world gallantry.

"Whatever your belief is today, the War of the Icons resulted in the loss of much great art, and that's what we're concerned with today, hah?"

Paul moved closer to Irene.

"Many glorious icons were destroyed in those difficult decades. Then the war that followed, in the thirteenth century, was another blow to art history, the destruction of Constantinople by the fourth crusade."

Was Paul religious, Beth wondered? Well, that was his business. Those of his generation were often religious. Her father, a general practitioner, was of the same generation as Paul, but not religious, definitely not religious. For Beth's father, science had been God. And literature. Beth had loved walking along the beach, when she was only a toddler, hand in her daddy's hand, listening to him recite nursery rhymes and chiming in whenever she was able, until she could recite them as well as he. She had written them too, her first verses. Later it was speeches from Shakespeare that they recited together and long, long poems.

If her father wasn't religious, neither was her mother. However, it was her mother who had insisted they belong to a church. They were a prominent family in the community and her mother had wanted the community's respect. After all, she had married the son of a wealthy Boston family. She had given up a promising career as a concert pianist to do so. And what had he done? He had taken a position as a small-town doctor. Well, the least her father could do, Beth had heard numerous times, was see to it that her mother had the social position to which she felt entitled.

"Most of the icons that we possess today are icons that belong to what we call the post-Byzantine period. In other words from after the middle of the fifteenth century. And then another war, in which Constantinople fell to the Turks in 1453."

An hour later the two groups were either sitting in small clusters on the broad marble steps of the Benaki Museum or standing on the sidewalk below. They were waiting for the arrival of their buses which would take them to the Museum of Cycladic Art and the reception that was to be given for them by Mrs. Goulandris, wife of the founder of the museum. The day was warm, sunny and clear with a mild, comfortable breeze.

Beth, starting down the steps, was greeted by Doris and Lucy. The two sisters were on the other bus and, therefore, with the other guide who had, Beth had noted, shepherded her group around the Benaki with firmness and officiousness.

"How is your guide?" Doris asked. And when Beth said she was very good, they said they would try to get on Irene's bus for the afternoon trip to the National Museum.

This is not going to be so difficult, Beth decided. You don't have to do anything but go where they send you, listen and look, that's all. And participate in a little polite conversation. She had met Doris and Lucy, had met Paul, and she had acted appropriately. You can do this, she reassured herself.

Beth reached the street level and stood on the sidewalk waiting patiently for the two 4-M buses to appear. She looked at the group of people sprawled out on the steps in the warm sun. You should begin to memorize faces, she told herself. After all, these individuals will be your companions for the next two weeks and two days.

So Beth began systematically to look at her fellow travelers who were sitting or standing on the steps above her. She had always been a good observer, could remember details. It was one of the aspects of her poetry that the critics had liked best, her sense of the particular. "In the particular, find the universal," her favorite teacher had told her years ago and she had not forgotten that.

"...Is this another example of your tendency, your need, to put everything into some manageable category?"

Her glance stopped first at the mother and daughter she had observed yesterday. They were talking animatedly. They looked so happy together, as if they really enjoyed each other. That gave Beth a sharp pang of loss. Stop it. Don't envy. Just look at your companions and try to memorize faces and forget about yourself.

Beth hurriedly moved her eyes away from the mother and daughter and stopped at a tall, broad-hipped woman, with grayish-brown shoulder-length hair and unflattering bangs on her high forehead. The woman was gesticulating with her cigarette holder and speaking in a loud voice to a group of people who had clustered around her on the lower steps. She was complaining about the "terrible destruction wrought by those horrible crusaders, and, darlings, they were Christians. People always say how horribly bloodthirsty the Turks were, but they were lambs compared to the crusaders. It was all about gold, of course, and land," she concluded in Oxford English, drawing little circles in the air with her cigarette holder. A few people clucked their tongues in agreement.

Beth's eyes moved on and saw her new friend Paul Burrows listening very attentively to an attractive, shapely, blond lady who was speaking to him. Paul caught Beth looking at him and winked at her. Beth smiled back. Then, standing just above Paul and the blond lady, Beth's eyes brushed unexpectedly over the face of Eric What's-His-Name from the Barry. He was leaning against one of the tall fluted columns just above the steps and had obviously been watching her for a time because he grinned at her and waved. Beth's heart began to beat faster and she pretended she hadn't seen him. Ever so casually she turned around to stare out at the street.

"I can't. I can't help it. I can't help myself. I'm like a man possessed."

"God, come up with a better cliché."

"Love is a cliché. It's a country-western."

"No. No, it's not. It's twenty-five years of living together..."

You idiot, Beth told herself. The man merely smiled at you. Why are you reacting so rudely, so angrily, with such panic?

It's because he's attractive, she answered.

It's not the man's fault if you are single again and available.

I am not available, she argued.

Before this dialogue could continue, the buses drew up. Beth quickly got into line and climbed back aboard her own bus and returned to her seat. Paul came down the aisle looking a little uneasy. He stopped and asked if he could sit next to her.

"Of course," she said, removing her sweater and carryall and placing them on the floor.

A few minutes later she noticed Paul's blond lady slowly making her way down the aisle. Paul nodded at the woman politely as she passed them.

"I have a feeling I've just rescued you," Beth said.

"Could be," he answered and then laughed. "My seat's in the back. She can have it."

The two tour groups came into the lobby of the Cycladic museum whose objects covered more than five thousand years of Aegean history. Beth was instantly struck by the elegance of the small marble figures and heads on display there.

Irene gathered her group together. "It was in these islands, as early as in the third millennium B.C. that we have this incredible civilization which we call Cycladic. We don't know where these people came from. The early Greeks appeared only at the beginning of the second millennium B.C. so you see how ancient a time we are referring to."

Irene led them to a glass case housing the idols.

Across the case Beth felt a pair of eyes watching her. She glanced up. Eric What's-His-Name was observing her but he did not smile. Beth blushed and turned immediately to stare at the idol under discussion.

"People usually work with the materials available to them. And what was abundant in the Cyclades was marble, all colors and all qualities of marble."

Why wasn't he with his own group, Beth wondered unkindly?

Because Irene is the better guide, she answered herself.

Irene was warming to her topic. "This is a period when men worship a female figure, Great Mother Earth."

"Raven wants to marry me. I don't know what to do."

When Beth looked up again, Eric What's-His-Name was gone. She looked around but couldn't find him. So what, she demanded of herself? And turned her attention on Irene.

"During the late stone age, agriculture was invented. The invention of agriculture changed everything. It had tremendous repercussions. Very shortly after that animals were domesticated which meant that the people's diet changed. When they began to use the whole animal, weaving was invented. Now they do something else, they take the earth and they mix it up with the water. What does that mean?" Irene paused. "It means that man intervenes in nature for the first time. He modifies the natural elements and by so doing he modifies himself."

Beth saw Paul move away from their guide to look at other objects.

"The earth." Irene was saying, "is directly associated with

the two poles of human life. And," she grinned and shook her head, "as you remember, the contribution of the male in procreation is still unknown."

"Raven wants to marry me."

"So the first important deity worshipped by man everywhere is Great Mother Earth. *Mother* Earth. She will be accompanied by a male god much later on."

"That's a relief," a man said.

There were a few titters.

"So all the figurines that you see here represent this great Mother Earth..."

A few moments later Colleen came up to Irene to inform her that it was time to go to the reception. The two groups were ushered into the small garden behind the Cycladic museum where a small speech of welcome was made by the museum's main benefactor, Mrs. Goulandris, and then they were offered refreshments.

Coffee and cookies in one hand, purse in the other, Beth walked through the small sun-soaked garden with its tiny, square mosaic pool and looked about for a free table. Paul was seated at one with Eric from the Barry.

Not there, she instructed herself, feeling an unwanted sense of panic.

She passed the two men by as if she hadn't noticed them. To her relief she found a seat with Doris and Lucy at a little round white table with white folding chairs. During the half hour they were seated there, Beth was careful never to look in the direction of Paul or of Eric. If she'd been rude, there was no help for it now.

"I'm hurting you. I'm hurting my kids."

The women were once again easy to be with. Enthusiastic as usual, they compared what they had seen that day with things seen in other museums on other trips.

Thirty minutes later, the group once again divided in two to finish their tour through the Cycladic museum. Then the buses returned them to their hotel for the lunch break. They were told to reconvene in the lobby at 2:30 for a tour of the archaeological state museum, the National.

Beth was about to head for her room and a rest when Doris and Lucy assailed her in the lobby and pressed her into joining them for lunch. She didn't refuse and had a pleasant enough meal with the talkative ladies in one of the hotel's restaurants. That left her with only fifteen minutes rest before she had to be aboard the bus. No point even going up to her room.

Sitting in the lobby of the hotel, Beth's sense of ease suddenly dropped away as if the ground had opened up. She could feel herself falling, a thin, rigid stick of a tree falling while her leaves were spinning away, deserting her all at once. She felt naked and abandoned, afraid to stand up. Breathe in-out, she told herself, in-out.

"...*picture the sun sitting in your heart and radiating light...*"

Beth was exhausted, that was it, really much too tired to go to the Museum.

"*Feel yourself bathed in a warm peaceful light.*"

She should go up to her room and sleep. She could do that. She could sleep and sleep and maybe no one would know. Through today, through tomorrow, through the week.

But they would come looking for her.

Someone would come looking for her. Colleen. Or the other tour guide. What was his name? Doris and Lucy would notice that she wasn't with them. Bill. He was called Bill Orbach. And Paul would notice. She would be assaulted from all sides and she was too weary to fight. She would cause people to be concerned. And she didn't want anyone's concern. Wasn't it better just to follow the schedule? Do what was expected, move through the museums following Irene, move through the hours, finish the tour, day by day and then go home? Her own home, her own bed. She would be careful then. Merle would never know. James would never know. Becky would never know. Why couldn't they all leave her alone? Alone, God, she was alone. So many people she loved taken from her. If only she could talk to her friend Mathilda Jones. But Mattie was in her cabin near Big Sur, tending her garden and writing her magnificent poems. And she was here in Athens on a trip that she had been coerced into. Well, she would get through it. And then when she got home... When she got home...

Beth stood up, headed toward the door and boarded the bus to the National Museum.

When Beth returned to her hotel room around 5 P.M., she tried to reconstruct the afternoon, but there were great gaps in her memory. Somehow she had managed to move around the National Gallery with her tour group. Irene's voice had been like a lead rope and she an obeying pony following, following.

Several times during the tour through the National, there had been an arm at her elbow and Beth had felt Paul guiding her around the exhibition. She knew he had spoken gently in her ear. What he had said to her during those moments, she was unable to remember as she sat in the chair in her hotel room, too drained to take off her jacket. But his soothing voice, his presence, his sensitivity, had helped her set one foot in front of the other.

She knew she had seen incredible treasures, evidence of "man's indomitable spirit". She had grasped at Irene's phrase that "What is wonderful is this inborn need of the artist of those days to beautify his surroundings, his life." Yes, that had once given meaning to her own life, that could be a good argument against the panic she was feeling. But then she remembered that she had barely written anything of value in four or five years, that she never intended to write again, that her faith in art, really in life, had vanished as Alicia's illness had taken more and more hold of Alicia's young body. Writing was, after all, an act of hope. And an act of hope was a futile gesture in a painful, meaningless world.

Beth needed to sleep. She pulled herself out of her chair, hung up her jacket, then undressed, washed her face and hands and brushed her teeth. Staring into the mirror she saw herself as if in a painting. One that was thick and globby, black and purple, a kind of passionate darkness. Surrounding her was a barely made-out landscape, surreal, where objects looked familiar but off-angled, a chimera, a deception. In it she was a tiny figure stuck in the color and stuck in the thickness. Any moment an abyss would open up in the Greek sunshine.

Stop it, Beth. Pull yourself together.

She reached for an orange soda from out of the small refrigerator and walked to the window to stare out at the traffic and the people hurrying in the street below. Where were they going? Home after work? Out for the evening? Who among them had lost loved ones? One in five? One in three?

Beth, don't.

In the National they had looked at many funerary reliefs showing people parting from their loved ones forever. She had barely been able to glance at the sorrow carved there for generations and generations to observe. She wondered if her own sorrow would last all her life. And then felt guilty that she had even asked such a question. If she couldn't carve a statue or write a poem that would outlast her own life, then at least she could carry the pain of loss, potently within, forever. In her mother's pain, Alicia would live. Her own poems, despite all the accolades she had received, were paltry things. Not like Mattie's. Surely if anyone's poetry would last into future centuries it would be Mathilda Jones's. If only she could write like her friend Mattie, perhaps she would not have given up.

Wrong! Her silence was her sacrifice to Alicia.

Beth opened the window. The air was warm and moist as a cloth on a fevered brow. Out there was Athens. Athens. She closed the window. Oh, Mattie, what am I doing here? She took a long swig of the sweet soda. Would you have done this? Would you have allowed your family to bulldoze you into something you didn't want to do?

She thought about writing Mattie a letter to let her know she was on this trip. But she was too tired to do that. So she emptied the syrupy drink into the sink, crawled into bed, rolled over on her back and thought about the time she had visited Mattie in her cabin in Big Sur.

The two women had taken part in a writers' conference in Portland, Oregon and afterwards Beth had driven with Mattie down the coast to Mattie's home for a few days of rest and good talk. Matthew was eight months dead. Beth had just started seeing Hank. Alicia had not yet been diagnosed with leukemia. And Beth's last book of poetry had recently come out, *America, Lost!*

The two women were curled up on the deep, heavily pillowed and roomy window seat in Mattie's cabin, stocking feet to stocking feet. They were talking and watching the rain stream down like sheets of metal, listening to it bang noisily on the window pane. Across the room, in the huge fireplace, a fire roared its comfort. The two women had finished a breakfast of oatmeal and coffee, and the dishes still lay on the table waiting to be whisked into the kitchen for washing along with their half-empty mugs.

The night before, Mattie had read *America, Lost!* while Beth had nervously leafed through a stack of country magazines and seed catalogs.

"Let me sleep on it, Beth," Mattie told her when she finally finished the book.

"Okay," Beth answered, and the two had gone to sleep.

They woke up late to the unrelenting rain. Sitting at breakfast in their robes they talked about the state of poetry in America. Breakfast done, sitting on the window seat, face to face, stomachs full, cheeks flushed with the intensity of conversation, they were speaking about Beth's new book. Outside, the surrounding mountains were nearly obliterated by the storm.

Mattie was questioning Beth's sudden interest in writing about America after so many years of poems centered on women's issues.

"Is it too much of a change of direction? Does it work? Will it be accepted—out there?" Beth gestured at the window.

Mattie stared down at her knees, her long ash blond hair falling like a water fall almost to the seat. "Actually, it doesn't seem like a change in direction. It seems to be pretty much in the same vein as your book on women." She looked up then at Beth, her blue eyes thoughtful.

"But how can you compare them? America and its lost ideals, it's indigenous people, its various waves of immigration from all over the world with their individual cultures. I thought I'd opened up a lot more, that I had looked at a broader range of issues."

"But that's just it, don't you see, it's still issues you're writing about. Is this really a new interest or the same quest? Is this another example of your tendency, your need, to put everything into some manageable category?"

"Why a category, Mattie? Why is looking at America and trying to discover its lost ideals, a category?"

"Wait, wait," Mattie said, "I didn't mean to imply that what you write about isn't important. Did I give that impression?"

"Go on."

"Everything is important. Everything." Mattie brushed her hair impatiently from her eyes. "And you write beautifully. You say what you have to say forcefully, clearly, yet with poignancy and grace."

"So what troubles you? Yes, I write about issues. Life is about issues. What else is there? Being a woman is an issue. Being Indian or Black is an issue. Being poor is an issue."

"What about being a mother or being in love or praying or having mystical experiences? Are those issues? Are qualities issues? I'm trying to understand how you think, don't you see?"

"Maybe you're trying too hard. I'm not as complex as you are, Mattie. I'm too down home Yankee. Surely my thought processes are not so esoteric."

"What I'm trying to understand is this need to categorize, to find large boxes to put things in, to carve up the world into digestible chunks. Sorry about the mixed metaphors."

"Are you saying that I infer simplistic answers?"

"I didn't say that, nor did I mean to imply that. I'm looking at our differences, looking at the way you organize your perceptions. You seem to need large, broad categories, to systematize."

"You mean I give things labels."

"No, no, that's not it. Good God, Beth, this is not a criticism. I hope you don't think I'm criticizing you. You're such an adventurous soul. You can't imagine how much I admire you, admire the way you go out and confront the world, the way you search for meaning. You try to classify whatever you're concerned with, so that you can bring some understanding to bear on it or even some solution."

"That sounds hideous," Beth's words were mild. She straightened out the twisted stockings on her feet. "You make me sound like someone who reaches for easy answers, who pigeonholes, who wants simple solutions. I see what I do in a different light. I don't think of categories or classifications, I think of contexts. I need to bring everything new I experience into the context of what I've learned so far."

Suddenly the rain stopped. The gray silence startled her after the thunderous downpour. Mattie could write about that, about the significance of the sudden quiet after torrential rain. Mattie could infer a whole life from such a juxtaposition, such a simple event. But she, Beth, could not.

She tried to explain. "If I see women suffer in Cambodia, for instance, I see it in the light of what I know about the suffering of women in Brazil, or in South Africa. If the Irish immigrants who came here voluntarily suffered dislocation, I see it in the context of the forced dislocation of Native Americans. And all of them fit, for me, into the general suffering, and degradation, and undervaluing of the poor in this world for endless centuries."

"What about your own suffering?"

"What do you mean?"

"Where does your suffering fit in?"

Beth wound her fingers through the multi-colored crocheted afghan. It was soft with a hundred washings. Her own suffering. It wasn't the stuff of poetry for her. "It doesn't, Mattie. My own suffering is too small."

"Yes, that I understand."

"What's bothering you about what I'm doing, Mattie? You worry me. You make my approach sound as if I were either naive, or worse, shallow."

Mattie looked over at her friend, startled, then remorseful. She reached for Beth's hand and squeezed it. "Oh, my dear friend, why do I have so difficult a time finding the right words? It's a terrible fault. It's amazing that I write at all. I'm interested in how a person knows what he knows. What tools he uses to know. It seems to me you have a set of concepts you bring to bear on everything you think about. You draw toward those familiar and accepted concepts, all your new experiences and you organize them according to what you already know." She whacked her hair away from her face. "Do most people do that?"

Beth stared out at the wet day, at the dark pewter anger of it, at the mountains standing mournfully in their misty shrouds. Then she pulled the afghan up over her knees and let out a long breath. "But that's not the way to come to anything original, is it? What you just described. God knows, every poet wants to be original, not just in *how* but in *what* he writes. And that's not what you do, Mathilda."

"Forget about me. We're talking about you now."

Beth ignored her. "You, my modest friend, take a single item, a stone for instance or a raindrop," Beth gestured at the window. "You observe it. You try to draw forth from that one small microcosm an entire macrocosm. In a raindrop, the whole world. Or you look at a single moment and crack it open. There's not a soul who writes like you today. Single things, single moments don't speak to me, only things in relationships, things in contexts. You're unique, Mattie. Next to you, I feel like a hack."

"That's nonsense. You're trying to put a good face on how I write. Unfortunately, it's the way I think," Mattie sighed. "But let's not talk about me, Beth, because I'm limited, far more limited than you with your categories or contexts. I like your book. If I could do what you do, I'd be thrilled. The sheer passion of your concerns, the driving force of your language. Your adventurousness, your fearlessness. My stuff is tepid compared to yours. Still, it's the only thing that I can do. I get caught up in a single detail, imprisoned in it's multifarious possibilities, its endless ramifications. That's no good, really, no good at all. I don't know very much of the world. Perhaps I should try to find the categories to which my details belong. I should go back to Aristotle."

"Mattie, you're the wisest person I know. Don't go back to Aristotle. Be Mattie."

"You're an ass, Elizabeth," and Mattie threw a pillow at her. They laughed, climbed down out of the window seat and began clearing the dirty dishes from off the table.

As Beth lay in her Athens hotel room wanting sleep to come and end another day, she felt once again that old nagging concern about how she organized her life's experiences. Was she truly only interested in issues? Had she eliminated all qualities from her life, all the things one couldn't taste, touch or smell? Were her concepts too rigid to allow for creativity and change? Was that what she had been worried about, a slow atrophying of her poetic powers, when she had turned from her subject of women and their difficult lives all over the world to write about America and its peoples, its lost ideals?

"You never risk yourself for yourself."

Had Hank been right?

Why think about that now, Beth? Why lie here in Athens and think about that? Two deaths have happened in your life since you wrote your last book. You're fighting for survival not for a literary posture. You don't have the luxury of worrying about the way you think or write. Survive. That's what you need to wrap your mind around, survival and how to accomplish that. Everything else is unimportant.

At seven o'clock Beth was pulled out of a troubled sleep by the phone's insistent ring. She answered it in a low, sleep-filled voice. It was Paul.

"My dear, I just called to see if you were all right."

"I'm fine," she said. "Thank you."

"Have you had your dinner?"

She paused to consider. "I don't think so."

"My dear, you should have something to eat. It will keep your strength up. Would you like to join me for dinner? I'm going to eat here in the hotel and then get to bed early."

"Thank you. I think I'll just stay in my room tonight."

"Then may I order you some dinner and send it up to your room?"

She hesitated. She could order her own dinner from room service. She probably wouldn't.

"Elizabeth, I can hear that you are tired and will probably not bother to order any food. So do give into an old man's whim. Let me order the food. I'll keep it light, and have it sent up to you. All you need do is answer the door and eat the stuff. What do you say? You can watch the TV. It has two English-language stations."

"Okay, thank you."

She hung up, went into the bathroom, washed her face, put on a bathrobe, came back into her room, fiddled with the TV until she got it working. Indeed, there were two

English channels. She selected the one with world news and sat there until her dinner arrived, half an hour later. She methodically munched on a club sandwich, a small salad, drank tea and left the ice cream untouched. Before she went to bed, she looked at her itinerary. Tomorrow the Acropolis and the Agora. And for those who still had energy, a walking tour of Old Athens. Tomorrow should be interesting, she told herself without enthusiasm as she set her alarm. She crawled back into bed and fell immediately into sleep, a vast dark cave that gave her no comfort.

Somewhere in the middle of the night she was startled awake by an angry female voice.

"Really, it's too much, simply too much!" the voice said. "Mankind *invented* agriculture, *invented* weaving, *invented* pottery. They leave out the gods, all the gods. They are too proud and intolerably foolish, these people."

Beth opened her eyes and sat bolt upright, her heart beating wildly in her chest. She turned on her bedside light. No one was in her room. She walked to the outside door and tested the lock. It was bolted. There was a door leading to another room. It, too, was locked. But the voices must have come from there. Probably from some member of the tour group. She looked at her clock. It was nearly three-thirty. Well, some people have lots of energy and probably there is some interesting night life in Athens. She went back to bed. Sleep returned mercifully with silence.

Paul was standing next to Elizabeth Layton just inside the entrance to the business and market place of ancient Athens, the Agora. They were waiting, as were the other 4-M tourists, for the American director of the first century archaeological excavations to come and speak to them. It felt good to be in Athens again, to breathe the Greek air. For a moment Paul longed to have Annie by his side seeing it all with her own huge and observant hazel eyes. But he pushed the thought away. He would do his best to take her through the trip, to think to her everything he was seeing and hearing.

Whenever Paul looked Beth's way she smiled, but there were dark shadows under her eyes. He couldn't help thinking of Penelope, Odysseus's wife, who had been charming and courteous with her suitors. Had they noticed the circles under Penelope's eyes as she had greeted them each morning, as she had dined with them, as she had engaged them in conversation? Yesterday at the National Museum, Beth had seemed distraught, caught up in some inner battle fought out in the lonely valley of her soul. Penelope must have done the same, in the hours after she had retired, struggling through her pain, then setting out on her nightly work to undo the stitches she had put in only that day on her tapestry. What stitches did Beth pull out all alone in her room? Who came to her aid? And who had allowed her to come on so strenuous a journey when she was so obviously troubled?

"Look over there, mother."

Two women were standing just to Paul's left. A tall, angular woman with teased champagne-blond hair was pointing in the direction of the trees.

"Where?" asked a very old and diminutive lady with a large sun hat. Her voice quivered with excitement.

"Can you see that temple?"

"Oh, now I see it. Yes, it's quite splendid, isn't it, Lolly? Whose temple is it?"

"It's the temple of Hephaistos"

"Who, dear?"

"He's the god of the smiths, Mother."

"Did we read about him last winter?"

"Yes, we did. Do you remember?"

"Of course, I remember. He is the god of the smiths." The mother fiddled with the binoculars and very quickly gave up. "I can see perfectly well with my own glasses. They're new. I purchased them for this trip. Did you know that, Lolly?"

"Yes, Mother."

"Here, young lady, you look," and the elderly lady suddenly thrust the binoculars at Beth.

"Oh," Beth said, "thank you," and she took them from the woman and held the binoculars to her own eyes. "What did you say the name of the temple was?" Beth asked.

"The temple of Hephaistos, god of smiths," Lolly answered. "He was a cripple, despised by the other gods, but they needed him and they used him. Aphrodite was given to him by Zeus as his wife, I've forgotten why."

The mother turned to Paul and to Beth and said, "How rude we are. We haven't introduced ourselves. We're from Palm Beach. That's in Florida. Isn't that right, Lolly?"

"Yes, Mother."

"My name is Ellen Parkington and this is my daughter, Leona Parkington. But everyone calls her Lolly."

Paul and Beth introduced themselves.

"I am eighty-seven years old and Lolly is sixty-six. Isn't this a splendid trip?" Mrs. Parkington said.

"Splendid," Paul and Beth said simultaneously.

The two women said, "Nice to have met you," and went to look at the map of the Agora that was posted under glass.

Despite the twinge in his left knee, Paul was relishing the wait. It gave him time to look around, to admire the view, to watch the people. Would he ever sort them all out? Ellen and Leona Parkington, Ellen and Leona Parkington, Paul repeated to himself. Lolly for Leona.

Beth, too, was looking at the Agora with genuine pleasure on her face.

"I don't think this is a good idea at all," a tall, heavy-set woman, with curls like a bonnet surrounding her plump face, was saying to a group of people near by. "We were supposed to do the Acropolis *first*, then the Agora. That's what it said on the schedule for Athens that we were all sent before the trip. You'd think they could make better arrangements than this." Her brown eyes shone hard as agates, and despite the attempt at a smile, her words were whiny. "We'll be too tired by the time we finish walking all over the Agora to make it up the hill to the Acropolis."

"Well, you see," a slight, middle-aged lady in a floppy white hat said, "the director could only meet us this morning. He has a very busy schedule."

"The Agora is not as important as the Acropolis," the first woman insisted.

"Perhaps," a tall man said, "you could just sit here and wait until the Agora tour is finished and save your energies for the Acropolis." He gave the woman a solicitous smile.

A breeze suddenly kicked up. "Oh, no dear," his lady companion answered, holding on to her hat. "I've already inquired. The buses are going to meet us on the other side of the Agora," she pointed in the direction of the Temple of Hephaistos, "so there'll be no hanging back."

"I see," her companion said.

"This is poor planning," insisted the first complaining lady, who, Paul observed, was only in her fifties. "There are elderly people here. Do they think all of them can manage that long walk?"

"Can you manage it, Paul?" Beth turned to him with concern on her face.

He smiled at her and winked.

"Will you all gather round?" It was Colleen MacMurray, the young woman escort from Smith and Smith.

"I hope you all can hear me but it's a bit windy," Marion Levitt, their lecturer from the Brilling, said in a shrill voice.

Paul noticed a rather distinguished looking man standing next to her.

"Talk up," someone suggested.

"I will, and I'll make it short," Marion said. "Today we are very fortunate to have the field director for the American excavations at the Agora here to talk to us about their most current work."

The director greeted them, then launched into his talk. "We are standing above the main street of ancient Athens called the Panathenaia, so named for the great festival given every four years. It was the primary religious festival of ancient Athens, celebrating the birth of Athena, the guiding goddess of this city."

"Of course, our modern parades derive from such religious processionals," Paul heard a lady with a cultivated British accent comment in a fairly loud voice.

After an hour's walk through the new digs with the American director, the 4-M tourists were taken to the on-site museum. There, the director bid them farewell and their Greek guides took over. The travelers were led rather quickly through the Agora Museum. Then despite the complaints of a few, they started off on the walk through what was now a park, up a small tree-lined hill, to the temple of Hephaistos. It was a pleasant walk, Paul thought, and really not too difficult, just a little incline at the end. The elderly mother and daughter whom they had just met, the Parkingtons, were walking with ease ahead of him, as were several others that Paul knew to be in their seventies.

"Isn't this lovely," Beth said, walking next to him.

She's keeping an eye on me, Paul thought, with both amusement and a twinge of pleasure. "Wait till you see the temple," Paul said.

The lady who had complained so bitterly made it up the hill. Her eyes looked sullen with anger and her face was red. But she was silent.

When her group gathered in front of the temple, Irene said, "The popular name for this temple is rather misleading. It is known as the Theseon. But we know that Theseus was only a hero of Athens and was never worshipped as a god."

Beth turned to Paul, "Wasn't Theseus supposed to be half mortal? Wasn't he a son of Poseidon, at least in some of the stories?"

"Yes," Paul answered, "but he was also the son of King Aegeus of Athens and it was he who destroyed the Minotaur in Crete."

"Therefore, the temple would not have been dedicated to Theseus. It was dedicated to Hephaistos as god of the blacksmiths and to Athena as goddess of arts and crafts," Irene launched enthusiastically into her talk. "Apparently some of the sculptural decoration of the temple depicted the exploits of Theseus and this is how people ended up calling it the Theseon."

Two people with tape recorders dogged her steps as she moved slowly around the temple. Several others diligently wrote in small notebooks.

"It's wonderful, isn't it?" Beth turned to Paul. "Is this the first time you've seen it?"

"Oh, no. I've been here a few times...with my wife. Theseus is a favorite character of mine. And," he added, "the temple is well preserved. It's really quite wonderful being near it. Something of its past still permeates the atmosphere around it. Can you feel it?" He smiled and walked away from the group.

Come, Annie, we don't need a guide for this.

Beth watched him go and thought, interesting man. And he is right, there is something wonderful about this place. She stared into the temple. The gods of the Greeks were so understandable, so human. Her own gods were too remote, too abstract. What kind of a god was the Holy Spirit? If she had to choose a god to believe in at this very moment she would choose the crippled god, the god of practical blacksmithing. Yes, he would suit her very well. She certainly wouldn't choose the Christian God she had been raised to venerate, that endlessly suffering God. Where was he when her own daughter was suffering, when she herself was nearly torn apart?

"This is the best preserved temple that you can see any-where. And the reason is that from the seventh century A.D. until the nineteenth century it was used as a church dedicated to St. George. This is a temple that has colonnades running on the four sides of it. The style is Doric."

"Come with me to Greece over the holidays. I want to show you Delphi and Eleusis, the Parthenon, the incredible architecture, the Greek light. You should see the Hephaesteon. You'd like it. It would inspire you to write great poems."

"Don't ask that of me, Hank. Don't make me feel bad. I can't leave my girls this Christmas. It's the first since their father died."

"Your girls are grown up, Beth. Share this one with me..."

"I can't. You'll have to go with one of your other friends. I'm sorry."

"At the far end of the temple proper you will imagine the two statues of the deities on two tall platforms. Sorry that we can't go into the temple. It's forbidden. But we can walk around it."

Beth tuned Irene out and allowed her group to go ahead. Staring into the exposed interior of the temple she imagined herself walking through it toward the great statues of the gods, votive offerings in her hand. It was an image that appealed to her. She might do a poem about a modern woman, a poet, coming to Athena, the goddess of wisdom, and to Hephaestos, the god of practical crafts, to ask for inspiration. As the modern poet walked through the long chamber, the temple would suddenly be restored, it's walls resurrected, its altar made whole. That would be the woman's gift to those old gods, given from out of her poet's imagination. That's a nice touch, she thought. She would describe the restored temple minutely. The gods would be so enthralled they would leave the heavens to see it, to be in it. Hail, Athena, personification of wisdom. Hail, Hephaistos, personification of...of what? Imperfection? The human condition?

"Come with me..."

What else?

What kind of questions would the woman ask of these forgotten deities? Perhaps walking through the temple, the woman would find the ghosts of her onetime lovers there. Hello, Matthew. Hello, Hank. How would the poet deal with that? How would she deal with the ghosts of all the lovers who had walked through that temple beseeching help? A luster basin for tears, for so many tears caused by lost love. But would they come to Athena rather than Aphrodite? Athena was Wisdom and wisdom can heal. Wisdom educates the head which you need when love goes bad. And Hephaistos, why come to him? Yes, to remind us of our mortality, of our imperfections, of the work that we must struggle to do.

For a few brief moments the idea engaged and stimulated Beth, until she remembered that she had no intention of ever writing again. She literally drove the burgeoning pictures, the beginning phrases, out of her mind.

Beth was amazed at how many people, singly and in groups, were at the bottom of the hill leading up to the Acropolis. She looked around carefully but didn't see Eric What's-His-Name. Halsey. His name is Eric Halsey. She had not seen him at the Agora either. Perhaps he had gone off on his own today.

So what, Beth?

Sew buttons, she answered herself, with Becky's favorite retort.

The two 4-M groups were given fifteen minutes to purchase drinks and to go to the bathroom before beginning the trek up the hill to Athens's most famous site.

"Isn't this just grand?" Doris said as she and Lucy overtook Beth who had started up the hill.

"Grand," Beth agreed.

"Hurry up, Doris," Lucy called to her. "We'll lose the group."

Doris hurried after her sister. And Beth followed the two of them, her eyes keeping the stocky figure of Doris in sight. Then Beth spotted a small temple above them and she stood riveted to the spot.

"That's the temple of Athena Nike," she heard a voice say just behind her. It was Paul, looking a bit winded but radiant with pleasure. "Athena who brings victory, that's what that means."

Beth took Paul's arm, and the two ascended the marble stairs together. They entered through the Propylaea onto the Sacred Way. They were at the top of the hill, on the Acropolis itself. Irene was leading her group along a path. And, of course, there it was, the great temple. Don't look at it yet, Beth told herself with mounting excitement. Savor everything. Take it slow.

Irene waited for her group at the site where the famous work of Pheidias, a bronze statue of Athena Promachos, had once stood. "Athena Promachos means 'Athena who preceded the warriors in battle'," she told them.

At the Hephaesteon she had imagined worshipping Athena, goddess of wisdom. A few minutes ago, she had been drawn to the temple of Athena Nike, she who brings victory.

Now she was enveloped in the desire to see Athena Promachos. What was it she longed for? Wisdom or a warrior's soul? "This famous statue was later carried off to Constantinople and, sadly, destroyed in 1203 during the crusaders' siege of the city. They say that the tip of the spear of the goddess could be seen for miles around, glinting in the sun. It was this spear tip glowing in the sun, a bit like a lighthouse, that told sailors they were nearing home."

Beth felt both a sense of loss and of rage because the statue had been destroyed. The terrible injustice of it. The loss.

Easy, Beth. Hang on. That was centuries ago.

Nevertheless.

Beth finally looked up at the Parthenon which now stood in full view. "But Paul," she said, "it's enormous!"

He nodded. She felt, from the tension of his arm which she still held, that he was deeply moved. "There will never be a repeat of this," he gestured at the Parthenon. "Never. Mankind's consciousness has altered too much."

Beth looked at Paul questioningly.

"Greek civilization is the central point in earth evolution. You can see it in its art. Man in perfect balance between heaven and earth. We still long for what the Greeks possessed."

"It's glorious," Beth said, staring at the magnificent hill on which they stood.

"My wife loved this place."

Beth turned back to him.

"I'm a widower." He smiled at her, gently removed her hand from his arm, and said, "Thank you for your help up the hill," winked, and walked off toward the temple alone.

Beth watched him go. Sometimes one had to experience important things alone.

Hank came here alone.

I couldn't go. Let's not think about Hank, please. It's four years and it was unimportant, an interlude. I never think about him.

You do.

Stop this.

Paul moved around the large temple, away from the 4-M group, keeping them in his peripheral vision. He had no need to hear a lecture on the Parthenon. After all, he had been here more than once with Annie. The sight of it made him feel alive, like the sight of the beloved after a long absence. All his fatigue, his aches and pains slid away as he stared once again into the splendid space.

How he loved the ancient Greeks, cherished their uniqueness, their remarkable transition culture. During their brief sojourn at the forefront of history, the transformation from image thinking to a lively philosophic thinking had been accomplished. Which, and he sighed at the thought, had eventually evolved into the dry abstract thinking of his own times. But no abstractions for the early Greeks. For them the gods embodied ideas. For them the gods personified qualities. Athena Nike, Athena who brings victory.

Paul longed to go inside the Parthenon, feel the great columns looming up around him, but that was forbidden now. He stared out across the hill that was the Acropolis trying to will it restored and whole, wanting to see the Greek people walking around in their togas and chitons, and the Greek gods firmly ensconced in their temples.

The Greeks had created a culture that was a fulcrum between the cosmos and the sense perceptible world. And humanity was still moved by their accomplishments. Well, why not? After all, the human race owed them much. The humanization of consciousness culminated with the classic Greek period. Before that time human beings walked the earth half dreaming. Before that time it was the gods who breathed across the consciousness of humanity. It was the gods who had thought in the human being.

Paul tried to imagine the inner life of an ancient Greek as he walked around a group of attentive Japanese tourists. But he was too much a man of the present epoch. He knew the gods, or what the Jews and Christians called the angelic hierarchies, had slowly moved away from humanity, leaving the human being inwardly alone. That loneliness he could experience, that inner abandonment. But then so could most of humanity. The angelic hierarchies had released humanity into its own care. You are past childhood, they had said.

Having circled the Parthenon, he stopped to take in the entire Acropolis. So many tourists. What did they see when they looked around at this religious hill? No doubt, most admired it and listened attentively to lectures on its architecture. But to reduce the Acropolis to great architecture was to diminish it. To laugh at the religion of the ancient Greeks but admire their philosophy and art was foolish, one-sided and self-serving. It was, after all, interwoven, all one.

He turned to walk past the old temple of Athena. Athena, goddess of wisdom. How he loved to read the Greek philosophers, how living their thinking was then. How dead our thinking has become. A corpse really, abandoned by the gods. Good only for looking at sense material reality. Even our so-called religious ideas have materialized the heavens. We can no longer penetrate the pictures.

Paul moved on to look at the caryatids at the Erectheum, thinking about what humanity had lost. But he caught

himself quickly. After all, this descent from a cosmic consciousness to a human consciousness with all its hard
sacrifices meant a step forward in evolution.

It is a hard but splendid road, Annie thought to him.

But sometimes we must remember what great spiritual gifts
we have given up in order to pursue the goal of genuine
freedom.

No regrets, Paul. On this side nothing is forgotten, nothing
lost. The past transformed still rains down on humankind,
integrated, sublimated into something new. The future is
coming toward humanity and the past is incorporated in it.

No regrets. Just remembrance and acknowledgment.

Paul turned back to look at the temple of Rome and Augustus. It was there that Colleen found him. They were about to
go into the museum.

"Yes, of course," he said and followed her to where Irene
was waiting.

Beth stared for a long time at the Parthenon, listening with
one ear to Irene. Then she turned to look with pleasure at the
other temples on the hill dedicated to other gods, then at the
various buildings, waiting for Irene to identify them. She
tried to imagine what it would have been like to have worshipped many gods, to have worshipped in temples of
exquisite beauty, in front of masterfully carved statues.

Why have I never come here before? Why has it been
Africa and South America and Asia, but never Greece? Why
not the cradle of western democracy and culture? Was I
afraid of something?

Without answering her own question, Beth followed Irene
about the Acropolis, her senses radiating out to claim everything on the hilltop. It was a familiar feeling. Insight came

from such feelings. And poetry. Something majestic and yet evanescent was in the air here, gently soaking into her like a steady rain. Yet she couldn't intuit what it was. She walked through the ancient site, now barely listening to the guide, just looking at everything and listening into the space.

There's essence in this light, she thought, there's being. If you breathe into it with your senses the air will fold back like a curtain and you will see...you will see...what? Something. This Greek light is a curtain. It wills to drape open. Something behind wants to shimmer through. What? Something. No good, Beth. Our senses are like closed curtains. We occult the light. Something behind the closed curtains. The Greek light is a curtain of veils. Who will lift them?

Not you, Beth. Leave metaphors to others. You're finished with that.

Leave me alone and let my imagination enjoy the day. It's okay, if I don't write it down. Really.

Beth kept track of the rest of her group, but just enough to keep from getting lost. She wandered past the temple of Rome and Augustus, then around the Erectheum with its famous porch where copies of the caryatids stood, then past the old Temple of Athena.

Finally, Irene led her group once again past the Parthenon toward the Acropolis Museum. And Beth followed.

As she waited for the stragglers to catch up, Irene said, "The nineteenth and the twentieth centuries have almost succeeded in blowing up the buildings on the Acropolis. Wars have nearly been the death blows dealt to our great antiquities. But now an even greater calamity than bombs. Our modern technology, including airplanes and millions of visitors, are causing more and more damage with their pollution. The gorgeous marble is slowly breaking down into gypsum."

"Damned shame," a broad, elderly man said.

"Come," and Irene led her group into the Acropolis museum.

Beth was already emotionally full but tried to keep her attention on the objects that had been found on the Acropolis and were currently being preserved there. Again, and irrationally, she longed to see the famous statue of Athena with its gold tipped spear. But that statue had been destroyed in Constantinople centuries ago. She could feel her anger rising because she and others like her had been robbed of its magnificence.

And then was amused at herself.

It was after two when the 4-M tourists returned to their hotel from the Acropolis. As they walked into the lobby, Beth asked Paul if he would join her for lunch.

"I'd be delighted," he said, with a little courtly bow.

Not wanting to change clothes, they chose the most casual restaurant in the hotel and found a table near a waterless, indoor fountain. The room was nearly empty. Just as they were seating themselves, an English couple that Beth had spoken to at the Agora, entered the restaurant. They were accompanied by a woman, the one whom Beth had observed holding court on the steps of the Benaki Museum. Seeing Beth and Paul, they asked if they could join them. Beth and Paul said they would be delighted and when everyone was seated, introductions were made. The names of the couple were Winifred and Melvin Winston and the single lady was called Barbara Churchill.

"How appropriate, don't you think?" Mr. Winston said, "Winstons meet Churchill," and everyone laughed.

After their lunch orders were taken, Winifred Winston said, "We're from Winnipeg."

"And Florida, darling," Melvin added.

"Yes, I suppose that's true," Winifred said. "Of course, we are originally from London and two of our three children still live there. We'll be visiting them as soon as this trip is over."

Barbara Churchill was from San Francisco but also originally from London. She didn't speak of any children and she wore no wedding ring.

When Beth mentioned that she was from New York the conversation quickly turned to everyone's favorite restaurants there. When Paul disclosed that he was from north of Boston, there was a discourse on sea food and various "exceptional" sea food restaurants in the Boston area.

"Does the Acropolis seem more crowded to you?" Barbara Churchill asked, pursing her lips thoughtfully and pointing her empty cigarette holder at Beth.

"I don't know," Beth answered. "This is my first visit to Greece."

"Really? Your first? How remarkable," Barbara said.

"Well, how marvelous for you, to see everything with fresh eyes," Winifred said. "Mel and I have been here more times than we can remember. Something mysterious always draws us back." And she took her husband's hand and he gave her an affectionate smile.

"I should say, yes, it is more crowded than in previous years," Mel answered the question. "But, Winnie," he turned again to his wife, "wouldn't you say that the restorations are marvelous?"

"Oh, yes, simply marvelous."

And they talked about the Acropolis for a while.

Barbara Churchill sat up in her chair, puffed on her empty cigarette holder, listened for a while, then said, "Of course, the Parthenon is exquisite, unique among temples. But I think somehow I prefer the Hephaesteon." Her bangs glistened waxily in the light falling directly on them from a skylight.

At this point, the waiter brought their food and after much discussion and rearranging of plates, they each had their own orders sitting in front of them.

It was Winifred who resumed the conversation. "I have to confess," she said, "I have never heard of that god. I meant to look him up the last time I was here."

"So you did, my darling," her husband said.

"Not well known," Barbara said. "He's spoken of in Homer, of course."

"My dear," Winnie said, "it's years since I studied my Homer." She laughed and her husband smiled at her fondly.

Beth noticed Paul waving at someone, motioning him or her to join them. She twisted around to see who was standing in the open doorway. Her heart quickened as she saw that it was Eric Halsey. Was it her imagination or had he taken a step toward them, but on seeing Beth had pointed to his watch and had turned and quickly retreated?

This is ridiculous, Beth scolded herself. You must make amends. You certainly have offended that man by your cold responses to what were obviously only friendly gestures.

"You know you're chicken shit," Hank scowled across the table at her. They were sitting in the cafeteria at the Museum of Modern Art, eating salads.

"What do you mean by that?" Beth asked him evenly, trying to ignore the raised eyebrows she saw on the elderly couple sitting a few feet from them.

"I mean that you lack courage," Hank articulated the words slowly.

"I know what chicken shit means. I'm not in my dotage. What I want to know is how you think I lack courage?"

"Good God, do you want a list?"

"Because I won't sleep with you?"

"For one, but that's not the essential point. The essential point is that you lack courage in life."

"That's ridiculous, Hank, and you know it. I won't sleep with you because you're twenty-four and I'm forty-eight. That's twenty-four years difference."

"Yes, I know, and you are old enough to be my mother. My God, your generation is hung up on age."

"Yes we are."

"Get over it. You're living in the La Brea tar pits"

"What?"

"With the dinosaurs. I'm talking about taking chances in life, not about sex."

"And I don't take chances? Who braved attack by the Shining Path in the mountains of Peru in order to talk to women about their lives? Who ducked bullets in the jungles of Brazil for the same reason?" She knew she was being defensive. *"Does that sound like a fearful lady? You'll have to come up with a better psychological profile than that. What are we getting today, Psych. 101?"*

His dark eyes stared at hers unflinchingly. *"Yeah, that's just my point. You've run all over the world just to get away from dealing with your own life."*

"I knew it, Psych. 101."

"No, I've read all four books of poetry by the renowned feminist writer, Elizabeth Layton."

That stung. *"First of all, I'm not a feminist writer…"*

He snickered.

She scowled. *"Why the hell are you trying to analyze me from my books? You know damned well I don't write about myself. Boring to both me and my readers."*

"That's precisely it," he grinned darkly and his smile said, *"I got ya."*

She relented. *"So what do you see as my main deficiency?"*

"You pull away from life and all its marvelous experiences..."

"Including you?"

"Including me. You hide behind your very remarkable capacities for involving yourself in the lives of others. Oh, you do that well, Elizabeth, you do that very well indeed. But, and this is the crux, kid, you don't pay attention to what's going on inside. Inside you're a scared rabbit. Adventure means other people's lives. Not your own. You never risk yourself for yourself. Maybe if you had, your husband wouldn't have looked to graze in other fields."

"Oh, shut up," she tried not to show how much that last jab hurt. *"I'm not going to sleep with you. Finish your lettuce. I want to see the Matisses before we leave".*

Beth looked at the retreating back of Eric Halsey and sighed. When we get on the boat, she told herself, I'll take the first opportunity to straighten this out. We can't be avoiding each other for no good reason.

"The temple of Hephaistos intrigues me," Barbara was saying, "especially its architecture. Of course, you'll find other Greek temples in Sicily and southern Italy that are in as good condition, but they are still provincial temples and do not, I repeat, *do not* have the elegance of proportion that the Hephaesteon has." And she launched into a ten minute monologue on the virtues of the temple's architecture.

"I find myself intrigued by the legends surrounding Hephaistos," Paul, who had been rather quiet, finally interjected.

"What do you find interesting?" Beth asked him, before Barbara could sail into a lecture on mythology.

"Isn't it in the legends, the stories of the people, that you find hidden truths about their lives, their thoughts, their beliefs, their consciousness?"

"Oh, but the mythology doesn't make any sense," Winnie said, "it's all pretty silly stuff. But, of course," she quickly added, "it still makes delightful tales, even today. I can imagine the ancients sitting around the fire, telling these tales to each other. After all, what other entertainment did they have?"

"Some tales are even contradictory," her husband added. "They can't seem to make up their minds, for instance, on how Athena was born. Who her parents were."

"I thought she sprang from the head of Zeus," Beth said.

"In one account," Mel said, "in the other..."

"...she comes from the sea." Winnie finished her husband's words.

"Wasn't that Aphrodite?" Beth asked.

"I think," Barbara said, in a commanding voice, "that these stories have psychological significance. They are about our own psychological struggles, what the Victorians used to call soul struggles. There has been very important work done on myths and fairy tales by noted psychologists and even philosophers. Therefore they are significant."

"All interpreted," Paul said, "out of the consciousness of our own times. After all, psychology is new. Myths are old."

"The study of psychology is new," Barbara said. "But psychology is as old as mankind."

"Do you believe in evolution?" Paul asked her.

"My darling, everyone believes in evolution. Only a fool or a religious fanatic denies evolution." And she poked at the air between them with her cigarette holder.

"Driven God or the gods right out of the universe, I'm afraid," Mel said with a chuckle.

Beth looked at Paul sitting next to her. Had they offended Paul's religious feelings.

But Paul seemed unperturbed. "Then do you also believe in an evolution of man's perceptual and conceptual life?" Paul looked across the table at Barbara Churchill.

"What do you mean, exactly?"

"I'm merely suggesting," he said, "that with our own modern consciousness that is so self-aware, so self-involved, it is hard even to imagine a different kind of consciousness for the humans of earlier times, before the classic Greek period, for instance, in the mythological epoch. Yet I feel that this recognition of a change in consciousness over the ages is the only way one can understand Greek art or the Greek religion. Or any early art or culture, for that matter. For instance, why in our times do we perform rituals inside our churches and cathedrals that once took place outside?"

There was silence.

Paul went on. "Can it be that man himself has become more inward? And as he moves into his own interior, into his own personal house, he moves his religious practices into the interior of his houses of worship?"

"There is simply no evidence of any change in man's consciousness for thousands and thousands of years, not since man became the human that we know and recognize. Simply none," Barbara said.

"But there is. The myths themselves tell you of another kind of consciousness."

"What do you mean, Paul?" Beth asked.

"I mean that before the time of the Philosophers and in some parts of the world even later, man must have had a picture-consciousness, a consciousness that was more participatory."

"Like some of the primitive tribes in Australia or Africa," Winnie said.

"Better than what the primitive tribes have now," Paul said, "because since it is past its proper evolutionary period, the present faculties of the current primitive tribes have become decadent. I'm merely suggesting that it is grossly unfair to only consider the value of these mythological pictures as symbols for our inner soul struggles. Battles against things like greed, falsehood, cowardice..."

"...fear, hate, anger, selfishness," Winnie added.

"Right," Paul said.

"Why, Paul?" Beth asked.

Barbara spoke loudly, "But they make perfect sense." Beth could see her struggle against irritation. "As psychologists have shown, as philosophers have almost proven. Are you saying that the myths can't be interpreted that way?"

"Oh, they can, of course."

"But...?" Beth urged.

"That misses the fundamental point."

"Which is?" Winnie asked.

"That myths give pictures of evolutionary processes."

"How do you mean that?" Mel wrinkled his brow.

"I mean, a kind of spiritual-humankind history."

"You actually believe that Zeus was real or that Athena existed?" Barbara's voice rose several decibels.

"Maybe he means that they, the ancient Greeks, really believed in the gods," Beth said. "Well, they must have. They built all those splendid temples in which to pay them homage." She wasn't sure she could follow Paul's thinking, but she had this sudden urge to protect him from Barbara Churchill's ridicule.

"What I'm saying is what Zeus represents is a *picture* of spiritual forces, spiritual realities, that the human of those times could see as Zeus. There was a time when the gods were very active in the lives of humans and also a time when that interaction ended, when the deities, or as we Christians would call them, the angelic hierarchies, removed themselves gradually from that activity. One sees that severance in many folk myths. For instance in the Nordic myths there is the twilight of the gods."

"Wagner," Mel said. "The Ring Cycle. Have any of you ever been to Bayreuth to see the Ring Cycle?"

And from there they embarked upon a discussion of Wagner, of music, of other trips.

Beth barely followed the new talk. She was still thinking about what Paul had said. A metaphoric consciousness. But not just for poets, artists and visionaries, for everyone. That was an idea that would certainly appeal to her friend, Mattie. But where was the proof? She turned to watch Paul who was attentively listening to Barbara's lecture on Wagner. He may indeed be religious, she thought, but he's also more complex and more interesting than I gave him credit for.

Not long after Wagner, the luncheon broke up. Paul asked Beth if she was going to go on the walking tour of the Plaka. She answered, no, that she intended to write some postcards, pack for their departure the next morning, and take a nap. Paul said he too intended to rest that afternoon and to pack.

It was close to 4 P.M. when Beth got up to her room. She took a shower, put on her bathrobe and sat down to write postcards, first to Merle and Phil, then to James and Nina, a few more to friends, then finally a letter to her daughter and her daughter's husband that would be waiting for them at their new apartment in Philadelphia when they returned from their honeymoon. To each, she wrote that it had been a wonderful trip so far, that she was very glad she had come, that she was feeling good. And she was. Today, finally past jet lag, she felt fine. This trip was really a very good idea.

I'll write a letter tomorrow to Mattie, after we get on the boat, she decided.

Ship, she corrected herself.

After the letters and postcards had been written, she lay back on the bed to think about the day. She had very much liked the Temple of Hephaistos, and Hephaistos himself intrigued her. Greeks had worshipped a crippled god, had actually built a temple for him, a beautifully designed temple. She got up, pulled out her suitcase, unpacked her guide books and read what she could about him. Then once again she lay back on her bed just to think through the lovely full day.

As she did, reveling in her satisfaction of it, guilt began to trickle into, then flood, her feelings. How could she feel good? How could she allow these pleasant, light-headed emotions to supplant the feelings of mourning she had promised Alicia? The whole year since Alicia's death, as she had stayed strong for all those around her, as she had entered as best she could into Becky's happiness and into her wedding plans, Beth had silently assured her dead daughter that she would indeed mourn for her, that she had only been postponing her grief for the sake of others. And now, she was being seduced out of her grief by old ruins built by a people she could barely understand who worshipped ungod-like gods and who bequeathed to us their quaint stories. How could she be so unfaithful? Really, how could she? It was appalling. The pain of her transgression hit her hard. She put her guide books on the other side of the room and lay down on her bed. It was six o'clock. She cried herself to sleep.

Paul, just as he was falling asleep, thought to Annie, I talk too much.

You spoke for Elizabeth Layton to hear.

Yes, but that's not all.

I know.

I couldn't help but put a pin prick in Miss Churchill's balloon.

You can't change everyone.

No. But I don't have to let pomposity rule the day. Was I too hard?

Were you?

I'll do better in the next few days. Sometimes it is best to be still and just to *think* another possibility.

Yes.

Beth seems better today. What is it that ails her?

You must find that out, my love.

Yes. Soon. Goodnight.

Goodnight.

Somewhere around ten o'clock Beth had a dream.

She was standing before the Doric Temple of Hephaistos in the twilight. She wanted to go inside but was afraid. There was no one else around. But Beth hesitated because the guide had told them that no one was allowed to enter the temple. As she stood there peering into its dark interior, uncertain as to whether she should go in or not, a woman walked past Beth, talking heatedly to a man who was accompanying her. The woman was very clear to Beth. She had a beautiful face, her dark hair was long and curled and she was dressed in a chiton like the korai Beth had seen in the Acropolis museum. The man accompanying the woman, however, was unclear in the dream, as if he were walking in mist. But Beth knew, as one does in dreams, that the woman's companion was male even though she could not see him.

The woman was angry. "It's really too appalling," the woman was saying in a familiar voice. "Such egotism, such arrogance, such gall. They pride themselves on their erudition, their so-called science, but I tell you their intellect is a puny thing, a crippled child compared to what they've lost." And she disappeared into the temple with her shadowy companion.

Beth longed to follow them into the temple but remembered the guide's warning.

"Beth, follow them," Hank called to her from inside the temple.

Beth tried to move her feet. "I can't," she said and felt a terrible loss.

"You pull away from life," Hank said.

Beth woke up.

Awash with frustration, Beth sat up and glanced at the clock. It was after ten. The dream was still so vivid that she decided to write it down. She dreamt frequently but usually remembered very little, only bits and pieces like the colorful fragments of a kaleidoscope. But her dream fragments seldom made a discernible pattern. However, this fragment, though short, seemed clear.

She reached for the notebook that she had automatically put by her bedside as she had done ever since her college days, even though after Alicia's illness, she had hardly written in it.

After she finished writing the dream down, Beth began to jot down the events and impressions of her two days in Athens including the people she had met and as much of the conversation at lunch as she was able to recall. She pushed aside her sense of guilt. After all, she wasn't writing a poem, only notes in a journal. At 11:30, she ordered a late supper from room service, picked up her guide book and read about the Monastery of Daphni, the only stop they would be making the next day on their way to Piraeus and the ship, the New Odyssey. At 1 A.M. she fell asleep and did not dream again.

Two large buses unloaded their passengers in the tree-lined driveway near the gate to the Monastery of Daphni. As the guides waited for all the 4-M travelers to enter the church's courtyard and then for the camera buffs to snap their pictures, Beth wandered through the arches at the far side and found herself in an adjacent courtyard where there were ancient ruins. Old columns stood there like sentries from another age. Were they from an older church or from the temple of Apollo alleged to have existed there in an earlier time? Her mind couldn't recall what she had read about Daphni the previous night.

To Beth's dismay, she had been pulled out of sleep that morning by the ringing of the alarm clock into a state of acute anxiety. Something was wrong and as she tried, through her sleep-befuddled mind, to latch onto the cause, she remembered that she was being pursued by a band of Furies who recited over and over the litany of her angers and sorrows. Whatever joy the previous day had given her had simply disappeared as if it had never happened. What had made her think that the beauty of ancient Greece could so easily dispel current sorrow? Really, how stupid she was to think she could be seduced so easily by a remnant of a remote past she certainly couldn't understand or even imagine.

Nevertheless, according to instructions, Beth had placed her packed suitcases outside her hotel room door with their 4-M labels in place. Then she had stepped into the shower where she had wept tears of wrath coupled with helplessness while methodically washing her hair with the hotel courtesy shampoo.

As she was raging and weeping and washing, a small voice inside her said, You don't have to go on with this trip. You can simply stay in Athens or go somewhere else, Rome or Paris. Or how about to some obscure Greek island? The idea intrigued her. She could do that. She could take control of her life by telling the Smith and Smith people she wasn't feeling well and that she would stay a few more days in Athens and then arrange to go home.

You've left your suitcase in the hall to be transported to the ship.

Oh, no. She was trapped.

Maybe they haven't collected the suitcases as yet.

Maybe if she hurried out of the shower and dressed quickly (her bathrobe was packed), she could pull her suitcases back into her room before the porters came to take them away.

Beth quickly rinsed off the soap, climbed out of the tub, dried herself with a large white towel, slipped into her denim skirt and white cotton blouse and opened the door to the hall. The suitcases were still there! Thank goodness, they were still there.

"You?" a voice asked in a thickly accented English.

She looked up to see a pair of opaque black eyes in a young man's face looking at her without interest. He was pointing to her luggage.

"Yes," she answered, and said nothing as he hoisted, first, her suitcase, and then her hanging bag onto his cart already piled high with baggage and pushed the cart with effort down the hall to the next group.

Beth closed her door with a pounding heart and sat in her chair until she reminded herself that she had to pay the extras on her hotel bill before the buses arrived.

"This is a beautiful spot, isn't it?" a man's voice said just behind her, pulling her out of her thoughts and back to the Daphni courtyard.

"Oh, yes," she answered politely. She turned to see Eric Halsey standing a few feet from her, a tentative look in his eyes, his body half-turned toward the archway, ready for retreat.

When she felt the blood rise to her face, she turned away from him. But so he wouldn't once again feel the brunt of her rudeness, she asked, "Do you know if those columns are from the old Greek temple or from the earlier church?" and she gestured toward the white pillars.

"Look," he said, walking up to her, "I'm sorry if I've intruded on your privacy. You've made it clear that you don't want to talk to me but you looked so utterly forlorn standing there, I couldn't help but come over."

Beth was both touched by his kindness and appalled at the revealing nature of her face. But he had come upon her so unexpectedly that he had caught the misery and the exhaustion mirrored there. She'd have to be more careful.

"But, please," he went on, "answer just one question and then I promise I won't bother you for the rest of the trip."

"Oh, I'm so terribly sorry," Beth said, and touched his arm and then blushed again, and finally asked, "What's your question?"

"Do you know me?" his brow furrowed and his light brown eyes, narrow with concentration, looked troubled. "I mean, have we met somewhere? At some party? Or club? Some opening? Was I rude? I've racked my brain trying to remember. But after my divorce I got pretty crazy and went to a lot of bars and parties and I drank too much and all I can think of is maybe we've met before and I made an insulting pass at you...or what?

Divorced.

Beth had to smile. "No, we've never met. I seldom go to parties and I never hang out in bars."

"Sorry, I didn't mean to imply..."

But Beth interrupted him for now was her opportunity and she grabbed it. "I'm sorry I've been so unfriendly. I can hardly explain why. I'm a little crazy myself now and I simply misread your smile?"

"Divorce?"

"No," she hesitated, but finally went on, "I'm a widow. It's not that. I mean my ill-mannered behavior is not that. Oh," and she gestured with relief at the archway, "Bill What's-His-Name has come to get us. They must be going into the church now." Beth started to move away.

"Wait," his hand caught her arm.

She paused mid-flight.

"Let *me* show you the church. The mosaics here are very special."

"Come with me to Greece over the holidays. I want to show you Delphi and Eleusis, the Parthenon, the incredible architecture, the Greek light."

"You've been here before?"

"Yes, a few times. Byzantine Art is a passion of mine."

"I thought you were an expert on Contemporary Art."

"I am."

And they walked together into the church.

"This is one of the most beautiful churches in the whole of southern Greece. It's a church known for the uniqueness of its priceless mosaics," Irene was saying with genuine enthusiasm. "Outside of Thessaloniki, there are only three churches in all of Greece where you can find this many Byzantine mosaics. Two are on the mainland, Daphni where we are today, Osios Loukas near Delphi and a third, Néa Moní on the island of Chios."

Eric took Beth's elbow and steered her away from the guide and group and maneuvered her past the vigilant guard who eyed them without curiosity.

"Now, look up there," he pointed to a corner of the softly lit church. "Isn't that extraordinary?"

Beth glanced up to where he was pointing and caught her breath as she saw the fragment of the Annunciation. "Oh," she clasped her hands to her chest, "It's exquisite, really elegant. Yes, that's the word for it, elegant."

"In an orthodox Christian church there were paintings or mosaics on every inch of the ceiling and walls. As much of the Gospels were depicted there as could be fitted into the interior. But you probably know that. Stop me if I begin to sound like a travelogue but I love this stuff."

"Do go on. I don't know very much about Byzantine art."

"Good. Then you're in for a marvelous treat. Irene is right, these pictures are indeed rare. In Istanbul, in the Hagia Sophia and in the Chora, there are mosaics of equal quality. Still, there is something here one can't find anywhere else."

Beth craned her head and turned to look at the panorama of glorious images. "What is it?" she finally asked.

"Can you see the influence of classic Greek style?"

"I'm not sure."

"Well, for one, look again at the Annunciation, look at the way the archangel Gabriel is standing, one foot out like that. Very Greek."

They moved about, their heads tilted up. Beth looked as Eric pointed out the details, absorbed in what she saw.

"Look how expressive the faces are."

And she answered, "Oh, yes."

They stopped under a mosaic called *The Baptism.*

"Good heavens," she said, "that's odd. I never saw a naked Jesus before?"

"Which," Eric grinned, "proves my point. They are still influenced by classic Athens and the Athenian love of and complete ease with the naked body. Not like us poor embarrassed Christians. But see how they've done the water. They've been able to give it, with mosaics mind you, the appearance of translucency." He was enthusiastically into his subject. "Meanwhile back in our old European homeland, the Normans had just conquered Britain. Here they were building this extraordinary church."

"Boggling, isn't it?" Beth said.

"Before this church, there was another one built in the fifth or sixth century. Am I sounding too much like a guide book?" he asked looking down at her interested face.

He was rather handsome, about 5'10" or so, with light brown eyes. And a beautifully shaped head with only a slightly receding hairline. And, she had to admit, a very nice body. "Oh, no, please go on," she said, glad for the dim light because the color was rising into her cheeks again. Beth turned to look up again.

"Okay, then... Before the early church there was a Greek temple here, most likely dedicated to Apollo. This site was one of the stops along the way to Eleusis. Eighteen miles is a long walk and so there were these shrines built all along the way from Athens. Some of the old temple stones were used in the first church and possibly even in this one." He took her by the elbow and maneuvered her toward a particular mosaic. "Here's my favorite," he pointed to a scene of the crucifixion.

Beth looked up.

"Look at the Madonna. Look at her dignified suffering. She's so human and yet so transcendent."

He was standing very near her, watching her. Beth had to work to control her breathing. Well, she had to be honest with herself, he was attractive. And she wasn't dead yet.

When she thought the word *dead* something drained out of her. Alicia was dead. To lord over her poor dead child her own *aliveness* was appalling. Her hands flew up to her face.

"What's the matter?" Eric asked her. "You just went white."

"Oh, sorry," she said, "just a bad thought. I'm fine."

"Shall we go outside? We've seen most of the mosaics." He took her by the arm and without waiting for a reply, steered her toward the door and out into the sunlight and back through the arches to the courtyard where they had met earlier. There was a ledge around the old ruins and he sat her down there. "Don't move," he told her. "I'll be right back."

Beth nodded and watched him as he disappeared back through the archway into the first courtyard. He must be somewhere between fifty and fifty-five, she decided. Just the right age.

God, why am I even thinking like this?

She shook those thoughts out of her mind and turned once again to her own feelings which were getting dangerously out of hand. Why was she responding so terribly to everything

91

today? A single word could set her off. Why had she become so upset at the reminder of death? Everything that they had seen and would see on this trip had been created by people long ago dead. All the events of history they were studying were dead events.

And her loss was not the first loss ever to be felt nor would it be the last. Was it death that was so upsetting to her or was it, in the presence of Eric, the realization that she was glad to be alive, that she could still feel human longing?

No, she cried out angrily in her mind, I will not have what Alicia could not have. It was unfair, utterly unfair, to take the child before the mother. She would not accept it, no, never.

But who was there to fight? Where was the enemy?

Beth bit her lip to keep the tears from welling up, got shakily to her feet and turned to look at the old ruins. She hugged herself to keep from falling, felt terribly chilled in the warm sun and closed her eyes against the insistent light.

She saw the temple ruins. The woman from her dream last night stood there staring at her, quizzically. Her black curls were piled high on her head and her white chiton dropped in flattering folds to her small ankles.

The woman's companion stood behind her and though the sun shone brightly on the ruins, he was obscured in shadow.

"I shall never understand it," the woman said, her black eyes shining opaquely.

"What's that, my dear Iris?" the man asked.

"This attitude toward death."

"The fear you mean?"

"They are not courageous," she shook her dark head, "that is a certainty. They don't even value courage and that is a mystery. But it's not that."

"What then?"

"If death is darkness, if death is shadow, if light after death is only for a few chosen as it was for us, why don't they value life as we valued it and give all their skill to it?"

"It is not possible for us to understand the twentieth century. Come away from her."

"But it has been said that even the realm of death has changed in their times, so distant from our own. It is said they can bring light into Hades' dark kingdom. Why then do they still fear death? And why do they not, at the very least, value life?"

"Come away. She cannot answer your questions."

The woman continued to gaze at Beth as if she were looking through a one-way mirror. Finally, she shrugged her delicate shoulders and turned around. Taking her friend's arm, she moved away.

Beth wanted to call out to her, to say...what? What did she want to tell them?

She lurched awake. "Oh, my God," Beth cried out.

"I'm sorry. Did I startle you?" Eric withdrew his hand from her shoulder. "You were standing there with your eyes closed and the tears running down your face. What can I do? You look so miserable."

She looked at his troubled face and felt moved by his sensitivity.

"I'm sorry," she said to him, and sat down again. She searched in her purse for some tissues. "That's never happened to me before. It's the oddest thing but I must have fallen asleep standing up, just for a moment or two. And I had the oddest dream. Really a very strange dream," and she stopped talking, recalling to herself just what it had been she had dreamt. When she returned to the bus or after she was on board ship, she would put it down in her notebook.

When she didn't go on, Eric said, "I tried to find you some water or a drink of some sort, but no luck. I did buy you a present."

Beth looked up.

"Some beautiful postcards." And he put the cards in her hands which had been clasped tightly on her lap and now opened to receive his gift. "The color is coming back to your cheeks. I swear, when I came back and saw you standing here, eyes closed and so terribly pale, I thought you had seen a ghost."

Startled, she laughed. "Really?"

"Not a bad spot for a ghost, you must admit. Perhaps one of the Cistercian monks who lived here is lurking about." He grinned at her tentatively.

"I thought Cistercians were Roman Catholics, not Greek Orthodox."

"So they are, but after the Franks conquered Athens in the early thirteenth century, they gave the church to the Cistercians."

My ghosts, she thought, were definitely not Cistercians.

"They kept it till the sixteenth century and then turned it over to the Greek Orthodox Church."

She felt how hard he was trying to engage her, to drag her away from her sadness, so she tried to meet his effort with the only tool she could muster, her interest. "I'm ashamed to say I don't know much about the history of Greece after Alexander. Somehow my history classes concerned themselves mainly with Western Europe."

"Mine too," he nodded. "If I hadn't studied Art History…"

"It's a shame, isn't it? I know a little about Byzantine art from our museums, but, frankly, I was never drawn to it. I hadn't expected to be so moved by mosaics."

"Wait until you see the Chora in Istanbul."

Several members of their party came out into their court-yard. Assorted cameras were clicking again. And the small video cameras.

"How did you become interested in Byzantine Art?" she asked him.

He stood with his hands on his hips staring at the columns that were part of the ruins in the courtyard. When he spoke there was a certain weariness in his voice, or was it regret?

"When I was younger, in my late twenties, my wife, ex-wife, and I spent two years living in Rome. She wanted to study opera. She was, is a singer. And I wanted to study art. So we worked a few years, saved money and came to Italy. We lived very frugally, but we did travel, staying in flea bag hotels and eating bread and olives," he half-smiled at the memory, "but we saw a lot of art and heard a lot of music. Because of this church and the two others I mentioned before, I got hooked on mosaics. I came back twice while we were studying in Rome. And once about ten years ago."

"Well, after today, I can understand why you would get hooked on mosaics." She made her voice light. Did he still miss his ex-wife? Had she pried too much?

"Why haven't you published another book of poems? It's been four or five years, hasn't it?" he asked suddenly.

"What?" Beth was astonished. How did he know she was a poet?

At that moment, Bill from Smith and Smith appeared in the courtyard to announce that it was time to return to their buses for the short ride to the ship.

Beth stood up quickly. "I guess we'd better get back to our buses." Surely Eric Halsey hadn't read her books. Beth moved toward the archway and through it into the first courtyard then hurried quickly across it. Could he still recognize her from those youthful, carefree photographs on the dust jackets? It had been more than four years. Four terrible years.

Eric Halsey walked silently behind her. They entered the driveway where the buses stood under full-leafed trees.

As she reached her own bus, she turned to Eric and said (was her voice too bright, too aloof?), "Thank you so much for the tour and for the postcards. It's been very nice talking to you."

"See you on the boat," he said, with a nod, but no smile. He moved quickly away from her and toward his own bus.

Oh, damn, Beth thought, I've done it again. Well, I can't manage him. And that's just the way it is.

"You pull away from life and all its marvelous experiences."

"You never risk yourself for yourself."

Go away.

The seat where she had left her belongings was in the middle of the bus and she slowly made her way there behind a talkative group who, one by one, struggled toward their seats. Beth finally slid into her own. She dropped her purse onto the aisle seat, leaned back in her own and stared out the window. She was sorry that she had offended Eric after he had been so nice to her. If she had been cold or rude it was because he had startled her when he had mentioned her poetry. But she didn't want to think about that right now. She wanted to think about that dream.

Curious, she must have actually fallen asleep standing up. How else explain that very coherent and lucid dream? She reached for her notebook but once again her thoughts returned on their own to Eric. The reason he had made contact with her was obvious now. She was a fellow artist.

Simple. End of worry. Eric Halsey couldn't be more than casually interested in her.

"...*you do have beautiful hair...no question, your best feature is your hair. Don't ever cut it.*"

Never a beauty, she was, at a weary fifty-three, not the least bit alluring. Well, that was all right, she didn't want to deal with a man in any way right now.

You're friendly with Paul, why can't you be polite and friendly with Eric. Who asked you for more?

Go away.

Beth began to write down her brief dream in her notebook.

"There you are," a familiar voice trumpeted.

Beth looked up to see Doris peering down at her with a wide benevolent smile on her large layered face.

"Where did you expect to find her? That's where she was sitting before," her sister Lucy said, coming up behind her. Lucy looked a bit warm.

Doris paid no attention to her sister's peevishness. "Did you like that church?" And not waiting for an answer, which she obviously knew would be in the affirmative, went on to say, "You were right about the guide, that Irene. She was great. Very informed. I really don't know how they do it, these European guides, they simply know everything, history, art, geography."

"Did you know," her sister barged in, "that the laurel leaf and the bay leaf are one and the same? Well, that's my new thought for the day."

And they passed by her not waiting for a response to sit in the last row. Beth had managed a smile. She tried to return to writing in her notebook. Odd, odd dream.

The three English travelers, Winnie and Mel Winston and their new friend, Barbara Churchill, slid into the two rows of seats just in front of Beth. Barbara was speaking in her cultured and authoritative voice, "One doesn't know, of course, if this place was called Daphni because they found so many laurel trees here to begin with, and so decided to build here—they were terribly superstitious, my darlings, as we know—or if they, I mean, of course, the ancient Greeks, planted the laurel here because this shrine had already been dedicated to Apollo." She was facing around the back of her seat in front of the Winstons and her large face with its flat bangs looked very pensive.

Beth tried to tune her out.

"Is that the legend about the water nymph that was turned into a laurel tree so as to keep Apollo from catching her?" Winnie asked.

Her husband laughed. "Well, the Greek gods were nothing if not virile."

"Not like the Greeks themselves," Winnie said.

"You mean all the homosexuality?" Barbara said, voice booming. "It was merely cultural with them, accepted as perfectly normal. Let's not forget it was a man's world, despite the female goddesses. Women kept their own company. They were breeding stock, really."

At that moment Paul showed up at Beth's seat looking a little flushed. "May I sit next to you?" he asked.

A short way down the aisle Beth saw the persistent blond lady heading toward them.

Beth picked up her abandoned notebook and purse and said, "Of course." She would write down her dream after she was aboard ship.

Paul slid into the seat next to Beth gratefully. On the trip to Daphni, he had been sitting a few rows behind her by himself. As the blond approached him, Beth was tickled to see a flash of annoyance cross her face.

She thinks I'm a rival, Beth thought with amusement.

Paul nodded and smiled pleasantly at the woman as she walked by.

"Now where was I sitting?" the woman drawled, trying to look confused. "Oh, yes, how silly I am. I'm down in front," and she turned then, and with great difficulty made her way against the still boarding passengers to her seat in the front of the bus.

"You have an admirer," Beth said.

Paul just shrugged his shoulders.

"Well, I'm not surprised."

"I simply do not understand it," a loud voice, that Beth recognized as belonging to the complaining lady at the Agora. "I don't understand why we're not going to Eleusis. We're so close." The complaining lady was aiming her irritation at Colleen MacMurray from Smith and Smith who had come down the aisle to count the passengers.

Colleen lost count but said cheerfully, "It's in awful surroundings, and there's not much to see there now."

"Then why aren't we going to Delphi?" the complainer demanded.

"Well, Mrs. Green," Colleen said, "we can't go everywhere, can we? We brought you to Daphni." And she went to the back of the bus and began her count once more.

"I, for one, would have gladly given up Daphni for either Eleusis or Delphi. We'll have our fill of churches and mosaics in Istanbul," Mrs. Green spoke loudly enough for half the bus to hear her.

Paul looked at Beth and raised his eyebrows.

Beth returned his look with a smile.

"Delphi was important, wasn't it?" Winnie, who was seated in front of Beth, asked her husband.

It was, naturally, Barbara Churchill, seated in front of them, who answered. She turned around and peered imperiously at the two. "For centuries, the great and near-great came to the Delphic Oracles to ask for guidance when they had important decisions to make, both personal and political. Lots of hocus-pocus, steam and sibyls foaming at the mouth and saying incomprehensible things that the priests interpreted, no doubt, to their own advantage. But the ancients were naive about many things. Even Alexander was alleged to have gone there..."

Beth listened to the familiar tale, but finally tuned it out to watch the scenery through her window as they traveled toward the Aegean Sea. With Paul sitting next to her she felt safe and so she allowed her thoughts to turn again to Eric Halsey. She decided that he was a disturbing element on this trip, one that she wished she didn't have to deal with. But really, she asked herself, what harm can he cause? She need never be alone with him. She was in the midst of dozens of people and it need never get out of hand. And hadn't she decided that he was just being friendly? That was his job, as representative of the four museums.

Beth turned her attention to Paul, "It looks like you're being chased."

He sighed and then winked at her, his blue eyes clear, amused and resigned, "It's part of being a widower. Women chase you."

"How long have you been a widower?"

"Six years," he said.

"I've been a widow for five," Beth said.

"Ah, but you're so young. Perhaps that explains why you have such sad eyes."

"Oh, dear, are they?" And without waiting for a reply she asked him, "Are you retired?"

"Yes, for ten years. I was a high school teacher."

"Really? I've taught, too. What did you teach?"

"History."

"Then you'll be a great help on this trip," Beth said.

"And you? What did you teach?"

She looked out at the ocean that the bus was now running along. "Oh, English literature, writing," she answered.

"High school?"

"No," she turned back to him. "College."

"Look," someone called out, "there's the ship!"

And all conversation stopped as everyone turned to look out the window at the New Odyssey.

Beth opened the information folder that she found in her cabin and studied the map of the ship. Then she started to unpack, but quickly gave that up, changed into white cotton pants and a green T-shirt, gathered up her sweater and notebook and left her cabin. She found a staircase just down the hall and climbed up one flight to A Deck. Beth wanted to see the ship cast off.

Many of her fellow travelers were also on deck to see the departure. The ship would sail north the rest of the day and through the night and arrive in Salonika in the morning. Thessaloniki, she had heard it called, the ancient Thessalonika, named after the half sister of Alexander the Great.

Beth moved to the stern, where the pool and its bar were located. She looked over the rail to the deck below. Greek sailors were busily doing their tasks with obvious pride, with cocky awareness of the scene they were playing for this new group of tourists. Finally the rope was hauled on board, the ship's whistle was blown, and they were on their way.

A few of her new companions had drinks in their hands, others had coffee, all obtained at the poolside bar. Many were sitting in the deck chairs around the still empty pool. Everyone looked excited and pleased, even, she noted, the grumpy Mrs. Green. Beth watched the retreating harbor and wondered as the ship turned north if she might catch a glimpse of the Acropolis. And the golden tip of Aphrodite's spear.

Piraeus, the port that they were just leaving, was an industrial town, no great beauty, but behind it were lush May hills and before it spread the fabled Aegean. Throughout their journey there would be Greek islands to sail past, reminders of the greats of Greece, like Sappho and Homer. A few screeching sea gulls careened through the air above them and then took off back to shore. Beth watched the coast for a while but could not see the Acropolis so she found a chair near the pool. She wrote quickly in her notebook, setting down the remainder of the odd dream she had experienced in the courtyard at Daphni.

At four o'clock Beth was seated in the large Poseidon Lounge along with almost all of her fellow passengers. Next to her were Doris and Lucy dressed in twin jogging outfits. Lucy's was a brilliant pink and Doris's a pale green.

"Isn't it amazing," Lucy leaned over Doris to say to Beth, "how many people didn't bring warm clothes. What do they think sea air means? Ships are chilly when they're out on the water."

Beth commiserated by shaking her head.

"Well," Doris said, "this is some people's first time on a boat. They'll learn."

Ship, Beth almost said

Marion Levitt lectured on Thessaloniki and its environs, showing them slides of the famed Macedonian treasure from the alleged tomb of Alexander's father, King Philip, with slides of Pella, his capital, and its various excavations. They also saw slides of the excavations at Vergina where Philip's tomb was ostensibly found.

"That wife of Philip's was something," Doris mumbled in Beth's ear. "She hated Philip."

Despite herself, Beth looked around for Eric Halsey. He wasn't at the lecture. She had seen him across the dining room at lunch engaged in lively conversation at his table. If he had been aware of her, Beth had not noticed it.

After the lecture, Beth wrote postcards by the pool. That done, she returned again to her cabin to shower and change for the Captain's cocktail party and dinner. She selected a black dress, low cut and sleeveless. Her mother had often said, "You can never go wrong with a little black dress." For a moment she wished she had a pale yellow dress, something her mother would heartily disapprove of.

"I wish Merle had picked another color for these bridesmaids' dresses, but you know how stubborn Merle can get when she makes up her mind." Beth's mother looked at Beth critically. They were standing in her mother's bedroom before the fireplace. "That pale yellow is definitely not your color. Turn around, Beth."

And Beth turned around.

"The shape of that dress doesn't do much for you. It's for girls with round behinds and a little more breast than you have. It will probably look perfect on Merle's friend, Eileen, or even on Audrey, who is much too tall to be graceful. But on you... Beth, I wish you'd put on a little more weight, it might give you some waist. Turn around again."

Beth's mother walked over to her and began pulling in the dress at the waist and flaring it out at the knees. "Perhaps we can get the dressmaker to put in some padding in the bust."

"I don't want any padding."

"And build up the pleats on the hips. Stand still, dear. You certainly take after the Laytons and not my side of the family. Your nose is just like your father's. Come here near the window." She pulled the shades up as far as they would go. *"That's better. Never, never, darling, wear yellow, lime or beige. It will just blend into your skin tones and make you look blah. Merle takes after your father too, but her height gives her an advantage. She has my breasts at least. James takes after me, in looks anyway. He's too serious. That's like your father. Still, I think the girls drive him crazy and he's only fifteen. Girls are so forward these days, don't you think? Stand still while I try to pin this."*

"The dressmaker is coming this afternoon. She'll pin it."

"I want her to see what I mean. Don't be so impatient. You can at least try to look pretty at Merle's wedding. I swear if you could get away with wearing blue jeans, you would. I hope you'll be as smart as your sister. If you're not a raving beauty, you can't afford to be too fussy, that's what I told her. Take what is offered, within limits of course, but you know what I mean. A good family is important, but I'm sure you know that. And a good career. Phil is a dentist."

"I know he's a dentist."

"Stop squirming. Merle is only twenty. She didn't wait. She saw something good and she grabbed it. Turn around. Let me look at the hem." Beth's mother dropped to her knees. *"Turn around slowly."*

Beth turned around.

"Phil will make a very nice living soon. And the Brodys are an old New England family, not wealthy but well off. Your sister will be quite comfortable. Of course at thirty she will get the Layton trust, as you will, and James. And a dentist's hours are better than a doctor's. That will be a blessing for her. If only you played

the piano with a little more talent. This hem is crooked. I'll let the dressmaker straighten it." She stood up, moved slightly away from Beth and looked at her daughter. Her eyes narrowed slightly. *"Elizabeth, you do have beautiful hair. Now that can carry you far. A few blond highlights and yes, no question, your best feature is your hair. Don't ever cut it."*

The following year, one month after Beth entered college, she cut her hair, keeping only an inch of it cropped around her head.

She had worn it short ever since.

Beth left her neck bare, but put on her longest silver earrings, of American Indian design, and looked at herself in the mirror. She was too thin.

"...you look so utterly forlorn standing there..."

She pulled open a drawer and took out the embroidered shawl that Matthew had bought for her the winter they had visited Mexico. Her mother had looked at it once and had said, "Matthew has the taste of a gypsy." Beth put the black silk shawl with it's embroidered brilliantly colored flowers around her shoulders. She felt safer under it.

"Raven wants to marry me..."

Go away.

She looked at herself critically in the mirror. "Not bad," she told herself out loud, "except for the bags under your eyes."

Who will even notice, she answered, and headed for the Poseidon Lounge.

People were seated at low tables, in chairs or sofas, talking in groups, drinking cocktails, wine and soft drinks. Beth stood for a moment, not knowing what to do, with whom to sit. When she saw Max and Sheila Birnbaum, the elderly couple she had met at lunch, motioning to her to join them, she gratefully crossed the room to where they were sitting.

"My dear," Sheila said, her gray hair curled about her pretty face, "do tell me your name again. My memory is not what it should be. We had such a delightful lunch together and here I've forgotten your name. I know you're from New York," she said.

And Beth introduced herself to the group and sat down.

Sitting with the Birnbaums were three other people. "I'm Donna Herder, from Santa Barbara, and this is my daughter, Jenna," an attractive blond woman said. "And this is our new-found friend, Jordan.

"Don't you just love this," Jenna said. Despite the fact that there were so few her own age Jenna was obviously thrilled at being aboard the ship.

Jordan, sitting next to Jenna, said that he was escorting his grandmother on this trip. "I'm supposed to be looking out for her," he grinned, "but she really doesn't need much looking after. She's very gregarious and half the time shoos me away, telling me to find my own friends. She's terribly independent."

Jenna laughed loudly at Jordan's remarks.

Well, Beth thought, the only two *youngsters* on this trip have found each other.

A waiter came and took Beth's order and soon returned with her white wine. A band from England was playing recognizable tunes. Some couples were dancing on the dance floor, an uncarpeted circle in the middle of the room. The sound of conversation and music was loud and cheerful.

Donna and Beth exchanged the requisite information, where they were from, where their cabins were, what had impressed them in Athens, where they had eaten there, what they had purchased. Beth found out that this trip was a college graduation present for Donna's daughter, Jenna. Donna mentioned a son but not a husband and wore no ring. Beth spoke about Becky and said she, herself, was a widow. Jenna listened to the conversation around her and piped in now and then with caustic and insightful observations about the passengers and staff.

Halfway through her second glass of wine, Beth began to feel a little light-headed. Don't drink too much, she warned herself, and set the glass down. Stress and alcohol don't mix.

"May I have this dance?" a voice behind her asked.

Beth, startled, glanced over her shoulder, then blushed. It was Eric Halsey who looked down at her without smiling. She didn't want to be rude. She didn't want to dance with him. She didn't want to reject him once again. She didn't want to create a *little scene* in front of all these smiling people, so Beth said, "I'd love to." And stood up.

"You know you're chicken shit..."

Eric led her by the hand out onto the dance floor. The band was playing something by Cole Porter, a slow fox trot. Beth had loved to dance when she was younger. Matthew had liked it also and they had danced often before the children came.

"Raven wants to marry me."

Stop it, damn it.

Eric held her firmly as the two moved around the dance floor to the languid music. He didn't speak.

Just inhale and exhale, she ordered herself when she became aware of the raggedness of her breathing.

In a moment Beth was resting her head on his shoulder. Their bodies were close (touch-dancing, her girls had called it), and his hand was tight against the small of her back.

Stop holding your breath. In, out, in, out.

When the song was over he nodded politely, led her by her hand back to her seat, bowed slightly, said, "Thank you," very formally. And left.

Donna raised her eyes questioningly at her.

"A fellow New Yorker," Beth said hoping that would be enough.

"He's that art specialist from that museum in New York," Sheila Birnbaum said.

"Mother, is it awful? Is it too soon?"

Beth didn't explain why her fellow New Yorker had caused such color to rise in her face.

Moments later, the gong announcing the dinner sounded, and they went down the wide staircase to the dining room. Jordan excused himself at the door, saying he and his grandmother had been invited to sit at the Captain's table. Beth caught sight of Paul standing alone at the door and motioned him to come join her and her cocktail companions.

There was plenty of wine, free this evening, and though Beth was feeling a bit light-headed she couldn't refuse the delicious drink. After all, wouldn't it help keep panic at bay? And she was enjoying both the company and the food. The special six-course meal, including both lobster and steak, was elegantly served and, judging from the buzz of laughter and talk in the room, people seemed in a celebratory mood.

By the time dinner was over, Beth felt dizzy.

As Paul and Beth left the dining room, he turned to her. "Shall we stroll on the deck? You look like you could use a little air."

"Why not?" Beth said.

The two climbed the stairs to the A level. Others had arrived before them and were standing in clusters talking, or sitting, or walking around the deck. It was chilly and Paul offered Beth his jacket.

"No, I'm fine," she answered, but she wrapped her shawl more tightly about her shoulders.

There were few stars. The sky was overcast. Still Paul could see the lights of the shore and the odd shapes of hills hovering in the background.

Paul and Beth began their stroll around the deck.

Be brave, Annie thought to him.

Or an old fool, he thought to Annie.

That too, she said.

"My dear, are you looking for something?" Paul asked, "or trying to get away from something?"

Beth looked startled, and then annoyance washed across her face.

Bad start, he thought, and tried again. "Forgive an old man for asking you so personal a question, but you have a face like clear glass and it does make one curious about you. I noticed you in the airport in New York. You reminded me of my Annie."

Beth's eyes widened and irritation was replaced by curiosity.

"Actually, you look nothing like her. It's your face with it's light-show of feelings. That's somewhat like Annie's. On the plane, I couldn't help wondering about you. I was convinced, because of those sad, anxious expressions, that you were not going on a pleasure trip. Frankly, I was surprised to find you on this tour. So if I've been tactless by asking too much, you can simply ignore an old man's curiosity and tell me to mind my own business."

Beth moved to the railing and stared down at the water. Paul stood next to her waiting.

"I don't think I'm looking for anything anymore," she finally said. "Why look? If you don't go looking, you won't find disappointment. And what's there to get away from?

Most everything I've loved has gotten away from me." She laughed, and Paul thought it a cold sound.

"Are you bitter?"

"I hope not." Beth said, moving along the deck again. Paul followed her. "I'd hate that. I'll admit to being an angry person. But that's not terrrible, is it? If awful things happen, why not be angry? And life is full of, really made up of, injustices, don't you think?"

"Oh, I would never say life is fair. No, that would be foolish. From a certain perspective, life is definitely not fair. But I would say it's ultimately just."

"You think life is just?" her voice teetered on the edge of shrillness. "You think everyone has the same advantages as you and I?"

"Considered from the point of view of one life, of course not. But looked at from a higher standpoint..." Careful, Paul, tread carefully, he warned himself.

"What higher standpoint?"

Paul gazed out at the shore, trying to make out the shrouded objects. Hills, trees, houses? He glanced down at his companion's tight face. Why was he pursuing this woman? Hadn't he come on this trip to get his own life in order?

Annie, what should I do?

"If you were to take into consideration more than one life," he heard himself saying, "you might see that in the long run, things will balance out..."

"Reincarnation? Really? How very comforting," she said in a tone that refuted her words. "I thought you were a Christian. What are you, a Buddhist?"

""Oh, I am a Christian, my dear. And I also believe in reincarnation."

I'm behaving like an old boor, Annie, I can't do this. It's unwanted.

He changed subjects. "Were you disappointed, as some others were, not to have seen Demeter's temple?"

Beth's tone lost its edge, "Well, not really. I mean it wasn't on the original list of sights we were given."

"I went once with my wife. My Annie was a teacher of world literature with a special fondness for Greece and Greek literature. We came as often as we could scrape the money together."

"Was it beautiful?"

"The temple of Demeter? It was as Colleen described it. But there is something in the air there, something that still permeates the atmosphere. Demeter is a very, very ancient goddess. She represents spiritual forces that are no longer possible for humanity to understand or take hold of."

"What do you mean? Why not?"

"Because of evolution, Beth. Humanity is not anything like it was when Demeter roamed the earth."

"Demeter roamed the earth?" He heard the derision in her voice.

"In a sense." Should he try to explain that once upon a time spiritual beings did indeed roam the earth, not in physical bodies, but in spiritual bodies that an earlier humanity with their clairvoyant faculties could *see*?

They walked again in awkward silence. It was Beth who broke it. "Do you miss your wife?"

He answered, "Yes," and he hesitated, "but she's not really gone, you see." He wasn't going to lie. "I feel her presence always. She's enjoying this trip, I think."

The look on Beth's face said it all.

He would say one more thing and then leave it be. "Any time in mankind's long, long history, Beth, right up until the modern era, if I had said that, it would have been taken as a matter of course that we live with our dead. But today I must sound, well, if not crazy then simpleminded. Perhaps in a few centuries people will again experience the nearness of those who have entered the spiritual world before them, without embarrassment or fear, in the natural course of things."

Beth excused herself then, saying she was feeling a bit ill and needed to get some sleep.

"Goodnight, Beth."

He watched her go. I've made a fool of myself, Annie. I interfered and she didn't like it. And, frankly, I have no idea what she needs.

She needs, my love, what all human beings need.

Alcohol and stress don't mix, dummy, Beth told herself as she stepped into the shower. Let's watch it from now on.

When she was lying in bed she thought about Paul. It was yet another cruel gift from the Furies to be given as a friend on this trip a man in his dotage who believed his dead wife was still with him. Alicia was dead and Beth would never see her again. Never. She didn't want to hear any more of Paul's odd religious prattle. Did he really believe that the old tale about Demeter was true?

But why was she carrying on like this? What difference did it make to her if Paul was eccentric. All in all he was a kind man. Old people get strange living alone. Besides, in a couple of weeks he would be forgotten.

Beth slept badly, waking now and then in a panic, feeling the room spin, falling back into ever-changing nightmares. Matthew showed up in one with that little slut of a student, Raven. He said it was all right for him to have a fling or two, but now that he was dead, Beth owed him allegiance. She tried to scream at him but no voice came out of her mouth. She nearly fainted from the effort. He had no right to ask faithfulness of her but deep down she felt she owed it to him, owed it to what had been the good years, or there would be nothing left of those years given to the marriage. Matthew was gone. He had no right to take the marriage with him, to obliterate half her life. She called to him but he disappeared down a corridor. Hank appeared for a moment, and shook his head at her. "Fool," he whispered and he too disappeared. Then it was Alicia who was standing at the end of the long corridor crying out to Beth, "Mother, listen…" "I'm coming to you, baby, I'm coming to you," Beth called to her but the words were flung back in her mouth and they tasted bitter. When she tried to run to Alicia, she was stopped by an invisible barrier. Then Paul appeared floating on a cloud above the ship, saying, "Really, my dear, it's easy. Just try." Try what? But again she was mute.

Suddenly the dream calmed. It was night, the sky illumined by a crisp, lucent moon. Beth stood at the ship's pool, across from her the lady from her daydream. Near the rail in shadow her companion waited.

Iris stared at Beth, without blinking. "Really, why do they do it?"

Beth tried to leave, to run. But her legs would not move.

"What's that, my friend?"

"Drink."

"Why did we do it?"

"It brought us down to the earth when we still hovered too much above it. But they are too much in it. Really they are immersed in the sub-earthly. There is no balance. Look at her. She's made herself quite ill."

"It's not just the alcohol. She's angry. It flows out in dreadful colors."

"Yes, yes, dreadful, it stains the atmosphere around her."

"Peace, my Iris, she lives at the end of the twentieth century."

"How blind they all are, it brings one to despair," the woman shook her head and her black curls bounced in the moonlight. "They have no courage, no honor, little pride. And to think we are so dependent on them. What heritage will they leave for us when we return?"

"Let it be, Iris, there is still time."

"Not much. Really, my old friend, not much." And the woman turned her back on Beth and the two disappeared around the poolside bar.

Beth woke from that dream sober. It was 5 A.M. She picked up her notebook and wrote it down. The writing of it helped her. She then added the other dream fragments, Matthew, Hank, Alicia, Paul. Once more her own frustration at not being able to reach them, not even in her dream, overwhelmed her. Then she thought about Paul and how rude she had been and how suspicious. After all, many people believed in life after death. Why should she assume he was nuts or in his dotage? Paul was still an attractive man. That blond woman was after him, and she was younger than Beth. And half the world believed in reincarnation. Why had she acted as if she thought he was crazy?

"To me reincarnation is self-evident," Hank told her with a shake of his head. *"Therefore, make the most out of life."*

"It's just fuzzy thinking," Beth answered him. *"You'll grow out of it."*

If anyone was crazy, Beth decided, it was she. It was hard enough to keep herself together when she was sober, when she was tipsy it was impossible. She had better leave liquor, even wine, alone. She got into the shower then and cried and cried. But all the bitterness and all the anger and all the frustration barely trickled away with the water. She climbed out of the shower exhausted and slowly dressed.

Paul was looking at a mosaic floor called *The Deer's Hunting* in the ancient town of Pella which had been Philip's capital and the birthplace of his son, Alexander. The mosaic floors were remarkably well preserved. They had lain for centuries buried like hidden treasure only inches under the earth.

Immediately after their arrival at Thessaloniki that morning, the 4-M tourists had embarked for a visit first to the Archaeological Museum and then out into the Macedonian plains to see the excavations at Philip's capital.

The floor Paul was looking at had been part of a large house in the fourth century B.C. The scene he was observing was a savage one. Two naked hunters were slaying a stag, one with an ax, one with a sword, while a dog attacked the spotted creature's underbelly. And yet the incident was beautifully rendered.

How different the consciousness of these people had to be, he thought to Annie. The art tells you.

If you look with open eyes, Annie said.

How little we understand them, those ancients. How baffling they seem to us.

Why should we understand them? Can we understand fully just one other person from our own times? Someone we think we love?

No, not even someone we love.

Paul described the mosaic floor he was looking at to Annie. What an extraordinary sense of beauty they had in ancient Greece, he thought as he moved on. They were words he had often said to her when she was alive.

Yes, Annie answered.

But like us they fought terrible wars, he said. And the gods joined them. Why don't we moderns puzzle over the role war played in their development? Why don't we ask if it was different from the role it plays in our times?

The human being then needed to learn courage, honor, loyalty, faithfulness. But that was long ago, Annie said. War no longer belongs to humanity's development. Yet we still engage in it.

Paul stopped at a mosaic floor called *The Lion Hunt.* He thought, But what has happened to those qualities we all learned in our past? They seemed to have disappeared.

Paul, I love that you are thinking.

It feels good, Annie, not to be dreaming and drifting.

It feels very good.

"Fascinating mosaic, don't you think?"

Paul looked up to see Beth standing next to him. She was smiling, much to his relief.

"Beautiful. Beautifully made," he answered.

"And yet so violent. Nothing disjunctive here."

"I beg your pardon."

"I was thinking of poetry, which I teach. How some say, in a disjunctive world where there is such upheaval and such terrible violence, poetry must use a language that is disjunctive, jarring, lacking in the harmony and the orderliness of formal poetry."

"That didn't seem to bother the Greeks. As you say, nothing disjunctive here."

"It's the argument of the New Formalists, that it's the job of art to order the disorder, to reign it in, to shape the chaos."

"And where do you stand?"

"In utter confusion," she said, and laughed.

Before they boarded their buses to return to the ship, Paul said to Beth, "I'm thinking of taking a walk a little later along the Thessaloniki waterfront. It's Sunday and the stores are closed but the outdoor cafés are open. Perhaps I'll get a cup of coffee at one of the cafés and try out my college Greek. If you haven't better plans, would you like to come along?"

"No better plans. And I'd love to, if it's toward late afternoon. I'm a bit tired. Too much wine at dinner. I didn't sleep too well last night. I must have been terrible company."

Was that an olive branch? "Then take a nap and let's meet in front of the purser's station, when?"

"Four?"

"Four is perfect," he said.

That afternoon, Beth and Paul disembarked and moved down the long dock toward the gate where a solitary guard sat watching those who walked out into the city from off their small ship. He stared at them with, what Paul thought was, a benign indifference. The two sauntered along the well-cared-for waterfront, past couples and strolling families, all dressed in their Sunday best, despite the heat.

"Paul, what made you come on this trip? I mean why did you choose to take *this* trip?"

"Why did I choose this trip?" he repeated her words.

"Yes."

Paul thought back to the days just before the invitation had come from the Brilling describing this trip, then he said, "I needed to come on this trip because I was dying."

Beth's feet stopped moving. "Oh my God, Paul, no!"

He looked at her, startled, then reached out to take her arm. "Oh, my dear, oh, my dear, you've misunderstood me. No, it's my fault, I phrased that terribly. I'm not ill or anything. Actually I'm in very good health for a man my age. What I meant...mean is that I was allowing myself to die."

Beth's face cleared. "Oh, I'm so glad you're all right." And she gave Paul a spontaneous hug which touched him deeply.

They began to move again. The sun was very hot and there was only the mildest of breezes spinning off the blue water. "What do you mean, Paul, that you were allowing yourself to die?"

"I guess you could say that I had lost interest in life. That's not good. The funny thing about it is that I hadn't realized it. I slowly glided into it." He shook his head. "Are you sure you want to hear this story? It's not very interesting."

"But you are interesting, Paul. And yes please tell me."

He stooped down to look in her eyes, saw concern there, and began his tale.

Actually it had been the communication from his dead wife that had convinced Paul that he needed this trip.

It was a winter morning, just past dawn. Paul drifted awake and heard this thought: You are allowing yourself to die too soon. It is a waste that you will regret later. Paul knew it was Annie. But the message astonished him. It bolted him awake, away from that fugitive border between sleeping and waking that he so loved of late.

He sat up. "Annie?" he called softly.

But there was only silence. If there was more to the message, he had lost it. But what he had heard was enough. The dawn had slid into gray. A raw, rainy wind was pummeling his bedroom window which faced the Atlantic. He stared out at the roiling water pounding the rocky cliff on which his house sat. The room was too cold. No good, he warned himself. He got out of bed and turned the thermostat up above seventy. Cold makes you sleepy. He put on his slippers and bathrobe, then climbed down the stairs. He stopped in the living room, then the dining room, and adjusted the thermostats there. He did the same in the kitchen. You are getting penurious, he scolded himself.

He prepared his coffee with the new coffee maker that he had received as a Christmas gift from his nephew, Barney, and Barney's wife, Harriet. Second only to his study alcove, with its large bay windows overlooking the ocean, the kitchen was his favorite room. It still had the old stove from almost forty years ago when he and Annie had taken the little inheritance Annie had received from an uncle and had combined it with their meager life savings to purchase this small two bedroom house high on the rocks overlooking the Atlantic in Gloucester, Massachusetts. Until their retirement it had been their weekend retreat, their vacation haven. While they were teaching, they rented a comfortable old apartment in Boston. When they retired they gave up the apartment and moved to Gloucester.

Paul opened the refrigerator and took out a carton of milk to use with his coffee. The refrigerator was new, bought twelve years ago. The original had simply died one day and they had replaced it with a more up-to-date model. Paul took out the butter and the jam, placed them both on the table to soften and warm for the breakfast toast that he would take with his second cup of coffee.

The kitchen table was his favorite piece of furniture. He liked it even better than his treasured desk. It was worn, made of oak, with lots of scars and stains, an old friend who had mediated many a wonderful conversation between him and Annie or between the two of them and myriad friends. It was here, at this table, that they had wept and had finally reconciled themselves to childlessness, to their task as teachers of other people's children. It was here they had talked over Annie's incurable illness, here years earlier that they had talked through that one indiscretion of Paul's. He sometimes thought he could see the tear stains her weeping had made then. It was at this table that they had planned their few trips to Greece, here they had studied their spiritual philosophy together, read the books and lecture cycles of the turn-of-the-century Austrian scientist and spiritual researcher, Rudolf Steiner. It was here they had worried about money or the lack of it, here they had had their last conversation—before Paul went off to the big war—and here they had had their first, when Paul returned with the Purple Heart from the Italian campaign. It was here, too, that they talked about and fretted over all the little wars that had come and gone since.

Paul poured his coffee, ran his fingers gently over the surface of the table to evoke Annie's face more clearly in his mind, then took his filled coffee cup and walked back through the hallway into the living room and finally to his study alcove at one end of it. He wanted to watch the storm while he thought of what Annie had told him. He never tired of watching the play of water against the rocks. There was no beach below the rocks on which his house sat, but that didn't matter. What mattered was this pounding of surf against stone and the invigorating sense of vitality it gave one. Life forces, that's what this hard meeting of water and land quickened.

Paul sat down behind his desk in his comfortable swivel chair and turned it in a half circle so he could face out toward the storm. Then he began to think of Annie's words, her urgent message. That was the way the thoughts felt, urgent and serious, "You are allowing yourself to die too soon. It is a waste that you will regret later." Somehow the message had the ring of truth about it. It had been a long time since he had heard Annie within, a long time since he had directed his own thoughts to her. Had he been living too much in the past? Their past?

"I had given up on life," he told Beth. "I had settled into a dull and rather rigid routine, had become miserly even though my nephew who is a stock broker has done wonders with my savings."

"It's hard to imagine you uninterested in life, Paul. You seem so, well, so lively. But tell me more."

He had never thought of the way he was living as a slow death. But hearing Annie's words in his mind, he knew them to be true. "It is a waste that you will regret later." That part was easy to grasp. It took no unwinding. Once in the spiritual realms after death, he could make no changes. Only on earth could change come about or something new begin or something old be repaired. In the spiritual realm after death all one could do was gaze at one's past life, see what was left undone, or done badly, and long for a new life in which to correct mistakes, fulfill old goals. It was a simplification, for there was more that one did in the time between two lives, but good enough for his present musings. The first part of the thought, "Paul, you are allowing yourself to die too soon," what could he say to that? Was he longing for death? Annie had been gone over five years. Had he given up on life? Was he only biding his time? Well, there was the book he was writing.

"You write, Paul?"

"Oh, well, not literature. No, as a historian. I've been interested in writing a book about myth as a key to pre-history. Over the years, I've gathered material. It's sitting on my desk and on my bookshelves. But I haven't written much, really."

"Why not?"

"I'm not sure exactly. Since Annie died, I guess my zeal is gone. I'm half way through and it all seems like presumption and a kind of impudence to think one knows anything at all that the world must have, must hear."

Hard gray rain slapped the windows of his alcove. He turned to look at his desk. Neatly stacked papers lay waiting. There were several books in ordered piles behind the papers. In a cup that said "I love you" on a big heart, given to him by his eight year old grand niece, Marcie, there were a dozen sharpened pencils. It was the desk of a man on the verge of writing, not the desk of one deep into his work. He sighed and turned back to the storm.

Before Annie became sick he had begun his book *Greek Mythology as Spiritual and Earthly History*. In the years since she had died he had written at it intermittently. It was the excuse he gave when Barney and Harriet called to invite him to Long Island for a visit or for a holiday. It was the excuse that he gave when he refused invitations for lunch or dinner with old friends in Boston, or when he stopped going into Boston for events at the spiritual-philosophical society to which he belonged. But the truth was that he was writing less and less and daydreaming more and more.

How often he had sat in just this way, or in warmer weather on the porch, beginning with a thought he was elaborating for his book then sliding into thoughts about the past or into reverie or sleep. Hours would pass and what had filled those hours would quickly escape him. Even when he read he would drift away into a remembrance of some past incident, usually with Annie, occasionally roaming and dreaming through his childhood. It was natural in one's seventies to remember. Yes, that belonged to old age, but was he giving into the dying process? Was there more he needed to do still in this lifetime? Well, there was his book. He knew he had a point of view that wasn't commonly articulated. And of course he knew that life was precious, that everything one could do while still here, should be done, that each moment on this earth was an opportunity for something.

He stood up, a twinge of familiar pain riding up from his knee to his hip, and moved through the living room, the hall, through the small dining room which contained his parents old dining set, pushed through the swinging doors into the kitchen again. His slippers made a shuffling sound. He drew his old bathrobe a bit tighter around him. The house was still chilly. How many times of late had he not bothered to get dressed, to bathe, to shave? Too many, he knew, and shook his head.

He took the bread out of the bread box, dropped two slices into the toaster and poured his second cup of coffee. When the toast was done, he gingerly pulled the slices of toast out and stooped slightly as he buttered them and then lathered them with jam. He had done all of this before in exactly the same way. His morning resembled a ritual, no, far worse, a thoughtless habit. This is not good, he warned himself. You are becoming a caricature. Annie is right. You're wasting your life.

He slid his 6'2" frame into *his* chair and took a bite of his grape-jellied toast just as he did every morning, then got up with a jerk that caused his coffee to slurp into his saucer and onto the wooden surface. He took his two pieces of toast and threw them out with only a twinge of regret. He opened his refrigerator and took out a piece of cheese, scraped off the mold, found some stale crackers in the cupboard and ate those.

He knew he had to do something about his life. Annie was right.

At ten-thirty that morning, showered and shaved, meditation completed, Paul came down the stairs and noticed the mail had come, pushed through the slot in the front door.

"In the mail, that very morning," he told Beth, "was the brochure from the Brilling announcing this trip. That very day I filled out the forms, wrote my check, and mailed it."

"Wow," Beth said. "You certainly were determined."

"Better late than never, my dear," he said.

He did not tell her how he had begun a program of physical fitness that very afternoon, after the sun had made a tentative appearance, to prepare himself for the trip. He began to walk daily around his neighborhood. By the time he left on the trip, he was walking two hours each day. Not bad for a seventy-six year old man.

When they arrived at a square filled with cafés and restaurants, Paul suggested they get some coffee.

"I'd love that," Beth agreed. She felt glad that she had come on this walk, despite her fatigue, glad that Paul had shared his story with her, glad that her rudeness of the night before had obviously been forgiven.

The two found a table at an outdoor café. Paul ordered coffee in his best Greek much to the waiter's delight. They sat and contentedly watched the passing parade of families dressed in their Sunday best. It was very warm, much warmer than it had been further south in Athens. But the velvety air around her was soothing.

Beth looked at Paul with his kind face and said to herself, you're not the only one to suffer losses. Everybody carries wounds, healed or open. Don't feel so special, Beth. You can manage another two weeks.

"Two things can happen as you get older," Paul said, stirring sugar into his cup.

"Tell me the two."

"Warn me if I get boring."

"Okay," she said, and smiled.

"Old people preach, you know. We all think we have something to say."

"I'll keep that it mind," she said. "Shoot."

"Well, one, you can become more creative because the forces that were working to keep your physical body going for years and years are finally freed from that task. Or you can become dull inwardly, a caricature of old habits, slip into too much daydreaming, into fixed ways of doing things, fixed ways of thinking and feeling. Then you become cranky and old. That's what I was doing."

"Hard to imagine that. You're the best company I've had in years."

"Ah, you are flattering me and I love it."

"I mean every word."

"My dear, you are a delight," Paul said, patting her hand affectionately, and then he announced, "I found one of your books of poetry after lunch and read it."

"What?" Beth said.

"My dear, I had no idea that you were a poet as well as a teacher of English literature. But yes, that fits somehow."

"My poetry? Where? On the ship?"

"You look surprised. Surely you knew that the ship's little library has all four of your books?"

"You're kidding," she said, feeling a surprising sense of panic. No more anonymity. No, that wasn't it. Worse, she would have to explain why she hadn't written anything of consequence in five years. She bit her lip in consternation.

Paul hadn't noticed for he was waving at someone on the sidewalk and beckoning to whomever it was to come over.

Beth looked up. It was Eric Halsey.

Paul noted the look of distraction on Beth's face as Eric Halsey wove his way through the tables toward them. He saw Halsey stop and hesitate a moment. The two New Yorkers had met, he had seen them walking through the church at Daphni together. So what was this all about?

Eric came up to the table and hovered there for a moment.

"You've met our host from the Barry, haven't you my dear?"

A hint of pink brushed her cheeks. "Yes, we've met," Beth said. "Do join us, Eric," she gestured at the free chair.

Eric sat down. "I hope I didn't put that look of panic there."

"Oh, no. Of course not. It's just that..."

Paul put his hand on hers, "What is it, my dear?"

She looked first at Paul, then turned to Eric, "Paul just told me that my books are in the ship's library."

"You didn't know that?"

"No."

The waiter came over and took Eric's order.

"My dear," Paul said, "I had no idea that would upset you."

"It's not my doing, I promise" Eric said. He looked at her curiously. "But Smith and Smith always put the works of authors who are traveling on the New Odyssey into the ship's library. Most authors are delighted."

"That was very thoughtful of Smith and Smith," she said.

"But interfering, no doubt," Paul said. "Were you hoping for a little anonymity?" He found her reticence rather appealing.

"Yes, I was," Beth attempted a smile. "I would have liked to have left it…that I teach, which I do, or have."

"Ah, my dear, it's too late, the word will be around the entire ship in a few days," Paul said. "You'll have to talk poetry and you don't want to do that, right?"

"Oh, why not? I love poetry. I know it. Of course, I can talk about it."

"Then, my dear," Paul said, "what I would like to tell you is how very much I liked what I read, how very gifted you are."

"Thank you, Paul, that's kind of you."

"Not at all."

"Very gifted but also very passionate and very political," Eric said.

"Oh really? Is that how you see my work?" Beth turned to him.

"I didn't mean that as criticism, merely an observation. Please don't get up and run off."

"I won't," she said.

The expression on Beth's face was one of amusement. It was a wonderful face, Paul thought, beautiful in its mobility, in the way the light and shadows played across it expressing whatever it was she was feeling. He wondered if she knew how lovely she was. He looked at Eric. Obviously, from the soft look on Eric's face, he thought so too. Annie, are they old friends, ex-lovers?

Watch and see.

Eric said, "But what is wrong with either politics or passion?"

"I have this dread of being polemical. I hate polemical poetry and the truth is I never thought of myself as a political poet. I write...wrote about what interests me. Oppression appalls me, has always appalled me."

"But that's admirable. Surely you don't have to apologize for that." Eric said.

Beth shrugged, "After my first book, I began to write about what troubled me most as a human being. A good portion of my second book was about oppression in the Third World. The one after that was more about the oppression of women, which in my travels struck me as worse than any other oppression that I had seen. The last book, my fourth, well, it's about America."

"*America, Lost!* That's a wonderful book," Eric said.

"You've read that?"

"I've read them all."

"But the first is out of print."

"I know a few people. I pulled a few strings. We tracked them all down."

Beth was staring at Eric, baffled "But why?"

"I was interested."

I see, Paul thought.

Yes, Annie answered.

And Beth blushed again.

Eric is why she is on this trip, Paul thought to Annie.

Perhaps. But what about your meeting with her, Paul?

"You must have traveled quite a bit," Eric said to Beth.

"There were years when I traveled for nearly three months every summer. My dad was a country doctor, not the banker my grandfather had wanted him to be. I think my mother would have liked that better. When my dad died, he left me and my siblings each an inheritance. And his parents were fairly wealthy," she rushed over that, "and they, too, set up trusts for us. So part of every summer while my two girls were either in camp or working, I traveled."

"I didn't know you had two daughters," Paul said. "You only mentioned one, the one who married recently."

To Paul's dismay, Beth's eyes filled up.

"My oldest daughter died a year ago. Leukemia."

"Oh, my dear, how insensitive I've been. I didn't mean to stampede through your life like that," Paul said.

Eric handed Beth his handkerchief.

"I'm so terribly sorry," she said. "I've simply not had the time to mourn properly."

That's the answer, Annie. Her sadness. She has lost a child.

Yes, but there is more.

"And you came on this trip to mourn?" Eric said.

"No, my family insisted I come on this trip so I wouldn't mourn. It was easier to comply than to fight them."

"There is no loss more terrible," Paul said, "than the loss of a child. Forgive me for being so callous."

What more is there, Annie? Surely this is enough.

Get to know her view of death, Paul, then you will see.

"It's all right, but can we talk about something else?"

So the two men talked about trips they had taken. The conversation was stilted in the beginning, but Beth finally joined in, talking about some of the places she had seen in Africa, in South America and in Asia. Eric, in particular, was well traveled. They compared notes when one or the other had also been to the same place. Soon they were laughing and all the earlier tension faded.

"It's odd," she said, "in those traveling days I never wanted to spend the money to come to Europe or Asia Minor. Oh, I don't mean that I've never been to Europe. When I was a child I came a few times with my parents."

She told them that her mother had been a concert pianist before marrying her dad and that they had come to Europe for some music festivals when she and her brother and sister were teenagers. "And I came a few times with my husband, but just for a couple of weeks at a time. We saw Paris, London, and naturally did the grand tour of Italy. I kept a journal, of course. But Europe seemed so worked, so mined, I guess. It just didn't pull at me."

Other than for its art, she told them, she had never been interested in the past. "I used to be singularly focused in on the present, on its current ills, its current solutions. Until..." she hesitated.

"Until what?" Eric asked her.

"Until I could no longer ignore that iron core that exists deep, deep in the folk consciousness of various peoples. I saw to my shock that it was I who was shortsighted. I was only concerned with the present. I hadn't reckoned with the weight of history. It was like a magnet that drew people, even oppressed women, back again and again to their collective past."

As she traveled more and more, Beth said, she found she could no longer ignore history the way she once had, the way that she had once encouraged others to do. "Everywhere people were stuck in its thick mud, or sometimes in its quicksand, unable to go toward the future. I saw old hatreds that stem from past centuries still working into the present, almost as if hate was buried unconsciously in their folk memory."

"You only have to look at what is going on in Europe today," Paul said.

"And then I began to realize that only Americans find it easy to ignore the past, to be indifferent to it. And that turned me eventually toward my own country." She paused. "I think I've been standing on a soapbox."

"Not at all. Do go on, my dear," Paul said. He had wanted to know more about her and now she was opening up. Eric, too, was listening attentively.

Will they fall in love, Annie?

Annie was silent.

But Paul knew that only the meeting was destined, not its outcome. But his meeting with her was also destined.

That's right, Paul.

For a few summers before her husband's heart attack, Beth had traveled all over America, driving through the heartland, through the big cities, the south, New England, the northwest. She had simply talked to people. Occasionally she had visited friends. Occasionally friends had traveled with her. "In those days I found people easy to talk with." She laughed and shrugged her shoulders deprecatingly. "It was in this period that I wrote *America, Lost!*. I saw something in America that excited me and also distressed me."

"What was that, my dear?" Paul asked.

"I saw how, as an immigrant nation, a melting pot nation, our roots in the past are really very shallow."

"And you think that's a good thing?" Eric asked.

"Neither bad nor good. Well, yes, good in a way, because it presents an opportunity for Americans, whose ancestors come from all over the world, to be something new, something freer, something creative. But were we living up to our potential? Oh, I've written about it better than I can say it now." She looked at her watch, then. "It's getting late, isn't it? We have to dress for....oh, it's your cocktail party," she said to Eric.

"Yes, this evening I will represent all four museums for cocktails and yet another gourmet dinner."

"Is there going to be another captain's table?" Paul asked.

"No, lucky me, I can eat with whomever I choose," Eric grinned. "So shall we three meet and have cocktails together, after I've greeted everyone? And then we can dine together. We can continue this talk about America or anything else that comes to mind?"

"Art," Paul said.

"I wax eloquent on art," Eric said, and motioned to the waiter for their bill and insisted on paying for their coffee.

That evening Beth put on a red chiffon skirt with a black silk shell and her red glass and gold faux earrings, then eyed herself critically in the mirror.

"Elizabeth, I wish you'd put on a little more weight..."

I have a good figure, she decided.

Yes, and a very plain face.

And I have good eyes, green and expressive.

That will have to do, she thought. There was no reason she couldn't be social. She had to get through this trip and being social was part of it. Paul was dear and comfortable to be with, just the kind of companion she needed on this trip and Eric was not really coming on to her. He was simply being nice to a fellow artist. It would be okay.

She didn't drink that night. But she did dance. At the cocktail party, after Eric had greeted everyone, he joined Paul and

Beth. They were sitting with Donna and Jenna, the mother and daughter from Santa Barbara. Eric ordered a drink, and before the waiter had time to return with his order, he asked Beth to dance. And they danced three dances, not talking, just moving. Finally, she whispered, "Don't you think, since you're the host at this party, that you should dance with some of the other women?"

"Ah, duty," he sighed, and led her off the dance floor and asked Jenna for a dance. Jenna was obviously thrilled. Then he danced with Donna.

Beth, in turn, asked Paul. He said, "I think I can manage one of the slower ones." Paul danced well, with more flexibility than Beth had expected and with charming dignity.

After that, Beth danced with some of the officers of the ship. And then it was time to go into dinner.

Beth, Eric, and Paul sat together as they had planned. At the table there were three others, a slight, elderly woman from New Orleans, with the eyes of a silent screen star, and with the odd but appropriate name of Daring. Ellen and Leona Parkington, the mother and daughter that Beth and Paul had met at the entrance to the Agora in Athens, were the other two. The conversation at the table was light and she was grateful that Eric and Paul carried most of it.

Beth was beginning to tire. The noise in the room seemed to become louder and louder, to seep under her skin. Even without wine, Beth was feeling dizzy and warm. She had slept badly the night before. The day had been long and filled with unexpected meetings and conversations. She didn't know what to think about Paul and his beliefs. She didn't know what to think about Eric and his attentions. She didn't know what to think about her own response to either of them. She didn't know what to make of her own ardor during the discussion she had had with the two men that afternoon or the revelations about her own life. She needed to get away and think. When the dinner was over, Beth excused herself, saying she was exhausted.

Paul said, "Of course, my dear. I, too, am going right to bed. Tomorrow promises to be a long and interesting day." He took her hand and bid her good night.

When she said good night to Eric, she could see a shadow of disappointment in his eyes. What did he want?

Beth left the dining room and hurried up to her cabin. She took another shower to wash off the dizziness and the confusion she was feeling, then set her alarm, climbed into bed and fell quickly asleep. She slept soundly until the dream she had just before morning.

She was walking around the mosaic floors that had been excavated near Pella. It was night. There was a full brilliant moon.

She was saying to Matthew, "When we redo our apartment, this is the kind of floor I want."

He answered, "It's hard to get good craftsmen in New York anymore. They've given up the old skills and have gone into the grocery business."

"We'll advertise in the *Village Voice*," she answered. "I want tile in every room of our house. I want all these hunt scenes. I adore the savageness of them. I want exact copies of these floors. Did you buy a book that shows all the mosaics clearly?"

"I've purchased some postcards," Matthew said, "but I'm not sure Raven will like these bloodthirsty floors."

From a small hillock that suddenly appeared, Beth saw Raven who called out in a light, musical voice, "Come away,

Matthew, this place is so boring, so old. Why are you interested in old things? Be young. Live in the present. Come away with me."

Matthew sheepishly shrugged his shoulders and giving Beth a sick smile he walked up the hillock to Raven. They embraced.

"They deserve each other," Hank said.

Beth whirled around, but it wasn't Hank she saw, it was Eric. He was standing a few feet from her. He wasn't smiling but he was holding out his hand to her.

"Is she your wife?"

"Of course," Eric said.

"She's a slut."

"That's why I'm free now."

"No one who has loved is ever free," Beth said. "The past imprisons you."

"That's garbage," Eric told her. "You're an American. You don't have to be held by the past. Focus on the future. That's where the action is."

"Alicia's dead," she said.

"Only in the past," Eric said. "She's waiting in the future. As I am waiting. Now let me tell you about these mosaics. I saw them when I was younger, with my wife."

"You've been here before?"

"Don't you remember?"

"Did I like them?"

"We measured them together, counted how many stones there were per square inch and compared them with the mosaics in your living room. Come, I want to share these things with you. Let me tell you all about the technique of making mosaics. Let's talk glue. Let me tell you where the stone is found, how many people worked on these floors, where they came from, who their families were, what they ate for dinner. Olives. And honey. And bread. Delicious bread. They were vegetarians. Cheese." His voice became louder. "And they were definitely Greeks, the Macedonians. Don't believe the rumors. It's not true that they were Bulgarians or Aztecs. I will recite to you by heart all that has been written about, not only these mosaics, but about all the mosaics in all the churches on the Greek mainland and on the islands," he said, seductively.

Eric was leading her around the site, holding her arm too tightly and talking with greater and greater intensity.

Beth tore herself free, and screamed at him, "Go away. You're complicating my life. I'm not interested in the quantity of stones per square inch of my life, not at all. Raven is beautiful. I am not. That's beyond measurement. Raven is radiantly young and I am teetering between middle age and old age. Raven is fresh. And I am stale. I shall marry Paul."

"That's a lovely idea," Paul said. "I'll ask my dead wife to see if she approves. We're very close, you know. We shall all be happy together as long as we all shall live and die, amen."

"A thing of beauty is a joy forever," now it was Matthew who called to her from the hillock, Raven on his arm, Raven's head on his shoulder, her long black hair billowing in the wind, looking like snakes.

"It's Medusa," Beth screamed a warning at Matthew. "Don't look at her face or you will turn to stone. Then you'll be crushed and used to make mosaics. I shall find you forever fixed on my living room floor."

But I've moved from that apartment. She would never find Matthew now.

Beth turned to Eric for help but he was gone. She had driven him away just as she had driven Hank away. And where was Paul? Beth walked alone along the row of invisible houses, angry and tired. Stones endure, she thought. They get buried, but if you dig for them, you uncover them.

My stones will stay covered. They were created with too little skill.

She stood staring at the mosaic floor called *The Deer's Hunting*. Two naked men with capes and red hair, one with a short sword, one with an ax, were striking at a buck. From below the dog was biting through the skin toward its heart.

One wound would have been enough, Beth thought.

Mattie said from behind her, "It's a question of balance, you know, my friend. If you can find that point where the leaf changes into another leaf or better yet into a flower you will know everything."

"There's no meaning in a leaf for me or in two leaves. I cannot be like you," she told Mattie and turned back to look at the brutal mosaic.

"She is hopeless. Balance is everything. It is beyond my comprehension," the woman called Iris strode across the mosaic floor Beth was observing and stopped, her small sandaled feet covering the top of the buck's face.

"What is, my friend?" her companion asked from out of the shadows.

"How they approach art with only thought and deprecate feeling as if it could not inform them of anything true."

"It is where they are in history, Iris. They don't know better."

"But how do they experience the joy of beauty or its rightness? One can't apply to beauty only the soul that thinks, the soul that weighs and measures. It is a dryness that is worse than a desert."

"For us, Iris, thought was a beautiful experience, for it was new in our times. To think, to open up to a cosmos of ideas that came into our inner life seemed like the breath of the gods across our souls. Thought was added to the soul that felt, like rain is added to the soil. Thought is something different for humans now. It arises from the aridity of the self, no longer god-breathed. Little did we know that the thinking-soul, for which we were so grateful, would eventually cause the loss of the capacity for beauty in humankind."

"A heavy price to pay."

"Indeed, heavy."

"What can be done?" Iris was now looking at Beth who pulled back from her stare into a patch of darkness.

"They have something we did not have in our day, a third soul capacity, given by the great gods. With it they could learn all lost things again, but with effort and only if they so choose. But they must choose, for the gods will not lead them in this."

Iris folded her arms and stared at Beth. "But will they choose? Will she, for instance. She is a poet. Will she?"

"Is she even interested? Come, Iris. Let's be on our way."

And Beth woke up. It was 5 A.M. Once again, she rose up from her bed, went into the bathroom, washed her face with cold water, climbed back into her bed, took her notebook and wrote as fast as she could everything she was able to remember of the dream.

Don't think about it now, she insisted as she wrote. Do what you have always done. Put down the facts. You can muse over them later.

A dream is not facts.

Just put it down, Beth.

Strange dream. Long and strange.

Who are they?

"My God!" Jenna exclaimed, plopping herself down on the seat in front of Beth, then turning around to face her. The 4-M bus was slowly loading it's passengers on board for the full day excursion into the countryside of Macedonia.

"What's the matter?" Beth asked.

"If you were a school child here in Salonika," Jenna said, "do you know how many years of history you would have to learn, just to know your own city? Forget about the rest of the country."

"Over two thousand years," Eric said from the seat behind Beth.

"My God!" Jenna uttered again, kneeling in her seat and peering over Beth at him. "Do you know how many mayors there have been or head honchos since the founding of this town? Hundreds and hundreds."

Paul, sitting next to Eric, spoke, "Do you know, young lady…"

"Jenna."

"Do you know, Jenna, who founded Thessaloniki?"

"Well, I looked it up last night," Jenna said. "In fact I read a short but horrendous history of Thessaloniki. Invasions, sieges, invasions. First the Greeks fight among themselves, then the Romans come, then Barbarian hordes out of the north, then the Turks, then the crusaders, or was it the other way around? Believe me, no one lived to a ripe old age. In all that mess of facts, I forgot who founded the city."

"It was Kassandros," Donna said, as she slid into the seat next to her daughter. "He was married to Alexander's half sister. Kassandros fought against, and took the kingdom away from, the man Alexander's mother backed to be Emperor."

"Right," Jenna said. "Olympia was her name, Alexander's mom. Imagine having her for a mother-in-law, or a mother."

"She sounds like some mothers I know," Eric said.

The bus began to move away from the pier.

"Keep your eyes open, Jenna," Paul said. "At one time Thessaloniki was surrounded by fortification walls. Maybe we'll see some of the remains on our way out of the city."

Jenna sat back down in her seat.

Their guide, Irene, announced from the front of the bus, that before they left the city to go to Vergina, they would stop off at two of the city's many important churches. The first would be the Hagia Sophia, or St. Sophia.

"St. Sophia is a very old church. The earliest date put forth is after the Ecumenical Synod of Nicaea, in 325. It was at this Council that Christ was acknowledged as Divine Reason and Wisdom. You know St. Sophia is not a *being*, not a saint, it means divine wisdom."

"Nonsense," Beth heard Paul murmur.

"Well, Jenna," Eric said, as the bus eased its way into traffic, "he certainly picked a beautiful site for his city, your Kassandros."

"Prettier than Athens, don't you think?" Donna said, turning to look at him.

It certainly is pretty, Beth thought, looking out at the horseshoe bay as they moved away from the sea. It was a beautiful day, the light was evanescent and the air warm.

She could certainly get through this day.

Despite the long and curious dream she had just before waking, she felt rested. Writing helped. Just setting things down on paper helped. Yes, writing brought balance, however momentary.

"She is hopeless. Balance is everything..."

"It's a question of balance, you know, my friend. If you can find that point where the leaf changes into another leaf or better yet into a flower you will know everything."

Those lines were in her dream last night.

Mattie had written those lines to her. They were in a letter Beth had found in the mail that had been held and then given to her when she and Merle had returned to New York to pack some things for her trip. What had she done with that letter? Hadn't she put it away to reread later? She thought hard and then opened her purse and unzipped a small compartment in the lining and there it was. She had forgotten about it in all the preparations for the trip.

She took it out and read, "Oh my good friend, I think I've discovered something important. You know how often I have spoken about balance, trying to understand balance and I think I am closer at last. It's so tied up with all those crossing-over moments in life and its processes. You know what I mean, when one thing is moving toward becoming another, for instance when a leaf is about to become a flower. But not just in those great moments of change, not just in those extraordinary transformations, but also in gradual changes, in

quiet and small metamorphoses. Can you see what I'm getting at? Those tiny spaces in-between before one thing
becomes another. For instance, before one leaf becomes
another and then another there must be this tiny moment of
balance..."

They had reached St. Sophia and Beth put the half-read letter into her purse. She stayed close to the guide while they
walked through the church but her gaze wandered time and
again after the figure of Eric Halsey who was walking on his
own through the church looking at the mosaics.

At one point Donna walked up to him. Then Beth saw
Eric point out something to Donna who was listening carefully, nodding in understanding. Beth felt a twinge...of what?

Jealousy.

Ridiculous.

*"I never meant it to go so far, Beth, really I didn't. I saw it
first as a little attraction that would pass..."*

"Go on."

*"It didn't pass. I thought if I had a little fling, the attraction
would disappear. It didn't."*

Beth, with Jenna walking companionably by her side, followed Irene. She looked up at the dome and was struck by
the magnificent mosaic called *The Ascension of Christ* and on
its periphery the twelve Apostles with the Virgin Mary. They
were beautiful. Beth felt the urge to go up to Eric and tell
him that she, too, saw how lovely the mosaics were. But she
didn't, couldn't.

"She is hopeless..."

Instead, she turned to watch Paul. He was standing on the
edge of the group, listening attentively, but his eyes glimmered with appreciation and...what? Reverence. That's it, he
becomes very reverent in a church. He is religious, she

reminded herself. And a Christian. And that belief seemed as distant from her as the worship of Hephaistos had seemed at the Agora in Athens.

Back on the bus, Beth once again took out Mattie's letter.

"...Look how this came to me, Beth. I was pacing the length of my little house, working a poem in my mind, getting it into my limbs, feeling its rhythms. Suddenly I became aware of myself walking, just walking. And then I found myself thinking, how miraculous it is that we humans can stand upright and walk, our heads pointing to the sky and our feet to the ground. Are we ourselves the great metaphor for that space in-between, that remarkable creative space in-between, say, heaven and earth? So I tried then to follow my own walking with great consciousness..."

Mattie, Beth thought, staring down at the graceful handwriting of her friend, you are unique. You worry about such strange things. Do you have a key to something I don't? Are my senses too opaque? Am I too shut off from the essence of things? Balance. I say I need it. You ask what is it?

"...I slowed my walking down and tried to catch the moment when my weight shifted from one foot to another. I couldn't do it. But I was convinced that there was some secret enchanted into that fraction of time, into that fragment of eternity when I was balanced! Over and over I tried to catch it until finally I felt, yes, here it is! And then immediately I fell, either to my right or to my left and thought, but, of course, this is the way of modern humanity. We fall either to the right or to the left. We move unconsciously through that balance point, unable even when conscious to sustain it. Then I remembered the Greek statues I had seen, those created before the classic Greek period which I consider part of the modern era. Look at an archaic Greek statue. Try to stand in that sort of balance. Feel it. But we really have lost it, haven't we, that capacity? We moderns stand with hip thrust out, or leg, or arm. We've given up the balance. But for what? I can't imagine for what! I'm in despair over it. I'll send you the poem, if I'm ever able to write it..."

Beth tucked Mattie's letter back into her purse pocket. If only she were more like Mattie. Mattie saw meaning everywhere while she was awash in a sea of meaninglessness.

Tired metaphor.

Well, she didn't want to think about that now. She wanted to see the church of St. Demetrius.

As the group stood near the glassed coffin staring at the remains of St. Demetrius, Irene said, "This church has been destroyed many times. Fires, invasions. But always it has been rebuilt. St. Demetrius is the patron saint of this city. And this church, though it is not the largest, is the cathedral of the city, its main church."

That these Byzantine churches and the Greek temple had originated from the same people seemed irreconcilable to Beth. She wanted to ask Eric about it but when she finally located him he was walking about the church, away from the group, with Donna. They were deep in quiet conversation.

Oh, well, she thought. But her stomach knotted uncomfortably.

"...when one thing is moving toward becoming another..."

The 4-M groups returned to the buses for the hour and a half trip to Vergina. Donna and Eric were the last to come aboard. As they did, Jenna turned around and grinned at Beth.

Paul was looking forward to this day in the country. He found Alexander fascinating and by association Alexander's father, Philip. The 4-M buses were heading to Vergina, the town where the so-called tomb of Philip had been excavated. All its treasures had been found intact which had caused much excitement. They were scheduled to see a second tomb open to the public and the excavations of a palace.

Despite the drought that covered much of Greece and its islands, there was a profusion of wild flowers to be seen, particularly the orange poppies that had sprung up like little question marks all over the countryside. Because he and Annie had not been to this part of Greece on their earlier trips together, he described carefully to her what he was seeing.

Irene's voice came over the loud speaker. "Before we leave the mood of Byzantium," she said, "and head back to the time of the Macedonian kings, let me say something about the word, *Byzantine.* Up to the fourth century A.D., the Eastern Roman Empire was part of the whole Roman Empire and it's only in 330 A.D. that we have the creation of the eastern part of the empire with Constantine the Great..."

They were out of the city now and traveling through the Macedonian plains in a northwesterly direction. Paul listened carefully as the woman continued her narrative, but her explanation seemed dry and date-ridden. She doesn't take into account the spiritual streams that work in history, he thought to Annie. But hardly anyone does in our times.

Your book will be different, Annie said.

"In the beginning the official language was Latin. But as the dominion of the Eastern Empire covered more or less the former dominions of Alexander the Great and the Hellenistic Kings, Greek was the language spoken by the people even during the Roman conquest..."

The bus was coming into an area of rounded hills. Mountains stretched tall beyond.

Tell me what you are seeing, Paul.

So he described the hills that were rapidly approaching.

"We've sent one of the buses back to the village to see if they can find the guard. The gates should be open on Monday, but..." Colleen shrugged her shoulders and grinned. The two 4-M groups were standing on the hilly ground in a very picturesque area, known as the Palatita, waiting to go into the remains of the little palace that was being excavated. Some people wandered away to take pictures.

"This is ridiculous," Mrs. Green said. "Do they expect us to just stand around in the hot sun?"

Paul winked at Beth.

Irene, after a brief conversation with Colleen and Bill, tried to rescue the situation. "If you want to look at the theater where Philip was murdered, follow me."

Beth, with Paul right behind her, left the roadside and followed the nimble-footed guide. Soon they were standing looking down at a grassy depression. All that was left of the theater were a few stone steps. Beth noticed Donna standing with Eric away from the group. They were talking cozily together.

Not your business, Beth.

But she continued to watch them.

Marion Levitt, the lecturer, and her husband approached the two. They spoke for a few moments and then Eric and Donna went off with Marion and her husband and disappeared from sight. Beth, trying to keep her sense of equilibrium, turned her attention to Irene.

"...this is the way of modern humanity. We fall either to the right or to the left. We move unconsciously through that balance point, unable even when conscious to sustain it."

You saw him first.

"You know, you're chicken shit..."

Shut up.

"Philip had come here to the palace for the wedding of his daughter. When he was visiting the theater he was murdered..."

"Was Vergina the capital of Macedonia?" Mel Winston asked, after Irene had finished her short talk. "I thought it was at Pella."

"Well, you're right. It was at Pella. And then it was moved, as far as we can tell, to a town called Aigai. It is now almost universally accepted that the royal town of Aigai was here in Vergina."

"Fascinating," Paul murmured.

When the guard who was to open the gate couldn't be located, it was decided that the 4-M group should continue on to the tombs. Some decided to walk the quarter of a mile down the country road while others chose to take the bus. Paul and Beth decided to walk.

Jenna and Jordan overtook them. "My grandmother's on the bus," Jordan told them, as the two youngsters strode past them at a brisk pace.

"My mom's disappeared," Jenna announced loudly over her shoulder. She grinned happily. "Along with Marion and Eric."

Paul called out, "I don't think we'll ride off without them. Our Mrs. Levitt is scheduled to lecture us tomorrow morning on Troy."

So he had noticed their disappearance, too. Beth felt color rise to her cheeks, which irritated her, so she didn't look at

Paul. May is a lovely month, she told herself severely. You should get out more into the country. You're too much of an urban person.

With whom would I go?

Eric.

Stop it.

"...this is the crux, kid, you don't pay attention to what's going on inside. Inside you're a scared rabbit."

They were strolling at a very leisurely pace down the road, past fields of colorful wildflowers. The land was dry and the mild breeze lifted a fine dust off of the road. With great deliberateness, Beth pushed thoughts of Eric out of her mind and turned to Paul and said, "Paul, can I ask you a question?"

"Of course," he smiled, his blue eyes twinkling. "It's one of the things old people love, to be asked questions."

"Paul, you're incorrigible," she grinned up at him. Why think about Eric when she had Paul as a wonderful companion.

"Sorry, shoot."

"Would you tell me about your wife, if you don't mind talking about her, that is."

"No, I don't mind talking about her. But can this be interesting to you?"

"Of course, it's interesting," she said, "or I wouldn't have asked."

"Annie was warm and caring. In looks she was a tall, statuesque woman, almost as tall as I am, so you see," he stooped a bit to look into Beth's eyes, "you don't really resemble her. Annie had wavy brown hair when she was younger, gray at the end. Hazel eyes, large, and what we used to call soulful. She was a wonderful teacher. She loved literature, especially Greek literature, and could make her students really excited about words, about the way they were put together, about the holiness of language."

Several people overtook them, walking briskly, and waved.

"We came to Greece several times, though never to this part of Greece, never to Macedonia. If she had lived, no doubt we would have come here eventually. She would have found this very interesting. Annie had a boundless enthusiasm for life, for nature, but especially for what human beings have wrought throughout their long sojourn on earth."

"She sounds lovely, Paul. I wish that I could have met her."

"You would have liked her, Elizabeth. Yes, you two would have taken to each other, I feel certain." Paul smiled at Beth with genuine affection. "Like you, my Annie was beautiful, I think."

Beth was startled by that pronouncement.

"Oh, not because she had such remarkable features, but because she had such an expressive face. Like yours, it showed everything. They say by the time you're fifty you have created your own face." He winked at her. "If that is so, then Annie did a splendid job. Her whole being shone through her face. Like you, my dear."

What a lovely thing to say.

"Annie was a marvelous listener. You really felt heard. It's a special quality, that. To be a good listener, you have to be unselfish, truly unselfish."

"I'm not sure I follow that."

"Are you sure you want to hear this? I'm about to get preachy, you know."

"Preach away."

"Then here goes. To be a good listener you have to let go of yourself, enter another, forget your own ego. Can you imagine how it's a little death? You die to yourself, if I can use such an expression. You wake up to another. If only for a moment. That's true listening. Out of that kind of listening can come real understanding. My Annie could do that."

"That's an odd way of putting it. But rather apt, rather poetic. Not too many people, unfortunately, are good listeners. Conversation is mostly about waiting until it's your turn to talk, isn't it?"

"It's because no one wants to let go of his own self, even for a moment."

"That's true. Ours is a terribly selfish age. It sounds like you had a perfect marriage, the kind that doesn't happen anymore."

"No, not perfect, not by a long shot. We had our difficulties." His voice shook slightly and he suddenly looked sad, even remorseful.

What imperfection lay in his past, in his marriage, to put that look there? Maybe she would ask him someday. Or would that be too nervy?

"We're here," Paul said.

At the chamber tomb, they were again divided into two groups. Irene gave Beth's group some details about the unearthing of the tomb and told them an anecdote about grave robbers. Beth, helped by Paul, descended the modern stairs to peer into the tomb so she could see the marble throne still standing in the antechamber. After everyone had their chance to look inside the tomb and the camera buffs had their fill of picture taking, the two groups loaded onto their buses once again.

"We'll go on to Veroia to see two little churches and to have lunch. If we can locate the guard, we'll go back to look at the palace excavations after lunch," Irene told them as soon as she boarded the bus. But the bus did not leave. Finally Irene and Colleen descended from the bus again.

It was Mrs. Green who finally spoke up, "There's the lecturer and that man from the Barry and some others." Beth looked out her window. "They're just now, after everyone is on the bus, going down to look at the tomb. That's extremely inconsiderate. What are we supposed to do, just sit on this bus and wait?"

No one bothered to answer her.

After several moments of delay, Donna and Eric boarded the bus, with apologetic looks.

"Why are you taking my class?" Beth asked the young man with the long dark curly hair who was insolently sitting on the corner of her desk at the New School for Social Research. Frankly, he had been a thorn in her side for the last six weeks. She couldn't figure out what he was doing there.

The young man, his black eyes half-closed and his heavy black eyebrows raised slightly, leaned toward her. "Ah, I didn't know you cared. You see," he said, "I have trouble with women and thought this class might help me understand them better."

Beth stared incredulously at him. "A class on Sylvia Plath?"

"Come have a cup of coffee and I'll tell you my sad, dissolute story."

Beth ignored the invitation. "I think you're in the wrong class, Steven..."

"Call me Hank."

"I think you're in the wrong class, Hank. If you want to understand women better, take a course on feminism. There are several very good ones offered at the New School."

"Oh, teacher, am I disruptive? Don't you like having students who disagree with you?" He stood up, tilted his head to one side and thrust out his hip. She thought him thoroughly impudent.

"*Disagree is one thing. But you take exception to everything I say. The other students in this class didn't pay good money to listen to us argue.*" *She decided to pull no punches with him.*

"*Sorry, teach, but this is the right one for me,*" *Hank said, hefting his book bag to his shoulder. He was dressed in the obligatory blue jeans and T-shirt with the picture of some heavy metal band on the front. He carried an old flight jacket left over from the second world war.*

"*If this is the right one for you, why are you so damned critical of everything I say about her?*"

"*Because Plath was a nerd. Anyway she's pre-feminism. She didn't live long enough to become Adrienne Rich. Frankly, she whines and that pisses me off. I hate women who whine.*"

And I hate men who talk as if they've had a lifetime of experience at what, twenty-three or twenty-four? "*So you've said numerous times. You don't like her. So why are you in this class?*"

"*I paid my money,*" *he shrugged.*

"*Answer my question, please.*"

"*Come have a cup of coffee with me and I'll answer your question.*"

"*Do you give all your teachers such a hard time?*"

"*Only the female ones.*"

"*Oh, come off it. Don't talk like you just stepped out of a low-budget movie. You're not impressing me.*"

He dropped the mocking tone for an instant. "*Why won't you have a cup of coffee with me? I don't bite, unless I'm bitten first. Come on. The lunchroom is one flight up, hardly out of your way.*"

"*Okay,*" *she said and wasn't sure why. Perhaps it was just to hear his story.*

A few minutes later they were sitting at a table in the near-empty dining room drinking coffee out of paper cups.

"I recently got dumped," he told her, stirring sugar into his drink.

"By a woman?"

"Hey!"

"I didn't mean that the way it sounded. You mean, you were in a relationship that just ended."

"I thought I said that."

"I thought you might have been referring to a job."

"No the job is okay."

"What do you do?"

"I'm a bartender." He watched for her reaction.

Beth didn't disappoint. She raised her eyebrows.

"The money's good. It's at night. Which leaves my days free for..." he didn't go on. "Is that the way you were also raised?"

"What?"

"To be a good little girl, to defer to men, to feel so trapped by life?"

She realized that he was back to Sylvia Plath.

"She'd be your age if she had lived, wouldn't she?"

"A few years older," Beth said. What right did this brash kid have to make her feel like an antique? Pre-feminism, my eye. "I don't consider myself trapped. Or whiny. Remember, it was my generation that started both the women's movement and the civil rights movement."

"Wow," he said.

Why she didn't get up and leave was beyond her understanding. No, she understood very well why she sat there. She sat there listening to this smart-assed kid because women of her generation were responsible, and she was a teacher and she was supposed to deal rationally with her students, no matter how irritating and impudent they were.

"Okay," he shifted around in his chair, "so why hasn't it worked? Why aren't women more liberated?"

"*You want them more liberated?*"

"*Of course. I don't want any woman hanging around my neck forever. I don't want to be responsible for the happiness of another, her well-being, her fulfillment.*"

"*That's why you broke up with your young lady?*"

"*My young lady, as you call her, broke up with me. She said I was going nowhere and that therefore we didn't have much of a future.*"

"*And how did you answer her?*"

"*I told her I was heading in the direction I wanted to go, and that if she wanted lots of bucks so she could spend her days in the mall, she should earn them herself.*"

"*That didn't go over too well?*"

"*Not well at all. But,*" he grinned, "*it's cool. Melonie was a wimp. She's barely heard of the women's movement. She needs a Jewish lawyer from Long Island, not me. Or better yet, some Guido from Queens who'll blacken her eye once a month.*"

"*Why are you taking this poetry class on Sylvia Plath?*"

Hank looked at her unblinkingly. "*Because even though Plath's a whiner and even though she's a class A wimp and a complainer, she's brilliant. There's no one who uses language the way she does. She absolutely breaks the damn words open and all your senses with them.*"

"*You write?*"

He shrugged.

"*What?*"

"*I'm working on a novel.*"

"*Then why are you...*"

"*...'taking my class?' Because I love words. Really, I do. And because you're teaching it.*"

Beth felt the color rise to her cheeks.

"Galway Kinnell is giving a reading at the Guggenheim next week. Do you want to go?" he asked, his head slightly cocked.

"With you?"

"Sure."

"I am going," she was suddenly uncomfortable. "With friends."

"Okay. It should be good. Maybe I'll see you there." He stood up and looked at her, his chin slightly raised. "Don't worry, Ms. Layton. I'll behave in class from now on." He reached over and shook her hand with mock formality and left.

Beth watched him go with an uneasy feeling.

The bus lurched into gear and they were off to the town of Veroia, known in ancient times as Berea. It was an old town, one that had been visited by Paul the Apostle who had come, as he had to other towns, to preach to the Jewish Community there.

"Where were you?" Jenna demanded of her mother when she slid into her seat. Her brown eyes glittered mischievously.

"Marion Levitt found a way to get around to the back of the palace."

"Really, what's it look like?"

"A dig," her mother's answer was dry, but her face was flushed.

"Marion loved it," Eric said from behind Beth. "And the countryside was beautiful. Sorry we made you all wait, but Marion simply would not leave until we had also seen the tomb with the marble throne. We do apologize for the delay."

"Veroia is a prosperous town..." Irene began.

Beth stared out the window at the approaching houses. She barely took in Irene's narration. Instead she was trying to cope with an emotion she was angry to find inside of herself.

Jealousy.

"After too many years of trying to make it as a painter," Eric said, "I went back to college and took my degree in art history. That took me first into teaching, then to work at several galleries, and finally to the Barry."

The outdoor and terraced restaurant where Beth, Paul, Eric and Donna were seated, overlooked part of the town of Veroia and the surrounding hilly countryside whose distant plateau shimmered blue in the heat. Beth sipped her wine and watched the busy waiters hurry in and out of the restaurant, carrying heavy trays filled with local dishes to the 4-M tourists.

"Do you miss it?" Donna asked Eric.

Beth turned her attention back to her own table.

"The painting?"

"Yes."

"I wasn't all that good. It was that realization that sent me back to school."

"Well, my story is just the opposite, in some ways," Donna laughed.

"How is that?" Paul asked.

"I desperately wanted to major in fine arts in college. But my parents said, absolutely no, get a degree in something that will earn you a living. And take a painting course as an elective. So I studied journalism. I work now as an editor for an engineering magazine. I've been doing that since I was divorced seven years ago."

Beth looked across at Eric. He was listening both attentively and politely.

"But," and Donna turned to Beth, "I've also gone back to painting, my first love, and I now belong to a society of women painters who are very serious about their work."

"Why just women painters?" Paul asked. He was sitting across from Beth next to Eric.

"Because they have a harder time getting recognition as artists. Art's been a man's world for so long, now don't deny it," she flashed a smile at Eric, "so we felt the need to organize, to let people know that we are here and that we are as good as our male counterparts."

"That's an old story," Eric said.

"Really?" Donna said. "How many women do you have represented at the Barry, for instance?"

"I never counted the women, nor counted the blacks, nor the Hispanics, nor the Asians, nor the American Indians."

"You're being patronizing," Donna said.

"I am not." Eric turned to Paul, "Am I being patronizing?"

"I've been told if I hold a woman's chair for her, or the door," Paul said, "that I'm being patronizing. I'm the wrong person to ask."

"I don't believe in quota systems to redress wrongs. Art should be chosen on its merit," Eric said.

"Oh, God, spare me the Old Boy Artist's cry." Donna mockingly clutched her heart.

"How do you choose the art for your museum?" Paul asked Eric.

"Nothing mysterious about it. We look for the best work currently being done that is at the same time on the cutting edge of art. As a matter of fact, after we finish this tour I'm staying on in Rome for a few days, maybe go to Milan, then off to Paris, Amsterdam and Berlin. Just to see what's going on there. The Barry considers itself a cutting edge museum. We have our detractors, boy do we ever, and I personally have been attacked in many an art magazine."

"I've read some of them," Donna said.

Eric shrugged and grinned. "Some say a museum should not be doing what galleries do, that museums should have the long view. But at the Barry, we do have the long view. We really do."

"So how do you choose what should be exhibited?" Paul asked him.

"I'll answer a question with a question. How does any piece of art become part of the mainstream, having value both for museums and for collectors?" And not waiting for an answer, he went on, "By engaging in a dialogue with art history. A piece of art has either to take what has gone before it and carry it a step further, or it has to rebel against it and try to abolish it and put its own approach to art in its place, like artists attempted to do in the middle of this century. An artist who doesn't know art history and who doesn't know his own times will never become a mainstream artist. He may make pretty wall hangings, beautifully crafted, but he will never become a major artist. We like to think of the Barry as a museum that continually pushes against the perimeters of fine art so that what was once outside the mainstream now becomes mainstream. A museum's responsibility is to bring

into its hallowed halls pieces of art that have a place in the
history of art, if only briefly, but still a place."

"Is that true for poetry, Beth?" Paul asked.

"I've never thought of it quite in those terms, but yes,
something similar goes on in poetry. You do have to be part
of your times. You can't write nineteenth century verse in the
twentieth century, as gorgeous as nineteenth century poetry
can be. You can't write today as if Modernism had never
happened."

"What about the return to poetic traditions that's so popular among poets today?" Eric asked.

"Yes, that's going on. One generation discards it's traditions, then another goes back and takes a look at them again
to see if something can be salvaged from them. I love free
verse, but I do try to work with old forms, in a new way,
sometimes. However I would never consider myself a New
Formalist. As more and more of our social structures break
down, I think we feel a need for a shaping element for what
might be a very unruly content. Isn't that what the Greeks
did? For instance those mosaic floors we saw yesterday at
Pella."

"Aren't the Greeks then an argument for your New Formalists?" Donna asked.

"We can't go backwards. I feel that's wrong. Unhealthy.
No artist wants just to be a copyist. It's okay to scoop up
something from the past and transform it so it works in the
present. Or meets the future. But free verse can do that too.
Free verse is not really free. If you look, there is structure, but
a more subtle structure. There's a demand on the reader to
be aware, awake."

"Something similar is going on in painting," Eric said.
"The juxtaposition of disparate parts to force people to use

their eyes in a new way. For instance the reawakened interest in figurative art after one generation was sure that abstract art had replaced it forever. But it has a very different quality and certainly a different purpose."

"To sense into one's times, that's a task of the poet as well as the fine artist," Beth said. "In an era of disharmony, of psychological as well as social upheaval, language needs to be harsher, the voice more disjunctive, the subject matter any and everything..."

"Is it poetry's task to speak the truth?" Paul asked.

"Definitely to speak the truth." Beth said.

Donna said, "I think truth is overrated in the Arts. The imagination isn't about truth. It's about invention. Truth is so relative. Memory is ultimately subjective and not about truth. I'm interested in that subjectivity and that memory, not in some abstract idea called truth. All those differences in how we experience our world bring all kinds of colors to an artist's palette." She turned to Beth. "How do you feel about women's issues?" Donna asked her.

"They're important. I've written about women and their problems..."

"I'm sorry," Donna said, "but I haven't read your poetry yet. I've looked for your books in the library but they're out. You seem to be very popular."

Beth shrugged. "I don't think of myself as a women's libber, even though I've been defined as that. That's too narrow. People should write about all phases of the human experience. I'm a human being, and I'm an American, a woman, a New Yorker and a poet and I live in the twentieth century."

"Bravo," Eric said. "Poetry sounds healthy but painting may be on its way out."

"Never," Donna said.

"Multimedia art, performance art, installation art, video art, computer art," Eric said. "I'm not sure that technology isn't going to so revolutionize art that museums will become obsolete."

"Books may be on the way out, too," Beth said.

At that moment their harried waiter, carrying a loaded tray, brought them a heavy meat-and-potato dish and the conversation returned to food and to lighter topics.

Beth noticed that Paul had listened very attentively to the discussion about art and poetry, but had contributed hardly anything. He has another point of view, she thought, another approach. I'd like to hear it.

It's probably religious. He probably thinks art should be frescoes or mosaics or icons.

That's not fair, you don't know anything of the kind.

The guard with the keys to the gate of the palace digs in Vergina couldn't be located, so they returned to their buses for the hour and a half drive back to the ship. As their bus rumbled out of Veroia, Irene spoke to them over the loudspeaker and mentioned the name of several churches with Byzantine architecture or mosaics in Thessaloniki that were worth seeing. The bus would let anyone off in town who wanted to visit any of these churches if they were willing to find their own way back to the ship.

Eric announced that he wanted to visit St. Athanasios and asked if any of them wanted to come along.

"I'd love it," Donna said.

"Well, I'm tired," her daughter said and looked out of the window.

She's getting out of her mother's way, Beth thought.

"Me, too. These old bones need a nap," Paul said.

"What about you, Beth?" Eric asked.

"Raven wants..."

Go, she told herself.

Why, she answered? I'm not interested in Eric. Why shouldn't I make myself as scarce as Donna's daughter and give Donna an open field?

You're not interested because you're afraid, Beth.

"You know you're chicken-shit..."

Shut-up.

"I think I'll decline," she said. "I need to do a little laundry, write a couple of letters, and bring my journal up to date."

"...you lack courage in life."

Eric didn't ask again.

Beth ignored the cocktail hour and came in late to dinner. Eric and Donna were at table together. Beth was seated with people from Denver and from Minneapolis on the other side of the room. The dinner passed in easy conversation.

After dinner, Beth went up onto the deck to watch the ship leave the port of Thessaloniki. She didn't see Eric there, but she did meet Donna. Her heart inexplicably lightened and she and Donna talked casually about the day's adventures and what they would be seeing tomorrow. The ship would be at sea all night, passing into the Dardanelles late the next morning. They would dock at Çanakkale and disembark by motor launches for the shore and the afternoon trip to Troy. Paul was not on deck either and Beth assumed he had gone to bed early.

After the ship had left Thessaloniki behind, Beth said good night and returned to her cabin.

Should I have said something? Paul asked Annie just after he climbed into bed that night. Should I have defended the idea of truth?

Do you think you should have?

I say too much. People think I'm peculiar.

Beth?

Beth, too.

What would you have said?

Something about language. Something about the way it changes. Something about truth and language.

Good.

The difference between literalness and truth. Literalness and language. How metaphor is under attack today, thought to be untruthful.

Donna.

That pains me. If she could really watch the development of a child, how it repeats all the evolutionary stages of humanity, perhaps she would understand.

Perhaps.

One can't help thinking these thoughts in Greece. It is here where the change from metaphoric thinking slowly metamorphosed into conceptual thinking. Should I have told them?

Tell me. Think these thoughts now. Here. That is what is important.

At one time we humans thought in pictures.

How can one know that?

We have evidence from all of the world myths.

Good.

But the pictures were not the ultimate reality. The reality stood *behind* the pictures. And yet they were true. The spiritual hierarchies, what the Greeks called gods, worked with the humans through metaphor. They were the original metaphorists. That belonged to a certain stage of our development.

Would you have said that ancient humans could sense the truth behind the pictures?

Yes.

Good.

People were inwardly much more flexible then and pictures elicited a certain response in the soul, a kind of knowing. But the ancients were less free. They still lived with a strong need for authority.

Yes. Good. But their sense for truth was stronger, just as a child understands on a deeper level the truth in fairy tales.

And I could have said that thinking has gone from a living thinking experienced by the Greeks, to an abstract dead thinking in our time where literalness and truth are confused with each other. I could have said we need to re-enliven our thinking, make it very mobile, and reclaim our picture-making capacity which is under attack by the ready-made pictures on TV, the movies, the computer.

But you didn't.

No, I didn't.

You will say it in your book.

Yes, in my book, Paul said and drifted into sleep.

Iris was standing several feet from Beth, looking down at what had once been the theater in Aigai where Philip had been murdered. Her companion was standing off to one side.

Iris said to him, "They have such strange ideas, my friend. It is impossible to understand them. They talk about art as if it were the property of their own souls to do with as they like, to shape as they like. They leave the gods out of it. They talk about art, about history as if both were exclusively within their purview. As if only they, the humans, created. Where are the gods? Why do they forget their origins?"

"Humankind loses something to gain something. We gave up our natural clairvoyance so we could develop the intellect."

"But we hadn't so lost our respect for where we came from, even in our questioning. But can't they see how deficient their intellect has become, how little they can know of the world or of themselves if they only depend on the intellect. The intellect can't make a painting or a sculpture..."

"No, Iris, nor can it write a poem nor offer a prayer."

"Why are they so proud?"

"A child is proud when it learns to walk. It doesn't think at that moment about all that it still has to learn and to do. Human beings have acquired a little freedom. Their egos have become more individualized, distinct from the group-ego of the times out of which our own fledgling egos developed. They have not yet suffered enough to see that without developing a new clairvoyance, a *clairthinking*, they will solve none of the great problems of their times."

"How long must it take? How long must they suffer?"

"That is not decided. Humanity is becoming free. No rank of god has that freedom in the whole immense cosmos. Even the opposers oppose out of the will of God. The gods of strife have no more choice than the harmonious gods. They must strew boulders along mankind's path. Else how will mankind know choice? This freedom is the special gift that humanity will bring to all the hierarchies of the heavens. The gods need humanity. Will humanity fail them, fail to go from being takers to givers?"

"So they must continue to suffer."

"To learn. To grow. Sweet Iris, you know that joy brings no growth. It is its own reward"

Iris turned to look at Beth. "She doesn't understand the nature of pain."

"No, she does not."

Beth wanted to scream at them, that she did know the nature of pain, that she was suffering it, that she could describe it minutely. Pain, she wanted to tell them, is losing a husband, is losing a child, is giving up, is losing those elements of life that give it meaning, coherence. I have lost everything because nothing means anything to me anymore.

But Beth was mute.

She woke up then in a rage, tears of frustration flowed out of her. She got out of bed and paced up and down, furious at Iris and her friend for not understanding her. After several minutes of anger it evaporated and she began to laugh.

Who ever heard of being angry at a figment of one's imagination? she asked herself. Write it down.

And she did. When she went back to sleep, she did not dream again.

As Beth was strolling around A deck the next morning, she heard a voice call out to her.

"Beth, wait up."

Beth turned around. Jenna was jogging down the deck behind her.

"Is this day great, or what?" Jenna slowed down to walk along side Beth.

"Great."

"I'm really looking forward to Troy even if Schliemann did make a mess of the digs. But what a man. Imagine finding the place because he believed in Homer. Awesome, isn't it?"

"Totally."

"Isn't he handsome?" she said.

"Who?" Beth asked, "Schliemann?"

Jenna burst into laughter.

"Jordan?"

"No, not Jordan. He's sweet but he's engaged. And I have a boyfriend back home. I'm talking about Eric," and she looked around to see if he was in earshot. He wasn't.

"Yes, I guess you could say he's attractive," Beth suddenly felt on guard.

"Wouldn't he be perfect?"

"Perfect for what?"

"Not for what, you silly, for whom. Perfect for my mother, of course."

"Mother, is it awful? Is it too soon?"

Beth was uneasy and wasn't sure what to say.

But Jenna plunged on. "He's the right age. He's divorced. He's traveling alone so he probably doesn't have a girlfriend or she would be traveling with him. They are both interested in art. Perfect. Wouldn't it be just perfect?"

"Well, they do live a continent away from each other," Beth said.

"What difference does that make nowadays? Mother's free. I mean her job is not the most thrilling job in the world. She could move to West Africa, for the right man. Listen, I'll see you later. I've got to run at least two more miles," and she took off leaving Beth a little disconcerted.

Well, what business was it of hers anyway? If Eric was interested in Donna there was nothing she could do about it.

Oh, really.

Please go away.

Just inside the gate at Troy, Beth's Turkish guide, Joe, began his lecture. He told them the well known story of Heinrich Schliemann's stubbornness, how he was convinced that the Troy of Homer was a historical town and how from carefully following the descriptions in the *Iliad* he had decided this location was the correct place. And he had proven his theory.

Beth knew the story and listened with half an ear. Neither Paul, Donna, Jenna, nor Eric had been on her bus that morning. Well, that was all right. They weren't joined to each other at the hip. Her absence probably was making Jenna happy, giving her mother a clear field.

Beth, stop it, she told herself. Look around and absorb something. The landscape was lovely, there were lush rolling hills overlooking the plains toward the Dardanelles. Asia Minor, the ancient Anatolia. Not a bad spot to live. So much history—biblical, Greek.

"Now, ladies and gentlemen, we are going to be walking up and down over at least seven different Troys," Joe was saying. "You will notice that the digging by Mr. Schliemann was not very scientific according to modern archaeological methods. He ruined many, many parts of the town. So follow me and I will try to point out some of the interesting places..."

The wharf at Çanakkale was filled with vendors. The 4-M group had been given some time on their own after their visit to Troy, so Beth walked around for half an hour, bought some pistachios from a street vender, and then went to wait at the dock for the first of two launches to come and take people back to the ship. When she arrived at the dock, she greeted Paul who was also waiting there. She didn't see Eric nor Donna. Perhaps they had decided to take the later launch. Once again she felt a slight twisting sensation in her stomach.

"It's not right, Hank. This has no future. I should never have gotten involved. You're a kid. You need a young woman who can give you a family."

"Shut up, Beth. Just shut up. What I don't need now is a Victorian lecture. I love you. That's the bottom line. Is that so hard to take? Don't you feel anything for me?"

"How was your guide?" Paul asked.

"Not bad, not as good as Irene. But then Irene was very special."

"This is Turkish territory. The Greek guides can't work here," he said.

Suddenly, before she knew she was doing it, she asked, "Paul, what do you think about dreams?"

"In what way are you asking that?" She could hear the caution in his tone.

"How do you interpret them? Do you go along with Freud? Or Jung? Do you have another theory? What value do you place on them?"

"Well," he said, "I think there can be many kinds of dreams."

"For instance?"

"For instance," he turned to watch the approaching launch, "I think that some dreams can be caused by something physical, a room that's too hot or too cold, or too much food, an upset stomach, a pain, that happens often when you're older."

He stopped. But she knew he had more to say.

"Paul, do go on. I'm really very interested."

"Yes, well then, a dream can also be a message from your subconscious to your more conscious mind, but in picture form, of things you've been concerned with during the day. In such a dream, I feel it's the gesture in the dream that's important, the movement, what follows what, its progression. Not the picture as symbol, there I disagree with Freud. Or," he rushed through his next words, "it can be a meeting with someone you once knew or perhaps someone who has recently died, or..." he paused.

Beth felt a pain in her heart as he once again referred to the dead as if they were alive somewhere. However, she said, "Go on."

"Or sometimes," Paul looked out at the water, "when a person is going through a particularly difficult period in his life, when he is, so to speak, at the end of his rope, or hers, the veil between this world and that other world becomes so thin that it suddenly tears apart."

"Mother, why can't you see that there is something other than this material world? Why is that so hard for you? Why are you so stubborn?"

"And when, Alicia, will you stop looking for the grand escape and pick some practical road for yourself?"

The launch docked at that moment. And Paul changed the subject. "Are you interested in cocktails or are you going to be on deck for the sailing?" he asked her.

"Oh, I wouldn't miss the sailing."

"Then I'll see you there?"

"It's a date."

Eric may have turned off of you, but Paul is still interested.

Yes, and Paul is seventy-six years old.

Don't be unkind.

They boarded the boat for the five-minute ride to the ship.

After watching the ship set sail at twilight to move through the narrow straits called the Dardanelles, the ancient Hellespont, Beth and Paul had dinner with Ellen and Leona Parkington, the mother and daughter who were from Palm Beach, Florida, and with Doris and Lucy. The talk all centered on Beth, a real live poet, the celebrity within their midst. The two sisters were particularly excited.

"My dear, we had no idea," proclaimed Doris, when they were all seated.

Even the usually calm and unflappable Lolly seemed affected.

Beth answered their questions as best she could. She had done it all before. She could do this.

When she told them about her early interest in nursery rhymes, Lucy said, "It takes all kinds. I used to think those rhymes were about as silly and as dumb as they could be."

"Lucy," Doris scolded.

"Well, I did," Lucy said.

When dinner was over, Paul was about to say good-night and turn in early.

But Beth said, "Paul, would you have a few minutes to spare?"

"Yes, of course."

"I have something I want to read to you, and I'd like your opinion on it."

"Oh, my dear, you know I'm not a poet nor do I know all that much..."

"It's not poetry. It has to do with dreams. Will you come to my room?"

He nodded and followed her to her cabin. It was a small room, like his own. Two beds were on opposite sides of the wall with only a small space in-between. Beth removed some of her things from off of one bed and Paul sat down opposite her.

"Remember the conversation we had earlier, about dreams?"

He nodded and waited.

"I've recorded some odd dreams I've been having since I came on this trip. And I'd like to read them to you if it's all right."

"Yes. Go ahead."

"I've labeled these, the *Iris Dreams*, you'll understand why after I've finished."

When she stopped reading, he waited for her to say something, to ask some question. When she didn't he asked, "What do you make of them, Beth?"

She shrugged, laughed uneasily and said, "Beats me. What do you make of them?"

"Are you sure?"

"Sure?"

"That you want to know what I think?"

"Of course, I asked you here, didn't I?"

"My dear, I am well aware of how peculiar my ideas can sound to most people. I wouldn't for a moment want to press them upon you."

"You're not pressing any of your ideas on me, Paul. I'm the one who is asking."

He nodded. She asked and he would tell the truth. That much he felt obliged to do. "All right then. Your dreams seem to be a breakthrough into another realm, something beyond all the ordinary kinds of dreams we were talking about this afternoon."

She screwed up her face thoughtfully. "One of your so-called other-worldly dreams, you mean."

"It's possible."

"But why? What's the purpose?"

"Well, I can't tell you that, why don't you ask them or her?"

"What? What do you mean?"

"I mean, should you dream of Iris again, ask her a question?"

"Really?" In the light coming from her desk lamp her face looked suddenly white. "I'm not sure I can."

"Afraid?"

"Maybe. Yes. I think I tried once. But I couldn't say anything. I guess I'm afraid if I let them know that I hear them, they'll go away."

She got up suddenly her knees banging into his. "I can't tell you how ridiculous what I just said sounds to me at this moment. Weird to hear them read out loud."

"Too real?"

"Maybe. It's funny but I feel like an interloper, that I've walked into somebody else's world, that it has nothing to do with me, that I stand outside it."

"Truly?"

She moved to the foot of the bed and stared out of the porthole above her desk. "But I know that's impossible. Whatever you think about dreams, if you dream them, they belong to you, right?"

"They do belong to you."

She turned to look at him. "Actually, I'm terribly intrigued by the dreams. I become very engaged. And when I wake up, I remember almost verbatim what I've heard. Why?"

Another question. What could she hear?

Speak what you know, Annie thought to him.

"Perhaps it's because the pain that you've been suffering these past five years has made the wall between that world and this almost nonexistent."

Beth chewed on her lip for a moment, "Another world. That goes against everything I've ever believed as an adult." She came and sat down again. "So I should ask Iris a question?"

"That seems to me a reasonable thing to do."

"What should I ask?"

"Beth, that's entirely up to you. What do you want to know?"

Beth shrugged. "They came to me. I didn't come to them."

Paul reached out and patted her hand. It was an awkward attempt at comfort. "Think about it, my dear."

"Yes, I will."

Paul walked to the door. "You know, Beth, you don't have to do anything you don't want to do."

"I know. Thank you, Paul, for listening to me."

"No, thank you, Beth, for trusting me enough to share this with me." He smiled at her and left.

Beth sat for a long time without moving. Somehow speaking about Iris out loud gave her dreams a peculiar reality that she suddenly didn't know how to deal with.

This is all ridiculous, she finally decided, and prepared for bed.

But she was afraid to go to sleep. She lay awake for hours. When she finally fell asleep, she didn't dream about Iris. She dreamt instead about Alicia. Once again Alicia was standing at the end of a long corridor calling to her. Beth couldn't hear her. She tried to tell her that she couldn't hear her, but her own words were blocked before they left her mouth. She tried to run down the corridor to Alicia but there was an invisible barrier which obstructed her. She banged and banged on the unseen wall with both fists. All the while she could see that Alicia was struggling to get to her. It was a dream of horrible frustration. And Beth woke up from it with tears of rage pouring down her face and her blankets wound up like corkscrews on her bed.

She got out of her bed and paced back and forth, back and forth until her tears subsided. She felt ill with hopelessness. Alicia was dead. And she, Beth, was still failing her. But how could that be? Would she ever get over the sense of her own culpability in Alicia's death? She knew it wasn't her fault. That is, her logical mind knew it wasn't her fault. But would the sense of wrongness in a mother outliving her child be with her for the rest of her life? Beth had the terrible feeling that it would. And would Beth's expiation for living longer than her daughter continue to be giving up the value of her own life? Maybe. Maybe that was the only way to live with that terrible sense of guilt and wrongness, the only way to cancel it out.

She wasn't able to sleep any longer. It was 5:30 A.M. Beth dressed and went up on the deck to watch the New Odyssey sail through the Sea of Marmara. She hoped that no one but sailors would be up at this early hour.

After Paul left Beth's room, he knew he would not be able to sleep as yet, so he went up on A deck and stood staring out at the yards and yards of velvety water.

And there you have it, Paul, Annie thought to him.

Startling, Annie. Those dreams are startling. Beth is being given information about evolution, about the nature of the human soul, from this Iris and her companion. It was amazing to hear.

Why amazing, my love. Like each human being, Beth has lived in spiritual realms between earth lives. And she has lived other lives where she was not so cut off from spiritual knowledge. You know all this. You know that spiritual knowledge and all the memories of her past incarnations live in her unconscious. And that her unconscious is not contained solely within her body, but lies also in a spiritual realm.

Yes, Annie, but Beth, like many, has blocked out such knowledge this life, has turned away from wanting to believe in, much less access, a spiritual reality. That turning away is also destiny.

We humans have lost many of the old god-given gifts, in the course of our evolution, for the sake of true self-consciousness, for the sake of clear thinking and independence. But in our times we must acquire that old wisdom again, in a renewed way, while retaining that individuality, that freedom, that marvelous earth-given thinking.

I know that, Annie, but each human has to want it, has to want to initiate the reconnection.

I sense a reluctance in you, Paul.

I confess it is there. Elizabeth Layton is in pain. I don't want to contribute to it. I can't be blundering into her life like a runaway truck. No being, spiritual or human, who values evolution, is going to force another into believing, into knowing.

Then Beth must want it. Deep down in her psyche she must want this, perhaps even planned for it before she came into this Elizabeth Layton life. Even planned to meet you, Paul.

Well, she has met me and what I say seems not to relieve her, not to ease her pain, but to push her further toward some crisis.

Why put it that way? Perhaps she herself wants the meetings with you in order to precipitate a crisis. Perhaps she herself wants to wake up, to conjoin herself to what is real, to what is true.

Perhaps on some level.

The most important level.

But if she is not up to it? If she breaks down?

And if it takes that?

I don't want to be party to that. No. I draw the line.

You merely answer questions, Paul.

I don't have to do that.

Even if you were silent, you are yourself.

At that point Paul disengaged himself from Annie and walked briskly around the deck. But when he had returned to his cabin, when he was lying in his bed, he called to her. Annie, I thought I came on this trip because I was dying too soon, not to speak of spiritual realities to someone who doesn't seem ready to hear them.

Beth also is dying too soon.

God help me, then.

Yes.

Fear wrenched Beth awake. Someone was bending over her. She blinked open her eyes, and heart pounding, gasped hoarsely, "Who is it?"

"Beth, I'm sorry. I didn't mean to startle you," Eric Halsey was standing next to her deck chair, looking down on her. "Wait, I'll get us some coffee." And he was off before she could say another word.

Beth looked around. She was seated on the deck of the New Odyssey where she had come after that terrible, frustrating dream about Alicia.

"You always hated lies, didn't you, Mom? I mean, you desperately needed people to be up front with you."

"Did I, Alicia? Really?"

Oh, Alicia! Oh, my lost child, I can't help you!

She took a few deep breaths and tried to shake off the unbearable sense of helplessness. It was this helplessness that she could manage the least.

It was morning. The sea green life scent of the ocean was all around her. The ship was still sailing the Sea of Marmara. Nothing around except water, deep, deep water. She could feel herself expanding out into the sea with its depths, expanding into its breadth.

But she pulled herself up short.

No, her soul was too large now, too deep, she was drowning in it. She must not go there, where the ocean called.

Beth glanced at her watch. 7:20 A.M. She had dozed off. While she was asleep several people had come up on deck, eager to watch the approach to Istanbul. Look around, Beth. Concentrate on what you can see, detail by detail. Doris and Lucy were there in another one of their numerous jogging outfits. Ellen and Leona Parkington were already dressed for shore in their pantsuits. The Winstons were there and several of the camera enthusiasts.

In a few minutes Eric had returned with two steaming cups of coffee. "Are you all right?" he asked, sitting in the chair next to her. "You look like you've seen a ghost."

Tears welled up in her eyes. "Just that," she murmured.

Eric found a handkerchief and handed it to her.

She took it and wiped her eyes. "Sorry, bad dream."

"About your daughter?"

She nodded and sipped the coffee.

"What a stupid remark I just made. That ghost business. I apologize."

Beth managed a smile. It was morning. She wasn't alone. There was a deck full of people who were no longer strangers to her. And here was Eric, sitting next to her looking concerned. Dressed in cotton pants and a blue shirt, he looked especially handsome.

He does have a nice face. Isn't that too bad.

Why too bad?

"I never meant it to go so far..."

"Mother, is it awful? Is it too soon?"

"I hadn't expected to find you up here," he said.

"Why not?"

"I mean, it's my good luck. I just slipped a note under your cabin door."

She carefully set the coffee cup down on the table between them.

"I have a proposition for you," he said. "Sorry, that came out wrong, I mean I have an invitation for you."

"What sort of invitation?"

"Well, a suggestion for today."

"I don't understand."

"We should dock about 9:30 and after the ship has been cleared through customs, buses will be at the dock to take the group to Topkapi Palace, then back to the ship for lunch, and then on to the Chora. Finally, some time in town for shopping."

He leaned toward her.

"Instead of going with the group, spend the day in Istanbul with me. I have a car and driver picking me up, courtesy of my boss, Mrs. Barry, and he'll be at my disposal all day. Come with me."

His proposal took Beth by surprise.

When she hesitated, he hurried on. "We'll see all the same sights, so you won't miss a thing. It's just that I want to show you the Chora. It's so glorious. I really don't want you to see it with a crowd. And I don't want to see it alone. Come with me."

"I don't know what to say. I haven't..."

"Is it too soon?"

"Say, yes. We'll go to the Chora this morning, while the others are at the Topkapi. Then we'll drive around the city, have lunch together, go on to Topkapi after that and come back to the ship when we feel like it."

The intensity in his voice shook her. "I think I'd like that," she said. "Who else is coming?"

"I'd like it to be just the two of us. Is that all right?"

Oh, dear, she thought. Oh, dear. Where's Donna? Jenna will be angry at me.

She swallowed and said, "Yes."

He stood up then. "Let's get some breakfast. And then come up and watch the sailing into the Bosporus. It's a spectacular sight." He held out his hand to help her out of her chair. She took it.

Beth couldn't identify the car they were in, some old European make, with an emphasis on the word *old.* Their driver, Dinc, spoke a fair English. "Mrs. Barry. This is a lady. Yes, yes, a very American lady. Very nice. Very generous." Then he asked Eric what he and his lady wanted to see first. Eric told him, the Chora. So they drove over the Atatürk Bridge from the New City to the Old City and into the heart of the old section of Istanbul with Dinc pointing out the important sights.

The city seemed so exotic to Beth, so venerable. Mosques and minarets gracefully pierced the sky. Istanbul didn't look like a Sydney Greenstreet/Peter Lorre movie. It looked like a fairy tale out of the *Arabian Nights.*

Dinc took a circuitous route, taking them past Valens Aqueduct, Faith Mosque, Yavuz Selim Mosque, and the Church of Pammakaristos, which had been the Greek Orthodox Patriarchate from 1454 until 1590 when it, like so many of the Byzantine churches, had been turned into a mosque. Dinc slowed the car down. "Very beautiful, very interesting for Christians," he told Eric, "You like to see? Your woman like to see? Very nice mosaics, very important."

"Let's do the Chora first," Eric told him. "We'll see how much time we have later."

"Okay, okay," the driver said, and picked up speed.

The Chora, or Kariye as the Turks called it, was in a corner of the ancient city. The words *Chora* and *Kariye* both meant *country*. When they reached their destination, Beth admired the wooden houses, many with vines of climbing roses.

"Very old," Dinc directed his words to Eric. "All saved, all restored." Then he asked, "Do you want that I show to you inside of church?"

"No," Eric said. "I've been to the Chora before. You wait here for us."

The driver gave a shrug as his two passengers got out of the car.

There were a few kiosks in the cobbled street selling post-cards, souvenir trinkets, and guide books on both Istanbul and the Chora. Beth saw two large tour buses parked up the street. The church would not be as empty as Eric had anticipated. She smiled at the children who watched them with open faces and mild curiosity as they walked the short distance to the entrance of the old church and mosque.

"It's not a church anymore nor a mosque," Eric told her. "It's a museum and a very valuable tourist attraction."

Eric took her by the elbow and they walked into the building and Beth stopped just inside the door. Her eyes moved appreciatively over the walls and the ceiling.

"Come," Eric said, "you ain't seen nothin' yet," and he took her into the church proper.

"This is unlike anything I've ever seen in my life," she said, at one point. "It's absolutely riveting. Is the whole of the Bible here on the walls and on the ceiling?"

"As much as they could fit on it."

"How old is all this?" her gesture was a sweeping one.

"Thirteenth century."

"Old."

"But not as old as the church itself. We owe these extraordinary mosaics and frescoes to a man called Theodore Metochites. He was very wealthy and very close to Emperor Andronicus II."

"A patron of the arts," Beth nodded.

"And a religious man. I love this place."

"I can see why. It's breathtaking."

The two walked heads up moving from one scene to another.

"Elegant," she remarked more than once. "So graceful."

"The mosaics that depict the life of the Virgin are not just from the Bible as you can see but also from the apocryphal writings," he told her.

Here was a Mary one could understand, Beth thought. Selected for a task that was too big for her. Accepting. Suffering. Growing. Losing a child in his prime. Suffering. Growing. Not only you, Beth. Mothers everywhere, throughout all of history.

Eric took her hand and they moved through the church without speaking. There were two mosaic fragments that Beth paused at for a long time. The first was called the *Mothers Mourning for their Children* and the second, *Herod Ordering the Massacre of the Innocents*. Both fragments were filled with the grief of mothers for their dead children.

You belong to a long line of mourners, she told herself. And the thought filled her with calm.

"'Then was fulfilled what was spoken by the prophet, Jeremiah. A voice was heard in Ramah, wailing and loud lamentation, Rachel weeping for her children; she refused to be consoled, because they were no more.'"

Beth turned to Eric. He was staring at the mosaic of the mothers mourning and reciting. He must have felt her eyes on him because he turned to her and said, "Matthew 2:17,18. I became acquainted with the Bible from looking up the mosaics in churches I love."

"It's a different Christianity, isn't it?"

"Different than the one I was taught back home in Chicago," he said.

He took her arm and once again they walked on in silence. He let her look without comment and she was grateful.

I'm living in my eyes, Beth thought, feeling something akin to pure joy. I'm a poet touching with my eyes. If anything could lift her above the world it was art. She pushed aside the warning voice that began to awaken in her solar plexus. I'm with Eric. And I'm having a glorious time. And she was discovering with his help the wonderful world of mosaics. One didn't have to be able to read the Gospels, one merely had to step inside the church and be moved by stones. Yes, stones were speaking, had spoken, would continue to speak.

She thought then of Mattie and of her book of poems that had come out a few months ago, *Speaking Stone*.

"Can we understand just one other person from our own times? Someone we think we love?"

She looked around her at the stories told in stone. These stones were different kinds of stones than the ones Mattie celebrated. Or were they? Were they?

One might become religious, Beth thought, if one came often enough.

Several times while they walked through the old church, Beth turned to look at her quiet companion. Eric's eyes were shining. And Beth knew that he watched her as much as he looked at the mosaics.

"I can't help myself."
"Can we understand…?"
Be careful, Beth. Be careful. Be careful.
Go away. Just leave me alone. I'm doing fine.

It was a perfect little fish restaurant in which to have lunch, one of several facing the Golden Horn. Beth thought the restaurant must be family owned because there was a strong resemblance between the manager, the waiters, and the woman who was the cashier. She imagined the kitchen peopled with cousins and aunts and children.

Dinc, who had recommended it, introduced Eric and Beth to his cousin, the manager with an unpronounceable name. "Ah, Mrs. Barry, Mrs. Barry," the manager said when he heard that Eric was a colleague. He took them to a table in the center of the outdoor courtyard where they would be seen by everyone, but Eric asked to be seated in a quiet corner. The manager looked at Beth, nodded at Eric, and reseated them. A soft gentle breeze blew in from off the water making the warm day comfortable.

There were several other parties in the courtyard as they sat down. None was speaking English. Beth recognized Italian, German, what she guessed to be Japanese, and possibly Rumanian. Istanbul was definitely an international city.

The manager asked permission to select their food. "What do you say, Beth?" Eric asked her. She nodded her assent and Eric in turn told the manager that they would be honored to place themselves in his hands.

The manager and Dinc both disappeared into the kitchen, the manager to select their dinner, and Dinc to visit with his cousins.

"He'll get a free meal for having brought us," Eric told her.

The manager returned almost immediately with two glasses and a pitcher of white wine. He poured the amber-tinted liquid into their glasses and returned to the kitchen.

Eric lifted his glass. "What shall we drink to?" His light brown eyes looked remarkably translucent in that light. Nothing hidden, Beth thought. Hank's eyes had been almost black, the dark angry eyes of intolerant youth. Matthew had hazel eyes, flecked with gold, changeable.

Beth lifted her glass. "Let's drink to Istanbul," she said.

"To Istanbul, may it stand forever on this spot, enchanting travelers from all over the world. And let's drink to two who admire it today."

They both took sips from their glasses.

"Delicious," Eric said.

"Delicious," Beth agreed. "I would have said, let's drink to Eastern Christianity for giving us such incomparable art, but that seems a little inappropriate in this Muslim land."

"You like to be appropriate?" he asked.

"It helps," she said. Feeling the intensity of his gaze, she turned to look out at the myriad small and large ships navigating the busy waterway.

"Helps what?"

"Helps one get through awkward situations. I've had a very waspy school girl upbringing." She forced herself to meet his eyes.

"Is this one of those awkward situations?"

"Yes," she answered, "no. Yes."

He laughed. "Two yeses, one no. Not conclusive, I would say."

"Mother is it awful? Is it too soon?"

"When were you in Istanbul last?"

"Too many years ago."

"With your wife?"

"No. Oh, I was still married but things weren't so good anymore. Nora stopped pretending to be interested in art or in travel. She wanted to stay home, study singing, raise the kids. Her mother would have taken them for a couple of weeks if she had wanted to come. But she didn't. So I came alone. There's too much to see in this uncertain world that's wonderful, that's food for the eyes. I needed to see both the world and its art. Still do, really." He laughed and shrugged. "Well, it's my field. But it's difficult not to have someone to share that passion with. Frustrating, like unrequited love."

"Where are they now?"

"Who?"

"Your children."

"I have two sons, both in college, one at Princeton and one at Duke."

"Good schools," she said.

"They both have jobs this summer."

"Are you close?"

"Yeah, yes. I'd say so. Particularly with my youngest, Kevin. I have legal custody of both."

"Really? How unusual."

"Do you want to hear my tragic-comic tale?"

"Comic?"

"A tragic-comic tale of trust and betrayal and retribution."

"I can't wait," she smiled. "This promises to be better than Oprah."

"Ah," he said. "You saw the show!"

"Now I know why you look so familiar," she said.

At this point two waiters brought out the first course which was a dish called *midye dolmasi,* mussels stuffed with rice and, to them, unidentifiable spices. It was served with a flourish under the watchful eye of the manager. When the two Americans had tasted the mussels and pronounced them, "exceptional," the manager left smiling and the waiters disappeared into the kitchen.

"I can see my marriage clearly now that I've been away from it for five years," Eric told her when they were alone again. "Too often we humans are like race horses rushing down a track with blinders on."

Beth was listening intently, her elbows on the table, her chin on her hands.

"Don't you like the mussels?" he asked.

"They're delicious," she picked up her fork again.

"Or we're like the three blind men in that fable, the ones who were asked to describe an elephant. One describes it as a large leg, one as a small tail, one as a long trunk. Not one takes in the whole beast. That's us humans."

"The mind is capable of infinite denial," she said.

The restaurant was beginning to fill up, but the manager put no one at tables near them.

"That pretty much describes me. I married Nora on the rebound. I was twenty-six, had gotten my heart broken by a beautiful but spoiled girl whose face I can no longer remember…"

"But the hurt lasted for years."

"Yes," he said. "But it was my fault that it did."

"How?"

"By keeping it in my gut undigested, by being so god-damned timid. I was afraid of getting hurt, so I became doggedly determined never to go through that kind of pain again, as if it were appropriate or even beneficial to hide from pain. Mind you, I didn't see that that's what I was doing. These brilliant, insightful observations are, of course, all in retrospect. At any rate, I quickly found a lady who was shy, not at all pretty, not very demanding, who seemed thrilled that I was interested in her. Someone I could depend on never to leave me, never to cause me jealousy or worry. What's wrong?"

"Nothing. I'm listening, that's all, and..."

"Raven wants to marry me."

"And what?"

"Trying to imagine you so cautious, so fearful."

"That's because you're now getting the grown-up me, a long time in the making." He half-smiled.

"Go on with your story."

"Well, Nora had always wanted to be an opera star, and I encouraged her to study, to dream. But in reality, she didn't have a great voice, and I knew it, not a voice with operatic potential. So for countless years Nora studied and studied and sang in an amateur choir, but her career went nowhere. She had always been high strung. She became increasingly bitter, became jealous of my work, blamed her lack of success on the fact that she had to take care of our children. Maybe that's why I stopped painting, I'm not sure. Maybe because I felt too guilty about her lack of success to have any personal success of my own. Our social life was limited. Nora didn't have too many girl friends. Our sex life was pretty awful. She stopped pretending interest in any of my work after we came back from Italy. Even after I stopped trying to make it as a painter and went into gallery and then museum work, she never accompanied me to openings or other functions that are so much a part of my business. Oh, once in a while, if it was very necessary that I have a mate in tow. But she resented it."

"Why did you stay in the marriage, Eric, all those years, if it was so awful?"

"Like I said, blinders. I didn't allow myself to see that it was awful. It seemed like most other marriages. A compromise. Normal. What was romance anyway, except a few okay years and then, like snow in spring, the meltdown? We had marvelous sons and I thought of her as a good mother. And in some ways she was. Nervous, and fearful, but doting and attentive. It seemed reason enough to stay."

"Are you a product of divorce yourself?" She was oddly touched by his story.

"How did you guess?"

"Those are the people who hang on to bad marriages when others would have walked away."

"Yeah, it's so classic. My dad left my mother for another woman. My mother raged for thirty-five years."

"How did it work out for your dad?"

"He lived happily ever after."

"Really?" she asked.

"Really. Happily ever after. Don't let your soup get cold," he told her.

She picked up her spoon and began to eat the delicious spicy fish soup called *balik corbasi* which had just been served them. "This is fabulous, isn't it? I wonder what these spices are?"

"There's a marvelous spice market here in Istanbul. We could see it."

"Maybe," she said. "So what were you trying to do by staying in a bad marriage, expiate your father's guilt? Make your mother happy?"

"Probably. The funny thing is, I don't know who I was really making happy. Amusing thing is, my mother never liked Nora, not from the beginning. She thought I was too good for her. And what craziness made me think that living with Nora for ever and ever would finally make my mother happy? She's a bitter lady, my mother, has always been a bitter lady. If she didn't have my father to blame for all her ills, she would find something or someone else to blame, something outside of herself. It is simply not possible for my mother to be happy."

"Seems so sad to have lived the way you lived."

"No pity, please. I made my own bed, and I've had a very interesting career despite everything. I've met some fascinating people and have watched history in the making, or at least art history. But most important, Nora and I have great kids. That's something I wouldn't change. And I probably wasn't good enough as a painter to make it. If I left painting earlier because of Nora, it was probably all to the good."

"Okay, so where is the comic part of this story and the betrayal?"

Suddenly there were loud voices from the kitchen area.

"Coming next, with the salad."

Out came a man carrying a large tray. Out came a young boy holding tightly two plates and some utensils. Out came the Chef who spoke not a word of English, along with the manager who then translated Eric's English words of praise into Turkish words of praise. Beth knew it was a good translation because the Chef flushed with pleasure. The soup dishes were removed under the manager's careful eye, instructing his cousins or children or whomever in harsh tones. Soon the table was cleared of crumbs, and dishes of cold vegetable *salata* were served them. Then the family left as quickly as they had come. Beth and Eric were again alone.

"Okay," Eric took a deep breath, "now for the comedy and betrayal part. Are you sure you want to hear this? I don't know why I'm telling you my life story."

"You want me to know I'm not the only person in the world to have suffered losses," Beth said.

"Maybe. Or maybe I need for you to know this."

She raised her eyebrows.

"No secrets. No surprises," he said.

"*...when one thing is moving toward becoming another...*"

"Do go on. I'm hooked."

"This is risky. You might not like me after you hear the rest."

"Eric, go on."

"Twenty years of marriage and life goes on and on. I'm a very loyal husband. No affairs. Well, a couple of one night stands. Honest, that's all. It's my Irish guilt, you see. I can't be like my father. So after twenty years I finally get involved with someone else."

Beth felt her own cheeks go cold. She looked away.

"Disappointed?"

"Raven wants to marry me."

"What business is it of mine to be disappointed? I'm not God or your mother."

"This is life, Beth. We aren't angels. It happened and I won't apologize for it." He reached across the table and put his hand on top of hers. "But I could stop talking about it."

"I'm sorry. I'm really not judging. Go on." And she pulled her hand out from under his and picked up her fork.

He apparently didn't believe her because he was silent.

So she said, "I've been a wife, Eric. I guess I feel loyalty to the whole specie. So this is the betrayal part."

"This is half the betrayal part."

She managed a smile. "Now I'm really intrigued. Please go on."

"Sharon was divorced and childless, in her mid-thirties. Our affair consisted of daily phone calls, and a few hurried meetings during the month where we would come together like love-starved kids. My guilt, you see, wouldn't allow me much more. After a couple of years of this, Sharon asked me to leave my wife and to marry her. She insisted she could give me the life I needed and deserved. She was probably right but I hesitated. I felt overwhelming guilt. I couldn't think beyond it. My kids would hate me, I convinced myself. My mother would hate me. God would hate me. My poor little Nora wouldn't make it through this very difficult world without me. So I made the correct and noble choice."

"Which was?"

"Which was to make no one happy, not Sharon whom I loved, not my wife whom I never loved, not my kids who would soon have lives of their own and certainly not myself…"

"And not your mother."

"No, not my mother. So I gave Sharon up and all hope for happiness. I stopped seeing her altogether and I tried to bury myself in my work. I had just joined the staff of the Barry then." He paused and looked at her with a mocking expression. "You're really going to love the ending, you and all the wives in America," he said.

"Tell me."

"A year and a half later my wife leaves me. Nora runs off with a piano player, the guy she was coaching with. And left me the kids. She didn't even fight me for them. The lady who I thought was afraid of the world wanted to be free of me who had kept her in prison, her own words."

"You're kidding!"

"Scout's honor."

"Betrayal number two. It cancels out the first?"

"Back to the first. After the shock wears off, I try to locate my old flame, Sharon, who had in the interim moved to L.A. I found her after weeks of searching. She had married a TV director, was expecting a baby and had never been happier in her life."

"Oh, Eric, how terrible. I mean for you."

"So there we have the sad and silly times of Eric Halsey."

"And now?"

"Now what?"

"No lady in your life. The world is full of women looking for men."

"Tell me about it. It's a jungle out there," he said, "and a single straight male with a good job is quarry to be stalked. But to answer your question, no, there is no special lady."

"Afraid?"

"Yeah. What about you?"

"Me what?" she asked. "A man or afraid?"

"Either."

"No man," she said.

"A great marriage and nothing looks good in comparison?"

Beth glanced out at the water and at a small boat sailing by. In the restaurant the tables close to them had filled up, mostly with tourists. And she was one. And Eric was another. Two strangers were having an intimate conversation half-way around the world from home. She looked curiously at the good-looking, obviously available man she had known for little more than a week. We all have our stories, she thought. Very few original.

"I never meant it to go so far, Beth, really I didn't. I saw it first as a little attraction that would pass…"

"Go on."

"It didn't pass. I thought if I had a little fling, the attraction would disappear. It didn't."

"You shit, Matthew! Twenty-five years of loyalty, companionship, family…"

"Everything you can say to me, Beth, I've said to myself. I have no defense."

"Not fair! Matthew, defend yourself. Fight, goddamn it. Don't stand there whimpering like a little boy. That's low. Give me something I can hit up against, not this."

"I can't. I can't help it. I can't help myself. I'm like a man possessed."

"God, come up with a better cliché."

"Love is a cliché. It's a country-western."

"No. No, it's not. It's twenty-five years of living together. It's twenty-five years of my life that you're throwing away. Don't give me that you can't help yourself."

"But I can't. I'm miserable. I'm hurting you. I'm hurting my kids. But…"

"But what? What do you want to do?"

"I don't know. All I know is I can't live without her and I can't keep our relationship a secret and I can't live a lie."

"Oh, my God, we're getting morality now. 'I can't live a lie. I can dump all over you but I can't live a lie.' What the hell do you want, Matthew?"

"I don't know."

"Too easy. Dump the garbage in my lap. You want me to make the decision?"

"No. Yes. Raven wants to marry me. I don't know what to do."

"Goddamn you. Well, my answer is I don't know. I don't know." And Beth burst into tears.

"I'm sorry, Beth," and Matthew left their bedroom.

"It was a good marriage for a dozen years, a so-so marriage for another ten and for the last two or three, it was terrible," she told him the truth.

"What happened?"

"There was someone else. Matthew was an English teacher at NYU. He was having an affair with a student. I think, if he hadn't...hadn't died, he would have left me."

"The bastard."

"That's not funny."

"I didn't mean it to be funny. How could a man want to leave you?"

"You're being patronizing."

"No, I'm not. You're bright and provocative, with something to say. You're witty, with the most eloquent eyes and the most expressive gestures I have ever seen in my life. I love your hand movements. They're delicate and float through the air with enormous grace. When you speak or when you look at something that engages you, your body language is absolutely captivating. I cannot see how anyone would want to leave you, particularly for a half-formed kid."

To Beth's relief, the waiters suddenly appeared with their main course, *kalkan baligi,* turbot. When it was all before them, the two began prudently to speak about the trip and their fellow travelers. Soon they were laughing at each other's observations. Beth hadn't felt this good in years. Her gestures, how lovely to be told that they were graceful and expressive. Far better than being told you are beautiful. A person inhabits her gestures. Beauty can be a mask.

When lunch was over, their driver suddenly reappeared. Eric paid for the meal and they were soon in the car again.

"Would you like to see more mosaics or Topkapi?" Eric asked her.

"Is there another church as beautiful as the Chora?"

"Probably not," he answered her. "Well, perhaps the Hagia Sophia."

"Which we are seeing tomorrow."

"Right."

"Then I don't want anything to dilute my impressions of the Chora. Let's go to Topkapi."

"Good," he grinned, took her hand, gave the driver the instructions and didn't let go of her hand until they had arrived at the parking lot of the Topkapi.

Beth strolled alongside Eric through the various courts of Topkapi Palace and up and down the terraces overlooking the water. They found their way to the rooms that held the sultans' famous jeweled treasures, and elbowed their way through the crowds, made larger by several groups of school children. They saw the Spoonmaker's diamond, the famous Topkapi dagger, and countless rare and valuable jewels. Beth loved jewelry but the crowds were beginning to make her feel anxious and dizzy.

"I think I need to sit down for a few moments," she said.

He took her arm and propelled her through the crowds and out into the gardens.

"Perhaps we should go back to the ship."

"Absolutely not," Beth said. "I'll be fine in a few minutes. And besides, what about the harem? I've never seen a harem and I'm not going to miss it now. I've met a lot of women in my life, but I never talked to one who had been part of a harem."

"They're not allowed out."

"Ghastly."

"Let's sit here until you catch your breath," he said, and led her to a bench.

"I'm really sorry," she said. "It's just crowds and noise. They get through the barrier of my skin, somehow. I can't keep them out."

"Depression," he said.

"Yes, but I'm having a wonderful day, really, I am."

"I know that, Beth. I can see that and I'm grateful that we've shared the day together. But one day does not depression dispel."

"Thank you."

"For what?"

"For the Chora, for sharing your story with me, for the lavish lunch, for the gorgeous weather, for the magic of Istanbul..."

"The only thing I can take credit for is my own messy life story."

"Shhh, don't disillusion me. I thought this whole place," and she gestured around the Topkapi gardens, "was your doing." Beth stood up. "I'm really fine now," she told him and they decided to go find the harem.

Eric, following his map of the Topkapi, led her to the small doorway. A guard stood there, unsmiling.

"It's closed to the general public. They're doing some sort of repair work," Eric told her after speaking to the guard who apparently knew a few words of English.

"Oh, no." Beth said.

Eric spoke to the guard again. "Wait here, Beth. I'll be right back." He deposited her on a nearby bench and went off. Ten minutes later he returned, followed by a short, smiling man with a large mustache. "This is Mr. Ozbay. He will show us the harem and make sure we don't get lost. The harem can be very treacherous. For Mr. Ozbay, we have Mrs. Barry to thank."

"An unusual woman, Mrs. Barry," Mr. Ozbay said, greeting Beth with a small bow.

Mr. Ozbay spoke to the guard, who unlocked the door. Ozbay led them through. In a few moments Beth was completely lost. The streets twisted and turned.

"It was done with purpose," Mr. Ozbay told her. "If someone came into the harem who didn't belong, it was not so easy to get out."

"Not so easy for the women, either." Beth said.

"Not so terrible for the women," Mr. Ozbay said. "It was quite a privilege to be chosen to be educated in the harem. And to become the mother of the sultan was a high honor. She was the most important person in the harem next to the sultan himself. A formidable figure, a little like your Mrs. Barry."

Mr. Ozbay chatted on amiably. He told them that the sultan's mother had forty rooms at her disposal, and many officials and servants to take care of her needs. There was always much scheming in the harem for even a slave girl could be raised to the level of the sultan's favorite. "Daughters of important families were brought to the harem at age ten or twelve," Mr. Ozbay said, "and if they pleased the sultan they were educated and raised in the harem.

A community of women, Beth thought, all dependent on the largess and whim of a single man.

"You understand," Mr. Ozbay said, leading the two down one of the many alleyways inside the harem, "that after a girl had completed her education, should she have chosen not to stay in the harem, a suitable husband was found for her and the sultan provided her with a dowry. He assumed the role of father."

"But," Beth asked, "wasn't she, or hadn't she been a sexual partner of the sultan while she was in the harem?"

"Yes, but try to understand, the sultan was considered to be a successor to the prophet and therefore holy. If he chose a girl for the night, the girl did not lose her virginity in the eyes of the public."

Beth looked around at the enclosed harem, a little city in itself, and thought how lucky she was to have been born in America in the twentieth century.

"The third most important person in the harem was the chief black eunuch. He supervised the other eunuchs and dealt with the finances of the harem."

They left the harem the same way they came in. Eric thanked Mr. Ozbay who asked to be remembered to Mrs. Barry. Mr. Ozbay bowed and smiled at Beth and left them.

"Istanbul is a beautiful city," she said to Eric as they walked toward the exit, "but it's not a city for women. I saw very few in the streets out on their own."

"Perhaps they're behind the curtains, peeping out at this man's world."

"Good to be an American, isn't it?"

"Very good. Beth, would you like to get something to drink before we return to the ship? I noticed some small restaurants not far from the parking lot."

"Yes, I'd love something cold," she said.

They found Dinc near their car talking to some other drivers. Eric told him that they were going to have a cold drink outside the palace. Dinc immediately suggested the best place and agreed to meet them in half an hour.

Beth and Eric walked out of the large parking lot and quickly found the little restaurant that Dinc had recommended. Soon they were drinking some sweet, cold concoction.

"Beth, will you tell me why you haven't put out a fifth book of poetry? I asked you that once before and you seemed angry at me for having mentioned it. Is it all right to ask you now?"

She looked up and saw that he was genuinely interested, and her heart gave a little unexpected leap.

"...when one thing is moving toward becoming another..."

I do apologize for that earlier rebuff," she said. "A new book is an idea that has simply been too painful to even discuss. You can't imagine how many times I've been asked that, urged that. But my life has been so completely altered, you see. The simple answer is, I don't have poems for a new book."

"You haven't written many poems since your daughter died?"

She toyed with the spoon, drawing water doodles on the wet table. "I haven't written much since Alicia first became ill, which was so soon after Matthew died that I guess one could say that I haven't written much since Matthew died. That's five years ago. *America, Lost!* came out only months after his death but it had already been completed before. It's been a time of losses and I can't write about that, won't write about that. Understand, I don't criticize those who do. Some who can and do are very good and noteworthy poets. But that's not me. I've never been able to put my losses or sorrows into a poem, never. I can't dig into my personal relationships with family or with friends in order to mine them for material for my poems. There's a line I can't cross. A line of trust, I like to think." She gave him a half-smile and said, "Some critics think it's what's wrong with my poems. They say I miss the personal touch, that I'm too objective, by which they mean removed or even cold."

"You mean something to me, Beth, everything. And now when things are rough you just throw us away? Am I so little to you?"

"That's ridiculous. You're such a passionate writer. Your poems are so felt. It's one of the reasons I looked forward to meeting you on this trip."

"Thank you for seeing that, saying that. I have felt passionate about what I've written, deeply passionate. I just haven't written about *me*. *Me* doesn't interest me."

"So write what you want to write, what you feel comfortable writing."

"That's the problem," she looked at his attentive face. "I've lost interest in all that interested me before."

"Because of your daughter's death?"

She nodded. "Because of that, because of Matthew's death, because of his betrayal which, God help me, I still can't forgive. Understand, perhaps. Forgive? Not yet. The things of value, all the *real* things of value have been taken from me. And all my other interests, all my worldly interests, pale beside them. I tell you that shamefully. And I can't explain it exactly." She shifted about in her chair, then took a long sip from her glass. "Actually, I can. There was a moment in a Woody Allen movie, where he finds out that the ailment that he thought he was going to die from is not going to kill him. He comes out of Mt. Sinai hospital practically dancing. He is so thrilled. He's not going to die!"

"*Hannah and Her Sisters*," Eric said.

"Right. And then it begins to dawn on him, that his reaction is ludicrous. He *is* going to die. Oh, not immediately, of course. Not from the disease that had caused him such fear. But someday. Someday he knew he was going to die. And what was the point of everything if someday he was going to die?"

"He had lost the meaning of life."

"Or maybe he had never thought about it before. He had just accepted life and had gone on doing what everyone else was doing, *imbuing* his life with meaning. But if there is no ultimate objective meaning, then *giving* it meaning doesn't mean anything, if you can follow what I'm saying. So he goes through all these various religions and they all seem ultimately unsatisfying. Because they can't explain to him why he has to die."

"Yes, Beth, but do you remember how he resolves it."

"Yes," she wrinkled her brow. "He goes to the movies and he sees something funny, an old Marx Brothers movie I think. And he decides..."

"...that life is it's own meaning. Just that. Life is its own meaning."

She shook her head.

"Then what was the message?" he asked her.

"Oh, I agree, that's the message of the movie. What I'm not agreeing with is that it's enough. Right now, it's not enough for me."

"Right now," he reminded her.

"Frankly, Eric, I don't see any end to it. For years I ran all around the world staring into people's lives and inferring meaning from what I saw. My meaning, not theirs. What does a woman starving in Colombia care for my poem? Or my extrapolated meaning? Or even my rage? I've lost a husband in the prime of his life and a daughter who had barely begun hers, and I can't tell myself that life is its own meaning. That's a worthless phrase to me, empty of all sense. I see pain all around, oh, not just my own. Look at the world, Eric. Everywhere there is fighting and hatred. Africa is on fire. The Middle East is still fighting a battle that began over five thousand years ago. There's a war in Ireland that is centuries old. And God knows what will happen inside the Soviet Union now that the Berlin wall has come down. And I haven't even begun to mention what we humans are doing to our poor planet in the name of progress. I see nothing hopeful, Eric. I see no salvation. I see only madness, hatred, anger. I see no rhyme or reason to our sojourn here. It seems futile. It seems meaningless. It seems, at present, only a difficult journey to get over with as quickly as we can." She stopped, picked up her glass and took a long swallow.

"Passionately said, Beth."

She didn't answer that.

He went on. "And, therefore, because it is a chaotic hell out there you see no room for, or need for, art." It was more a comment than a question.

"Art in the scheme of things seems mostly a frivolity. I can't fight for it any longer. Art was my faith and I lost it."

"The Chora seems frivolous?"

"What is wonderful is this inborn need of the artist of those days to beautify his surroundings, his life."

It took her a while to speak. Finally, "All I can say is that the Chora was built, and the art inside it created, in another time."

"It, too, was a difficult time. History is filled with difficult times and often just in the middle of them, art thrives."

"People had faith in God. Art reminded them of that faith. Art was integrated into their lives the way our bones are integrated into our bodies. They still had a sense for beauty. It served. We have lost all that."

"I saw your face today. You still have a sense for beauty. Why is that so, if art is so frivolous, so feckless?"

"Because," she answered, with a sigh, "I'm a sentimental fool. There's a part of me that hasn't learned it's lesson. There's a part of me that still hopes. It's a foolish part of me, Eric, a childish part of me."

"And what do you think about love? Do you think that is also foolish?"

"Can we understand just one other person from our own times? Someone we think we love?"

She looked at him without smiling. "What it brings you ultimately is suffering. Why look for it? It will throw fairy dust in your eyes for a while and then tear your heart out. Nothing and no one causes you as much pain as those you love."

"It's twenty-five years of my life you're throwing away. Don't give me that you can't help yourself."

"Can we understand...?"

Beth bit the inside of her lip, "I don't think I could try love again. I'm too raw. I don't trust it. I don't believe in it."

Eric didn't say anything.

"And that's why, to answer your original question, I haven't put out a fifth book of poems." And then she consciously changed the subject. "Are you going to the dinner at the Sultan's lodge tonight?" she asked.

"Yes, aren't you?"

She shook her head. "I need some time to myself. I told the concierge that I would be dining on board ship tonight. There'll be a few of us, not many."

"Won't you change your mind? I've so enjoyed our day. I hate to end it so soon."

She shook her head.

"Well, I have to go with the group," he said. "I do represent four museums and I have to do a little work for this free trip. I can only get off on my own ever so often."

"It should be fun," she said.

As they were walking from the car to the ship, Beth said to him, "Eric, you *have* given me a wonderful day. Really, the best day I've had in years."

He didn't answer her.

"I mean it. Everything about it was perfect. I can't thank you enough..."

"But?"

"But what?"

"But don't bother me again?"

"...is it awful? Is it too soon?"

She looked alarmed. "No, certainly not. What gave you that idea?"

"That little speech on love," he said.

"All I know is I can't live without her...and I can't live a lie."

"Someone we think we love?"

"Oh, Eric, it wasn't personal. It wasn't about you. It wasn't said as a weapon against you. You are so very nice. I like being with you. It was about me, the way I feel now. Don't, please, withdraw," she put her hand on his arm. "Please don't do that. Just understand why I act so peculiar half the time. I'm in a terrible mess right now. I can't pull myself out of it yet..."

"Raven wants to marry me. I don't know what to do."

"I'm sorry that I always seem to say something to hurt you," Beth rushed on. "That's the point, can't you see? I'm all mixed up and I haven't had the time to sort it out. No one lets me do it," she ended on a note of despair.

They were almost at the gangplank to the ship. Eric stopped, took her by the shoulders, and turned her to face him, "Beth, maybe other people could help you sort things out, maybe even one other. Don't shut the door to that."

"It's a question of balance, you know, my friend. If you can find that point where a leaf changes into another leaf, or, better yet, into a flower, you will know everything."

She slowly nodded.

And then they walked without touching up the gangplank and formally said "so long" when they got inside the ship.

That night, there were only about a dozen people at dinner. Beth was glad to see Paul there. "I've got to spare these old bones for the good things. My partying days are over." They were joined at their table by Lolly and her mother, Ellen. Both women were in good spirits after their day in Istanbul. Lolly was wearing a bracelet she had purchased and Ellen was sporting dangling earrings. She looked odd, old, and dear. The two women had braved the Turkish Bazaar and felt quite pleased with their adventures there.

Beth's mind was all ajumble but she kept up with the conversation. It had been a wonderful day. But had she said too much to Eric, been too open? Why had she been so discouraging? She liked him very much. At least she had been honest. Wasn't it better to begin with all one's cards on the table? She was, after all, not twenty-one.

Yes, but if you put all your cards on the table from the very beginning, sometimes you find yourself out of the game.

Go away.

When dinner was over, the ladies said good night and Paul asked Beth if she would care for a little stroll around the deck. "I need to move around a little before I take such a full stomach to bed," he told her.

She agreed and they went up on deck. "Did you enjoy your day?" she asked.

"The Chora was worth the whole trip," he said. "You can see in pictures so much of what Christianity in the west has forgotten."

"Yes, it does seem to be a different kind of Christianity," she agreed. "Do you like Istanbul?"

"Istanbul interests me," he answered. "But then I'm a terribly nosy man. Most places interest me."

They talked for a while about the city.

Then without forethought Beth asked, "Is your wife enjoying this trip?"

Now why had she done that? Why had she asked about his dead wife?

Paul didn't answer her but he stopped walking and moved to the rail. Beth, feeling a bit chastened, followed him and they stood there looking across the water at Istanbul. "Our senses do not give us the whole truth, my dear," he said, turning finally to face her. "I feel Annie's nearness. She's as real to me as you are standing there. That's all I can tell you."

"Sorry, Paul. I'm a terrible skeptic. I didn't mean to belittle what you believe." She slipped her arm through his and he patted her hand. What had she expected him to say? Sorry, Beth, it was all a joke. Or, she's having a wonderful time?

The two started around the deck again.

But Beth knew the answer. It wasn't about Paul's wife that she was asking. It was really about Alicia. Beth would have to stop this impossible probing. She couldn't bear to hope, to allow yet more vulnerability. She would fall apart if she met with a single ounce more of disappointment.

It suddenly felt cold and Beth shivered. Dead was dead. That was what she knew, she, Beth. Yes, that was important, what *she* knew, not what another person believed. She would stop asking Paul questions, about his wife, about dreams, about another reality. It just created confusion and confusion was the last thing she needed now. She needed to feel the ground under her feet. It had been such a nice day. Where had it gone?

"I'm feeling a bit chilly," she said. "I'd best go in."

He looked at her sadly. "Good night, my dear."

She hurried down to her room, took a shower. In bed she burst into tears, of loss, of confusion, of helplessness.

I'm losing my grip on reality. I must stop asking Paul questions. Keep it light, she told herself. People don't have to get serious on a trip.

But it wasn't only about Paul. It was also about Eric. She couldn't handle Eric. Really, she couldn't.

When Beth finally fell asleep, she didn't dream.

Paul didn't turn on the lights when he returned to his room. He threw his jacket across the second bed and lay down on the first.

Annie, this is not going well.

Beth?

I don't want to speak to her again.

You intend to avoid her?

I won't speak about this. About her dead daughter, about you, about dreams, about something other than this physical world. It causes her pain and I can't bear it.

It's why she came on this trip.

No, I don't accept that. She came on this trip to meet Eric. There is a match for her. If she can let him into her life she will find solace in his companionship. That will pull her out of this crisis.

She needs more. All humans need more. They need to connect with reality. Nothing else lasts.

I am making her more ill. I am not helping her.

You are looking only at the surface. Deep down she wants to hear what you have to say. She herself wants this. Yes, Eric, too, fits into her destiny. But so do you, my love. Spiritual economy. Do you think you came on this trip only to renew your love for Greece? Only for your book?

I am too old. Too tired.

Are you dead?

Annie.

Are you dead?

Please.

Paul got off the bed and undressed. He stepped into the shower and stood under the water a long time.

When he finally got under the covers he thought to Annie, I will answer her questions, but that is all. I won't do more than that.

Annie was silent.

"We didn't see you last night," Barbara Churchill said to Beth, pointing at her with her fork. Beth was lunching on the deck of the New Odyssey with Barbara, with Daring, and with Paul Burrows.

The 4-M tourists had returned from the Hagia Sophia and the Blue Mosque only half an hour ago. The ship had just set sail. They would be traveling through the rest of the afternoon and night, back across the Sea of Marmara, back through the Dardanelles, and would arrive at Kuşadasi on the coast of Asia Minor for their visit to Ephesus the following day.

"I was tired," Beth said.

In the bright, clear, warm morning, Beth's panic of the night before had vanished. During their visit to the Hagia Sophia, when she had seen Paul looking polite but uneasy at the unwanted attention he was getting from "that blond lady," she had hurried over to him.

"Paul, you promised to tell me the history of the Hagia Sophia," she said. Then with a sweet smile for the blond lady, Beth took Paul's arm and walked away with him.

He was obviously relieved.

"Thank you," he whispered, stooping down to her when they were out of earshot.

"What are friends for?" she said. "Now don't make a liar out of me. Talk."

So Paul had given her a brief history of the construction of the famous church.

Now she looked up and caught him watching her. She smiled back at him. No question, she had become very fond of Paul. He was complex, interesting, kind and sensitive. And a remarkable historian. She didn't have to buy any of his religious ideas. He wasn't pushing them on her.

"The cocktails were undrinkable," Barbara said, referring again to the night before, "but the Turks are Muslims, after all. Drinking is against their religion."

"What I found most interesting," Daring, the tiny, energetic lady with the eyes of a silent movie star, finally spoke, "was that troupe of dancers from the Black Sea region. Those dances were very old." She directed her words at Beth. "They did them with great stomping of feet. And the music was mostly drum music. They pounded on them like tom toms. I could understand, watching them, how stirred up it can get you, such dancing and drum walloping." She rolled her green eyes mischievously. "It could lead you right into battle filled with passion and frenzy. Oh, it was grand!"

"Did you see the Blue Mosque today and the Hagia Sophia?" Barbara Churchill had taken aim at Beth once again.

"Oh yes," Beth said, "I haven't missed any of the excursions."

"All that tile. Quite impressive. Ninety-nine different shades of blue, or so they say," Barbara turned her eyes, flickeringly, on Paul. "The Blue Mosque was an attempt by its architect to create something grander than the Hagia Sophia built by Sinan," she told him.

"Did any of you buy a rug at the market?" Daring asked

No one at the table had.

"Well, one of our party bought a rug for their living room, costing, I think it was, twenty-five thousand. That couple from Minneapolis, I forget their names."

"I found the mosaics in the Hagia Sofia interesting," Barbara said, picking up her sandwich and her subject once again. "To think of them under plaster for centuries. Of course, much of it is poorly made. After the War of the Icons, it must have taken a long time before the art was again perfected."

"But the deesis in the south gallery, *Christ flanked by the Virgin Mary and John the Baptist,* even though it's only a fragment, is extraordinary, worth the whole trip, don't you think?" Paul asked her.

Good for you, Paul, Beth thought.

After a pause, Barbara said, "Agreed."

Beth's attention wandered away from the conversation at that point. She had not seen Eric Halsey that morning. He had not been with them on their visits. That had surprised her and some irrational fear had said it was to avoid her that he had not come. It had taken some effort to dispel the ridiculous idea. He had been in Istanbul before and had simply gone to look at something else.

Barbara Churchill was now giving a comparative history of the architecture of the Hagia Sophia and the Blue Mosque. "Of course, the Blue Mosque was never a church but it does have it's similarities to the Hagia Sophia..."

Beth thought about her own strange reaction to the Hagia Sophia and the Blue Mosque. In both places she had felt weight, as if she were in a cave. They were both stunning to look at with their tiles and rugs and daintily strung lights. But her sense of satisfaction was troubled by a slight heaviness. It was exactly the way she had felt in the Byzantine churches in Salonika. She couldn't relate to the space as a place for the worship of God or gods.

Beth was brought back to the table conversation by Daring, who asked her if she intended to write poems about this trip. Beth answered her, as she had others, saying that she was taking notes and that when she returned home she would decide what could be done with them.

As Beth was leaving the dining room she saw Eric sitting at a corner table deep in animated conversation with a group of avid listeners. He didn't look up as she left.

Oh, well, she thought. Why shouldn't he enjoy other people's company? Yesterday was yesterday. She didn't have to expect something beyond that.

After lunch, Beth decided to go to her room, get the book on Ephesus she had taken from the ship's library yesterday, then go up on deck to read and watch the ship's progress until it was time to hear the lecture at three-thirty. But when Beth reached her cabin she realized that she was tired, so she decided to take a short nap. She lay down on her bed and fell almost immediately into a dream-filled sleep.

After leaving the dining room, Paul took a stroll around the deck. Half-way around the ship he saw Eric Halsey. He was standing at the rail staring out at the sea, but it wasn't the water that he was looking at, Paul felt certain, looking at the man's pensive face. He decided not to disturb him.

But as he passed Eric by, Eric turned, called him by name, and fell into step along side him. "You haven't noticed Beth on deck, have you?"

Paul shook his head. And waited.

"I wondered how she liked the Hagia Sophia."

"She's quite a lady, isn't she?"

"She terrifies me," Eric said, and then he laughed. "Did you like the Hagia Sophia?"

"I wouldn't have missed it for the world."

"Did you see the deesis?"

"Yes. Wonderful."

"The best."

They walked in silence for a while. Eric greeted people as he passed them. In those moments some of the old swagger came back, the public man. But when Eric spoke now, all of that was gone.

"I can't stop thinking about her, I can hardly explain it. Makes me feel like a high-school kid."

"Destiny."

"It does feel like that, ridiculous as that sounds. Kismet or some such nonsense."

"What terrifies you about her?"

"Me. My reaction. I don't think I have ever in my adult life pursued someone in this way. I haven't had to." He shook his head. "God, that sounds arrogant."

"It sounds honest. So you're afraid of women."

"Am I? Probably. If you had met my mother you would understand why. Or my ex-wife." He shook his head. "No, that's unfair. My behavior is my responsibility. I've been divorced five years and I've known lots of women, but..."

"But..."

"...but, frankly, Paul, I've never allowed them to get too close. I've kept it light and pulled away when they wanted something more."

"You have the thin skin of the artist."

"Or the spoiled nature of a single, working, availabe male. Don't excuse me too much, Paul. I've loved twice and neither worked out. I'm fifty-three years old. I have two marvelous sons. A great job. Enough money. What else do I need? Oh, well, a little sex now and then. But do I want this?"

"Beth?"

Eric nodded.

"Do you?"

"There is something so extraordinary about her. I fell in love with her books. Isn't that nuts? With the lady who wrote those marvelous poems. I couldn't wait to meet her."

"And now that you have?"

"Now that I have, she terrifies me and excites me and intrigues me. I find something so unique about her, so beautiful..."

"Yes, that I can understand."

"I think I've had this same conversation with my son, Kevin, only then the shoe was on the other foot."

"Love is a great leveler."

"Love's a big word."

"Very big."

"My mother would laugh at this, ridicule this."

"And your father?"

Eric stared out at the sea. "My father...my father would probably understand." He walked over to the rail and Paul followed him. "I don't know how to read Beth, what she wants, if anything. She pushes me away time and time again. We share something and then she pushes me away."

"She's going through a difficult period."

"I know. I know."

"But if you give it time..."

"I'm not good at rebuffs. And I'm also afraid..."

Paul waited but Eric was lost in his own thoughts. Paul was about to head to his own cabin when Eric said, his voice barely audible, "How do I know if I can stay the course, that I won't run if she allows me to get closer, that I won't pull back as I have a dozen times, that I won't add to her pain?"

How to answer him?

"Perhaps the fear of ourselves and what we are capable of is the begining of wisdom."

"Am I falling in love? Is it possible?" Eric chuckled and clapped Paul on the shoulder. "Forgive me, Paul, for dumping all this adolescent stuff on you. It must be the sea air. I'm positively drunk." And he walked off with a grin.

Annie, what will he do?

But Annie was silent.

Beth was standing in the Hagia Sophia, peering out into its great hall from behind a thick pillar, trying, at the same time, to keep herself from being seen. No one was in the old church except for Iris and her companion. It seemed to be twilight. The two were standing in the middle of the hall looking up, first at the arches flanked by pillars with their ornate capitals, then at the graceful strings of tiny lights crisscrossing the vast space and finally at the various domes with their many windows. Iris walked about like any tourist and her friend followed her.

"I don't understand it, my friend," Iris shook her black curls in consternation.

"And what is that, my Iris?" her friend asked in a mellifluous voice.

"The architecture. It shouldn't be as this is."

"What do you mean by that, Iris?

"Oh, I see that the space is grand, vast. And, of course, grandeur is what they wanted to achieve. But as a space to approach the gods, no."

Right on, Beth thought, with approval.

Iris's companion didn't speak but waited as Iris strolled about, her eyes busily taking in the details of the old building. Beth watched her too.

Her movements are as lithesome as a dancer's, Beth thought as she listened eagerly from behind her column. She knew, as one does in a dream, that Iris was about to tell her what it was she, herself, had felt was missing in the architecture of the building, despite its admitted splendor and despite its grandeur.

"This place of worship comes in history after our own Greek temples," Iris said. "In the design and execution of our temple, in the way the space is arranged, it is a perfect meeting place for gods and men. Balance and harmony are our greatest achievements. Gods can meet the human being and the human being can meet the gods, but this..." she flung her arms in a wide gesture. "All the curves enfold the space. Over and over this enfolding feeling like a mother holding her child."

"That describes it well, my Iris," her friend said. His voice resonated like a cello.

I've felt that also, in Salonika, Beth thought with satisfaction. I was right. Beth leaned out to see if she could make out his face, but could not.

"In the time of Greece's greatness," he went on, "a period one can liken to the fulcrum of a scale, there was perfect balance between heaven and earth."

He led Iris around the space and as they drew closer to Beth, Beth ducked behind a pillar.

"Soon after this period the turnaround began, marked by a great cosmic and earthly event. Humankind was again to ascend, to claim its cosmic inheritance."

Beth moved with them around the circumference of the old church so that she wouldn't miss a word.

"But, alas, the descent of humanity could not be stopped immediately. Sheer momentum carried them further into matter and in these world days even below matter. They stir around now in sub-matter."

"But how terrible!" Iris cried. "Such ghastly beasts lie in that realm. Will humanity turn them loose?"

"They have already turned them loose. And yet be patient with them, Iris, this turn back toward the heavens is difficult and needs time."

He's like a teacher, Beth thought. Like a Greek teacher. Didn't teachers walk around Athens, or wherever, with their students, expounding their philosophy and relating it to everything they saw?

"So now humanity has sunk deeper into the earth and into its bodily nature. It would appall a Greek to have to live in the bodies that are available today. They have a density the earlier Greek could not endure. So you see, little sister, because of the persistent force of their descent, human beings continued to build in their places of worship the forms that drew God earthward."

"And this is the result?" Iris again stopped and looked around her.

"Yes, but it has the beauty of an embrace, as you yourself saw. See that and admire it for what it is. Here we are all children of the gods."

Iris looked again turning slowly but she was silent.

That's it, Beth thought, there is protection here in this remarkable church, and I can admire that, but there is no soaring up of the soul. She thought of the Gothic cathedrals of Europe and longed to take Iris there to show her.

"Humanity today doesn't seem at all inclined to rise toward the spirit," Iris took up her familiar theme.

"Because they have acquired a new soul quality, and with it humanity's long-awaited freedom. But this new soul quality has been in the world only a little more than five hundred years. For all the crying of 'freedom, give us freedom,' humans struggle against it, oppose it. They don't want to be mature. In relation to the gods, they want to lead the life of children."

"Is there hope?"

"There is always hope. We must never lose hope, my Iris. We nourish the gods with our hope."

"What about for that one who follows us about and cowers in the shadows," asked Iris and pointed toward the pillar where Beth was hiding.

Iris's companion looked straight at the pillar as if he could see right through it. "I don't know," he answered.

From outside the dream Beth watched herself cower and felt a terrible shame. She was supposed to be doing something. What was it Paul had suggested she do? Ask them a question. She could only think of one question and so willed herself to step out from behind the pillar, her body racked with fear. She was determined not to let this opportunity go by.

Beth called out, "Why are you in my dream?"

Iris turned around and looked at her in astonishment.

Beth had spoken and Iris had heard. Beth took courage and walked closer.

Iris said to her companion who had remained in shadow "The sleeper has crossed over. How remarkable."

"In these world-times much is possible because of the new soul force," Iris's companion told her.

"You talked once of a feeling soul and a thinking soul and now a third one? What is this new soul force that you speak of?" Beth demanded with more fervor than she had intended.

"What name shall we give her, my friend? What would suit the sleeper?" Iris asked her companion but stared unblinkingly at Beth. "She seems so needy. How strange her being feels to me." She shook her head.

"Endure the strangeness, Iris. She is suffering because in the times that she lives, her thoughts no longer come from the gods. They arise out of her own psyche. That is why she feels strange to you. That and the new soul element. Consciousness, once heavenly, has now become completely human."

"Is that possible?"

"It is accomplished. Look at her. The new soul element sits in her psyche like a Janus-Being, in her and in all others of her time. It faces in two directions. It points upward toward a reuniting with God. And it points downward to the dead forces of sub-nature that she must overcome in order to sustain her self-consciousness."

Beth tried hard to follow the ideas Iris's teacher was setting forth.

"We might call the new soul element, the Awareness Soul, because it does give great outer and inner awareness. In her times, individuals can search out the doings, the feelings, the thoughts of their personal psyche as never before in the history of humanity."

"But how marvelous," Iris said, and clasped her hands to her heart.

"Ah, but they suffer because they have not the right concepts to comprehend what they see there, in their inner depths. They look for the riddle to who they are on earth."

"But how foolish," Iris said, "the answer is not to be found on earth."

"Where is it to be found?" Beth asked.

"Why in the spiritual realms from which you descend at birth and to which you return after death," Iris glared at her, her hands on her hips.

"We study humanity on earth. We have great sciences that study the human being on earth," Beth said.

"Yes," Iris's companion said, "you give many explanations to elucidate the riddle of the human being but it is mostly fantasy. You find only what is animal in humanity on earth. But the human being is also soul and spirit."

The teacher whom Beth saw only in a dim haze turned to Iris. "Yes, let us call it the Awareness Soul and add it to the Thinking Soul developed in our time, Iris, and the Feeling Soul developed by the Egyptians, the Babylonians and the Chaldeans in an even earlier time."

"Will that do for you, girl?" Iris asked her.

"I don't understand it, but yes, it is good to have a name, even two names," she answered.

"What are you called?"

"I am called Elizabeth," Beth told her. "And you are Iris. But I don't know your teacher's name."

It was not forthcoming.

"I don't understand why you tear apart the soul into so many portions," Beth said to Iris.

"It is because that is the truth of it," Iris said. "Why else would we speak of the soul so?"

"Iris, she is from another time," her companion said, "don't expect her to be as you?"

"Yes, the sense for truth is gone. I had forgotten that."

"That's not right," Beth's words were heated. "People in

my time long for the truth as much as they did in your time. At least some do."

Iris shook her head impatiently. "I did not say that the longing was gone, only that the sense for it was gone."

"Oh. But we don't think of the soul the way you do."

"No, you believe only in the evolution of the body and think it creates the soul. How is it you do not believe in the evolution of the soul?"

"But there's no evidence for that," Beth said.

"That's because you have become dull in your thought life," Iris said. "Have you read Aristotle or any of our poets?"

"Yes, I have," Beth said.

"Can you not see how they loved thought, how new and glorious it was, how the joy of conversation and the building of rational thought was a thing of freshness for them? They used thought to explore the true. You, in your time, are bored with true thought. You use it to justify opinion. It is not the same at all. You are a poet. Are your senses so asleep that you cannot see something as simple as that?" Iris was passionate and angry.

Beth couldn't answer.

"If you would look clearly at the long history of humankind, you would see how the three soul elements developed one after the other. But you, in your time, instead of uniting all three, are in danger of losing all of them. It is you who tear them apart, you who value one over another, or none. It is a pity."

"What do you want from me?" Beth cried. "I'm struggling as hard as I can."

"But why should you complain about that?" Iris asked. "You are on earth. That is what each sojourn should be, a struggle, should it not?" Her dark eyes glimmered with irritation. They reminded Beth of Hank's eyes.

"You are a poet this life. That is a great responsibility. Surely, a poet must search for the true, the good, the beautiful. Art of any sort must be like a Greek temple, a balance between man's world and the world of the gods. If we can no longer depend on our poets, what shall we do?" And Iris turned from her without waiting for an answer and took her companion's arm and walked away out of sight.

Beth was too flabbergasted to call out. She stood in the middle of the Hagia Sophia, looked around at its womb-like walls, and suddenly panicked, wondering how she was going to get back to the ship. As apprehension took powerful hold of her, she woke up.

For a while she lay there, allowing the fear to flow away. She sat up in utter amazement at the dream, and then took out her notebook and began to rapidly write it down. Once again she was astonished at her recall. Afterwards, when she reread it she felt satisfied that she had indeed put down the bulk of the dream.

I have to read this to Paul, she decided.

I thought you didn't want to listen to what he had to say about these things. You said it confused you, made you more anxious.

But to whom else could she turn? What else could she do with this stuff?

As she locked her door to go to the lecture, she thought regretfully, this is probably the last of my Iris dreams. I certainly seem to have offended her.

When Beth entered the lounge where the lecture was to be given, Eric broke away from the group he had been standing with and came over to her.

"Did you see the Hagia Sophia?" he asked her. For a moment he looked tentative, searching her face. It disconcerted her.

"The Hagia Sophia?" The dream was so full in her mind, she couldn't separate out what she had actually seen and what she had dreamt. "Yes," she answered. Yes, she thought, twice.

"What did you think?" Eric led Beth to a seat and sat down next to her.

Beth thought for a moment, trying to recall what she had seen in reality. "There was a face that struck me. A fragment." Stones speaking again. "The face of the Virgin in the deesis, I think it was." Paul had pointed it out to her. She saw the pleasure in Eric's eyes and it gave her a little whoosh of joy. "Sorrow with dignity, yes, I liked that very much."

As she spoke the dream began to recede. Here she was, after all, talking art with Eric in the twentieth century. Her century. She was on a ship taking her from port to port to look at remnants of the past. In the twentieth century. She very definitely had a human consciousness. That's what mattered. And the man in front of her was flesh and blood, definitely not a figment.

"You have such a good eye," Eric said. "That's a gorgeous piece. Will you save this seat? I have to speak to Marion for a moment."

She nodded, put her sweater down on his seat and watched Eric as he moved through the 4-M crowd with the confident strut of someone used to people, stopping to talk on the way. She looked around her at the room, at the faces of her traveling companions, at what people were wearing.

She tried to dismiss the dream.

I'm on a trip, lifted out of my own life, that's the explanation. Why did she need to look further than the world around her? She was safe, sitting in a room filled with people in slacks and sport shoes, in shorts and jogging outfits. No togas, no chitons. And she was about to hear a scholarly lecture by a woman whose prosaic style she could relate to from all her own years as a student and as a teacher. A dream was a dream. Dangerous to confuse it with life. All the art they were looking at were merely fragments of the past, artifacts strewn along the endless road of history. And every yesterday was gone. Over and done. She had only this world, this day, nothing else. But what else did she need?

Still, she would speak to Paul.

Yes, why not? Really, why not? I am free to believe what I choose.

"I spent the morning looking at some smaller churches that I had not seen on previous trips," Eric said when he returned. "But I did come into the Hagia Sophia for a moment just to see that one mosaic. What did you think of the Blue Mosque?"

Before she had time to answer Eric's question. Marion Levitt came to the lectern and began her talk on Ephesus, which they would be visiting tomorrow.

Beth concentrated on the information Marion was giving in her plain but intelligent manner. But, for the first time, Beth felt a bit disturbed by the superior stance Marion seemed to take as she looked back at the glorious and remarkable culture that had emanated from Ephesus.

Children do not produce sophisticated art, Beth wanted to say. Why do our discoveries in science and in technology make us so condescending to those who lived their lives without them? It is so small of us, she decided, and so self-serving. Perhaps Iris and her friend were right and those in the past did have different faculties than we possess now. Maybe those faculties had been even greater than ours. Why can't we be just a little humble?

"So will you, Beth?"

Beth was pulled out of her reverie by Eric who had just asked her a question. The lecture was over and people were making their way out of the lounge.

"I'm sorry, Eric. I was lost in thought, what did you ask me?"

"I asked if you would join me for a drink before dinner?"

"Oh, well, yes, I'd like that."

"I've some paper work to do in my cabin until then, but I'll see you around 7:15?"

"Fine," she said.

They said their good-byes. Beth hesitated only for a moment and then went to look for Paul. She found him up on deck.

"Paul," she said in a low voice. "I had another Iris dream and I spoke to her."

His eyebrows arched slightly.

"I fell asleep after lunch and had a dream. I wrote it all down. Would you come to my room and let me read it to you?"

She saw him hesitate. "Are you busy? We could do it later."

"No, I'm not busy. I'll come."

In a few minutes they were sitting opposite each other on the two beds. Paul felt claustrophobic in the tiny stateroom. It was too small, too warm, no place to pace and think. He thought of his own home, longed for it, for the porch that overlooked the Atlantic, for his rocking chair, his own uneventful life. He dreaded this conversation. He was old, why couldn't he just have some peace?

Annie, he called, as Beth began to read him the transcript of her dream, her voice shaking.

Listen.

And Paul turned his attention to Beth's words.

It was an astonishing dream. A powerful dream.

When she finished she looked up at him.

He was silent, sober, and moved.

"It's weird to hear it out loud," Beth said. "It gives it so much substance. What do you think?"

He looked at her furrowed brow, her tense face. "What do you think, Beth?"

"I don't know. I really don't know what to make of it all. It's all so tied up with this trip, don't you see?"

"How do you mean?"

"Well, on a trip you're pulled out of your own day-to-day life. A kind of separate reality takes hold. You're thrust together with strangers. You share precious moments with people you will likely never see again." Beth shifted around on her bed, kicked off her shoes and tucked her legs under her. "If I was home, in my ordinary life, I don't know if I'd think much about these Iris dreams except to note that they were interesting and clearer than most. And…"

"And what?"

"And if I were home, safe at home, I'd probably view the content of the dream as a hodgepodge of stuff I had heard or read over the years. As if the garbage can of memory had suddenly been kicked over and its contents strewn every which way, if you know what I mean."

Paul carefully crossed his aching left leg over his right and rubbed it absently. "So, then, why can't you leave it at that and view it the way you would if you were back home?"

"I don't know. It's because of this trip. The dreams are a part of it. Dreams can be very intense."

Paul nodded.

"Sometimes you dream you're having an important conversation with someone. You wake up with a sense of satisfaction. But when you try to analyze what was said in your dream conversation, you either can't remember it or it doesn't make much sense. Has that ever happened to you?"

"Yes. Is this one different?"

"A couple of things are different." Beth frowned, chewed on her lip, then stared at the open notebook lying next to her on the bed. "First, and perhaps the most remarkable, is my ability to remember the dream afterwards, as long as I get it down on paper quickly. The other is that the thoughts *seem* to make sense, and I emphasize the word *seem*, but I can't recall thinking them before. Or at least not organized in that way. Can I be having original thoughts in a dream?"

"You said that it might be from things that you have read, things you've stored in your memory garbage can," he half-smiled at her metaphor.

"I know I said that. But there's something else that I must take into account. I'm very stressed, depressed is probably a better word. I...I could simply be losing it."

"Going crazy?"

"Well, something like that, if not crazy exactly then prone to visions or hallucinations or something of that nature."

"Do you think you're going crazy?"

"Do the crazies ever think they're crazy?"

"Oh, yes, some know it very well."

"What do you think, Paul?" She pulled her legs out from under her and put her feet on the floor.

"What do you want me to say, Beth?" Annie, help me.

"I want to know what you really think."

"Are you sure?"

"Yes. No. I don't know. Tell me anyway."

Paul thought about his kitchen table, about how many thoughts he had shared there with his wife. Times that were sometimes pleasurable, sometimes hurtful. Why was he here with a stranger forced to answer questions that would cause her pain? Wasn't it better to let her alone? Let Eric help her?

But it was to him that she had turned.

He sighed. Perhaps in helping her he would help himself. He had given up on life. Now he was thrown back into it, no, given the opportunity to get back into it.

Or walk away.

That much freedom he had.

But he heard himself say, "All right, then, if that's what you want. This is my sense of it. Much of this dream and much of the other Iris dreams appear to contain genuine thoughts from a supersensible world. You talked about a memory garbage can. Maybe you have knocked over such a memory garbage can, only this one extends beyond this one life to different memories from other lives."

"Is that the only answer you can give me?" Beth said and her voice shook.

"Beth, I'm sorry. You've put me in an awkward spot. You're afraid to hear what I have to say, yet you ask. You know I won't lie. If I tell you the truth as I know it, you'll be hearing what you don't want to hear. Perhaps you'd prefer it if I told you were going crazy."

"You're right. I'm sorry."

He waited. "Do you want me to leave?"

She shook her head.

He sat there silent, watching her. She looked as if she were about to cry.

Instead, she began to laugh, "I suppose it would be easier if I thought I were crazy, if you corroborated that. *Crazy* is this world. It has reality." She reached for the box of tissues on her desk. "Why am I, a non-believer, having such a, what shall I call it, such a mystical experience? In your opinion."

"How to give you a short answer, Beth." Paul stood up, and moved toward the porthole. Through the thick glass he could make out the Sea of Marmara. He loved the vastness of an ocean, loved the sheer grandeur of it, the way the air felt brushing across it's unsteady surface, the way it pulled you out and out until you grew as large as the world. But this ocean caught in a small round thick glass seemed limited, gave him no comfort. He turned back to look at her.

"It's hard to speak of these things simply. Let me say at least this, everyone carries, deep in his unconscious, memory of the spiritual world, the world he lived in and participated in before he was born."

"Reincarnation, again."

"Yes, imagine it for the moment, will you do that?"

"But it's just this that I have trouble with, Paul. If I've lived before, if I've been in your spiritual realm before my birth, why is memory of it so buried? If I could remember something of either my previous life or my pre-birth life, I certainly wouldn't be such a doubting Thomas now, nor would most of the others in this world be. That would certainly make things easier for your gods."

"That's true, and a fair question. There is more than one answer, but the simplest is this, our current bodily organization obscures these memories. Man can't ordinarily pull them out of himself without undergoing a strict and cautious training. It can take years to achieve anything through the training that is right for today. Without such a cautious training one can come up with the most ridiculous junk and call it one's past lives. However..." he paused.

"However what, Paul?"

"However, as I think I said to you once before, the threshold in our times is like a thin veil fluttering between us and the spiritual world which is all around us. Things waft through and hover there between the subconscious and our ordinary consciousness. We lack the faculties to perceive them. But they are there, nevertheless. And sometimes it happens, more and more often today, that individuals, because of severe shock or pain, are thrust over the threshold. Or to put it another way, the lid over the unconscious is ajar and what you experienced before as a pre-birth reality or even another life drifts up to confront you in symbolic form. The pictures are from this world but that doesn't matter. It's the gesture that matters, the content."

"That can happen in a dream?"

"Yes, but not in every dream. And not only in a dream. It can happen as one is sitting alone thinking or struggling with a problem. The self that has created for its life on earth, a personality, a temperament, a family history, a career, thoughts, feelings, values, this earthly self now clothes this content coming from the spiritual world in pictorial elements from the earthly world. It's real, but it's not literal, if you know what I mean."

Beth sat staring at her hands. "Oh, Paul, I don't know what to think about what you've just said."

"You want a different explanation?" he said, sitting across from her again. "Then why ask me, Beth? I can only tell you what *I* know. Ask someone else, then, if what I say is so painful to contemplate."

She shook her head and he saw tears begin to flow down her cheeks. "It turns my world upside down, you see, and that's almost too difficult to contemplate."

"Then speak to someone else, Beth," Paul felt his leg begin to throb, and its ache move through all his skeleton. He was too old for this.

"I mean, to lose my loved ones is bad enough, but to lose what little belief system I have left may be more than I can bear. It feels like all the ground is gone from under my feet. To accept any of what you have told me would mean that I'd have to rethink, no, unthink everything I've ever thought. I don't know if I can do that. I've depended all my life on what I could see, hear and touch. Like my father, I'm a pragmatist. This is all too much, you see." And she rubbed hard at the tears flooding her cheeks.

Paul came over and sat next to her on her bed. He took her hand in his. "My dear Beth," he said, "all right, then, all right. Since it is to me that you have come again and again, let me say only this much more. Your world is already upside down. You've lost faith in it. You've lost faith in your ability to participate in the world again or even to hope. To lose hope is a terrible thing. Perhaps if you can just endure this appalling upheaval, your world will be restored to you and perhaps, Beth, those you have loved and have seemingly lost will also be restored to you."

And now Beth sobbed and sobbed. Paul took her in his arms and held her until the sobbing subsided.

"Perhaps you'd like to be left alone, now." he said.

She nodded. He rose to leave. She reached out to touch his arm. "Paul, thank you."

"Beth," he said at the door, "I'm truly sorry for your pain."

Beth lay back on her bed feeling as if she were in a thousand pieces. Instead of getting better on this trip, she was getting worse. Even her dreams seemed to be attacking her sanity. Why was she constantly pursuing Paul for his odd opinions when each thing he said only made her more and more uneasy and less and less sure of the perimeters of her own world? Wasn't that a sign of her own insanity? She was having a difficult enough time hanging on to the reality of this world. She certainly couldn't contemplate another world. It was all too much. She was not sure she could hold herself together long enough to finish the trip. Beth felt herself afloat, tossed about by big waves of uncertainty. The anxiety became so acute that she finally had to vomit.

At seven o'clock Beth called the steward to her cabin and gave him a note to take to Eric Halsey's room. In it she told him that she was not feeling well and was going to skip supper and the cocktail hour preceding it. Would he please excuse her? She asked him not to call as she was going to go to bed immediately. That done, she took a shower, put on her nightgown and crawled under her covers. She fell, miraculously, immediately to sleep.

It was a long time before Paul could fall asleep. Annie, I will do no more, say no more. I cannot.

You said what needed to be said.

I am causing pain.

She asked. You merely answered her questions.

I am too old for this.

You are alive. Treasure it.

It is easier to sit on our porch and dream.

Nothing, my love, is more important in all the worlds than others. We are here each for each.

I've forgotten about the pain.

Now you know you are alive.

Many people were on deck of the New Odyssey to watch the docking at Kuşadasi and Elizabeth Layton stood among them feeling rested and frankly sane. She had woken up calm. If something had transpired in her dream life to bring that about, she couldn't recall it. All she knew was that she was thinking quite rationally this morning. She had laughed a lot at breakfast. Daring had regaled her and her companions with outrageous stories from her days in a modern dance troupe. And at this moment, staring through the translucent Mediterranean light at the sparkling blue water, breathing in the crisp air, Paul's ideas didn't seem so strange. She had heard weirder things in the jungles of Brazil, or in the mountains of Peru. She didn't believe them then, so why should she believe them now? Paul's ideas were certainly interesting, but what could she do with them? She couldn't force herself to believe, even if she wanted to. She couldn't merely appropriate someone else's faith, as deeply felt as that faith might be. And, if it caused her confusion now in her rather fragile and erratic emotional state, then it was best that she leave Paul's ideas alone. But not Paul. She liked Paul very much. He was kind, full of interesting historical facts, and pleasant to be around. She simply would stop asking him impossible questions. What was so hard about that? There were only eight more days till home. She would be fine.

She looked around for Eric Halsey but didn't see him. Well, Eric was nice, but she couldn't manage him. Let Donna have him. Istanbul was only a lovely interlude, nothing more.

"Mother, is it awful? Is it too soon?"

She saw Paul halfway down the deck and walked up to him. "Beautiful morning, isn't it?"

Paul turned to look at her and his eyes crinkled with relief. He must have been worried about her and that touched her.

"Quite beautiful" Paul said. "You're looking well."

"I feel well. I needed a good night's rest and I had it."

"Good."

If only Paul were ten years younger. She really liked him. He would be a lot easier to deal with than Eric.

Don't be so sure, she answered herself.

"Are you going walking in Kuşadasi this morning?" she asked him.

"Yes, it's a good place to buy some small presents, I understand."

"Good. Are you going into town with anyone? Your blond bombshell, perhaps?"

"I think she's given up on me. I saw her recently arm-in-arm with that man from Philadelphia."

"How fickle. Well, then are you interested in a little company?

He searched her face.

"Am I about to be turned down?" she asked

"Certainly not. I would be honored to escort you through Kuşadasi."

"Good."

Kuşadasi was a pretty vacation town, hugging the coast, with a multitude of shops for tourists and vacationers. Beth strolled up and down the streets with Paul, peering into windows, entering stores to bargain for earrings and other gifts. Paul purchased a wallet for a friend, two scarves for his niece and nephew, a locket for his great-niece, and a belt for himself. Beth bought a blouse for Becky, wallets for her brother, James, and for her brother-in-law, Phil. She found a silver bracelet for Merle and one for her sister-in-law, Nina, two extraordinary shells for Mattie and several other trinkets for various friends. Paul was good company, and most important, he had a firm manner with the over-anxious shopkeepers.

And he never referred to the conversation they had had the previous night.

Beth suffered only two bad moments during the morning. One was when she found a perfect set of earrings for Alicia and almost asked how much the shopkeeper wanted for them, and the other was when she saw Donna with Eric in tow at the end of the street she and Paul were crossing.

From the first difficult moment, the earrings for Alicia, she recovered quickly. But she must have looked a bit unsettled when she saw Eric and Donna together because Paul said to her, following her gaze, "He's a very nice man."

"Who?" Beth tried to make her voice light.

Paul didn't answer her directly, "Someone must have hurt you rather badly, my dear, to make you pull away so consistently from an exceptional man who is obviously interested in you."

"Paul," she said, "are you flirting with me?"

"My dear, if I were a dozen years younger I would consider it. But I'm long past the need for permanent companionship."

"That, my dear friend," she said, "is because you have had a perfect relationship, the perfect marriage."

"Either you are an unreal idealist, Beth, or an unhappy perfectionist."

She was surprised at his chiding tone.

"No couple who has lived together as long as Annie and I did, forty-six years, ran down a smooth track the whole way."

Glancing up at him, Beth was struck by the sadness she saw in his face.

"Oh, my dear, don't paint this rosy picture of my marriage even in your imagination. It would be unreal and untrue. I hurt my Annie very badly once, very badly."

"You, Paul? That's hard to imagine."

They stopped to look in the window of a jewelry shop. She watched him studying his own reflection there. "Well, I wasn't always white-haired and fatherly," he smiled. "It may be hard to imagine but I was quite handsome in my day and there were always attentions from the ladies."

She tried to imagine Paul as a young man. He would have been tall, with very regular features, a wonderful smile, and large blue eyes. "You're still very handsome."

He winked and they resumed their walking. They crossed a street, turned the corner and there were Doris and Lucy, package encumbered, looking very happy, coming toward them. The sisters stopped the two of them to tell them about the leather shop they had just been in and then asked about the stores on the street Paul and Beth had just come from.

After the two sisters had moved on, Paul said, "Child, shall I paraphrase a poet that you seem to care so much about, Sylvia Plath?"

"You know her works?"

"My wife taught literature, you see."

"...even though Plath's a whiner and even though she's a class A wimp and a complainer, she's brilliant. There's no one who uses language the way she does. She absolutely breaks the damn words open and all your senses with them."

"Go on."

"It's something like this, 'Perfection hath no children.'"

Beth nodded in recognition.

Paul's voice tightened. "I had a love affair once that nearly wrecked my marriage."

He looked down at her, no doubt expecting the surprise he saw in her face.

"A young teacher. I had been married to Annie for twenty-some years and things between us were steady, easy and no longer very exciting. Diane was new, enthusiastic, worshipful, as well as young and beautiful. I felt rejuvenated, important and appreciated."

Beth felt a little knot in the pit of her stomach.

"I think you know this story, Beth."

"I can't. I can't help it. I can't help myself. I'm like a man possessed."

Beth glanced up at him. Surely she hadn't mentioned to Paul, Matthew's affair with Raven.

"I forgot all the things in my relationship with Annie that I had come to rely on, those dependable elements that had been like the ground under my feet. I got swept up in the excitement of the new."

"How did you resolve it?"

"Annie found out about it. Looking back, probably I wasn't too careful. Remarkable soul that she was, she gave me the choice of leaving her for my new love or staying and working it out."

"You stayed?" Beth's voice caught.

"All I know is I can't live without her. And I can't keep our relationship a secret and I can't live a lie."

"Yes, and I am grateful to God that I made the right decision, but..."

"But, what?"

"But at the time it was not so clear, not so easy. No, not at all. I wish I could say that it was. I struggled for days before I decided, while Annie waited in what must have been terrible pain."

"Raven wants to marry me. I don't know what to do."

"You have regrets, Paul, that you didn't go off with your...your..."

"Paramour? With my young love?"

He took her elbow as they crossed the street. "I have regrets, Beth, but the regrets are not that I didn't go off with Diane. Oh, yes, I felt tremendous loss at the time, some marvelous, potential-filled idyllic future that was not going to be. Oh, it hurt. But, no," he said, "my regrets now are all for Annie. My shame is that I hurt my Annie so terribly. I still wake sometimes in the night filled with the pain of those regrets."

They were heading for the ship now.

"What happened to the marriage after that?"

"It altered."

She nodded.

"And yet I have to say, in some ways, things were eventually better."

"How's that?"

"The marriage became more conscious. What I had come to depend on as my due I began not to take for granted. We carefully built the bridge between us again and this time it was a bridge standing on mature and deeper pilings. We became greater friends and even better lovers. We saw each other more wholly, with more appreciation for our good capacities and more tolerance for our faults." He looked up at the Turkish sky as if searching for a cloud. "And, of course, I regret that I hurt Diane, that I led her on."

"But she was at fault, too. She knew you were married."

"Yes, but if I had not allowed it, it would not have happened. Ah, well, pain brings remorse. It can also bring growth."

They were on the dock near the ship.

"Matthew and I never had the chance to work things out," Beth said, "He was trying to make a decision about whether to leave me for Raven or not, she was his student. He never had the chance to resolve it. He died of a heart attack before anything was decided either way."

Paul nodded as if somehow he had guessed her story. "Difficult," he said. "And now you don't trust any of us."

She didn't answer.

He took her arm as they headed up the gangplank to the ship. Once on board she said, "Thank you, Paul, for sharing your story with me. It helps, somehow."

He cocked his head questioningly.

"Really, it does." And she leaned over and kissed him on the cheek.

"Now, I am going to blush."

"Good. Shall we lunch in the dining room or on deck?"

"Let's do it on deck," he said. "Half an hour?"

"Half an hour," she agreed.

Beth and Paul had a buffet lunch on the deck of the ship near the swimming pool. Neither Donna nor Eric were there. Perhaps they had taken their lunch together in the dining room or perhaps in one of the little restaurants in Kuşadasi that was on the list given them by Colleen and Phil. She wondered why it was that Paul thought Eric was interested in her? Wasn't he spending as much time with Donna as with her? Didn't he seem as interested in Donna? She could ask Paul that. But Paul was speaking with Lolly in his kind and interested way. And it was a dumb question, she assured herself.

Would Matthew have stayed with her? Would they have worked things out, had even a better marriage? Perhaps she, Beth, wasn't as forgiving as Annie.

"You always hated lies, didn't you, Mom?"

Was she too much of a perfectionist? Probably. Still, she would have fought for her marriage. Yes, she would have done that. Was she avoiding Eric because of Matthew? Surely not. Surely it was because she was worn out from the losses she had not yet mourned fully.

"Perfection hath no children."

Surely it wasn't bitterness and distrust that had kept her from responding adequately to Eric's interest.

"You pull away from life and all its marvelous experiences."

"Including you?"

"Including me...You never risk yourself for yourself. Maybe if you had, your husband wouldn't have looked to graze in other fields."

Was she too demanding of life? Was she angry because life had not gone the way of her expectations? But did it go anyone's way? Was Hank right? Was she only a voyeur because life could seldom be controlled? Was she scared of Eric?

"You never risk yourself for yourself."

Scared or not, she had sent him too many negative messages. Perhaps Eric would avoid her for the rest of the trip if he were annoyed at her for canceling their date last night. Donna would be more amenable to his interest than she was.

"Shall we get on Joe's bus for the drive to Ephesus?" Paul drew her out of her thoughts.

"Yes," she answered him.

Then I'll meet you in ten minutes on the dock."

Paul and Beth boarded the bus to Ephesus and sat next to each other. As he glanced out the window, he saw Eric and Donna board the other bus. From the look on Beth's face she had seen them, too. Well, if she was interested in Eric, she was making little effort. Too much fear, he decided, and thought it a great shame. Destiny provided the opportunity. The human being was free to pick it up or walk away.

That's right, Paul.

"Beautiful country, isn't it," Paul said to Beth as they left Kuşadasi behind and drove out into the countryside.

Her face looked like glass again, so many emotions played in the reflection there. But Beth answered him. "Yes, but so strange that we have to go into the interior to get to Ephesus when it was at one time on the coast. I just can't take that in."

"Nothing remains constant," he said, "not even the land we live on."

"Excuse me, ladies and gentlemen, but as we are driving to the famous town of Ephesus which has been under excavation for over one hundred years, since 1866, I would like to tell you a little about the countryside that we are passing through," Joe, his mustache twitching, his eyes bright with pleasure, was speaking into his microphone.

"It is about nineteen kilometers to Ephesus from Kuşadasi. The climate here is a warm one. There is six months of summer and the other months are not cold either."

There was a small ripple of laughter.

"It is sometimes very rainy. This is an important agricultural area for Turkey, in part because of the land available and also because there are many rivers here which run down into the Aegean…"

Joe went on to describe the town of Selçuk which was the name given by the Ottoman Turks. "What we call Selçuk today is outside the ancient ruins of Ephesus. In Selçuk you can see all that is left of the famous temple of Artemis, ladies and gentlemen. There, too, you can find now the museum with many artifacts from the site of Ephesus. There are many Christian sites here. We will see none of the Christian sites today, ladies and gentlemen."

There were some groans from the passengers.

Joe went on, "I tell you this in advance so that you won't be disappointed. But Ephesus is very, very large and very, very important in what it has to offer the visitor. You will be thoroughly satisfied with what you see of the ancient city, and thoroughly tired by the end of the afternoon, I promise you that also." A wave of laughter ran through the bus.

"So I guess we're not going to see St. John's church," Beth said to Paul. She pointed to the brochure on Ephesus that they had been given.

"Not according to our schedule. This is strictly a pagan trip," he laughed.

"Paul, the Apostle, came to Ephesus, too, didn't he?"

"Yes, and almost lost his life here."

"I vaguely remember that. Sorry, but my Christian church history is very shaky."

"Paul was imprisoned here but eventually escaped from Ephesus with the help of friends, and moved on to Macedonia."

"I read in the guide book I took out of the ship's library that the Virgin Mary died in Ephesus," Beth said. "Could that be true?"

"It's possible. Mary was put into the hands of John the Divine by Jesus at the crucifixion. John came here, so it's not unlikely that he brought her with him. She could have been here, at least for a time. There were terrible upheavals in Jerusalem for decades. The Jews were not too happy with Roman rule. But there's a tradition that Mary died in Jerusalem, also."

"Let the believer beware," Beth smiled.

Paul nodded. "There's a house in the countryside not too far outside of Ephesus where Mary is supposed to have lived in her later years. I guess we won't see that either." He looked out of the window at the gently rolling hills, the wild flowers, the clear yet poignant light.

"It's not a bad place to live out your years," Beth said, and then she laughed, "if you forget about all the wars and the earthquakes that have torn this area apart, and about the various diseases."

"Ephesus is the place I've most wanted to see on this trip," Paul said.

"Really, Paul, why?"

"Because in Ephesus, at the temple of Artemis, that Joe just mentioned, there was a great Mystery School." He turned to look at her but she was listening with obvious interest so he went on. "Mystery Schools were very important in the ancient world. Modern history doesn't give them their due. Much wisdom flowed out from them and they affected the practical and cultural life of the people around it in a way that would surprise scholars today."

"Ephesus was important?"

"Very important. A lofty, esoteric wisdom was taught at its temple for century upon century, right up until it was burned down on the day Alexander the Great was born."

"Curious coincidence," she said. "Tell me more about your so-called Mystery Schools."

She was watching him with genuine interest. It's history, he told himself. She isn't threatened by history. Keep everything clothed in history.

"Myths were, in a sense, the religion of the masses. But for those selected to be trained in the Mystery Centers, the truth which stood behind the myths was taught. But not only taught, those who could qualify were prepared through a long training to ascend into the heavens and become witnesses. They were Mystery Schools of initiation. What happened there was kept strictly secret. On penalty of death."

"Why?"

"Because of the danger. To enter the spiritual world unprepared was extremely dangerous.

"You obviously don't think they were centers of superstition."

"Hardly that," Paul said. Better pull back. Stick to known history.

"It's been a dream of mine to walk those streets of Ephesus and to look out at the hills that those great individuals looked out at. Though, of course," he added, "we will be seeing mostly the city that Lysimachus built in the third century B.C. The earlier city, the Ionian one, became swampy after the river silted up. The malaria was terrible. Lysimachus moved the city, not far, to a valley between Mt. Pion and Mt. Koressos. So the ruins that we'll be seeing are the ruins from the Hellenistic, Roman, and Christian times. But the hills will be the same. And the air."

"I'm looking forward to seeing this, too," Beth told him. "They've excavated and restored quite a bit, so my guide book tells me. It should be very interesting."

Beth looked genuinely relaxed and excited. That made Paul feel enormous relief. Perhaps if he didn't speak about her life, her dreams, her sorrows, it would be all right.

But right now he didn't want to think about that. He wanted to think about Ephesus.

Annie, this is going to be something.

Yes, Annie said.

While her guide, Joe, handed out tickets and maps to his busload of travelers, Beth looked out at the ruins of Ephesus and felt a thrill of expectation, a slight quivering between her shoulder blades. They were free to wander through the excavations on their own or to accompany him, Joe told them. He pointed to his watch and told them when they were to be back at the buses and where the buses would be parked.

Something was going to happen here, Beth felt the certainty in her bones, and she suddenly wanted to go off alone. She was about to tell that to Paul when he touched her arm, saying, "My dear, I think I am going to walk around on my own. Can I do that without seeming unsocial?"

"Oh, Paul, how funny. I was about to ask you the same thing." She gave him a hug. They walked through the gate together and headed off in different directions.

Beth had seen Eric enter the gate with Donna and Jenna. For a moment she felt a shadow of regret. But with resoluteness—nothing was going to spoil this day, she turned away from thoughts of Eric and gave herself up to the old and well-excavated Greek city.

Map in hand, Beth located where she was standing, then began her excursion. She walked slowly past the Odeon, past the Upper Agora with its little temple of Isis, then down a street called Curetes, past various buildings that were being excavated, along columns and pedestals for statues, toward the Library of Celsus. She inhaled deeply, as if by taking in the air around her she could be part of the old city, feel something of its past glory. Living with all her senses into the space around her with its art and architecture, she felt like her old self again. And it was good. She drove away the familiar burgeoning warning signs. Nothing, no, nothing was going to spoil this day. Beth had two precious hours until she had to be back at the bus and she meant to use every moment.

Something is going to happen, Beth thought. It was a welcome and familiar feeling. She was standing on a precipice, tipping toward creative discovery. If she was depressed, she was also acutely responsive. Her body was empathic, all sense organ, alive to everything—the flowers growing haphazardly over the ruins, the wild speech of birds, the imperious noise of insects, the warm breeze gently slapping her face and pulling her hair, the sunlight runneling down her bare arms, the unidentifiable smells in the air, the sensation of old stones, earth's little histories beneath her shoes.

As it had on the Acropolis in Athens, she felt the air ready to part and reveal the past. She was standing before a stage with curtains that could open, that would lead to other curtains and to others, opening one after the other to her receptive and willing probing. A poem will come from this place, she thought, and didn't argue it away.

When she came to the square in front of the Library of Celsus, she stood there close to tears. How civilized, she thought, a people who valued books, literature, poetry, philosophy.

And war, another voice said inside her.

That, too, she acknowledged, but it was a war where you saw your enemy's face. You didn't just drop a bomb on him, or worse, nuke a whole city.

They were as ugly in war as humans are today. Don't romanticize.

Okay, okay. But they also valued art and art was for everyone not for a few elite. Please go away. This is not the time for the critic. You will close all the curtains and I will see nothing except the limits to my imagination placed on me by your constant harping.

Having dispelled the unwanted voice, Beth walked up the steps past the Corinthian columns to look at the statues in the niches between the doors. She leafed through her guide book until she came to the correct page. The statues represented wisdom, knowledge, intelligence and virtue. Perfect.

She felt at home here. Perhaps I've been here before, she postulated. And Beth smiled, wondering what Paul would think. Was she actually entertaining the idea of reincarnation? No, but perhaps there were ancestral memories embedded in some cell in her. After all you didn't have to go back too many generations before you discovered that you were related to everyone in the world.

Beth moved through what had once been a doorway to look at the large marble interior. To come to such a library, she thought. Had Heraclitus come here? No, he had lived in an earlier incarnation of this city. She looked at the pamphlet she was carrying, leafing through it until she came to a picture of the library. She scanned the text. The library had been built at the turn of the first to the second century by Celsus, who was the Roman proconsul in the area.

Beth walked back outside to once again stare at the two-story facade, then left the square in front of the library and followed the Marble Road, a colonnaded street, heading for the Great Theater.

She wondered what would it have been like to be in Ephesus when pilgrims, those ancient tourists, had filled the theater in celebration of the festival of Artemis. And what would it have been like to go to the stadium to see great sporting events? Or to stroll down the street as an artist and meet other artists, to socialize with them? Where did they socialize? Were there coffeehouses or bars? Were there private clubs? She thought for a moment. They must have socialized in the baths, athletes and sculptors and painters and dancers and musicians.

She stared at the marble beneath her feet. Streets of marble with colonnades everywhere. How wonderful to walk on marble streets. What would it have been like to be part of a procession to the temple of Artemis? Where was that temple? Paul had mentioned a Mystery School here dedicated to Artemis. He called it a great school. What would it have been like to study in such a school? Did women study there also?

She smiled as she passed Sheila and Max Birnbaum, a couple from her tour.

"Isn't this something?" Max said as they passed each other.

"It's exquisite," Beth answered.

"Gorgeous," Sheila added

Beth moved past them. It might be interesting to write about a woman who lived here in Ephesus in the second or third century B.C., before Christianity came on the scene. She had seen a statue of a doctor. What would it have been like to be a woman doctor in so sexist a society? Was doctoring like mothering, a nurturing occupation, and therefore open to women? And women wrote some exquisite poetry here as well as on the islands near here. How is it that they loved poetry so, those Greeks? Beth stopped to stare out at the lush hillside, thinking about the kind of poem she might write. Perhaps she could do a sequence poem, several sections about the different aspects of a woman poet's life, here in Ephesus.

All of that's been done before, Beth.

Go away. Everything has been done before. But I haven't done it.

It would take research, she thought. It's been too many years since I studied any of this in college. She gazed about her, contented for the moment with the prospect of so interesting a project.

Perhaps St. Paul had walked down this street and St. John. Two certain Christians taking on the glorious pagan world. And perhaps Mary, a stranger in a strange land, had stepped where she was stepping now. Mary, the archetypal suffering mother.

I could do an exposé on the hard life of women and what they suffered but managed to achieve despite all the handicaps. No, I've done enough exposés. Do I really want to write about the past? Do I really want to delve into history? Wouldn't it be more interesting to write about the present? Wouldn't it be more interesting to write about a modern woman poet who is visiting Ephesus and encounters the ghost of a woman poet who once lived in Ephesus? Getting there. Wouldn't it be interesting to write about, say, Iris, whom the modern woman poet encounters in Ephesus?

"Yes," Iris said. "That would be very interesting."

"Ah, there you are," Beth said, looking up to find her standing before her on the Marble Road. Beth tried to bring her into sharp detail but her imagination was more difficult to control than the dream image. "Do you know Ephesus?"

"Of course, I know Ephesus. It was a great city in my day. But this one is new to me," and she gestured all around her. "Let's look at it together." And she came over and took Beth by the hand and led her down the Marble Road to the Great Theater. They climbed the steps and entered the auditorium overlooking the stage. "Look, is this not resplendent?"

"Oh, yes. It's stunning." Beth looked about her. The theater was magnificently restored. She sat down, away from the three groups of visitors who were being variously lectured to in German, Japanese and Swedish, and wondered what it would be like attending a play by Aeschylus or Sophocles, say, or wearing the togas or the chiton that Iris was wearing sitting next to her.

"At Artemis's celebration there were many plays given here. That was in the spring," Iris told her. "Twenty-five thousand people attended the performances."

Beth tried to imagine the masks on the players, the sense of catharsis the audience felt after the performance. Ah, that would be good, to feel catharsis. That's what all of us tense twentieth-century people need. She turned to Iris and said, "I understand that this theater is in use again."

"Is it?" Iris murmured and stood up.

"Ray Charles performed here recently," Beth said.

"Come, Elizabeth, and let us walk toward the harbor. Once the Aegean flowed past here. Strange that it should be gone. So many things gone. Can you understand, it is the glory, the nobility of spirit that I miss. Come, let's walk down the Arcadian."

Beth followed Iris down the theater steps and across the stage and out a door opposite the one through which they had entered. They started down the lovely old street to where the Harbor Baths were and the Harbor Gymnasium, walking amid the stone and marble ruins belonging to the Roman period. Iris looked on with curiosity too.

Beth tried to picture ocean where there was now only land. "This was built after the Romans conquered this part of Asia Minor," she told Iris and showed her the paragraph in her pamphlet.

"Ah, yes, the Roman barbarians who came out of the west," Iris nodded. "The Romans are as strange in feel to me as you are, Elizabeth, even though they are closer to my own times. There was no light in them, none at all. They loved our art, but they didn't understand our soul. They are more like you, heavy and hard. Laws where there should have been compassion and dialogue. Come," she said, pulling Beth by the hand up past some ruins to a small hillock.

Iris sat down on a large piece of stone that seemed to be an old architrave and Beth sat down next her, turning to watch the beautiful woman who had so little substance in her mind's eye. Light is without substance, only shine, reflecting its own innate...innate....what? Creativity? Meaningless.

"What is it you are trying to achieve as a poet?" Iris asked, turning to stare at her. Beth could feel the intense glance of those dark violet eyes even though she could not bring them clearly into focus.

Only Elizabeth Taylor has violet eyes, Beth. Hers should be brown, a very dark brown.

"Trying to achieve," Beth said. "Well, I guess you could say that I have tried to bear witness to my own times."

Iris looked at her long and thoughtfully. "Strange," she said.

"Why strange, Iris?"

"Your times are very alien to me, my friend. In my times such a task would not have seemed the purview of art."

"That can't be right, Iris," Beth said. "I've read much of your literature and your poetry and indeed it does seem as if your artists also bore witness to their time, to its joys and sorrows, its struggles, its large and small defeats, its inequities. Much that we know of your era comes from your literature as well as from your art."

"We are talking about something more subtle, I think. It has to do with a different sounding of soul." Iris rose up.

Beth tried hard to keep Iris in focus.

"Knowledge addresses the head in rest. Art, as the great educator of the soul, must address the feelings which are always in movement." She began to sway, to dance, gesticulating gracefully with her arms as she spoke.

"Art must lead the feelings, step by step, *through* the piece of art whether it be a painting, or sculpture, dance, a piece of music, a drama, or a building. In motion, always in motion. In doing this, art connects the individual to his own rhythms. And as you know all the rhythms that are in you, such as breathing and heartbeat, all these wonderful rhythms are connected to the rhythms of the cosmos and, therefore, with the spiritual realities from which we are born."

Iris paused in her own movements and looked down at Beth, fixing her with a clear glance. "Therefore, the purpose of art cannot be to witness, even though that can happen as a consequence of art. That is too pedestrian. No, the purpose must be to lead man from his ordinary feelings to and then through his loftiest feelings into a connection, a balance between his earthly self and his higher self, between earth and heaven. That is what art must do."

"We've given up balance. But for what? I can't imagine for what! I'm in despair over it."

"But what about thought in art, new concepts in art, in other words, art that makes you think?"

"They are of secondary importance. They come after the direct encounter of art through your feelings. If thought is of first importance you can go into the Odeon and address the people directly. If feeling is of first importance, you go to the Great Theater and you see a great performance, or if you are the artist you give the people a great performance."

"These are ideas that I will have to think about, but I do thank you for them."

"No need. These ideas are not mine. To me they are self-evident. They come from the thought realm and are available to any who chooses to draw them down."

"Oh, dear," Beth said, "let's not get into this idea of an objective thought realm. That's a hard one for me."

"Yes, so I've been told," Iris said with a shake of her curly head.

"And let me say that it is not a widely held belief in my times that the rhythms of the body are connected to the rhythms of the universe."

"No?" Iris said. "How much you have lost! How can such cripples lead us into our future?"

For that Beth had no answer.

They returned back along the Harbor Street to look more closely at the gymnasium of the theater. The excavations had not been completed there.

"Oh, what a grand place Ephesus was," Iris told Beth as they walked about it.

Beth looked at the ruins and then at her pamphlet. The gymnasium of the theater was the largest school ever built in Ephesus.

"All destroyed," Iris said. "Will there ever be a place like it?"

Beth tried to imagine what the school had been like. Like Oxford, she wondered?

"I'm sorry that we won't be seeing the great temple of Arte-mis," she told Iris.

"It used to stand near the sea. A great temple where the Mysteries were celebrated and taught to those who were chosen. Impossible to imagine Ephesus without its great temple."

"Tell me what was taught there," Beth said.

"Does your world not remember?"

"History has not recorded it. But maybe there are hidden scrolls somewhere, like the Dead Sea Scrolls that they found in Qumran," Beth said.

Iris stared at her unblinkingly, her violet eyes becoming black. "Great cosmic secrets were taught in Artemis's temple. How the human being is a microcosmic reflection of the great macrocosm. You must understand the unique quality of this great Mystery Center. In the east the temple wisdom had fallen into decadence. In the primitive west it was hidden and secret. The temple of Artemis stood facing both east and west, a balancing point really.

"We've given up balance...I'm in despair over it."

"Like Greece has always been," Beth said. "Torn between east and west."

"Yes, that is Greece. But there was no question of *tearing* in the Mystery Center, but of balance. The highest knowledge available to humankind was obtainable there to those who trained, who underwent the sacrifices necessary to become one with the Goddess. It was she who could lead you into an experience of the entire cosmos, show you directly how the human being is membered into that cosmos."

They began to walk again.

"It is at the temple of Artemis that the great creative Logos was experienced and its connection to our own human word, to speech and the speaking and writing arts. This, you see, is the great difference from my times to yours, Elizabeth. Humans simply did not learn the Mysteries through their heads alone, nor even through their feelings. Then, humans *experienced* the cosmic realities within their own being, those who achieved their great goal. But for this, one underwent a rigorous training."

"What about women?"

"Women, too. They were admitted equally into the Mysteries.

Good, Beth thought with contentment.

"But only some students reached the zenith of its possibility. Those few experienced a union with the Goddess and through Artemis also the heavens. You will see a copy of the cult statue in the museum in Selçuk, no doubt. Ah, now this figure is for all to see which means that it has lost its cultic power. But in those times before the burning of the temple, it had great power."

Beth looked suddenly at her watch. She had half an hour before she was to be on the bus. When she looked up, Iris was gone. Beth felt tired from the long walk and the sustained imagining. She sat down on a piece of marble and pulled out her notebook and rapidly wrote down what she had seen and her conversation with Iris.

At the appropriate time Beth was on the bus, feeling a great sense of satisfaction with her afternoon in Ephesus. The bus would take them into Selçuk, a short drive, and they would spend about forty-five minutes in the museum. Paul sat next to her lost in thought. Beth did not disturb him.

Inside the museum, Beth bought herself a cold drink in the small cafeteria, and thought about her conversation with Iris. She suddenly longed to write, to use words, to move deeper into words, and with them into another human being, and with them into her own interior. Could she now? Should she now? Given all she had been through, given this wonderful day in Ephesus, given Iris?

Beth made her way into the Artemis Hall and stood for a long time in front of the first-century adaptation of the cult statue of Artemis. To believe. To be able to believe. In something.

Paul stood a few feet from the bus staring out at the ditch near the Selçuk-Kuşadasi road. It was all that was left of the temple of Artemis. Once it had been near the ocean. Now it was five kilometers away from the water.

Oh, Annie, this has been one of the most profoundly moving days of my life, and one of the most terrible.

But why terrible, my love?

I have been so moved by this great city, by what has been salvaged, by the beauty of the architecture, the glory of the sculpture. But I have also been filled with loss, with longing, with love, and so lonely, so bereft of your company. Why could we not have seen this together?

But you have shown me well, my Paul.

Today it is not enough.

But, love, why does your heart weep? Do you think that I haven't seen this place, haven't known this place, haven't been here together with you?

Is that possible, Annie?

What do you feel, Paul?

I feel, yes, this is possible. Something about this land, this lost Anatolia. When, Annie?

You must ponder that, Paul. Don't mourn what is gone. We had what is gone. Just try to understand it again, to recover it, with your modern day consciousness.

Yes.

I, too, have loved this day.

On the bus Beth once again sat next to Paul. His eyes were shining. "How was your day, my dear?"

"Wonderful," she said. "And yours?"

"Indescribable," he answered. "Too short, of course, but it's a memory I shall always treasure."

They were quiet on the way home. Beth watched content-edly out of her window. This day was worth the whole trip, she decided, and felt a little more amiable toward Merle.

Back in her cabin, Beth was about to get undressed, take a shower and a little rest before dinner when she heard a knock on her door. She opened it and was surprised to see Eric standing there.

"Listen, please," his words were rushed as if he expected her to slam the door in his face, "and don't say no right off the bat. I have a proposal for you, an invitation." He looked at her with an air of uncertainty.

"Come in," she said, backing away from the door to allow him to enter. His face had darkened in the sun and he looked very handsome. He stood just inside the door.

"I'm sorry to barge in on your privacy like this, but it couldn't wait until dinner because I've been invited by the captain, along with the rest of the staff, to have dinner in Kuşadasi."

Beth nodded and waited.

"Tomorrow, thanks to Mrs. Barry, I have a car coming to take me to Aphrodisias, about two and a half hours from here. I would very much like it if you would accompany me."

Beth was perplexed by his offer. All she could say was, "We're supposed to go to Didyma tomorrow and to two other towns."

"Yes, I know," he said, "but Aphrodisias is a temple city that promises to be the equal of Ephesus when its excavations are completed. It's only been open a couple of years and it's not usually part of the itinerary of tourists who come by ship because it's a long ride into the interior. Mrs. Barry says it's "a must see" and she's pretty much on the money about these things. I would very much like you to come with me."

Beth stared down at her bare feet and made little circles in the carpet with her big toe, and then asked. "Who else is coming?"

He looked at her directly, his eyes unreadable. "It will be just the two of us. I hate to press you for an answer so soon but I won't be here tonight..."

She wanted to ask him why he was inviting her and not Donna. Why he seemed cool and then warm? Why he wanted her company? What he wanted from her in general? She didn't. "That sounds intriguing. I've read a little about Aphrodisias," she said. "I'd like to go."

The relief on his face shook her.

"Good, we'll meet after breakfast at eight. It's a long drive and we have to be back at the ship by four-thirty. Then it's off to Crete. See you in the morning, Beth, and thanks," he backed out of the door grinning foolishly.

Beth closed the door and sat down on the bed and tried to think through what was going on.

Just go with the flow, Beth, she told herself finally, go with the flow.

After dinner, as she was preparing for bed, she took the presents she had purchased that morning out of their bag. She wanted to unclutter the small room and to pack the gifts in her suitcase. She looked over her selections with satisfaction, then remembered the pair of earrings she could not buy for Alicia. There would be no more gifts from exotic places for Alicia. Beth burst into uncontrollable tears and sobbed and sobbed.

When she finally fell asleep, her dreams were chaotic but she was not able to bring any of them into clarity the next morning.

"I *can forgive him, then?*

"He didn't injure you, honey. He injured me."

"You're wrong, Mother. He injured us all. But 'we always hurt the ones we love'..."

"What are you thinking about?" Eric asked Beth. He shifted in the back seat of the large, vintage Cadillac to look at her more directly.

"Nothing, really," she said, turning toward him. What a nice face he has. He listens with his eyes.

Well, he's a painter.

She had been staring at the landscape they had been driving through, at the soft yet angular hills, the rolling valleys filled with orchards and cultivated fields, at the colorfully pantalooned women with their patterned vests and shoulder-length head scarves working in the hot spring sun. "I was trying to think away the people, the Turkish people in their costumes." She smiled somewhat apologetically. That was at least partly true.

He raised his eyebrows.

"It's ridiculous, I know, unkind, in a way. The Turks have been living here and working the land for hundreds and hundreds of years, far longer than we Americans have squatted on our continent, which we took from the Indians. Yet that's what I've been doing."

"Why?"

"Well, on this trip we've been immersed in all those Greek periods, the Classic, the Hellenistic, the Byzantine. So I've been trying to imagine what it would have been like to see people in the fields in Greek costumes, with Greek faces."

"Have you been successful?"

"Not really, which is okay. Cavalier of me to want to wish away a thousand years."

"You're obsessed by the weight of history."

"How can changes come about when history drags us back? This may seem foolish, but it troubles me."

"You don't admire or long for, just occasionally, the certainty of, say, the French or the English, their confidence in who they are?"

"Oh, yes, I do. At times that certainty seems wonderful," she said, "but after a while I sense that it doesn't come from choice but from something built into the collective folk memory."

"Is that so terrible?"

"It's not that it's terrible," she said, "it's just that it does away with freedom, doesn't it?"

He squinted. "How do you see that?"

"Where does individual choice come in? What's different about the folk instinct from any other instinct?"

"Hey," he grinned, "let's hear it for the instincts."

Beth's mouth hardened slightly and she turned away from him.

Eric leaned over and patted her hand. It was an awkward gesture. "I'm kidding, Beth."

"All of this is my own musings, Eric," she said, "not of much interest to another. Let's talk about something else."

"Beth, my teasing wasn't meant to put you down or to squelch your thoughts. Really. It was a lousy male thing to do."

"Yes," she said, "it was."

"There are better ways to tell you I find you attractive. That's a statement, Beth. It's not meant as a come-on. I didn't lure you on this trip to make a pass at you."

"So what do you see as my main deficiency, Hank?"

"You pull away from life and all its marvelous experiences."

"Including you?"

"Including me."

Beth looked again at Eric's tan face, his light brown eyes. "Why did you invite me on this trip? Why didn't you ask…?"

"Why didn't I ask Donna?"

Beth nodded.

He took a moment to answer. "Donna's a very attractive woman. Beth, I meet women like Donna every day in my work. She's feisty and independent. She's ambitious. That's fine. She's opinionated, which is okay, too. I like people who know what they want, but…" he paused. "Beth, this is going to sound crazy. This is going to make you mad if I say it out loud."

"Say it."

"I'm attracted to your suffering."

The color rose in her cheeks. "That's disgusting."

"See, I told you this was going to sound crazy. Beth, look at me."

She didn't. She turned to look out the window again. A young boy stopped his work to wave at the passing car.

"Look, I live in a world of appearances, in a world that judges everything by the way it's packaged. There's great value placed on externals, on the presentation, the wrapping. In my world the way you look is the way you expect to be judged. Men as well as women take a great deal of pride in their appearance. Look at my clothes, designer stuff, these khakis and T-shirt. I haven't been to a plastic surgeon, probably won't go, but I admit I've thought about it."

They were driving through a village. Men were sitting at a café drinking something and staring phlegmatically at the car as it passed. Where were the women, Beth wondered? Working, no doubt. I could get out here. Get a cab. Stay.

"Okay, none of this is news to you. But it's part of a picture, so bear with me. Please. We appear at the hottest clubs, the newest restaurants, at all the important art and theater openings, so we can display ourselves for all to see. We read the latest reviews on books, theater, art, so we can talk, and talk well. But, other than concerning ourselves with what gives us pleasure, hardly any time is given to cultivating a rich inner life."

Beth turned finally to look at him. He was leaning back on the high seat, his eyes were closed. She could hear him struggle to say the words. Why? Why did he want her to hear these things?

"All right, that's a little overstated, but I tell you nothing is of consequence compared to the impression we can make on you with a look or an outfit. I can't say that I don't enjoy some of it. I do love anything visual. But it can be very empty. All day long I am surrounded by people who want to look good, make it big in their careers. We skim over life like skiers."

He opened his eyes and saw that she was watching him. "Am I being simplistic, Beth? Am I crying over too much rich food when so many don't even have bread? If so, that would be cheap. This is hard to say without sounding like a privileged kid who doesn't like cocoa. I love my life but something is missing."

She stared past him through the windows at the lush fields. What were they growing out there? So many fields. Thousands of miles away from New York strangers in strange costumes were working in their fields. And she was driving through them with a stranger. Was he? A stranger saying strange things.

"Beth, there is something special about you, even something noble, the way you struggle, the kinds of things that trouble you, the way you search for meaning. You're deep, so terribly deep. It's a place that as a man I suspect I'm afraid to go, maybe because I'm too shallow. But, oh God, I admire it. When my marriage broke up, when my affair turned sour, I felt plenty sorry for myself. I drank. I dated and dated and dated... But you, you're not self-pitying. "

Beth shook her head, "You don't know, you just don't know...me."

"Can we understand just one other person...?"

"But I want to," he reached for her hand. She didn't resist. "Beth, please don't put up walls. Please hear me, hear me out."

The set of Eric's mouth told her he was serious. "What's hard for me is that you shut people out. I'm drawn to you. I'd like to get to know you better. I'd be glad just to be your friend, though I think I'd like to be something more."

"You mean something to me, Beth, everything. And now when things are rough, you shut me out, you just throw us away? Am I so little to you?"

Beth felt unsettled by his declaration. How should she respond?

"You see, Beth, when I found out you were going to be on the trip, on impulse I bought one of your books. I read it. I told you that before?"

A quick nod was all she could manage.

"I was really impressed by the lady who wrote those poems, who stood behind those words. I looked all over New York, used all my connections, until I had all four of your books. After I finished reading them I couldn't wait to meet you."

"That's someone else. I don't think I'm that lady any longer." Beth's words were low, pushed out from behind a closed throat. "She seems light-years away."

"No," he said, "that lady is there, that passionate, caring lady is there. But something has been added. That's thrilling. You grow. You metamorphose. You move forward. Not like me. Stuck."

"You astonish me. If you're stuck, then I'm coming unglued. I'm not in a place that I would recommend, Eric. You wouldn't want to be here in this psyche, now, and I wouldn't want to drag you there, not for all the comfort in the world. Don't you see, I've lost the sense of life. That's a terrible thing."

"You haven't lost the sense of life, you question the sense of life."

"No, lost. That's the word."

"If you had lost it, you wouldn't be struggling so. You wouldn't be able to say what you said before, about the weight of history. You're disturbed by life. You can't find the 'whys' and 'wherefores' but you *are* giving battle. You haven't gotten into bed with the covers over your head."

"I tried."

"You tried to allow yourself a period of mourning. You would have gotten out of bed after a while and picked up your sword."

"Oh, Eric, please don't see me in that light. You're romanticizing me. I'm no warrior."

"Oh, Beth, we see our own selves so little."

Beth said, "There I agree."

"Good."

Outside, the hills meandered away then returned like waves in an incoming tide. "Because I think you're the one who underestimates himself. You talk as if you were a shallow, insensitive person. I haven't found you so. On the contrary." She hurried on, "Why are you stuck?"

"How to answer that question?" .

"Try words," Beth said when he didn't go on.

"I'm a painter, Beth, not a wordsmith."

"Protestations from a man who has written more than a few articles on art, from a man who has given numerous lectures."

"I even taught a class on collecting art at the New School."

"There, you see, you are a wordsmith," and she gave him a full smile. "So?"

"So why am I stuck, mired down, bored, rudderless?"

"Why?"

"Because what I do doesn't interest me anymore."

"Collecting contemporary art for Augusta Barry?"

"Searching for and collecting contemporary art for Augusta Barry, yes. I'm thinking of quitting my nice cushy prestigious job."

"Really?"

"Really, and that's why Mrs. Barry has sent me on this trip, I think, to rejuvenate me, to get me enthusiastic about art again, a trip to the source of Western Art as a balm for burnout."

"And has it gotten you enthusiastic about art again?"

"Yes, and that's the problem, don't you see?"

She thought about it for a moment, thought about his love of mosaics and frescoes. "The wrong art?"

"The wrong art. You'll hate this probably, but I'm one of those people drawn to the past, to its cohesive and explicable art."

"But there's nothing wrong with that. Every American tourist comes to Europe or Asia looking for the past, looking for some secret that's been lost to us. No doubt the Greeks went to Egypt for the same reason. They probably thought the Egyptians knew something they no longer understood. And they were probably right. But you know all this, Eric. You know that everyone idealizes the past, forgets its struggles, sees only its achievements."

He was silent so she went on, "I'm also, finally, trying to understand what the past can say to us in the present. Everyone who goes in search of history is looking for that. All artists who travel the globe looking at the art of the past are trying to engage themselves in a dialogue with the art of the past, isn't that what you said once?"

"But it's more than just a dialogue for me now, Beth, it's the sad fact that I feel nourished by the art of the past and…"

"And not by the art of the present?"

"Not in the same way," he said. "The art of the present, and I love it, don't misunderstand me, hasn't chosen nourishment as one of its tasks. It's me that's the problem. I'm not blaming contemporary art. It's me. At this point, now that my kids have flown the nest, and now that the road ahead looks shorter and shorter, I have need of something,

something else, some way-bread to sustain me on the road. Nothing in my present life does that."

"What would you do if you quit the Barry?"

"Well, I have a little money saved up and a fairly valuable collection of paintings, so I wouldn't have to worry about money. I'd probably travel for a while. And then I might…I might even go back to painting."

"But, Eric, how fabulous."

His eyes lit up. "Do you think so?"

"Yes," she said. "You have, well, the soul of an artist."

"And not the soul of an entrepreneur?" he laughed.

"Well, I don't know about that. The rumor is that you bought a rug in Istanbul?"

"Ah, the rumor mill. After only a week the gossip starts."

They laughed and the laughter made Beth feel good. Shared laughter, she thought, what is better?

"Where were you born, Eric?"

"Chicago. Haven't I told you that yet?"

"No."

"Good God, I've missed out on the opportunity to tell you the story of my life. Well, now you know why I asked you on this two and a half hour motor trip. You're a captive audience." And when she smiled, he launched into an account of his middle-class childhood, his parents, his older sister and younger brother, his schooling, his discovery of art in high school—thanks to a perceptive and inspiring teacher, his parents' divorce when he was seventeen. His mother's bitterness, his own sense of guilt.

"Where does your mother live now?"

"Palm Springs. My dad and his wife live in San Francisco. My mother still won't come to any family function that my dad is invited to, which of course creates havoc whenever there's a special occasion."

"Has your mother ever had a lover?"

"Not to my knowledge."

"Not like my mother. After years of marriage to a doctor, after being a pillar of Beverly society, an upholder of all good New England mores, my mother really let loose. After my dad died, she sold the house and moved to Miami. Did I tell you that she was a concert pianist before she met my dad? A child prodigy really. Well, she gave that up for marriage and after he died she went back to the piano."

"That seems reasonable."

"She began to play in small jazz bands, in night clubs."

"Not quite Chopin."

"No. And she took a series of young lovers and went through as much of Dad's money as she could get her hands on. Lucky that there's a trust, or she'd be homeless."

"You don't approve?"

Beth shrugged her shoulders. "She long ago stopped being much of a factor in my life. My dad was the one I was close to. My mother was a beauty, still is in her seventies. She always had an entourage of sycophants around her, even in Beverly. She didn't have much time for us kids. Actually, it wasn't time, it was psychic energy. Dad was the better mom."

"What did he think of your mom?"

"He adored her, was besotted by her, I think. But he knew she wasn't great with us and so he stepped in. He was immensely kind. Doctoring was perfect for him."

"You miss him?"

"I do."

"It was my dad who was the social butterfly," Eric said. "My mother was the daughter of German immigrants. Intellectual achievements were what she demanded from us, and a knowledge of culture, and good manners. Don't go out to dinner with my mother without a jacket or tie, not even in Palm Springs, not even in the summer when everyone else is in T-shirts."

"Have you stopped trying to please her?"

"I think so. I hope so. Pleasing her just ain't possible.

The travel time was passing quickly. Beth felt drenched in a lovely shower of fairy dust. Eric was interested in her. And despite feeling that she was not in shape emotionally for an involvement, she was immensely attracted to Eric Halsey. He was bright and sensitive and mature. Ah, well, she told herself, when she felt in danger of drowning in the fairy dust, enjoy the day. Why not?

Eric finally looked at his watch. "We should be there in half an hour," he told her. "Do you know very much about Aphrodisias?"

"Just from a quick glance at my guide book, that's all."

"Do you want a small synopsis of what we're going to see?"

"Yes, please."

He opened the guide book that had been lying on the floor at his feet, "Okay. First, we'll be about 230 kilometers southeast of the Aegean on a plateau that is 600 meters above sea level.'"

"Oh, dear, can you translate that into miles and feet?"

"No," he answered. "'To the east are the mountains once known as the Salbakos range but are now called Baba Dag...'"

"Fascinating."

"You're obviously not a geography buff. Okay, let's skip the geography," he ran his forefinger down the page then turned it. "Do you want to know when the excavations started?"

"Of course," she sank back comfortably into her seat and watched him as he began to read.

Such a very nice face.

"'Though the site was surveyed as early as 1904, the real excavation started about twenty-eight or twenty-nine years ago, partly under the aegis of New York University.'"

That was Matthew's school.

So what.

"The site is beautiful, I've been told, Beth," Eric looked up from his book. "Somehow the ancients just had a natural sense for beauty as well as a sense for what was practical. I always find that amazing."

"Me too," she answered.

"Now what attracted my interest in the city..."

"...was the insistence of Mrs. Augusta Barry that it was a 'must see.'"

"Besides that," he said. "What attracted me were the amazing finds, the statues and sculptural bits and pieces. They're at the museum there. They uncovered statues of exceptional quality lying where they had fallen, buried under the earth?"

"What happened there?"

"Earthquakes probably. But no new city has been built on top of the old and so the building stones and sculpture are still there where they fell."

"Remarkable."

The site where the old city of Aphrodisias lay, was perfectly located on a plateau surrounded by hills and filled with wildflowers, mostly the dainty little poppies that were everywhere in this part of the world. Aphrodisias itself was now a tumbledown city but one could still feel its grandeur. "Art and nature, art and nature," Beth's heart sang to her.

Eric proved to be a good guide. They walked for nearly two hours looking, commenting, speculating. Beth wasn't sure whether she was high from Aphrodisias or from being with Eric. When they finally entered the museum they fell silent. They walked through it holding hands, stunned by the magnificence of the statues, the reliefs and sarcophagi.

What will they dig up from our world, she wondered as many had before her? Plastic, she answered, as many had before her.

After three hours they were again back in the old Cadillac with their driver driving at breakneck speed toward their luncheon rendezvous, an old house which offered a fixed menu, served in the backyard under arbors to tour groups and other travelers. Eric and Beth ate, drank wine and talked through a rapid meal.

After half an hour they were again in the car. They spoke for a while about what they had just seen, and then both slept, Beth lying comfortably against Eric's chest, his arm around her shoulders.

As the car began its descent into Kuşadasi, Eric woke Beth up.

On board ship, just before they parted, they made plans to meet for dinner.

Beth changed into a green print dress, with a short full skirt. She put on dangling earrings and her highest heels. If she wasn't beautiful, she decided, she had a good figure and, apparently, eyes that he seemed to like. And, of course, her gestures. She tried gesticulating to see if she could ascertain what it was he found so interesting. She couldn't. She stared at her green eyes trying to get them to look deep. They seemed dull to her with their little crinkles on each side and two deep lines above her nose that gave her so serious a demeanor, or worse, made her look old.

Cool it, she warned herself. He likes you as you are.

At dinner she and Eric sat with Doris and Lucy and with Sheila and Max Birnbaum. Eric played host and talked attentively with their table companions. Beth was quiet, barely following the conversation. She hardly ate. She was full of delicious feelings, savoring each one as it rose up in her. There was little room for anything else. The waiter asked her twice if anything was wrong with the food as he took away course after course with only a few bites taken out of each. She told him with a little laugh that, no, the food was really quite extraordinary that evening, but that she was not too hungry because of the large lunch she had eaten that afternoon.

She couldn't really observe Eric because he was sitting next to her. For the most part she let the conversation flow about her as she gazed out the window at the dark Aegean. The ship was on its way to Crete. Beth felt a little like Alice in Wonderland, her head soaring up and up and her feet and body tiny and somehow anchored to the ground. She hadn't felt like this in years, these delicate beginning feelings that might tumble into that state called falling in love.

With Hank?

No, it had been different. She had felt too foolish from the beginning. It's eventual end had been factored in at the start. No, with Hank it had been something else.

And now Eric was interested in her. Eric was not interested in pretty, bright Donna. And it was all possible. Something with Eric was really quite possible. Why not? They both lived in New York, they were the same age, they were both artists, they were both free, both ready for a new relationship.

Then the inner dialogue began.

That's not true, Beth. You're not ready for a new relationship.

But this is serendipity. Why can't I change my mind?

Why should you suddenly trust another man? You hardly know him. Eric could be another Matthew. He already told you that he had cheated on his first wife.

That was a bad marriage.

All marriages are bad when the husband wants a reason to cheat.

Every person I meet doesn't have to be a potential Matthew.

You can't handle it. You'll ruin it. You're too stressed. You're too emotional. You need time to mourn for Alicia and time to heal before you begin something this important. You'll blow it.

Stop it. Every time something good comes into my life you want to stomp on it like an elephant on a tender plant. Get out of my garden.

And she pushed away the unwanted voice and turned to look at Eric. He was smiling down at her and her heart lifted out of her like a cardinal and flew away.

After dinner, Eric and Beth went up on the deck for some fresh air and to look out at the sea as the boat steamed south toward Crete. They walked around the deck, greeted people, stopped to talk now and then. They spoke about Aphrodisias. They heard about Didyma and Priene and Miletus. Eric asked Beth if she wanted to dance. She did. They left the deck, went inside the ship, stopped first at Beth's cabin so she could change into lower-heeled shoes, and made their way to the lounge.

When they entered the lounge, a few people had already gathered. Some were there for a nightcap, others, mostly couples, were there because they obviously loved to dance. Some of the officers were present and a few of the single women.

The English band was playing old standards. Eric found a table as far from the door as possible, ordered them both brandy and then took Beth out on the dance floor.

For over an hour they danced. Eric asked no one else. They didn't talk much. Beth felt as happy as she had ever felt in her life. She was intoxicated, she knew, on wine, brandy, Aphrodisias, the Aegean, Greece, Turkey, fairy dust, and Eric, Eric, Eric.

They were the last to leave the lounge. Eric walked her to her door. When they arrived, he asked if he could come in for a moment.

"Well, for a moment," she murmured.

The door shut behind them, and Eric took Beth in his arms and kissed her, first lightly, then as she didn't object, long and passionately.

Beth returned his kisses willingly.

At five the next morning, Eric stood over Beth, leaned down and kissed her on the bridge of the nose. She stirred and murmured, "What?"

"Beth, I'm going to leave now while it's still early, to protect your reputation from the gossip mongers." He kissed her mouth.

She opened her eyes. "Does anyone care?"

"You will, when you wake up. I'll see you at breakfast," he told her.

"Uh, uh," she shook her head, "I'm skipping that and sleeping in. I'll see you when we disembark at nine, okay?" she closed her eyes.

"Okay, lazybones. I'll see you then." He bent down and kissed her once more and left.

Beth heard the door close softly behind him. As she began to drift slowly back toward sleep, she stretched out toward the warmth his body had left and was jarred awake by the sudden emptiness of the bed.

All night they had slept arms and legs entangled, his quiet breathing blowing feather-like across her shoulder and breasts. They had come together with such tenderness, with such ease, like two people who already knew each other. There had been no uncertainties, no awkwardness, no apologies, no need for caution. They had been friends and lovers. For Beth, all sad memories, all fears, all concerns for past or future had melted away. As their bodies had come together, meeting, touching, embracing, it was as if they had passed through each other. No borders, no boundaries, no limits, every inch of skin a gateway.

Not with Matthew. Not with Hank...

And now the bed was empty. He was gone and she felt the loss of it. As she slipped back into sleep she comforted herself by saying. We'll meet soon, at nine, a few hours. Together. Eric and Beth.

It was still dark outside. Undulating shadows were slipping out of the ship's smokestack, leaving a trail of indecipherable writing on the dark air, gray text on black sky. Beth, walking around and around the deck of the New Odyssey, was trying hard to keep euphoria wrapped around her like a cloak in the cool air. Eleven times makes a mile. She had felt good. She had felt happy. Then why was anxiety dogging her? How had it overtaken her? It was moving up and down her spine like a cold hand on a bone xylophone. What could be wrong? She hurried past the life boats and was about to turn into the bow of the ship when she saw Eric standing there in the white moonlight. He was holding Donna. He was kissing her.

Horrified, Beth shrank back into the blackness of the bulwark. The dark felt wet and icy.

"Well, I did it," Eric said, holding Donna by the shoulders. He smiled down at her.

"What's that, my love?" Donna asked, looking up into his face.

"Seduced Elizabeth."

"Did you, my love?"

"She was a tough nut to crack. I wasn't sure I could find a way. But I finally hit upon it."

"How did you manage it, my darling?" Donna's fingers moved toward his hair like snakes about to strike.

"I told her I admired her suffering." His laugh was a machine-gun firing.

Donna broke away from him. "You're joking! And she bought it?"

"No, I'm not joking, my love. Am I smooth or what? It was an inspiration. An angel kissed me on the forehead. It worked. I convinced her that I was attracted to her depth of soul. She bought it hook, line and sinker. Do I get a medal for this? I conquered the ice maiden." He put his arm around Donna's shoulder and the two began walking away from where Beth hid.

"What was it like?" Donna asked him.

"Like sleeping with a desperate virgin," he told her as they disappeared around the bulwark wall and out of sight. "It must be years since she had any."

Beth felt sick with rage and betrayal. She wanted to scream, to run after them and shout invectives at them. No, she wanted to disappear into nothingness before she drowned in a cesspool of humiliation.

Beth heard laughter, deep male laughter. She stormed out of her hiding place and there in the bow of the ship, where Donna and Eric had been, stood Matthew. He was doubled over with laughter.

"Stop it!" Beth shouted at him. "How dare you laugh at me!"

"You are laughable, my sweet. Did you really think anyone

else would want you after I discarded you? What a dumb idea. You're no good for anything anymore."

"I am, I am," Beth screamed. "There was Hank."

"Hank was a boy. Hank doesn't count. I told you that. You mustn't betray me. You belong to me. After me, there is no one for you. How could you expect anyone to want my leavings?" Matthew's voice echoed loudly off the roiling water.

"You! You!" was all the cry Beth could get out of her mouth before she felt the sound dam up in her. There was a caldron of fury bubbling inside her and it had no outlet.

"Beth, why are you ignoring your child? Why have you once again forgotten your child?"

Beth whirled around, and down the long aisle of the deck toward the stern, she saw Iris.

Beth tried to walk toward Iris but she couldn't move her legs.

Iris said, "But this is unseemly, Beth, that your child should need you and that you should ignore her plea." And she gestured toward Alicia who stood some distance behind Iris, her arms held out in a silent, pleading gesture.

Beth's heart almost broke inside her chest. She tried to call out to Alicia. She tried to run toward her. She couldn't.

"I do not understand your times at all," Iris berated her. "Has all mother love disappeared in your times even as the sense for beauty has? Even as the sense for truth has?"

From somewhere near Iris, Beth heard her companion speak in his low melodious voice, "Iris, the times have changed. Beauty is not a natural capacity in her world. In her century, the artist must struggle between beauty and ugliness, must create art out of the tension between the two. She is not like you. Be gentle."

"I do not understand her or her times," Iris said over her shoulder then turned again to Beth. "You live in terrible times. Can you not answer your child? Why are you mute? Why are all of you mute?"

Inside herself, Beth screamed and screamed. The voice, stuck in her throat, was tiny and tinny.

Alicia disappeared. Iris shook her head and disappeared.

Behind Beth, Matthew's laughter roared louder and louder. "Useless," he howled. "You're as ineffectual now as you were as a wife and as a mother. I was the better mother. You were always leaving us to go off to places to hunt for poetry. I was the one there for Alicia and Becky. You are useless."

"As a lover," Eric said, standing next to Matthew.

"As a woman," Donna said, standing next to Eric.

"You ran from me, Beth. Why did you do that?" Now Hank joined the other three.

"You're an exploiter, Beth," Matthew wagged his finger at her. "You exploited the third-world poor for your poems. And you ignored your family so you could go off and write your simpy little verses that only a few college kids read."

"Attention, please."

"You left me when I could have helped you. That was a terrible thing to do," Hank's dark eyes blazed. "You were cruel and treated me shabbily."

"Our papers are being examined by the port authorities."

"Nooooo!" Beth hollered and sat up in bed.

Her heart was pounding and her head throbbing. She was dripping with sweat. Something was screaming in her stomach. She tried to breathe rhythmically. In out. In out. It was just a dream, she told herself over and over. In out. In out. Just another bad dream.

Really? that other self asked.

"...something other than this material world?"

Over the loudspeaker came the announcement that the ship which had been dockside in Crete since 6 A.M. would be ready for disembarkation in half an hour. First stop would be the museum and then on to the palace at Knossos. Beth pushed aside the blanket and began dressing. Blue jeans and a T-shirt. Sport shoes. She did, at that moment, what she so often did in a crisis, tackle the thing in front of her. She had to get dressed. She had to be on deck. Eric would meet her there. But Eric loved Donna. He was only using her. No, that was the dream. But was the dream a message?

"...dreams appear to contain genuine thoughts from a supersensible world."

From whom?

Beth methodically brushed her teeth and combed her hair. Get on deck, see Eric, go to Knossos, her brain told her limbs.

As she was tying her shoes, she noticed that an envelope had been slipped under her door. She picked it up and opened it. It was from Eric. Heart beating frantically, she read it.

New Odyssey, 6 A.M.

My darling, blasted news! When I returned to my room this morning, I found a note under my door. Mrs. Barry radioed the ship last night. It seems she wants me to fly immediately to Naples to check out a young artist that she's considering for her collection. He has a show that is closing in a few days and she needs me to see it now. Damn! Well, she pays the bills so I couldn't very well say no. By the time you wake up (from what I hope is a wonderful sleep) and disembark, I'll be in an airplane on my way to Naples. I'll meet the ship either in Reggio di Calabria or in Sicily. I can't say for certain which. Enjoy the next two days. I'll see you when I get back. Sorry. It's terrible timing. Eric.

Beth stared and stared at the note. This couldn't be happening, she told herself. He's left me.

"Do you know me…have we met somewhere?"

"Raven wants to marry me."

Not true, he has to do something for his boss.

"I don't know what to do."

I've been abandoned again. It was just a conquest for him, another conquest and I was easy. I fell for his line.

"I can't help it. I can't help myself."

"…have we met somewhere?"

Beth, he had to go. Mrs. Barry wanted him to look at a new artist.

He could have told her "no". He could have stood up to her. He didn't have to leave right at this moment, the morning after. I feel used.

"If you're not a raving beauty, you can't afford to be too fussy…"

You're putting a wrong face on this, Beth. He left. But he's coming back.

How do I know?

"Do you know me?"

It's in the note.

He's buying time. Another abandonment. Someone else making me trust him and then betraying me and disappearing.

"Raven wants to marry me."

Beth, you're seeing it all wrong.

Matthew was right.

Matthew is dead.

I've disappointed Iris.

"Such egotism, such arrogance, such gall.."

She doesn't understand you or your times. She's only a figment.

Alicia is angry because I've promised to mourn for her and I've abandoned her for a few hours of lust.

You haven't abandoned Alicia. She's dead. She left you.

"You always hated lies, didn't you, Mom...?"

"Beth, why are you ignoring your child. Why have you once again forgotten your child?"

Because I couldn't hang onto her. Because I couldn't make her well.

You have your own life.

"You never risk yourself for yourself."

No, life's without meaning.

Eric could bring you a little joy.

That's not possible. Eric loves Donna.

"How do you feel about women's issues?"

That was a dream, Beth.

Dreams can have reality. They can be messages.

"Why can't you see that there is something other than this material world?"

"...the threshold in our times..."

Humpty Dumpty sat on a wall.

Beth.

Humpty Dumpty had a great fall...

Beth.

"Will everyone please assemble on C deck. The ship has been cleared for disembarkation. The buses and guides are waiting at the dock," the loudspeaker said. "First call for disembarkation."

Beth picked up her sweater and left her room. She locked the door behind her. She descended the stairs to the disembarkation deck feeling as if she were moving in slow motion. That was good. She would need to be careful.

"Good morning, Beth," a cheerful voice said as she stood waiting to be told to leave the ship.

She turned her head. It was Paul who greeted her with a big smile which faded quickly when he saw her face.

"My dear, is something wrong? You look dreadful. Sorry, I didn't mean that the way it sounded. Are you all right?"

"If you were to take into consideration more than one life..."

She blinked at him as if to bring him into focus, then nodded slowly. There was a screamer inside her solar plexus and it was howling.

"Shall we sit together on the bus?" he asked.

"We lack the faculties to percieve them."

"Yes, thank you. That would be nice." She could barely hear her own voice.

"Then let's go," Paul took her by the elbow and steered her down the gangplank toward the bus.

We're in Crete, she told herself. But this can't be it. She squinted and looked around her. It's all askew. It's wrong. The colors are off. The colors are too bright.

"She's angry. It flows out in dreadful colors."

Look at those shapes, those hills, they are menacing. Are we going there?

"...the sense for truth is gone. I had forgotten that."

The screamer inside her stomach wailed even louder.

"Friends," their escort was once again Irene, "while we drive the short distance to the museum located here in Heraklion to see the Minoan finds from the various excavation sites in Crete, let me tell you the story, briefly, of the Minotaur, the monster who dwelt in the palace that we shall be seeing after a short visit to the museum."

Paul squeezed Beth's hand. She stared at him without smiling, then turned to look out the window at the dock in Heraklion, Crete. How far away the ocean seemed. How distant the dock through which they were driving. Another dock, another country, another day to push through. Hickory dickory dock...

"You've run all over the world..."

"You're such an adventurous soul."

It's all so useless.

I want, the screamer wailed.

"We are now on the island where European civilization was born," Irene said. "You will be amazed at what you see when we get to the palace at Knossos, not far from the museum. The legends say that there were over three thousand rooms..."

There were audible intakes of breath.

"But we think the number is more like fifteen hundred."

There were some appreciative giggles.

"We believe that the Minoan society was a happy one, that women were equal to men. There were athletic events, religious rituals and celebrations, a theater, delight in clothes, jewelry, crafts, love of the slender body, long hair. It seems to have been one of the most vivacious civilizations ever to have been on earth. And for many years a peaceful one."

"...an artist who doesn't know history and who doesn't know his own times..."

"What is wonderful is this inborn need of the artist..."

"Minos is not the name of just one King but was probably the title of every king at Knossos in those many centuries when the Minoan civilization was dominant in this part of the world. The Minoans were great sailors with very advanced ships for that time. And they were great artisans as well."

"...engaging in a dialogue with art history..."

"...to beautify his surroundings, his life."

"At any rate, our tale of the Minotaur is a tale that comes at the end, or near the end, of that fantastic civilization just as the Mycenaean Greeks are beginning their rise to prominence and power.

"...how deficient their intellect has become..."

"What heritage will they leave for us when we return?"

"Here is the story and I'll make it brief for I see that we are nearing the museum."

Listen to the story. One word. Then another.

"Androgeus, the son of King Minos, went to Athens to partake in the games there and was very successful. But on his way to Thebes with the nephews of King Aegeus of Athens he was killed by the Bull of Marathon who was ravaging the countryside there. King Minos did not believe the story but was certain that his son had been deliberately murdered by the Athenian King's family out of envy. After many adventures and several attempts to bring other countries to his aid, Minos finally attacked and conquered Athens.

"I'm no warrior..."

"They don't even value courage and that is a mystery."

"The tribute he demanded of the Athenians was that every nine years seven youths and seven maidens be sent to Crete for the funeral games. But the Athenians knew that the Greeks would be fed to the Minotaur who was a monster that lived in the cellar below the palace of Knossos. This beast, with the body of a man and the head of a bull, was the monster son of the king's wife and a magic bull."

"...is like a thin veil fluttering between us..."

Listen carefully, Beth. Every word counts. Every word is a stepping stone to home.

"Theseus, the son of King Aegeus and a proven hero, decided to take on the Minotaur. He persuaded his father to let him go to Crete as one of the youths. With a reluctant heart the king sent him. Theseus distinguished himself at the funeral games. The young daughter of Minos, Ariadne, was smitten with him so she helped him find his way through the labyrinth."

"...the contribution of the male..."

"I love you...Is that so hard to take?"

I'm in a labyrinth. Should I warn them all? We are in a labyrinth. She looked at Paul with frightened eyes.

He patted her hand and held it tight.

Yes, Paul is here. Paul will know what to do.

"They have no courage, no honor, little pride."

"Theseus also received help from the palace architect, Daedalus, who happened to be Greek. These two gave Theseus a sword and a ball of thread. Theseus entered the labyrinth, unraveled the thread, found and bravely killed the Minotaur and followed the thread back to safety."

Paul will have a ball of thread. Paul will know what to do.

"Theseus set his fellow Greeks free and, according to some accounts, set fire to the palace. He took Ariadne, who was in love with him, and his companions back to his boat."

"I didn't lure you on this trip to make a pass at you."

"...of the male in procreation is still unknown."

"And with a weeping, suddenly regretful Ariadne, he set sail for Athens. On an island where they had stopped for rest, he deserted the grief stricken and lamenting Ariadne."

"...you look so utterly forlorn standing there..."

"This was the great hero who had pledged undying love and marriage to the young girl when he needed something from her."

"Can we understand just one other person from our own times?"

"So he went back to Athens without her."

"Someone we think we love?"

"Ariadne cursed him and wished him the same grief as he had caused her. And he got it."

"Good," someone called out and the others laughed.

"I'm attracted to your suffering."

Deserted, Beth's mind registered. It is always the women who are deserted.

"How do you feel about women's issues?"

"Life is about issues. What else is there?"

"An eye for an eye is the way of the ancients," Irene said with a smile. "Anyway, Theseus had promised his father that he would change the black mourning sails on his ship to white if he had been successful in Crete. He forgot to change them. His father Aegeus waiting on a cliff over the Aegean saw the ship return. But, sorrow, the sails were black. He thought his son was dead so the king jumped over the cliff and committed suicide."

"I can't help myself."

All the king's horses and all the king's men...

"Oh," someone said, "it's the parents who always suffer."

"She doesn't understand the nature of pain?"

Yes, that's right. It's the parents who suffer.

"...why are you ingoring your child?"

"No," someone answered from down front, "it's the women."

"Right on," was another response.

It's the women who suffer.

"He injured us all"

The screamer inside Beth wept inconsolably for the parents and the women.

"Well," Irene said, "Ariadne did all right for herself. Dionysus, the god, who was roaming the world as he often did, just happened at that moment to be passing the island where Theseus had deserted Ariadne. He saw Ariadne and fell in love with her."

"I love you...Is that so hard to take?"

"They married and they both lived happily ever after."

"Mother, is it awful? Is it too soon?"

There was applause.

"We've arrived at the museum, friends. I just wanted you to hear that story because when we walk through the palace at Knossos, we will be moving from room to room in a structure with seemingly no plan to its layout, no symmetry. One can well imagine how the less civilized Greeks, at that time, thought of the palace with its hundreds of rooms as a labyrinth."

Beth allowed Paul to guide her down the steps of the bus and into the lobby of the museum. It was easier to be led. Paul would know the way out of the labyrinth. The labyrinth didn't matter. This was just another day to get through. A diller a dollar. One step. Then the next. How many days was it till home? One step. Then the next. Beth shivered.

I'm too tired to walk, the screamer moaned.

"Are you cold?" Paul asked. "Perhaps you'd better put on your sweater."

Paul took the sweater from her hands and helped her into it. Then he escorted her into the museum.

Paul's helping me set one foot in front of another. I'll let him. I can listen. I will forget each moment after it passes. What does it matter what we think? We look at drawings on vases and create a whole civilization. But how right are we? We can't imagine what that civilization was like. Perhaps they didn't think like us. Who said that? That's someone else's thought. Is it from Iris's thought realm?

"I tell you their intellect is a puny thing."

It doesn't matter. What matters is one foot after the other. Jack be nimble… I move this heavy reluctant body, step by step through the day and soon this terrible trip will be over and I can go home to New York and get into my bed and never get out.

"But you, you're not self pitying."

"Have we met somewhere?"

"We've given up balance. But for what?"

They were heading up the stairs to the room with the frescoes that had been taken from Knossos. Who said that? It must have been Paul.

Beth entered the room on Paul's arm. "Look, my dear, at how remarkable these frescoes are, really quite different from anything we've seen so far." He stopped in front of one.

"I am well aware how peculiar my ideas can sound to most people."

"Look at the Madonna. Look at her dignified suffering. She's so human and yet so transcendent."

Beth looked at the picture of the slim-hipped boy with the Minoan codpiece, wearing a fantastic crown of lilies and peacock feathers on his head.

Eric would love these, she thought.

"I'm drawn to you. I'd like to get to know you better."

Liar.

Eric has deserted you like Matthew and Alicia deserted you. Like your father deserted you. Like the gods deserted you.

"I can't help it. I can't help myself. I'm like a man possessed."

"That's called *The Prince with the Lilies*. Whatever it was he was leading is now lost to all but the imagination," Paul said. "It's from the palace at Knossos, fifteen hundred years before Christ."

"He's beautiful," Beth said. Hank was beautiful, slim hipped.

"Don't you feel anything for me?"

"Come look at *The Ladies in Blue*," Paul said, steering her toward the fresco.

"Look at the Madonna."

Beth allowed herself to be led till she stood before the partially restored fresco with the blue background. Little boy blue... How happy the ladies seemed, their black hair filled with jewels, and with bracelets and necklaces adorning their lithe figures. But what good did it do them, their momentary joy? They are long in their graves, three or four thousand years under the earth, their stories blown to dust. Ashes, ashes...

"You're allowing yourself to die too soon. It's a waste..."

"Why do they still fear death? And why do they not, at the very least, value life?"

Paul led her to a famous stone sarcophagus called *The Haghia Triadha.*

Look at the pictures. You will be safe if you look at the pictures.

Yes, yes. I can do that.

It was a scene of a bull sacrifice in honor of the dead king. Do I like this? It doesn't matter. A musician playing a double pipe was leading a procession of women. Little boy blue, come blow your horn. Look at the details, Beth. One foot in front of another. One item after another.

"But that's not the way to come to anything original..."

"Are we ourselves the great metaphor for that space in-between..."

Paul put his arm around Beth's shoulders and said, "Come, look at one more fresco..."

What is he doing? What does he want?

"...the one where men and women are taking part in a ritual sport. See," he said when they stood in front of it, "the athlete stands still, facing the wild bull as it plunges toward him. Then as it reaches him, he grasps the bull by the horns and somersaults over its back and lands behind it."

"She is hopeless. Balance is everything."

"It's a question of balance, you know, my friend."

What is Paul doing? What does he want? Jack fell down and broke his crown and Jill came tumbling after. Paul was trying to pull her out of the long dark corridor of her self into the small details of life. But that's not it. Jack be nimble, Jack be quick... I can do that. I know about the accumulation of details, heaps and piles of particulars. Life's little accretions. Jack jump over the candlestick. But I don't want to do that. There is no end to those piles. Hills. Jack and Jill went up the hill. Categories. They signify nothing. I want to stay in the corridor, stay in the dark of oblivion, stay near the screamer who understands me. Jack be nimble.

"...I've lost the sense of life. That's a terrible thing."

"We've given up balance. But for what. I can't imagine for what! I'm in despair over it."

One step in front of another. Speak. "It looks very dangerous," she said. "It's very beautiful." Jack Spratt could eat no fat...

"...you lack courage in life."

Life. His wife could eat no lean.

"Yes," Paul said. "It certainly is that."

Finally, they returned to the bus for the short ride to Knossos.

Irene told them, "The excavations at Knossos are quite extensive. We won't be able to see all of the palace."

Listen, Beth. Carefully.

"It is large, but I think what you will see will impress you greatly. We'll be there about an hour and a half."

You used to come at ten o'clock and now you come at noon.

"Because Knossos really is a maze and is difficult to find your way through, it's best if we stay together. But should anyone get separated from the group, you will find the bus exactly where we leave it."

"Beth," Paul said as the bus pulled up in the parking lot at Knossos, "if you don't feel well, I'm sure we can arrange to send you back to the ship. It's not that far."

Beth looked up at him. "I don't want to go back to the ship," she said. What an absurd idea. "I have to be here. You see, if I put one foot in front of the next, then I'll get through the day. That's the best way." A diller a dollar, a ten o'clock scholar...

"...your need, to put everything into some manageable category?"

"If I go back to the ship, I won't know what to do," her voice rose a little. "Here, I know what to do."

"...let's hear it for the instincts."

"I just follow the guide, follow you all." What makes you come so soon?

Paul looked grim. "Then, if you don't mind, I'll stick close to you."

"If you're stuck, then I'm coming unglued."

"That's perfectly fine," she told him. "I don't mind that." You used to come at ten o'clock and now you come at noon.

The group moved up some elegant steps and onto a terrace.

They knew about beauty, too, the Minoans. Look, Beth, the land is beautiful. The sheep's in the meadow... The palace is beautiful. But everything here is odd and off center.

"Our senses do not give us the whole truth..."

"...the first important deity worshipped by man everywhere is Great Mother Earth."

How strange this all is, Beth shuddered. The queen was in her counting house, counting all her money. She looked at the red columns with their black capitals, at the garishly painted walls. That's not right, not natural. Enticing. Seductive. Maze.

"She will be accompanied by a male god much later on."

"Beth, we'd better keep up with the group," Paul said, taking her by the elbow.

Why was he always intruding into her thoughts? She was trying to make sense of it all, was searching for meaning and Paul was always breaking into her thoughts pulling her this way and that way. Along came a blackbird and snipped off her nose.

"You make me sound like someone who reaches for easy answers..."

"Yes, Paul," she answered and allowed herself to be propelled after the group.

"...who pigeonholes, who wants simple solutions."

They walked up some steps and onto a terrace. The sun was bright and hot. Mary, Mary, quite contrary, how does your garden grow? The sun wants to swallow everything. Everyone. Maniacal sun.

"This is something else," Doris said, moving past Beth and Paul with a grin.

"It certainly is," her sister, Lucy, said and hurried after her. "Those ancients knew how to live. Picked the prettiest spots, too."

Little Miss Muffet sat on a tuffet.

"We're going to look at one of the storage areas, first," Irene told the group when they had once again gathered around her.

The group walked in the sun looking at the rows and rows of dug-out square holes and the lines of large earthen jars. Listen, Beth. Irene described what was kept in the storage areas. Details again. Nothing but vast containers for life's details. Is that all there is? History an aggregate of shards? The king is in his counting house counting all his money...

"He modifies the natural elements and by so doing he modifies himself."

Beth looked out at the vast area that was the old palace. Somewhere in his dark, gloomy cellar the Minotaur had once waited for his prey. Theseus had come, had killed the beast, had found his way out, then had abandoned his helpmate. The sun was glaring across the gaudy surface of the red and black pillars. Along came a spider and sat down beside her.

"I'm in despair over it."

Beth stared out across one of the many terraces at the sun-saturated landscape. Wait a minute. There was Iris! Yes, it was Iris and she was looking away from Beth and out at something or someone. Iris obviously didn't see Beth. It upset Beth that Iris didn't see her.

"But will they choose? Will she, for instance. She is a poet. Will she?"

"Come," Irene said to the group. "We're going into the east wing to see the throne room and the private chambers of the King and Queen and even a bathroom with its remarkable plumbing arrangement."

"Is she even interested?"

"You'll see some of the same frescoes that you saw in the Museum. Don't be confused. They're only copies.

"Is she even interested..."

"I'm in despair over it."

"There is much restoration here which is controversial. The original frescoes, most of them, are now in the museum where they are protected from the elements." And Irene set off at a good pace and the 4-M Group set out at a good clip behind her.

"Come, Beth," Paul urged, taking her arm.

"Wait," Beth said, pulling away from him. "I have to go to the bathroom."

Clever. He can't follow you there.

"She is a poet…"

Paul stopped, uncertain.

"It's near the entrance where we came in," Beth said, gesticulating in the general direction of where they had entered.

"You're such an adventurous soul. You can't imagine how much I admire you, admire the way you go out and confront the world…"

"I'll go to the bathroom and then afterwards I'll go sit on the bus. I'm a bit under the weather today," she said, backing away from him. "See you later," and she turned around and ran back the way the group had come, and away from where she had spotted Iris.

Paul watched Beth go. He felt uncertain. Should he follow her? No question, she was better off on the bus. What had happened to her? Last night sitting with Eric she had looked so happy, like someone falling in love. He had watched her across the dining room with a sense of contentment. Eric would be wonderful for her, he had decided then, and had felt relieved. His task with her was ending. Eric would help her the rest of the way.

But now, watching Beth run back toward the bus, he was anxious and bewildered. What should he do? She was so disturbed today, so tense, so near the breaking point. What had happened to her?

It is the beginning of her crisis.
Should I follow her?
It is her struggle now. Wait.

Beth ran. Away from Paul. Away from the group. Away from where she had seen Iris. She would turn back as soon as the 4-M group had left the storage area. Paul didn't follow her, much to her relief. It was a piece of brilliance to tell him that she was returning to the bus. That must have eased his mind.

"...admire the way you go out and confront..."

Beth ran until she could no longer see her tour group, then stopped not quite sure where she was. She stood against an ocher wall behind a red pillar, her heart beating wildly, and waited. She had to see Iris, had to speak to her.

When Beth felt she had delayed long enough, she slid out from behind the pillar and looked about. She saw another tour group in the direction that she wanted to go but decided it was best to avoid them and to find another route to the terrace where she had seen Iris.

Be clever, Beth. Be clever.

"You can't imagine how much I admire you..."

"She is a poet..."

She turned and hurried in a parallel direction to where she had come from. Nothing to worry about, she assured herself. She was out of doors and couldn't get lost.

Beth moved up a flight of stone stairs, walked along a wide street or corridor and kept her eyes open for Iris. But had she really seen her? Of course, she had. She wasn't blind. She had seen her.

The screamer inside her gut said, Scream!

Beth ascended a flight of stairs and found herself on a terrace and there, to her relief, was Iris.

"Iris," she called. "I'm here."

"…the threshold in our times is like a thin veil…"

Iris turned around and looked at her with surprise. "What are you doing here?" she said. "This is no place for you. You don't belong here. There is a terrible beast here. You shouldn't have come."

"They stir around now in sub-matter."

"Such ghastly beasts lie in that realm."

Beth felt devastated by Iris's reprimand. "But don't you understand," she said, "I had to come. I have to put one foot down after the other. This is on the schedule. I have only six more days till home."

"…to put everything into some manageable category?"

Iris called out to someone standing out of Beth's view. "Old friend, she is here. I have told her it is a terrible mistake to be here. This is no place for her."

"Will humanity turn them loose?"

The familiar voice of Iris's companion spoke from the shadows. "She is not like you, Iris. She is from a different time. The gods no longer compel her. She is here because she needs to be here, chooses to be here."

And while Beth tried to make sense of his remarks, out trotted a figure that caused Beth's breathing to stop momentarily and her heart to skip a beat and then pound rapidly. For the first time, Iris's companion came out into the direct sunlight. He was huge and handsome with a beautifully muscled and naked torso, with reddish ringlets for hair and emerald green large eyes. But from the waist down he was horse. He had the lower body of a white stallion. In his left hand he carried a bow and arrow.

"She absolutely breaks the damn words open and all your senses with them."

"...a thin veil fluttering between us and the spiritual world. Things waft through and hover..."

"But you're a centaur," Beth cried out in alarm. "How can that be? I never realized that before. How can that be?"

"What is the matter with her?" Iris asked.

The handsome green-eyed man-beast trotted toward Beth, stopped a few feet from her and looked directly down at her.

She began to back away in fear.

"...need to categorize, to find large boxes..." *"Fuzzy thinking."* *"Things waft through..."*

"It's all right," the centaur told Beth. "I'm your friend. What harm can come from me?"

"Centaurs are mythological beasts and are not real."

"...tears apart..."

"What is reality, my friend?" he asked in the rich deep voice that had become so familiar to her. "Only what is common to your herd, to your times, to the organization of your senses. That constitutes reality. I am not mythological. Nor were the griffins that you see on the walls in the throne room of this palace mythological, nor the dragons of other cultures. Nor is the Minotaur unreal. Nor the beasts within you unreal."

"Your dreams seem to be a breakthrough..."

"I'm going mad. One step in front of another. One step."
Beth began to inch back but found herself against a wall. "I
shall die here, disappear into a hole or shatter into a thousand
pieces."

"They have no courage, no honor, little pride."

"What is wrong with her, my friend?" Iris asked the
centaur.

"She has no concept in her reality for me as a reality."

*"...wants simple solutions..." "...can't you see that there is
something other than this..." "...veil..."*

"But how curious. Does she not look at you and see in you
herself?"

"Myself?" Beth's voice grew dangerously shrill. Where were
the others? Her group? Any group?

"Inside you're a scared rabbit..." "...just fuzzy thinking..."

"But, Beth," Iris walked toward her with a questioning
look on her face, "surely you recognize before you, in all his
magnificence, the human being?"

"He's not human. He's half beast."

"As you are. As I am. He is striving to grow out of his animal self, as you are, as I am. Surely that is still known. Surely
it is known that with his great bow, his great arrow, he can
aim toward the future, as you do, as I do."

"...before one thing becomes another..."

"No, no!"

"You pull away from life and all its marvelous experiences."

From behind Iris at the far end of the terrace Beth suddenly saw Alicia standing there in her loafers and jeans and
Mickey Mouse T-shirt. Alicia was looking with wonder and
delight at the centaur. Beth tried to call to her but there was
no voice in her. Even the screamer was silent.

Beth broke past Iris and the centaur and ran as fast as she

could toward Alicia, but Alicia had turned around and was walking slowly away. Beth ran after her and tried to call Alicia by name but nothing came out of her throat. Now scream, she pleaded inside herself. Now scream! The air had become thick as glue. Beth could barely move through it. Alicia strode ahead, seemingly unaware of her mother's attempt to reach her. She moved purposefully along the walkways of the palace.

Suddenly, Alicia turned to her right and plunged down the stairs. She disappeared out of sight. Beth finally reached the stairs and rushed down them after her. She couldn't see Alicia. One foot in front of another. One foot... Beth ran through a crooked corridor and came to a room that had been used for bathing. A group was listening to a guide who was speaking to them in German. A few heads turned as Beth stumbled into the room.

Beth stopped to ask a woman standing in the back of the group if she had seen a young dark-haired woman in blue jeans and a Mickey Mouse T-shirt pass through here. The woman shrugged her shoulders but her companion told Beth in excellent English that no one other than their tour group had come by since they had arrived.

Beth said, "I'm sorry," and ran into a room that must once have been a small shrine holding clay votive figures. No one was there. She turned, desperate to find Alicia, ran past a lustral basin, then past colonnades in a corridor. She was lost. But she didn't care. Her every cell was centered on finding her daughter. She stumbled into a room that had a double ax design on its wall. Beth hurried out another doorway. She tried to call her daughter's name but that name was stuck in her throat. She entered a room with columns and with frescoes of dolphins, fish, sea urchins. But Alicia was nowhere to be seen.

Beth was aware of more stairs. She was descending. How many flights did this palace have? How many rooms? She had to catch up with Alicia. She had to tell her to beware, that this palace was a maze and that she could get lost, that it was dangerous here.

Why dangerous?

Because of the Minotaur. Don't you know that? Deep in the bowels of this palace is a Minotaur with the head of a large bull and the body of a man. Like the centaur, she told her frantic mind.

No, not like the centaur. The centaur is striving out of the bestial toward his own humanity. The Minotaur is struggling away from his humanity toward his own bestiality.

Yes. Good. Write that down.

Beth was descending, down, down. Too many flights! She shuddered and slowed her pace. Weren't there only supposed to be four flights here at the palace? Where am I? Where is everyone? There are no groups here, only winding stairs, only this close suffocating air, only these old bones beneath my feet. No, no. They are stones. Bones. Stones. Suddenly she heard a cry from way down below her, from the bowels of the earth. It was a terrible but familiar wail.

"Mother, where are you? It's so dark here. I'm afraid. Help."

With a miraculous burst of will, Beth found her voice. She screamed, "I'm coming to you, baby! Don't give up. Don't let go. I'm coming." Beth flew down the staircase as fast as her legs would carry her. Once, she slipped and slid on her rear end down several steps, but she picked herself up and plummeted down again, all the time calling, "I'm coming, baby. Hang on. I'm coming to you."

Beth tripped when she reached the bottom and landed on

her knees and hands. She stood up once again. It was gray and dark where she stood but she could see.

"Mother, Mother." The voice was closer. Beth rushed toward the sound, heart beating, down a dark corridor. To her relief she came to an open door and almost fell through it.

Beth's heart nearly stopped.

"You're deep, so terribly deep. It's a place that as a man I suspect I'm afraid to go. But, oh God, I admire it..."

The large room was filled with a brown light trickling down from a dirty window near the ceiling. The walls were earthen, and jagged rocks protruded from them. The floor, too, was earthen and strewn over it was old, soiled straw. In the corner of the filthy room, whose fetid stench almost gagged Beth, stood a large man, dressed in skins. His head and neck were the head and neck of a gigantic bull with two huge horns. From the corners of his mouth saliva dripped and glistened.

"Oh, my dear God," Beth whispered.

"...this is the crux, kid, you don't pay attention to what's going on inside. Inside you're a scared rabbit." "You pull away from life and all its marvelous experiences." "You've run all over the world just to get away from dealing with your own life."

In his claw-like grasp, the beast held Alicia. She was white with fear and struggling to free herself from his grasp.

"Mother, Mother, help me please."

"Mother, why can't you see that there is something other than this material world? Why is that so hard for you? Why are you so stubborn?" "If we come here after supper, we maybe can pick up a couple of soldiers, what do you say, chickie..." "But 'we always hurt the ones we love.'" "Oh, it's dark."

Beth stood there paralyzed. All the terror she had ever experienced in her life was suddenly a horrible, deformed shape in front of her. This was a nightmare beyond any nightmare she had ever dreamed. He was the archetype of ugliness, the epitome of foulness. He was evil made flesh, a mockery of everything human. And she, Beth, was afraid from her short gray hair down to the red nails of her toes. The screamer screamed in her solar plexus, or was it she herself? Screaming and screaming and screaming!

"Mother, please! Help!"

"Why is that so hard for you..." "But will they choose?...She is a poet. Will she?"

Suddenly, something broke inside of her and a geyser of rage roared through her veins, unleashing a wrath of will as if it came not from her but from the earth itself. Beth felt it spreading through her limbs with amazing power and she bellowed in a voice that she barely recognized as her own. "Let my child go!"

The beast whirled, loosening his grip on Alicia. Alicia slipped out of his claws and backed away against the far wall.

"Who is it that comes to deny me my tribute?" The beast turned about until he finally located Beth. He fixed a hard bull eye on her.

He's near-sighted, Beth noted coldly. From behind her she could hear pounding on the staircase.

"So it's you," the beast growled. "I've been expecting you. For years I have waited for you to come. And now I have you."

"Let my daughter go."

"Why should I do that? She will make a splendid little appetizer. And you will be the main dish. Come to me, my love."

"You're no longer a menace in my world," Beth told him, focusing her rage on him like a laser. "You were killed years ago by Theseus."

"Theseus, a cheating human whom history calls a hero." The beast spat and the stench almost made Beth lose her nerve. She could hear the banging sounds on the stairs grow louder.

"I never die. How can I die when I am resurrected in each human life? I live forever!" The bull beast once again turned and lumbered toward Alicia.

"No!" Alicia screamed.

The Minotaur laughed. The pounding was now in the corridor.

"Don't touch her, you foul beast! Come to me first." And Beth ran toward him, fists clenched.

"Wait, Elizabeth! You will need this."

Beth whirled about and there was the centaur with Iris on his back. He threw the bow and an arrow toward her. She caught both in mid-air.

The beast was slowly and cruelly stalking Alicia who slid along the far wall trying to keep away from him.

Carefully Beth placed the arrow in the bow. Carefully she aimed and let loose the arrow. It shrieked through the air and struck the back of the Minotaur's bull head.

The beast lurched around screaming his fury and started lumbering toward Beth.

The centaur threw her another arrow. Beth caught it.

With meticulous deliberation, she took aim again. This time the arrow pierced the monster's neck. Blood burst from his throat like a fountain. The Minotaur fell to the ground. Dead. Beth walked over to him and stood looking down at him.

The centaur galloped toward Alicia. Iris leaned down, gave Alicia her hand and Alicia leapt up on the back of the centaur. The three galloped toward Beth who stood staring down at the beast. His face was contorted in death, and putrid blood flooded the ground and around Beth's sneakers. She stared at the blood with cool curiosity, the rage seeping slowly out of her. She had killed the Minotaur.

"Come, Beth, the centaur said. "We must leave this place of death. Climb on my back."

Beth shook her head. "You have two on your back. Lead on. I'll follow you."

"Grab my tail."

"She's brave. Like the fabled women of Amazon," Iris said, smiling down at Beth.

"Mother, you saved me. Thank you." Alicia looked at her with love in her eyes.

"I owed you that," Beth answered.

"Mother, don't mourn me," Alicia told her. "Your anguish gives me more pain than I can endure. I am near you always. Know that. Remember me with joy. We'll meet again."

"Yes," Beth said, "yes." And her eyes filled with tears of happiness.

"Away we go," the centaur said and began trotting up the corridor to the staircase.

Beth followed, jogging behind him. He was swift and she could not hold onto his tail. But she kept them in sight. Up and up the stairs they climbed. Up and up. It was a hard climb and Beth was becoming winded.

"Wait," she called out once as she saw the distance between her and the others widen. But they didn't hear her. She tried to increase her speed. Once, the centaur left the stairs to gallop through rooms and corridors with strange spiral wall frescoes and shafts of light pouring down from openings in the ceilings. Beth was out of breath. She couldn't keep up.

She came to another set of stairs and wasn't sure which way the centaur had gone. Was it up the stairs or down the corridor? She thought she heard sounds of voices above her so she decided on the stairs. She entered a room and there was a group of English tourists standing and listening to their guide. On one wall was the fresco called *The Ladies in Blue.* And on another there was *The Toreador* fresco. Copies, she reminded herself. There was no sign of Iris, Alicia or the centaur. For a moment she felt agonizing disappointment. Then the moment passed.

No, Beth. This is right. They have to go back to their world and you have to go back to yours.

"Which way is out?" she asked an English lady standing on the edge of the group.

"That way, dearie," the lady said, "at least that's the way we came."

Beth thanked her and went out a door. She took a few more turns, climbed some stairs. Soon she was outside and in the bright sunlight. How welcome the sunlight was. She looked about her. Now, where have I gotten to? She glanced at her watch. Oh, dear. She should have been back at the bus ten minutes ago. Now which way was it?

She stood there trying to make up her mind which direction to head in when she heard someone calling her name. It was Bill Orbach, their tour escort from Smith and Smith.

"There you are. We've got the troops out looking for you," he said.

"Sorry," she said, walking toward him.

"Well, there are three other people still to round up," he said with a smile and a shake of the head. "You haven't seen anyone from our group have you?"

"No, sorry," she answered.

"Look at you, you look a bit bruised. Are you hurt?"

Beth looked down at her blue jeans. The knees were filthy as were her hands. "I fell down some stairs," she told him.

"Nothing broken, I hope," he said.

She smiled. "Nothing broken."

"Look," he said, pointing off in a direction, "the bus is that way. Stop at the restroom and wash up. You look like you landed on your face. In the meantime, I'll see if I can find our lost ladies and gent."

On the way to the parking lot, Beth stopped at the ladies restroom. She was surprised at the dirt on her face. After she had finished washing her hands and face, she scrubbed at her pants knees and at her rear. I'll be dry in five minutes in the sun, she told herself as she appraised herself in the mirror. Her sweater had only a little dirt on it that she was able to rub off.

Except for the scrape on your right cheek you look well enough, calm enough, considering you just killed the Minotaur. My God, I killed the Minotaur. She grinned at herself in the mirror. No matter how crazy it all was, she had killed the Minotaur and she felt elated.

When she neared the bus she could see Paul peering out of the window. She climbed on board and called out, "Sorry, everyone, but I think I got lost."

"That's easy enough in this place," someone down front answered her.

"My dear, I was worried when I didn't find you here waiting," Paul told her as she sat down next to him.

"Sorry," she told him, "I decided to take a look at the palace after all, and went back." She gave him a dazzling smile. "I'm feeling much better. Something about this place," she told him. "Now am I on the right bus for Phaestos?"

"You are," he stared and stared at her. "Are you sure?"

"Haven't felt this good in a long time," she said and squeezed his hand.

Paul settled back in his chair. "Well, I had hoped to persuade you to get on the other bus and to go back to the ship for lunch and a leisurely afternoon. Apparently there is no need."

"I wouldn't miss Phaestos for the world. Particularly when we have to go straight across the island through mountains and valleys to get there. Now where is this box lunch? I'm ravenous."

After the bus got under way, Bill distributed the boxed lunches. Irene once more took the microphone to speak to the hardy souls who had chosen to take this additional excursion. "Friends, I'm only going to speak for a few moments. The views will be gorgeous, I think, and more eloquent than I am. But let me tell you only a few facts. We will be traveling around mountains, through gorges, until we finally arrive at our destination on the southern shore of Crete. The history of Crete is varied, with many migrations or conquests. There was the Neolithic period, the Minoan, the Mycenaean, the Greek, the Roman, the Byzantine, the Arabic, the Venetian, the Turkish, the Cretan-Greek state, the German conquest…"

She inhaled audibly and several people laughed. "I'm sure I left some period out, but you see how long the history here is and how many wars and battles and revolutions there have been. It all looks very peaceful and even idyllic, but the battles here have been bloody.

"A few words about Phaestos. It is the second major palace after Knossos. It is not as large and we will only have an hour there, but it is worth seeing. The excavations there have been done by Italian archaeologists. We know that there were two palaces and probably both were destroyed by earthquake..."

Beth listened with one ear to the description of Phaestos. She turned to watch the landscape with its cultivated and terraced mountains, its steep gorges. She found the land bathed in a radiant light and it gave her a comfortable and warm feeling to be traveling through the ancient winding roads. She didn't notice when Irene stopped talking. She was aware that Paul had fallen asleep next to her. After a while she herself fell asleep and woke only moments before the bus parked in Phaestos.

During the tour of Phaestos, Beth stuck close to the guide, listening attentively. She had no need to wander off. She did not look for Iris or her companion. She did not expect to see them there.

On the ride back to the ship, she listened around her at the various quiet conversations. Paul, obviously tired from the long day, fell quickly asleep. Beth didn't sleep nor did she think much on the long ride back. She merely watched the scenery contentedly.

They returned to the ship by four in the afternoon and it set sail immediately for Reggio di Calabria in southern Italy. They would be at sea all day tomorrow. As soon as Beth returned to her room, she took out her notebook and began to write in it everything that had happened to her from her dream that morning until Bill found her in Knossos. She wrote until dinnertime, had a pleasant dinner with Daring and two couples she didn't know too well. After dinner she returned to her writing tasks until she was bleary-eyed. She went up on deck to get a little fresh air and to watch the Aegean roll by. After half an hour, she returned to her room, showered and went to sleep. She didn't dream. She hadn't expected to.

Beth spent the early part of the morning completing the record of her adventures in Knossos. She wrote without editorializing or embroidering, as factually as she could remember the events. When she was satisfied that she had written everything down to the best of her recollection, she closed the notebook, put it in a drawer, and went up on the deck.

Again, sun and the promise of warm weather. Again, a cool morning breeze. Beth dropped her tote, which contained a book, postcards and stationary, on a deck chair, flung her yellow cardigan on top of the tote and then began a leisurely walk around the deck. She needed the exercise. She needed to clear her head, needed to come into the morning, into the day, the first after she had killed the Minotaur. She needed to come into reality.

She stopped to look over the rail at the frilly green water. Perhaps she was dead, had died in Knossos, and was now crossing the river Styx or its modern equivalent, sailing out to that unknown land of the dead, accompanied only by memories. Could she indeed be crossing the last waters? If so, she was calm. If so, the sea was beautiful, a vast and age-wrinkled transit that was carrying her off to that other world. If so, what was she taking with her of any worth? A notebook. A letter from Mattie. What else? Her books of poetry, placed aboard ship by the hand of some unknown organizer at Smith and Smith. Some pretty but inexpensive bits of jewelry...

"Well, Beth, you look perfectly fine considering..."

"What?" Beth was startled out of her contemplation by a familiar voice.

"Considering you had a spill at Knossos. Nothing broken or sprained, I hope." Doris, bundled in her coat, was smiling up at Beth from her deck chair, strategically placed out of the sun along the narrow side deck of the ship.

"No, no, I'm perfectly fine," Beth said.

"Sorry if I startled you, my dear. You did look lost in thought. Has the Muse struck you?"

"No, just enjoying the ocean. See you later," and Beth moved on.

"See you later," Doris sunk into her chair and put her sunglasses back on.

Beth continued her walk down the narrow deck. She had just moved past the lifeboats, heading toward the pool, when she heard a familiar voice.

"Well, I think its very poor planning, really very poor planning, not even to spend a single night in Crete," Mrs. Green complained to Daring. "Yesterday was a terrible strain, seeing both sides of the island in one day," she said. "Don't they think the Minoan civilization important enough to give it at least two days?"

Beth smiled at them and walked on as Daring rolled her eyes and said, "I suppose they do the best they can."

Beth finally stopped in the bow where several people were taking photographs.

"Look, look," someone shouted. "There are dolphins following the ship."

Beth hurried to the side of the ship, leaned over the railing and peered toward the stern. There they were! Four, no, five of them cavorting in the wake of the ship. Beth caught her breath. They're acknowledging us, acknowledging our right to the sea, welcoming our own big metal, black smoke-spouting, pollution-making ship. They're affirming us as a specie, and they want affirmation back, and acknowledgment.

Exhilarated, Beth watched the frolicking dolphins, then walked to the stern hoping for a better view.

"Of course, everything we know of their civilization comes either from their palaces or from their tombs," Barbara Churchill's voice hammered through Beth's pleasure.

She quickly moved past her and the Winstons until she found the deck chair where she had deposited her things. She leaned out over the rail and watched until the dolphins turned away.

Slipping into her cardigan, Beth sat down near the pool. One by one people returned to their previous occupations. Some wrote postcards or in, what looked like, travel diaries. Some read. A few slept in the sun. A few sat at tables drinking coffee, talking cozily with companions made on the journey. Everyone seemed glad for the day of rest, the day at sea. Across the pool from Beth, Lolly Parkington was rubbing suntan lotion or sunscreen on her mother's back. The older woman, Ellen Parkington, looked wrinkled and vulnerable in her bathing suit and straw hat, and Beth's heart went out to the spunky little lady. Lolly, too, was in her bathing suit, and Beth noticed two other women in theirs.

Hardy souls, thought Beth, and pulled the sweater around her. There was a cool breeze. No doubt the sun on bare skin felt warm. She had no intention of finding out.

Beth closed her eyes and leaned back, letting the sun caress her face with warmth and light. She was feeling remarkably well and the reason was simple. And strange. She had killed the Minotaur. Somehow in Knossos Beth had passed through a crisis, the way one does in illness. And Beth had killed the Minotaur. It had happened. She didn't question the fact of it. Not exactly. She knew something had been lifted off of her, some heavy blanket of sorrow, of loss, of madness, of meaninglessness. And she felt a deep sense of gratitude.

She was not ready to think too much about Eric. That, too, was falling into its proper place. Beth had been terribly needy. He, too, had been needy in his own way. They had comforted each other for a couple of days and for a night. That was okay. She didn't have to give it a significance beyond that, didn't have to feel either anger or expectation. She didn't have to think about it at all. Not today.

Lying on the deck chair, the sun warming her head and hands and the smell of ocean air deliciously around her made her think of Alicia and of their time together in Collioure. They had gone to southern France, near the sea, just north of the Spanish border, to give Alicia a time of rest after a difficult chemo treatment. Beth could look back on it today with poignancy, but without that dreaded sense of loss.

Beth and Alicia were sitting on deck chairs in front of one of the several cafés along the beach, drinking café noir and watching the soldiers who were stationed in the town go through sea rescue maneuvers.

"Who do they expect to invade this town, do you think?" Alicia asked with a grin. "Hannibal?"

"Probably, with a boatload of elephants," Beth said.

"Don't laugh, kiddo, Hannibal did come through here and with his elephants."

"You're making that up."

Alicia shook her head with an amused look in her dark eyes.

"But how did they get them here? Surely not by boat?"

"Beats me. Look, they're starting all over again. They're inflating their rafts. What is this, the third time?"

"The fourth, I think. It's ludicrous, isn't it? I mean why are they worried about an invasion by sea? If someone attacks this little town it will come from the air. They'll drop men by parachute after they level the town with bombs."

"Probably," Alicia answered, sipping her café noir. "Everything is obsolete now, isn't it?"

"How's that?"

"I mean in this time of airplanes and missiles," Alicia said, setting down her cup on its small saucer, "everything that was built to fortify this town in the past is meaningless—the castle, the fortress, the walls. All the old dependable values are gone. Who will they shoot at with their bows and arrows, or their rifles, the sea gulls?"

"Sad, isn't it? They built those edifices of rock to last forever and now they are, like dinosaurs, extinct. Everyone of them. Yet there they stand, heavy with age, solid as time, with dead eyes waiting, waiting." Beth looked to her left at the old fortress church.

"I wonder what they would have thought of the twentieth century?" Alicia asked, as she rubbed more sunscreen on her pale legs.

"Who, dear?"

"The Majorcan kings who summered here."

"They'd probably hate it."

"Why do you think that?" Alicia looked over at her mother. How thin she is. How I miss her long, thick black hair.

"Because all the old recognizable virtues are gone, such as chivalry, such as facing your enemy if you are trying to kill him, such as the faith in a person's word, little items like that."

"You always hated lies, didn't you, Mom? I mean you desperately needed people to be up front with you."

"Did I, Alicia? Really?"

"Yeah, really. When we kids fibbed, as kids will, you were always at a loss, really quite disoriented." Her dark brown eyes looked enormous in her small face. "It wasn't easy to get you to trust again. It was as if the ground had been removed from under your feet."

"That bad, huh?"

"Yeah, that bad," Alicia closed her eyes. "Tell me," she said, "if Dad had lived, do you think you could have forgiven him? Or do you think he would have gone off with that girl?"

Beth's back arched slightly, her lips pressed up against her teeth. "You knew?"

"Yeah, we knew." Alicia opened her eyes and looked directly at her mother.

"How did you find out?"

"Dad wasn't always careful with his phone calls."

"Oh."

"You were terribly, terribly hurt?"

"Oh, baby, do you really need to know?"

"Yes, you see I loved Daddy very, very much, and it was terrible for us too."

"Becky knew, too?"

"Yes, Becky knew, too. We had to console each other. We didn't want you to know that we knew."

"Why not, Alicia?"

" I'm not sure. We thought it would cause you more pain. So we consoled each other. When people you love hurt other people you love, it's...it's, well... its indigestible."

"I can't get rid of the anger yet, Alicia. I won't tell you I can. But I wouldn't take away your love for your father for anything in this world. You girls were the most important people in the world to him."

"I can forgive him, then?"

"He didn't injure you, honey. He injured me," Beth said.

"You're wrong, Mother. He injured us all. But 'we always hurt the ones we love.'" Alicia sang the last phrase.

"Yes, we do," And Beth knew she was speaking about them now.

"But we never stop loving them."

"No, we never stop loving them." Beth reached out and put her hand over Alicia's.

"Look, they're pushing those rafts out to sea again." Alicia sat up. "Aren't they cute in their tight wet-suits. If we come here after supper, we maybe can pick up a couple of soldiers, what do you say, chickie."

"I say why only a couple, why not the whole platoon."

About an hour before lunch, Beth decided to return to her room to wash a few clothes. But when she entered her room, she went instead to the drawer by her bed, pulled out the notebook and reread what she had written there.

It was then she decided to speak to Paul. The account was accurate. It wasn't that. It was that she was bathing in an afterglow she had no right to expect would last. She needed some thoughts, a context to put it all in when she finally said to herself, You did what?

I killed the Minotaur.

That's insane.

Nevertheless, I killed the Minotaur. That's what I think I did.

It's not rational.

Not everything in the world is rational.

No? Then how will you live in this world? Clear thinking is all you have.

By keeping my options open.

You're nuts, Beth.

No, I'm a poet.

Beth took lunch on deck and it was there that she found Paul. He told her that he had spent the morning catching up on his correspondence and his laundry. When Beth asked if she could speak to him privately, to tell him what had happened to her yesterday, he said, "Yes."

After lunch, Paul followed Beth into the Poseidon lounge. Yesterday, he had been convinced that she would not be able to finish the trip. He had been alarmed at how distracted she had become, how ill she had seemed. He had been afraid for her, and sick at his own role in her sufferings.

But Annie had said that she was passing through her crisis.

And when he stood there at Knossos and watched her run off, all he could hang onto was his faith in the ever-present help of the spiritual world.

And now he was more than a little curious to know what had happened after she had left him.

Beth selected a table in the far corner along the side of the bandstand. Only one other couple was in the lounge and they were absorbed in their own intimate conversation.

"Paul, this is embarrassing, but I want to tell you what happened between Eric and myself."

"That's not necessary," Paul said.

"Yes, it is, or you won't understand what happened to me yesterday and I would like you to understand. I'm telling you this before I give you my notebook to read, so you'll comprehend better my dreams and my...what happened yesterday. I don't want to ask your opinion of all of this," she gestured at the notebook that was sitting between them on the table, "without putting you clearly in the picture."

"Then, of course."

So Beth told him what had transpired between Eric and herself. When she finished she handed him her notebook and asked him to begin with her account of Ephesus where she had encountered Iris and to read all the way to the end.

Paul read slowly, now and again asking her to decipher a word.

He barely looked up when she left the table or when she returned with the waiter who carried their two cappuccinos on his tray. When Paul put the notebook down on the table, he folded his hands, and looked at Beth.

The ever-present help of the spiritual world. How remarkable.

"Well?" she finally asked. "What do you think? I mean what do you make of it all?"

"Oh, there's much that can be made of it. But what's primary, I should think, is how you feel today. You seem to be amazingly well. You look as if someone had taken a cross from your back and a shadow from your face. Not very original metaphors, I must admit, but you understand what I mean."

"Yes, I do feel incredible, light as light. I haven't felt this...well, healthy in years." She leaned in toward him. "Maybe it's foolish to say this out loud because this euphoria may all be temporary. But since I faced and killed the Minotaur, I feel like a new person. And with his death went all the terrible anxieties, guilt, sadness, anger I've carried around for years."

"Beth, what do you want from me?"

"I want to know what you think?" She sat back in her chair and stared at him.

"Because I have some odd ideas?"

"The honest answer to that is, 'Yes', Paul, and because you talk about your dead wife as if she were still with you, because you believe in some sort of non-physical reality. I guess that's most of it. No, there's something more. Despite the fact that I've always considered such beliefs ridiculous, you seem to me perfectly sane, perfectly normal. And I, with all my armor of skepticism, with all my earth-rootedness, have been nearly insane for years."

"Of course," he said, "I can't do more than hazard a few guesses."

"That's all I ask."

"Shall we start then with Knossos?"

"Yes. I killed the Minotaur there." Beth looked him steadily in the eye. "Of course, that's crazy. I know. But right now I'm as certain of that as I am of you sitting opposite me. How?"

"I beg your pardon?"

"How? What did happen in Knossos? I killed the Minotaur. A centaur tossed me his bow and arrow and I shot two arrows and killed it. I also know that the Minotaur and the centaur are beasts out of mythology and are not real. And that I can barely catch a ball without dropping it. Nor have I ever in my entire life held a bow in my hands nor shot an arrow. Yet I did it all, perfectly. Can you explain it to me?" Paul heard her voice quiver.

When she seemed calm once more, Paul said to her, "I can give you some ideas about what happened in Knossos. Mind you, I'm not saying this is exactly what happened, but let me give you something to consider. If you like."

"Please."

"In our times the veil between our world and a spiritual realm is very thin. Many things catapult us, not into the spiritual world proper, but into a border region between the two worlds. A realm we must first traverse after death."

"Okay," Beth said.

"In that border world lie the beasts of our own making."

"What do you mean, the beasts of our own making?" Beth picked up her coffee cup, then set it down again because her hands were shaking.

"Call them our own demons. You're a poet, Beth. You can understand this. In that border world, all ideas have substance. Ideas are not simply pale images drifting around in our brain or psyche, but actualities. Each thought is a being. Each of us, during our earthly sojourn, creates a beast or demon that belongs to him or her. That beast is the sum total of all our hatreds, our fears, the undeserved angers we vent at others, our doubts and uncertainties. In a land that might be called analogous to the one you call your imagination the Minotaur exists, and you did battle with him. And won."

"You mean the Minotaur belonged to me."

"Oh, yes. And you killed him. And you may have to kill him again and again. Oh, perhaps not so literally, so dramatically."

He took a sip of his near-cold coffee. "What I'm trying to say is that in the realm of the psyche, or what we old-fashioned ones still call the soul, you fought a battle just as real as any ever fought in all the wars of mankind."

"You're saying I fought a battle in my imagination."

"Yes, I am saying that. When you enter your own subconscious, or unconscious, you enter a spiritual realm, a realm not contained merely in your own mind, but an objective realm. It's something a poet can understand. How else create something that touches another? You crossed a boundary and experienced the pictures that belong to the soul battle, and you experienced them in all reality. Just as the ancients did when they described adventures and wars, for instance, as Homer did in the Odyssey."

"So when I write or create, I draw from this objective realm of the imagination?"

"Ah, when an artist is good, he can draw from there. But, of course, all art or poetry no longer comes from that realm."

"Then Alicia was just part of my imagination," Beth said. Paul heard the disappointment in her voice.

"My dear," Paul put his hand on hers, "your imagination has as much reality as this sense-perceptible world. An objective reality. I can't say that with enough emphasis. And sometimes when one is stressed the gateway to it opens.

"So I did fight the Minotaur, you think."

"Oh, yes, you did and, my dear, you won. It happened on the soul's deep ground. The emotional stress you were in pushed you over the threshold and you saw in pictures what was going on in your own soul."

She sat thinking about what he said for a moment and then asked, "Why was the battle with the Minotaur all mixed up with Alicia?"

"I think you had to fight your own beast in order to free her to move on in the spiritual realm. And you knew that. You didn't hesitate. To save one you loved, you were willing to put aside terror and act decisively. Alicia was bound to you by your grief. Now you have set her free by killing your Minotaur."

Beth felt relieved. "Yes, I can feel that. Right now I can feel the rightness of that. What I'll feel like tomorrow, I don't know. But at this moment, what you say seems right. At Knossos I found Alicia again in a way that is healthy. I can let her go and hope that we will meet again in some other reality when I, too, die." She started to giggle. "My God, I can't believe I'm saying this."

They sat silent for a while sipping coffee. Then Beth asked, "Can I ask one other question before I let you go?"

"As many as you like, my dear Beth."

"How should I look at Iris and at her companion, the centaur? They came to me over and over again. Yet I think now they will be gone for good. We're leaving Greece. I don't think they'll accompany me further."

"Let me put this in a way a poet would understand. You believe in metaphor? You believe that a picture can stand for something else?"

"Of course I do. Poetry is built around metaphor."

"Then Iris and the centaur were perhaps metaphors. Something or someone stood behind them, found this way of communicating with you."

"Like what, a Greek god?" Beth laughed a little hollowly.

"Why not? Or perhaps your own guiding genius, or to put it in more familiar terms, your guiding angel. You need only consider whether what they said makes sense and then…"

"…leave the door open?"

"Yes, that's a good beginning, to be willing to consider something other than what is already familiar. But you're an artist. Take what I'm saying merely as a possibility."

"Yes. I think I can at least leave that door open. I feel somehow that killing the Minotaur and saving Alicia has released us both from excruciating pain. I feel ready to let her go, at least from my selfish, guilt-ridden grief that has suffocated us both. I'll miss her. I'll love her always. But I can let her go now."

"And go on with your own life?"

"Yes, I think that too."

At that moment some of the stewards came into the lounge to set it up for the afternoon lecture on Etruscan Art.

"Shall we stroll on deck until the lecture begins?" Beth asked Paul as she gathered up her notebook and purse.

"I'd like that," he said, following her toward the door.

"Tell me, Paul," Beth said, "are you getting what you need from this trip?" She took his arm.

He laughed and smiled at her with great affection, "Far more than I expected." He squeezed her hand as they started up the steps.

She returned his warm smile with one of her own. "I meant, is this trip serving to stimulate ideas for your book?"

"No question. I am looking forward to getting back to work. This trip has been just what the doctor ordered. Annie knew." And he winked.

You did that well, Paul,

Thank you, my dear.

Then Paul asked Beth, "What do you intend to do about Eric?"

When they were up on the deck, walking under a cloudless sky, she answered him, "Whatever happened between Eric and myself happened when I was too ill to know what I was doing. It seems light years away, now that I have come through my crisis. He is very nice. He was very nice to me. But I don't feel he owes me anything because two needy people spent some time together on an idyllic trip."

"And vice versa?"

"Yes, that too. I'm under no obligation. I'm not sure we will ever see each other again." She stopped speaking until they had passed some people walking in the other direction. They nodded their greetings.

Paul then asked, "Isn't he supposed to meet the ship in Italy."

"So he said. But you know how things can be. It's possible he won't."

"Surely he has luggage here."

"It can be sent on to Rome. He's staying on in Europe."

Paul didn't say anything more.

Eventually the two of them joined a group of other strollers and talked companionably about the trip. At four-thirty they went down to the lounge to hear the lecture.

That night Beth had dinner with Mel and Winnie Winston, Barbara Churchill, and a couple from San Francisco. Despite an attempt on Barbara Churchill's part to turn the conversation to serious considerations of Minoan civilization, the talk that evening was gay and relaxed. Beth felt buoyant and at ease. When she fell asleep that night, she didn't dream.

When the 4-M group left the square to follow their Italian guide toward the Greco-Roman theater in Taormina, Beth broke away from the group, as others had, to stroll the long street of shops and cafés. The day had already been a full one and she felt no need to see yet another Greek theater. After all, they still had Paestum to visit tomorrow. Suddenly she was feeling very selective. The trip was nearing its end and she was filled to near bursting with all that she had seen and experienced, a bit like a French goose being prepared for pâté. How much more could she stuff into her senses?

That morning the ship had docked in Reggio di Calabria, a city located on the straits of Messina in southern Italy. The tour group had been taken to the National Museum to see the two bronze warriors that had been found off the coast at Riace in 1972. They were extraordinary. Beth studied them carefully, admired them and then blocked out everything else. The two great statues were all her mind could take in.

The 4-M travelers returned to the ship at 11 A.M. and the ship had set sail immediately for the port of Messina in Sicily. Beth had taken her lunch on deck, sitting with Doris,

Lucy, and Paul. How fond she had become of the two sisters, she realized. She would certainly ask for their addresses before they separated in four days.

The four of them watched the docking, then just before 2 P.M. two buses appeared on the shore to take the 4-M tourists up the hair-pin winding road to the quaint town of Taormina. It had, as had so many other towns they had visited on the trip, a long history of conquests and occupations. Each conquering people had left its mark on the buildings of the town. Beth listened with half an ear to the Italian guide on the bus.

To her discomfort, she had been disappointed when Eric had not boarded the ship at Reggio di Calabria. Nor had he been waiting in Messina in Sicily. Oh, well, emotions often lag behind, she reminded herself. Just because you're seeing clearly doesn't mean that your feelings have caught up with your brain as yet.

Still, she wondered if he would be aboard the ship when they returned to it later that afternoon.

Paul stood looking down at the Greco-Roman theater in Taormina. Ocean stretched around it and to the left. Mount Etna, surrounded by a large white shawl of snow, loomed ahead and to the right. Paul was tired, yet he felt a great sense of satisfaction. The trip had enlivened him inwardly in a way that he knew had been just right, for all that it had been unexpected. Elizabeth Layton, whom the gods had placed in his path, seemed to have come through her crisis recovered. Whatever role he played—he hoped more for good than bad—was now over.

All through the trip he had looked and listened and thought. He had taken no notes. He hadn't needed to. But deep in his heart he was fired with enthusiasm, a low, long, burning desire to finish his book, to reinvolve himself in his spiritual-philosophic society, to renew old friendships, to visit and invite his nephew Barney and his family. All in all it was good that he had come. No years you are given should be wasted, he thought.

Not a single day, Annie said.

You are right, as usual, my love.

Now describe to me what you are seeing with your earthly eyes.

Beth strolled down Corso Umberto which was lined with cafés and shops of all kinds. She went in and out of stores looking at jewelry and at linens and leather goods. She purchased some postcards of Mount Etna flaring up behind the theater in Taormina, felt a twinge of guilt for having missed seeing Etna from the theater, but not enough to make her decide to go back and look at it.

She didn't buy anything. She had enough gifts for family and friends. She did window-shop. She knew a few words of Italian, so she could ask prices and tell storekeepers that their merchandise was beautiful. In one of the linen shops she met Donna and Jenna. They were trying to purchase a tablecloth for Donna's mother. Beth was pressed into negotiating. She was glad she could help the two women whom she liked. If Jenna or Donna felt any strain over Eric, it didn't show. They seemed genuinely glad to see her.

After the tablecloth was wrapped and paid for, the two women continued on their shopping expedition and Beth wandered off to see the cathedral dedicated to Saint Nicholas. Its exterior had the look of a medieval fortress. Inside it there were granite columns each carved out of a single piece of stone. The style was Doric and the columns were rumored to have been taken from the Greco-Roman theater that Beth had not gone to see. Well, she told herself, wryly, now you've seen some of the theater.

As Beth stood in front of the altar she suddenly had the urge to pray. But pray about what? To be spared from yet another ending to yet another relationship? Well, it had hardly come to that. She could hardly consider her encounter or encounters with Eric a relationship. Therefore, if it had not been a relationship, it could not be coming to an end.

And suddenly she thought of Hank and a terrible wave of guilt, no not guilt, unhappiness swept over her.

"I can't believe you're saying this to me, Beth. How could you be saying this to me." Hank was sitting half-naked on his bed watching Beth. Beth was dressing rapidly and crying. He didn't get up to comfort her. "You need me now more than ever."

"No, no, I can't see you anymore. Don't you understand? My daughter has leukemia. I have to help her." She was fumbling to get her blouse on with all its little buttons, but her hands were shaking and it was taking too long. She hadn't meant to sleep with Hank that night. She had only meant to talk to him, to tell him that they couldn't go on seeing each other. Why had she slept with him? Damn, this was difficult. "Alicia is moving home until she's better."

"Of course, you have to help her. Of course, she has to move home. But what does that have to do with us? Let me help you. You're going to need support now, babe."

"It's not right, Hank. This has no future. I shouldn't have gotten involved. You're a kid. You need a young woman who can give you a family."

"Shut up, Beth. Just shut up. What I don't need now is a Victorian lecture. I love you. That's the bottom line. Is that so hard to take? Don't you feel anything for me?" His voice cracked. "Alicia's illness is a tragedy and I want to be there for you the way you are there for her."

"No, damn it, you don't understand. Why do you refuse to understand? This is a time for the family to rally, not for...not for..." She stopped and walked over to the window to stare at the wall of the next building only a few feet away.

"Not for what, Beth?" Hank asked, "not for young gigolos, for schoolboys who are only good for sex, is that it?"

"Oh, for Christ's sake, Hank. Why are you refusing to understand what I'm trying to say to you?"

"Because what you're saying is pure shit. I thought we'd gotten past all those New England, nineteenth-century hang-ups of yours. I guess not. You mean something to me, Beth, everything. And now when things are rough, you shut me out, you just throw us away? Am I so little to you? A breeze that came by and got caught in your sails for a few miles?"

"You need someone younger."

"I want you."

Beth sank down into the large stuffed chair with the broken springs. "Hank, I don't want to analyze this. Maybe you're right, maybe it's all hang-ups, or maybe I don't love you enough, but I can't handle you now, handle this relationship, and Alicia and her sickness all at the same time. And that's my bottom line."

"Oh, babe, you're such a fool."

Beth walked out of the church a bit shaken but determined. About six months ago, she had received a book in the mail from Hank. It was his first published novel. It had been dedicated to her. She had cried all that afternoon. In it he had written in his big scrawl, "To Beth, with love, Hank," that was all. It was a month before she was able to read it. How proud she had felt afterwards, for it was a beautiful novel about one summer in the life of a ten-year-old boy. She had cried again after she had finished it. She decided as she walked down the steps of the cathedral that she would call Hank's publisher and see if she could get his address. She wasn't sure where he was living now. She wanted to do two things. First to apologize for the way she had ended their relationship. And then to thank him for the beautiful months they had together and for helping to pull her out of her depression after Matthew's death.

Is that all you want, Beth?

Yes. That's all I want. Really, all. It would have ended sooner or later.

Alicia's illness only precipitated it. I am not, was not capable of making a life with Hank. That, too, is clear now.

At the fixed time Beth was on the bus. She found Paul there ahead of her.

"Are you all right?" she asked. He looked exhausted.

"Oh, yes, just tired. Too much to metabolize, I mean all that we have seen, don't you think?"

"Yes," she said, sliding into the seat next to him. "I feel part of my body is winging its way home and I am only half here, finishing up the trip. Paul, can I ask you a question?"

"Ask away?"

"You have some...well, some interesting beliefs. How did you come to them?"

"Well, I'm a student of anthroposophy, you see."

"Anthro...what?"

"Anthroposophy. Say it."

"Anthroposophy. What is that exactly?"

"Well, at the beginning of this century there was an Austrian man called Rudolf Steiner, who was a scientist, an educator and a philosopher. He was also clairvoyant, in the modern sense."

"In the modern sense?"

"In full consciousness. Without entering into a trance the way mediums do."

"Oh."

The bus was beginning to fill up.

"He lectured extensively around Europe on his scientific research into spiritual realms."

"I've never heard of him."

"Haven't you?"

"Perhaps I'll look him up when I get home."

"Yes, perhaps."

They arrived at the ship on schedule. If Eric was aboard the ship, he hadn't let her know. No note was under her door. She didn't see him at dinner. She felt more than a pang of regret. He had not kept his word. He had said in his note that he would board the ship at either Reggio di Calabria or Messina. He hadn't. Good thing she had it all straightened out in her mind because there was nothing she could do about it. It was over. But it was all right. She was entitled to a little shipboard flirtation. That's all it had been. It was all right.

That night she slept deeply as the ship sailed to the bay of Sorrento. Again no dream troubled her sleep.

There was something comfortably familiar about the landscape that the 4-M group was riding through on their way to Paestum. Compared to Turkey, Beth decided, it seemed almost like home. The farther east we go, the farther from the familiar, she thought. The Greeks seemed exotic compared to the Italians, and the Turks seemed beyond exotic…they were…they were… She couldn't think of the words or phrases to describe her feelings, which meant that she was burnt-out. Not burnt-out in a terrible way, she assured herself, but in the way a wrestler might feel after a difficult match. She was ready to go home. She had seen enough, had accomplished much. Her sister had been right. The trip had done Beth a world of good. Once in a while, despite herself, Merle had a good idea.

Still, there was a nagging disappointment.

"What makes Paestum valuable," Beth heard a didactic voice somewhere behind her, "is not its place in the long march of history, but the fact that its grand Greek monuments are still standing. They're better preserved than most that you can see on the mainland of Greece or on its islands."

Barbara Churchill was no doubt speaking to the Winstons. "Of course, the Greeks colonized this part of the world. They had many settlements in southern Italy."

"I don't know if I can look at another Greek temple," Mel Winston said. "I'm all templed out."

"Well, I'm looking forward to the Etruscan tombs we will see tomorrow on our way to the airport hotel," his wife, Winnie, said.

"Don't forget Pompeii this afternoon," Barbara said.

"We're not doing Pompeii," Mel Winston informed her.

"Not doing Pompeii!" Barbara's voice moved a notch higher.

"Oh, we've been there half a dozen times, I think," Winnie said. "We've decided on the trip up the Amalfi Drive instead."

"Surely, you've done the Amalfi, too," Barbara said.

"Oh, yes," Mr. Winston said, "several times..."

"...but it's going to be easier on the feet," his wife said, "and besides we have never visited the gardens of the Villa Rufolo in Ravello. Supposedly Wagner got his inspiration for the Klingsor character there."

"Parsifal," Barbara intoned.

The three continued to talk but Beth turned her attention to the busy road they were traveling on. She stared at the trucks and at the small cars zooming by. It would take an hour to get to Paestum. They would return to the ship for lunch, then the group would split into two bus groups, one going to Pompeii and the other to Ravello up on the Amalfi Drive. Beth was going on the Amalfi Drive excursion. She, too, had seen Pompeii but had never taken the fabled Amalfi drive.

The day after tomorrow, I'll be home, she thought.

After visiting the museum, the 4-M group crossed the street to the lovely grassy field containing all that was left of the city of Paestum. The two temples that had been dedicated to Hera and Poseidon stood like old respectable sentries, side by side, amidst a landscape of farms. The weather was warm and sunny. A few clouds meandered across the sky. Paul wandered off from the group. He had no need to hear the history of Paestum nor to have the architecture explained to him. He was very tired. The trip was complete for him in a way. Seeing Greece again had awoken in him the desire to finish his book. He had met Elizabeth Layton. Perhaps had even helped her.

Who has helped whom, Paul?

Quite right, Annie. Beth has reminded me of the importance of life, of people. She has given me more than she knows. I must thank her.

Yes. She won't quite understand it, but do.

And thank you, my dear Annie. Life is too precious to let it just drift away.

So very precious.

Come let us go visit the temple of Hera. It is quite a magnificent ruin. He walked slowly over toward the old temple where Hera had been worshipped.

The land was old here in Paestum. Beth felt the urge to walk the tired land, the story-filled land, alone, away from conversation and lectures. She wanted to feel the earth and stones and grass beneath her feet. In a few days she would be in the New World. The land beneath her feet there, where she would walk near a different ocean, would have fewer stories to tell. But into that earth she could write her own. All Americans, unburdened by countless centuries of war and hate, could write their own stories into its waiting soil. And that was a comfort.

Beth stood a long time looking at the huge Doric temple dedicated to Hera, she who was guardian of hearth and home, upholder of old values, of that which the tribe claimed to be legitimate, enemy to those who stepped out of the traditional ways, a goddess who hated the new, the different, the deviant. So much of her temple was still standing. Those great pillars that had witnessed rituals long neglected and forgotten, as so many hearths and homes had since been neglected and forgotten.

Hera's time was definitely gone.

Beth walked all around the temple, then climbed up the stairs and walked into it, past the inner columns, until she stood finally in the inner sanctum where once only priests and the candidates for initiation had been allowed to come. Only priests and their acolytes had been permitted into the presence of the goddess who had resided in the cult statue that had once dominated the interior space. Where in Paul's pantheon of gods was Hera, she wondered?

Just as she thought of Paul, she spotted him standing at the other end of the temple. His body was listing slightly to the left. He looks like a tired warrior, she thought, and for a moment imagined him in armor leaning on a sword surveying the remains of his final battle. Yes, definitely, Paul was an old warrior, for all his gentle ways. Perhaps this would be his last trip. Perhaps it wouldn't be many more years before he joined his beloved wife in the afterworld. Beth walked over to him.

"So," she said coming up behind him, "you've escaped from the guided tour. I shall report you to Bill and Colleen."

He turned around at the sound of her voice with a grin of delight.

"We are two truants," he said. "But I don't think I can hear another word spoken about anything. Well, maybe I've just room for Pompeii."

"You're going to Pompeii? That's a lot of walking, you know."

"I wouldn't miss it for the world. My wife and I never made it down this far. We had planned it, however. Now I'm taking her through, keeping a sort of promise," he said.

"Paul, can I ask you a rather personal question?"

"And what would that be, my dear?"

"About your wife. How do you... How do you actually speak to her? Or she to you?"

"Yes," he nodded, and took her arm as they walked through the temple. "It's a very delicate process. It's more like thought than speech, if you understand the difference. In a sense, Annie thinks in me. The thoughts are akin to my own but are not my own. They can feel like one's own thinking, but that's how the dead communicate with us. And they do communicate with us, my dear. We need only pay attention. Annie thinks in me and I bring Annie's thoughts into words, clothe them in language."

"Then how can you be sure...?"

"By paying attention to the content. Does it make sense? Does it leave me free? I test Annie's words against the reality of my life. Believe me, I know myself, and the thoughts that come from Annie are far wiser than my own."

"A delicate process, indeed. Perhaps a creative process?" She smiled up at him. They walked about in companionable silence for a while. As they were about to descend from the temple, Beth said, "I'm still amazed at how huge the Greek temples are, were," she corrected herself.

"They were central to the life of the people."

"Paul, you know, for a Christian, you make a great pagan."

"Do you think so? But all this had its time and place in the history of humankind. It was all preparation."

"For what?"

"Why for the Christ," he answered.

"That's a hard one for me."

"Then don't get me started."

"Okay," and she took his arm to help him down the stone steps.

The two strolled back in the direction of where the buses were parked, crossed over the Piazza Del Foro, now a large concrete slab but once the Forum Arcade with many buildings around it. But instead of turning out of the gate, they walked off to see the little temple that had been dedicated to Athena, or to Ceres. "From whom we get the word cereal," Paul said.

Finally, at the requisite time, they returned to their bus.

On the return trip to the ship, Paul slept in the seat next to Beth. She wasn't tired. She was content to look out at the farms with their fields of nodding artichokes and finally at the scenery along the highway that was taking them back to Salerno.

Late that afternoon, when the buses had returned from Amalfi and Pompeii, the New Odyssey steamed away from the port town of Salerno. Before returning to her room, Beth decided to go to the lounge to get something cold to drink. As she was sitting at one of the small tables in the lounge sipping iced tea and watching the casting off, Jenna came in and plopped herself down across from Beth.

"Did you get a chance to say good-bye to Eric?" she asked, her bright eyes all innocence.

Beth merely raised her eyebrows.

"He's gone," Jenna announced with a smile. "He had to go on to Rome. Something about his work. His boss has him running all over Italy, it seems to me."

"When did you see him?" Beth asked, forming her words carefully.

"He stopped at Pompeii," she told her. "He was traveling in a car with a driver and he caught up with the group, wanted to say good-bye, I guess. He stayed only for a few minutes and then he headed back to the ship to pick up his things. He was in a terrible hurry because he had to be in Rome before evening for some appointment or other. Too bad you didn't get to see him. You two hit it off pretty well, like Mom and him. He told us both to look him up at the Barry if and when we come to New York. I'm going to try to get Mom to make the trip to New York in the fall."

That accomplished, Jenna told Beth about the afternoon in Pompeii. Beth listened politely as she forced herself to drink her iced tea slowly. But her stomach was in knots. Then it was true. It was over. Done. Finito. Eric was gone with all his belongings.

Beth, buck up, you expected it. Don't make a federal case out of this little shipboard romance.

Yes, that's right, I didn't expect him to come back. What I didn't count on was feeling this bad about not seeing him again.

Her tea finished, Beth stood up, gave Jenna her best smile, told her she would see her at dinner and escaped back to her cabin.

When Beth entered her cabin, she saw two envelopes that had been slipped beneath the door. She picked them both up, turned one over. It was from Eric. She quickly opened it and read it.

My dear Beth,

I feel like I'm in *The Comedy of Errors*. Mrs. Barry has decided that I don't need to see Italy on a tour as I am here three or four times a year anyway. She has put me to work and I have been running all over the country. I tried to make it to Reggio di Calabrio but it didn't work out. I had to go to Barletta on the other coast. I'm terribly sorry. I stopped at Pompeii, on my way to the ship to retrieve my things, hoping to have a few words with you, but more error or comedy, you were on the other excursion and I didn't have time to chase you up the Amalfi Drive. I have to leave right away. An appointment in Rome. But when you get to Rome I'll be in Milan. Damn. Without seeing you. Beth, I don't have your address nor do I know whether you have an unlisted phone number. And Smith and Smith will not violate your privacy by handing out the addresses of its clients. So I'm leaving you mine. Please call me in New York. I'll be back at the end of June. I'm sorry this has all gone the way it has. But please call me. Eric.

Beth's heart was beating fast. What did this mean? He had tried to see her, had stopped at Pompeii. He wants her to call him in New York, but that's four weeks from now. Surely by then this encounter will have faded. But he's behaving like a gentleman. Not like the oaf in my dream. She didn't know what to think. Don't think about it now, she told herself. Leave it alone. Pack. She could make up her mind in four or five weeks whether she wanted to call him or not.

The second envelope contained an invitation to dine at the Captain's table tonight at the farewell dinner.

Beth packed, showered, then dressed in her finest black dress, put on gold dangling earrings, then her highest heels, made her face up carefully, and went down to the Captain's cocktail party.

She sat in the lounge with Lucy and Doris.

"I can imagine what my house will look like when I get back," Doris said with a shake of her head. "My husband will probably have piled up all the dishes we own in the sink and there will be tons of dirty clothes in the basement waiting for me to wash them. It will take me a week to dig the place out."

Beth thought, It's over, the trip, people are talking about home.

"Doris should join a consciousness-raising group," Lucy said. "She's a veritable slave to that man. The two of them don't know the world's changed since they were married."

"Oh, tosh," Doris said. "Frank and I have made a pretty good go of it. He has his tasks and I have mine. Between us we get along better than most. What's a little dust now and then."

Paul came in a few minutes before the gong rang for the farewell dinner. He found Beth and sat down on the arm of her chair. The music was loud now and so was the laughter. Drinks were free and everyone was taking advantage of it. Paul leaned down and under cover of the noise said, "I saw Eric."

Beth was startled.

"He came to Pompeii expecting to see you. He was terribly disappointed when you weren't on that excursion. Did you get a chance to see him before he took off back to Rome?"

"No, but he left me a note."

"Good."

"He wants me to call him in New York when he gets back at the end of June."

"Will you?"

She hesitated. "I can barely imagine what I'll be doing or feeling in a week from now, how can I know what I'll be feeling in four or five weeks? Or more important what he'll be feeling. Lots of water will have passed over the proverbial dam by then."

"The best way to find out is to make the phone call. Nothing ventured, nothing gained. How do you feel right now?"

"Confused. It's been quite a trip."

"He's a good man, I think."

"Yes, I think he is. Well, we'll see."

The gong rang and Beth stood up. She said to Paul, "I've been invited to sit at the Captain's table."

"Me, too," he said. "You'll get a chance to talk to some of the officers."

After dinner, Beth returned to the lounge to watch the dancing. She, herself, danced with several of the officers who flirted outrageously. Oh, well, she told herself, it's the last night. After an hour of dancing, she returned to the cabin, packed the rest of her things, tried not to think of Eric, set her alarm and went to bed. For the third night in a row she did not dream.

Staring back at the New Odyssey as the bus pulled away from the dock at Civitavecchia, Beth felt a momentary pang of melancholy. This time they would not be returning to it as they had so many times before. And so much had happened there. She looked now with heightened interest at her fellow travelers.

How curious a life is, Beth thought. It moves along a seemingly meandering, even haphazard path. Then at certain points that path converges with others, and strangers meet and share experiences. Then the roads separate again. All of these people are part of my crisis and my epiphany. Most I will never see again, yet they have become an indelible part of my biography. And none of them know it. No one knows that this trip has been a sharp turning point for me. Except Paul. She glanced at the man sitting next to her. He, too, was studying their fellow passengers.

Across the aisle, Doris was trying to photograph the ship, a last reminder of a grand experience.

"You won't get a good picture through the glass," Lucy said.

Even Mrs. Green, who was sitting in front of them, said, "This has been the nicest tour I've ever been on."

Paul grinned at Beth.

"Well, how could it not be lovely with so many wonderful people as traveling companions," Mrs. Winston said in her clipped British English.

And her husband said, "Hear, hear."

After that the group settled down for the forty-minute drive to Tarquinia where they would visit some Etruscan tombs.

Yet another vital culture, Beth thought, that has come and gone, another small notch on the yardstick of history. What kind of notch will we make, we modern westerners?

"Paul," she said, "I'd like to keep contact with you. Would you mind?"

"No, I'd like that very much myself."

"I have relatives in the Boston area, so maybe I can visit you when I get up there."

"Yes," he nodded. "Or perhaps a note or letter now and then?"

"Absolutely."

They exchanged addresses and phone numbers, then settled back for the drive to Tarquinia. The suitcases and belongings of the 4-M travelers were stored in the belly of the bus to be unloaded that evening at the hotel. Tomorrow at this time they would be at the airport waiting to go home.

Outside the town of Tarquinia, they visited the necropolis of Monterozzi, one of the major sites of Etruscan tombs. Then the 4-M group was taken to a museum which was housed in the fifteenth century Palazzo Vitelleschi to see, among other items, the great terra-cotta grouping called the *Two Winged Horses,* then on for a final lunch at a tavern in Viterbo. It was their final meal together.

Soon the 4-M tourists were back on board the two buses and heading for the nearby town of Bagnaia for a visit to the Renaissance gardens of the Villa Lante. An hour at the gardens, an hour and a half drive to Rome. Then dinner, sleep, the airport and home.

That's the way it would be.

But in the gardens at the Villa Lante, something unexpected happened.

Senses satiated, Beth had moved away from the guide, who was giving the history of the gardens and the villa, and had climbed the stairs to the top of the meticulously sculpted terraced garden. She had almost reached the final level where the two houses were located and was about to walk toward them to peer into the dark windows, when she heard a voice call out to her.

"Beth, wait up."

Beth turned and running up the steps was Eric Halsey. But that couldn't be! Eric was gone! That was over, was fading into the past to take its place among all the other mementos of the trip. This was not the scenario she had mentally written for her last two days before home. She stared at him in astonishment, and her stomach went in two directions. It plopped down around her feet and it soared up through her head to float in the clear blue Italian sky.

He arrived at her side, and with barely a pause, took her by the hand and said, "Come with me." Then he led her back down the steps oblivious to all the stares of the American tourists, some of whom had said good-bye to him in Pompeii. Eric approached Bill Orbach, who was pointing out the remarkable irrigation system that had been worked out for the gardens, and said to him, "How long before you leave here?"

Bill glanced at his watch, "Oh, about forty or forty-five minutes."

"Where are the buses parked?"

Bill told him.

"Okay, I'll have Beth back on the bus by then." He turned away and still holding Beth by the hand, led her out of the gardens and down into the village. She followed wordlessly. There was so much going on inside her that she couldn't have managed to say one intelligible word. Eric stopped at a near-empty outdoor café, held out a seat for her. She sat down. He ordered two coffees and then finally began to speak.

"First order of the day, I want your phone number and your address. I left you mine, but knowing you, you'll probably never call, not after four or five weeks."

He was right, of course. She gave him both.

"This has happened all wrong. Of all the miserable timing," he said, gently lifting her chin so that she had to look at him. "Something was finally beginning and if we had had a few more days together it might have held until I return to New York next month."

All she could say was, "Did you come here just to find me?"

"Well, of course." He ran a finger down her nose and then took her hand. "I'm going to be very late for my appointment in Milan. But to hell with it. I was sure that if I didn't get a chance to talk to you face-to-face you'd never make contact with me again."

"You're probably right," she said.

"See, aleady, I'm getting to know you. That's what I want, Beth. I want to get to know you. I want that opportunity."

"Hmmm."

"That's all you can say is 'hmmm'?"

"I'm so baffled by this, I don't know what to say."

"Well for starters you could say, 'I'm glad to see you. I'd like to get to know you, too.'"

"I'm glad to see you. I'd like to get to know you, too."

"Well, I'm glad that's settled." He leaned back in his chair and looked at her appraisingly. "Hey, you look terrific. I mean you look, well, terrific. What happened?"

She laughed. "I went through a crisis, like one does in an illness, and I came out the other side."

"Tell me." He smiled and she thought, My, what a nice face.

"If I tried to tell you at this moment, I'd miss my bus. Let's save it until you get back to New York. By then I'll have digested it and hopefully will be able to make sense of it. If not sense, at least some poems or even a novel."

"Now I'm really intrigued. Can't you give me a hint?"

"Let's just say that I fought a demon, one of my demons, and I won."

"Now it's my turn to say, 'hmmm.'" And then his eyes widened and he leaned back in his chair and grinned at her. "Did I hear you say that you're going to write something?"

"Oh, yes. A writer writes," she said. "What did you expect me to do, paint?"

He laughed. "But this is terrific. Can you at least give me a hint about your new project?"

"No, sorry," she shook her head, "I hardly ever talk about a project while I am working on it and never, never before I *start* to work on it. The Muse will slip away." What great eyes he has. He's really very handsome.

"I think I'm going to call Mrs. Barry and tell her I have to be home, right away, for personal reasons," he said. "All she could do is fire me and I'm thinking about quitting anyway."

He was serious.

"Don't do that," Beth put her free hand on top of his. "Don't make that kind of gesture. When and if it's right for you to leave the Barry, you'll know. Don't leave on my account. I'm not a kid. I can wait."

My God, she *could* wait!

"You won't dismiss all of this as tourist fever, as something that belongs to a trip but not to one's real life?"

She stared into his concerned face. "No, truth is I'm interested in you, just as interested in you as you are in me. Why should I give that up? Why shouldn't I give this a try as long as that's what you want, too?"

"I do."

"Eric, after Matthew died I had an affair." She paused, surprised that she had spoken. What did she want to tell him? After all, she had been free to do as she pleased. It wasn't that.

When she didn't go on he squeezed her hand and said, "Of course you did."

She tried again. "But only a small part of me really participated in that affair. Only a tiny part of me got involved. That was unfair to myself as a woman and certainly unfair to the man involved, who was very dear and really deserved better. I became involved with a younger man, knowing it had no future, not letting it count."

He was listening without judgment in his face.

Thank you for that, Eric, she thought, and plunged on. She knew what she wanted to tell him now. "I had to stay loyal to Matthew, you see, despite the fact that he had been disloyal to me and despite the fact that it was he who had untied the marriage knot that year before his death. It's hard now to understand what I thought I was accomplishing. Something for my girls. Some gesture. Keeping the structure of family in tact. And trying to retrieve for myself my history, my individual worth."

"No one can fault you for that, Beth."

"Perhaps not. But I didn't save my children pain. And I looked in the wrong place for my sense of worth."

Eric squeezed her hand and held on tight.

She smiled slowly at him. "Somehow on this trip I've learned that no one can take your history, your biography from you."

There was a slight breeze beginning to sweep through the square bringing with it the scent of dinners cooking. Across the square, in front of a souvenir shop Beth saw Paul looking at the postcard rack. How fond she had become of his tall, lean, slightly bent figure.

Beth plunged on. She had to talk, to tell Eric things. It surprised her but it also made her happy. "What was between Matthew and myself was good for a while. And then it wasn't. But that relationship isn't or shouldn't be the measure of all things. I can finally say I want to know about love again. And in order to do that, I have to let go of my anger at Matthew, in a sense, to free Matthew. I shouldn't remember only the bad times allowing that to cancel out all of the good times. I now want to put everything alongside everything else—the good, the bad, the in-between—in all their shades and hues, in all their richness, because all of it is part of my history. All of it."

She looked at him and he was watching her intensely and soberly. "I held on to my sorrow at losing my daughter. And I've let that go, too. Eric, I can't bring her back. I think I tied her to me with my grief. I think now I can love her deeply but release her. I can remember that I once loved Matthew and release him. And importantly, I can allow myself to love again, if that's in the cards."

"Oh, Beth…"

She put her fingers on his lips to stop him from saying anything and blushed slightly. "I'm feeling very brave right now, Eric. Something happened to me on this trip and I'm saying things to you that I couldn't have said, even a few days ago, and might not be able to say in a few weeks. Does that scare you? Am I projecting too far?"

Eric leaned across the table and kissed her lightly on the mouth.

More and more of the 4-M group were coming down the street and entering the square. A few had found their way to the café she was sitting in with Eric.

" Look, Beth, I don't know how you came to all of this in the past few days, but I'm so happy… Am I glad I took this chance and found you today. You give me…"

"What…?" she shook her head but smiled.

"Hope. Yes, that's what it is, and that's something I've been without for years. Life's not much good without it."

Beth leaned toward him and kissed him. "This is Italy. It's expected."

They spent the next twenty minutes talking as more and more of Beth's fellow travelers found seats in the café. None approached the two. Eric told Beth about the places he had been, about the artists he had seen. He would be crisscrossing Europe for the next few weeks.

At the very last minute, Eric walked her to the bus. All of the others had boarded. "Next time I do this, perhaps you could come with me. I understand a writer can travel with just a little notebook and a pen?"

"Well, a toothbrush. But wouldn't that be fun."

He took Beth in his arms.

"Remember," Eric whispered, and left quickly.

She stood watching him as he walked off across the square to his own waiting car.

"Beth?" Bill Orbach called to her softly.

She turned around, brought out of her reverie.

"We're waiting."

"Oh, sorry," she gave him a big jubilant smile.

As Beth entered the bus, she received a round of applause. She blushed with enjoyment, then slid into her seat next to Paul.

"Straightened everything out, I see."

"Yes, we'll see each other and get to know each other when he returns from Europe."

"Of course. That will be good for the two of you."

"I hope so, Paul. I really hope so."

Beth and Paul had managed to get seats together on the airplane to New York. He was going to visit his niece and nephew on Long Island for a few days before returning to Gloucester. About half of the 4-M group were on the return flight to Kennedy airport but their seats were scattered all around the plane. The tour had broken up. The participants were on their own now.

Sitting in her aisle seat, Beth watched, with mild curiosity, the other passengers maneuver down the narrow aisle, pushing carryons and children ahead of them. She wondered where some of them had been. If she had been a betting person, she would have bet that no one had had the kinds of experiences that she had had on her trip.

Oh, Beth, you can't know that. Everyone's life has its own epiphanies.

But has any of them slain the Minotaur? Answer me that.

There was no answer.

And how many people have an Iris in their lives?

No answer.

Right, Beth thought with satisfaction.

The plane finally roared into motion and they were up and away and over the Mediterranean, flying west toward America.

Eighteen days had been just enough. Beth was eager to be home. She would, after a few days of coping with jet lag and after attending to her mail and her bills, train down to Philadelphia to visit Becky and Ed for a day or two. She wanted to see the newlyweds and to hear about their honeymoon in Hawaii, Australia and New Zealand.

And she wanted Becky to see that she was all right.

Then she would return home and begin the internal dialogue that would eventually lead to her new writing project. In little over a month Eric would return. Oh, what a lovely summer this was going to be!

Beth and Paul spent the first hour talking about their trip and about future plans. Then drinks were served, then lunch. When the shades were finally lowered for the movie, both Beth and Paul fell asleep. They woke only an hour out of New York, ate a sandwich and an apple, filled out their duty cards, then waited for the landing.

Paul was to be met at the airport by his nephew and niece who lived in Westbury, L.I. Beth was to be picked up by her sister, Merle, who would no doubt be waiting anxiously, ready to whisk her off to Scarsdale if Beth looked the least bit shaky.

Won't she be surprised. What fun to rattle the unflappable Merle.

In Kennedy airport, Beth helped Paul find his luggage at the crowded carousel and accompanied him through customs. Together, they walked through the double doors, wheeling a large cart with both their belongings on it. A young man and woman moved out into the aisle, calling,

"Uncle Paul, Uncle Paul." There were hugs. There was a quick introduction. Paul's nephew removed Paul's luggage from the cart. Beth gave Paul a bear hug, said she would call or write him soon.

"Beth," Paul said to her, "thank you."
She looked up in surprise. "Thank me for what?"
He looked down at her surprised face, her beautiful expressive face, filled with affection now as she gazed up at him. Ah, if only he were a dozen years younger. But what foolishness. "For your friendship, for trusting me, for sharing yourself with me," he said, bending down toward her, "but mostly, for proving Annie right, for reminding me that people make life so very precious."
She kissed his cheek then. "You'll hear from me soon."

From beyond Paul, Beth could see Merle barreling down the long open corridor toward her. She pushed the luggage cart toward her astonished sister. They touched cheeks and embraced.
Merle looked her over carefully and seemed relieved with what she saw. She then asked, "And who was that I saw you kissing?"
"Merle, you are never going to believe this…Where's the car?" Merle pointed in the general direction of the exit. "This has been quite a trip. You couldn't have picked a better thing for me to do. Merle, there are now two very special men in my life."
And with an amazed Merle hurrying after her, Beth rolled the cart toward the exit.